ABBREVIATING

Ernie

ABBREVIATING

Ernie

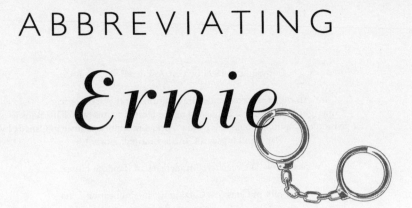

A NOVEL

PETER LEFCOURT

VILLARD

NEW YORK

Library of Congress Cataloging-in-Publication Data
Lefcourt, Peter.
Abbreviating Ernie / Peter Lefcourt
p.   cm.
ISBN 0-679-43950-1
I. Title.
PS3562.E3737A63   1997
813'.54—dc20   96-34450

Random House website address: http://www.randomhouse.com

Printed in the United States of America on acid-free paper
24689753

Book design by Victoria Wong

A Terri
pour tous les jeudis de ma vie

"This . . . thing just happened overnight. What reason it happened, I don't know, but it's from a higher source so I don't make a biggie out of it."

—Brian "Kato" Kaelin

ACKNOWLEDGMENTS

I'd like to thank David Rosenthal and Amy Edelman, the best editors in the business; and Joel Finer, a lawyer with a heart of gold, who explained the arcana of criminal law to me.

ABBREVIATING

Ernie

Chapter 1

"I'm afraid this is going to be just a little bit uncomfortable," he lied.

It was going to hurt. In fact, it was going to be thirty to forty seconds of fairly excruciating pain. But he said it, as he always did in this situation, in the hope that when his turn came, as it invariably would, it might somehow turn out to be less painful.

Ernest Haas looked at the thin old man bent over his examining table, boxer shorts around his ankles, spindly legs bowed, varicose veins trellising his distended scrotum, and wanted to tell him that the prostate gland wasn't designed to do the job for more than seventy years. The simple fact was that he had outlived his equipment. But instead he reached into the cabinet for the box of disposable rubber gloves and the tube of lubricant.

Outside the snow was beginning to melt under the faint rays of the late-March sun. Spring was edging its way north. The digital wall clock noiselessly changed numbers. There were four old men with hypertrophic prostates stacked up in the other examining rooms, sitting in their shorts, reading back issues of *People*, waiting for their turn to bend over the table.

I'm afraid this is going to be just a little bit uncomfortable . . .

Meanwhile the day was dissolving into a puddle. Before long it would be May, and the lawn would need mowing, and he would go down to the mall to check out the spring line of clothes at Jordan Marsh. The

sap was rising and the salmon spawning, and he, Ernest Haas, diplo-
mate in urology from the Cornell medical school, was standing in his
office on State Street in Schenectady, New York, with his finger up an
old man's ass.

"Jesus, Doc . . ."

"Just a little longer, Mr. Nemic. We're almost finished."

He thought of Audrey, in the aquamarine kitchen of their Dutch
Colonial on Van Schuyler Lane, watching *Oprah* on the nineteen-inch
Magnavox, drinking decaf instant coffee, and clipping coupons.

At least she was out of bed these days. Since she'd gone on Prozac,
things had been better. She got up and dressed before noon and even
went out now and then, though he had no idea where. He checked the
odometer on the Camry to verify that she drove it, but when he asked
her where she went, all she would say was "Out."

"Out where?"

"I went for a drive. I went to the mall. I went shopping." And so on.

Audrey. The beautiful depressive with the milky white skin and the
febrile eyes. Audrey, the fair. Audrey, the absent. Audrey, the languid.
Audrey of the almond-shaded areolae and the cupcake crumbs on her
lips . . .

"Jesus, Doc . . ." Mr. Nemic groaned.

"Just finishing up," he said, then slid the finger out, removed the
glove, tossed it in the toxic waste bin, and crossed to the sink to wash
up. He carefully scrubbed each finger with surgical soap, all four surfaces, then tore off exactly three sheets of paper towels, dried his hands.

"What's the story, Doc?"

"We'll talk about it in my office."

"You want to go in, don't you?"

Ernest Haas flexed his cheeks in a noncommittal reply and headed
out past the nurses' station, where Denise, his receptionist, sat beside
her wooden sign that informed his patients, IT IS CUSTOMARY TO PAY
FOR MEDICAL SERVICES WHEN RENDERED.

"How many more out there?" he asked.

Denise opened the sliding glass panel. "Six."

"How did we get so backed up?"

"It's always like this on Friday."

He went into his office, glanced over the urinalyses and PSA results
on his desk, and picked up the phone.

It rang eleven times before she picked up.

"Hello . . ."

The voice was liquid and remote. As if she had been woken from a nap.

"Were you sleeping?"

"No."

"What were you doing?"

There was no answer for a moment, then, "When are you coming home?"

"Not before seven. I've got four inside and six more in the waiting room."

"Bring take-out Chinese."

"Okay . . . anything special?"

"Lemon chicken and steamed dumplings with Szechuan noodles."

Mr. Nemic appeared in the doorway of the office. Ernest Haas motioned for him to come in. He wrote *lemon chicken*, *steamed dumplings*, and *Szechuan noodles* on the pad with the old man's lab results.

He was about to hang up when he heard "Ernie?"

"Yes?"

There was a long silence. She often left long, agonizing silences between sentences. It drove him crazy. Sometimes she didn't continue at all but left the words hanging in the air.

Mr. Nemic was staring at him from the black Naugahyde chair across the desk. They were going to have to do a biopsy.

"Audrey?"

More silence, then just as he was about to hang up she said, "Get extra soy sauce."

She hung up softly, the way Barbara Stanwyck did in an old movie she had watched earlier that afternoon on the Nostalgia Channel. Audrey liked hanging up the phone with a femme-fatale air of mystery. She found the number of a local movie theater, dialed it, got the recording, and then, pursing her lips, whispered a breathy "Good-bye" before hanging up softly, like Barbara Stanwyck.

The kitchen clock read 4:07. Approximately three hours before Ernie got home. She picked up the remote and ran the channels, stopping on the Weather Channel. There was a low-pressure system over the Great Lakes that could bring snow flurries to the tri-cities area by tomorrow evening. This fact was announced by a short pert woman in a light-blue wool suit with an ivory-colored brooch.

Audrey wondered if you needed any qualifications to work for the Weather Channel besides a clean suit and decent posture. She watched the high and low temperatures flash on the screen, listened as the woman in the blue suit read them off in a nasal voice: "With lows from the teens in the Berkshires to the low twenties in downtown Albany . . ."

Siggy, the Rottweiler, wandered into the kitchen and stared pointedly at his bowl. It was too early for his dinner. And he knew it. Still, he went through the starving-dog routine until she said to him tartly, "Get lost, Siggy."

He glowered at her, as if to say that he was making a list of all the indignities that she had visited upon him and that one of these days he would retaliate. He was Ernie's dog. She had never liked him. He made her uncomfortable with his radish eyes and bad breath.

Siggy held her look a little longer than usual, it seemed, before he turned and exited through the doggy door and out into the backyard.

It hadn't been a very good day. She had stayed in bed till ten, trying to find an activity for the early afternoon. Eventually, she hit upon the idea of going to Kitchenalia at the mall and buying a new salad spinner. The thought of this excursion imbued her with sufficient energy to get out of bed, shower, file her nails, tweeze her eyebrows, put on a pair of spandex tights and a big fluffy orange sweater, make a cup of instant Medaglia D'Oro decaf, and sit with the morning paper and a couple of Hostess Twinkies.

Things were going decently well until she made the mistake of calling Kitchenalia to find out if they had salad spinners. When she was informed that they didn't have any in stock at the moment, her entire day collapsed around her.

She sat there with the remains of the Twinkies and the dozen clipped coupons and tried to figure out how many hours were left till lunch. And then she picked up the remote and started to scan the hundred and thirty-six channels that their cable system delivered, and before she knew it she was watching Barbara Stanwyck hang up the phone softly.

She hadn't liked the accusatory tone in Ernie's questions: *Were you sleeping? What were you doing?* It was like Dr. Zadek, sitting in his overheated, knotty-pine office, with the faux-leather furniture and the box of Kleenex, folding his bony, hairy fingers together and asking: *How do you feel? Are you angry?*

Click. It was 4:28. She was beginning to feel the first signs of a sugar crash from the Twinkies—the sudden dip in altitude that began the descent. She walked into the den and looked vacantly around her until she noticed that the gold-and-white print of the ducks over the nonworking fireplace was askew about a sixteenth of an inch.

She made the adjustment and then stepped back to verify it. She had overcompensated. She went forward, moved it the other way, went back to check. It was still askew. Shit!

Audrey burst into tears and threw herself onto the couch.

It was 6:23 when Ernest Haas finally left his office. He had spent the last two hours giving old men bad news, and he was exhausted. All he wanted to do was go home and get into bed with the March issue of the *New York State Journal of Urology*.

But as he pulled the Mazda into State Street traffic, he saw a woman walking out of Jorgensens wearing a pale-blue raincoat, unbuttoned, over a burgundy linen suit and a lovely lavender blouse with a light-green-and-gold silk scarf. She had on a pair of narrow white heels—a little early for the season, but they went very well with the suit and scarf.

So taken was he with this sight, that he nearly rear-ended the car in front of him. He jammed the brakes on just in time and, heart pounding, waited for the light to change. In the forty-five seconds it took for the light to go from red to green, he readjusted his itinerary.

He drove quickly through State Street traffic and out Route 5 east till he reached the Mohawk Mall, located halfway between Schenectady and Albany. Parking in a handicapped zone, he put his MD ON CALL sign on the dashboard.

The mall was uncrowded at this hour, and he was in and out of Kmart in under ten minutes. He got two pair, one light-cream, the other sheer.

He returned to his car, moved back into the thinning traffic on Route 5, exited at Poltroon Road, and drove the three and a half miles to the little pod mall that housed Ming Sun's Take-Out Chinese Cuisine.

He ordered lemon chicken, steamed dumplings, and Szechuan noodles. Helping himself to a handful of soy-sauce packets, he paid and was out the door and back in his car, negotiating the windy road that led through the subdivision, turning right onto Van Schuyler and left into the driveway of 474.

The automatic garage door responded to the radio signal, and he pulled the Mazda in beside the Camry. He got out and went over and unlocked the front door of the Toyota with his spare key. The mileage was 24,569, the same as that morning.

He opened the door to the service hallway and walked past the washing machine and dryer into the kitchen. The Weather Channel was on on the small TV in the breakfast nook. There were dirty dishes on the table, the morning newspaper open to the shopping pages, Twinkie wrappers on the floor.

Ernest put the Chinese food down on the kitchen table and went into the den, where he found Audrey asleep on the couch, facedown.

"Audrey?" he said softly. "I'm home."

She stirred, turned her head away from him.

"I brought lemon chicken."

After a moment, he heard her voice, faint and liquid, "What about the extra soy sauce?"

"I got a whole bunch."

And a pair of sheer and a pair of light-cream pantyhose . . .

But he said nothing about his stop at Kmart. He would save that for after dinner.

They ate right from the containers, chasing the lemon chicken with Diet Coke. Sitting at the breakfast-nook table in front of the TV, they watched an Asian woman with an overbite trace the pattern of high- and low-pressure areas across the country. High pressure over the Rockies. Snow turning to rain in the Ohio Valley. Flurries across New England.

They finished dinner in silence. Ernest pushed back his chair, wiped his mouth with a paper napkin, and said, "I stopped at Kmart on the way home. Light-cream or sheer, what do you think?"

"Ernie, maybe . . ."

Fifteen seconds went by. Audrey was stalled again in the middle of a sentence, drawing a blank, spinning her wheels without traction.

"Maybe what?" he asked.

But she didn't say anything else. She just left the words hanging in the air like a puff of stale cigarette smoke. He excused himself and, leaving Audrey alone with the empty Chinese-food cartons, walked out of the kitchen.

He closed the bedroom door behind him and went to Audrey's underwear drawer. He took out an assortment of panties and carefully laid them out on the bed. Then he opened the closet door. Scanning the rack, his eye was drawn to the beige knit suit with the faint coral-colored check pattern and stitched pockets. He held it up for a closer look, then laid it down beside the panties.

He took a long time choosing a blouse, finally settling on a yellow silk with high collar and ruffled sleeves. So far, so good. It was all up to the shoes now.

The yellow pumps were just a bit too much. He needed something a tad subtler and decided on the off-white open-toed high heels. When he had the entire outfit assembled on the bed, he sat down at the dressing table.

He went through Audrey's jewelry box carefully. There was a new pair of silver jade earrings that he had gotten for her in Cincinnati during a nonintrusive-urethral-surgery convention in January, but they didn't work with this outfit. Instead, he chose a pair with inlaid amethysts and then a simple strand of pearls to go with them.

He put the jewelry on the bed beside the suit, then took the pantyhose from the Kmart bag to make the final choice. He hesitated for a long time before going with the sheer. The light-cream was overkill.

Then he got a pair of scissors from the night table and began very carefully to go to work.

Audrey sat there picking her teeth, with no idea what to expect. It was always something different with Ernie when he came home with a shopping bag. She didn't discuss it with Zadek. It was, frankly, none of his goddamn business.

If Ernie hadn't insisted that she continue to see Zadek, she would have stopped long ago. She didn't need to sit in his overheated office three times a week and pick herself apart. Why couldn't he just mail the Prozac prescription to her?

There was a TV movie on at nine. Meredith Baxter playing a woman who gets an unnecessary hysterectomy from a manipulative doctor and then sues him. It was based on a true story. Maybe they'd be through by then and she could get into bed with the remote and a cup of chamomile tea and watch Meredith Baxter sue the doctor blind.

But as soon as she heard the sound of the high heels on the hardwood floor of the hallway, she knew she'd be lucky to see any more than the last hour of the movie.

He stood in the doorway, one hand on his hip, a dark-brown patent-leather pocketbook hanging from his shoulder. He was wearing too much mascara. He had been sparing with the lipstick—the Revlon crushed roses—but not the mascara.

"The bag goes great with the shoes, doesn't it?" He smiled before reaching inside the pocketbook and bringing out a pair of handcuffs. "They're padded inside. They don't leave marks," he added, showing them to her so that she could see for herself.

"I got them in the mail. From Santa Monica, California."

As he bent down to kiss the back of her neck, she could smell the mixture of mouthwash and perfume. He had gargled with Scope and put a dab of Narcisse behind his ears. As usual, he had used too much of both.

He dangled the handcuffs in front of her. There was a foot of chain between the two shackles.

"For mobility," he explained as he led her across the kitchen, slipping one end of the handcuffs around her left wrist and attaching the other to the oven-door handle of the restored antique O'Keefe and Merritt stove.

Then he walked away, teetering a little on his heels, took out a key from his pocket, and put it down on the breakfast-nook table beside the extra soy-sauce packets.

In the liquor cabinet above the microwave he found the bottle of Harveys Bristol Cream. He took two juice glasses from the dishwasher, which Audrey had neglected to empty, and poured a glass for each of them.

"Cheers."

They clinked glasses. He bent down and kissed her neck again. Then his lips slid down her front, and he caressed her breasts through the material of her fluffy orange sweater.

He lifted the sweater gently over her head, but couldn't remove it all the way because of the handcuffs. It dangled from her wrist, sweeping the floor in front of the stove. She was wearing a standard, no-frills Maidenform.

He studied her for a moment before going over to the odds-and-ends drawer near the phone and taking out a pair of scissors. Gently, almost tenderly, he lifted the front elastic of the bra away from her body, slipped the scissors beneath, and snipped it in two. It hung there, hugging her breasts loosely, functionless.

He moved back a few steps to get perspective. Like a painter at an easel, he hummed to himself, rocking on his heels, studying his subject.

The spandex didn't work, he decided. He kneeled in front of her and rolled the black tights slowly down until they lay around her ankles, Toulouse-Lautrec fashion.

"I adore you, Audrey. You know that, don't you? There is nothing I wouldn't do for you," he whispered before taking out his compact and brushing up his lipstick, smacking his lips together expertly.

Then he took the TV remote and flipped it to her. "Put something good on," he said with a wink.

She flipped through the channels, stopping for a moment on C-SPAN to watch the undersecretary of transportation address a house subcommittee. She switched to TBS and saw Dean Martin chasing Indians on a horse. Then she found the Home Shopping Network and admired a set of twelve supposedly mother-of-pearl-handled steak knives for only $19.95, wondering how they could be mother-of-pearl at that price.

When she looked back at Ernie, he was ready for action—his skirt hiked up over his hips, his thing sticking out of the hole he had cut in the sheer pantyhose.

It didn't quite work. Not with the sheer pantyhose. He would have done better with the light-cream. Especially with the white shoes. He needed the color.

By the time they were finished with the foreplay, such that it was, the mother-of-pearl steak knives had given way to a floor-to-ceiling halogen lamp that came in black, white, and gray. She thought the gray would go well in the den with the dark-gray Levolors.

Ernie was making a lot of noise. More noise than she could remember him ever making before. She had to grab hold tightly to the elastic band of his pantyhose to keep from falling.

"OhgodbabyJesus," he moaned in her ear, his lips pressed deeply into the flesh of her neck. He kept losing traction as his heels slid against the Mexican tile floor, and each time he slid, he pulled himself back up and into her with a desperate war cry.

There was an additional technical problem caused by the spandex tights rolled around her ankles. Her legs were so constricted that she had trouble holding him between her thighs.

Nevertheless, she made the best of it, kissing him on the earlobe and sliding her free hand beneath the elastic band of the pantyhose to caress his frantic little buns, which were going a mile a minute. He went at it with such purpose and diligence that she felt a great tenderness for him. There was her Ernie, wearing her clothes, emerging from another pair of tattered pantyhose, going about his business with such seriousness and determination.

If only they could do it in bed. So that when it was over, they wouldn't be locked together in an awkward position in some uncomfortable place. The women's clothes no longer bothered her. In fact it was convenient. When they went shopping, Audrey would try things on for him, and he would nod or shake his head to the saleswomen, who never guessed that the clothes were for him as well as for her. They were both a perfect size 8.

Ernie was beginning to ascend the summit. It wouldn't be long now. She reached down to tickle him in the special place that, she knew from experience, would release the safety in preparation for firing.

"OhgodbabyJes . . ." He didn't get the name of the Savior all the way out. It stuck in his throat. Instead of the usual triumphant, piercing high note, he uttered a horrible, gurgling screech as his fingers clutched the flesh of her buttocks and didn't release.

There was no Hallelujah chorus. Nothing but a grinding halt, as if someone had yanked the plug suddenly out of the wall. He didn't deflate as he usually did, dissolving into a puddle of mumbling gratitude.

If anything, he seemed to inflate. His whole body seized up like an engine that had run out of motor oil. And he didn't move. He didn't bat an eyelash. He leaned on her, with his chin on her shoulder, rigid, motionless, and speechless.

"Ernie?" she whispered in his ear. There was no response. Not even a grunt.

"Ernie?" she called louder, moving her free hand up from the linchpin to his back. She caressed his neck. Then squeezed it a little less gently.

"You okay?"

She squeezed him harder, digging her nails in, finally pinching him.

"Ernie, what the hell's going on?"

Ernie wasn't talking. He held her tightly in his powerful grip, pinned against the O'Keefe and Merritt, his hands riveted to her flesh, his thing stuck up inside her like a champagne cork.

Chapter 2

Audrey did not immediately consider the possibility that Ernie was dead. He was clinging to her tightly, his weight pressing her against the surface of the stove, balanced precariously on his high heels. It was as if he had been dancing the tango, done a dip, and thrown his back out.

She tried to pull his face back and get a look at him, but there wasn't enough hair to get a decent grip. She searched for a pulse, jabbing the finger of her free hand into various parts of his neck, looking for signs of life.

Nothing.

Jesus!

What the hell was going on here?

As Ernie continued not to move or, for that matter, to breathe, as far as she could tell, it slowly dawned on her that she could be locked in an embrace with a dead man.

Oh, god!

How could he be dead if his thing was still wedged inside her? If he was dead, he would have shriveled up and slipped out, as he usually did very soon after the Hallelujah chorus. And then he would have fallen on the floor. That's what dead men did. They fell down.

But Ernie wasn't falling down. He apparently was being held up by his thing, though she couldn't tell whether it was her gripping him very tightly or him expanded beyond her capacity to accommodate him. Whatever it was, it wasn't coming out.

Ernie would have known the answer to that question. He knew everything there was to know about those things. But Ernie wasn't talking right now.

When it finally occurred to her that she was manacled to her stove, her tights around her ankles and her bra hanging in shreds, penetrated by a dead man in a beige knit suit and open-toed shoes, Audrey fell apart. She began to cry. But her crying, violent at times, didn't dislodge Ernie. On the contrary, his body shook and vibrated along with her, as if he, too, were crying.

The sound of her sobbing brought Siggy in through the doggy door. He stared at the two of them locked in their bizarre tango and then went over to his empty water bowl and stood there in silent protest for a moment before heading for the bathroom in the hope that someone had left the toilet seat up.

She didn't know how long she had been crying. Maybe five minutes, maybe fifteen minutes, maybe an hour. When she finally got her wits back and tried to consider what to do next, the Home Shopping Network was featuring a 14-karat-gold brooch with matching earrings.

The brooch, in the shape of an ancient scarab from Egypt, was $379.95, plus shipping and handling. It would look nice with her lavender cocktail dress.

She looked back down at Ernie and shuddered. He wasn't budging. She tried to raise her knee to push against his thigh, but the tights constrained her. She stuck her free hand between Ernie and her and pushed with all her might, screaming from the exertion. She tried to change the angle so that she would be leaning on him, but there was not enough play in the handcuffs.

Marshaling what was left of her strength, she tried as hard as she could to reach the refrigerator. But the handcuffs kept her six inches from the door handle. She screamed out in despair and sank back against the stove.

The key to the handcuffs was beside the soy-sauce packets on the table, well out of reach. She couldn't get to the phone. It was Friday night. Ernie wouldn't be missed until Monday morning.

His office would call. They'd get the machine. Hi, this is Ernie and Audrey. Leave a message at the beep. They'd leave a message at the beep. Hours would go by. A day. Two days. A week . . .

Doltha had a key, but she didn't come till Wednesday. And Doltha was a zombie. If by some miracle Audrey was still alive when she showed up, the cleaning lady would probably just clean around her. There was Tuesday and Thursday this week with Zadek. But he wouldn't blink an eyelash. He'd just bill her for the session. "I make this time available for you, Audrey. I'm here, ready to go to work. If you choose not to come, that's your decision."

Her mother would call from Tucson to complain about her father, a retired State Farm salesman. Lately she had been keeping Audrey on the phone for hours with her lamentations. "You'd think maybe once a month we could eat someplace where they have tablecloths and no salad bar."

Hi, this is Ernie and Audrey. Leave a message at the beep.

Eventually they'd be discovered—Ernie in the beige knit suit and sheer pantyhose, she, dead from starvation, handcuffed to the O'Keefe and Merritt with her spandex pants down around her ankles, the TV remote in her hand.

It would all come out, the whole business with the handcuffs and the women's clothes. They'd be on TV. Schenectady urologist and wife in bizarre sex suicide. Details at eleven. . . .

They would be buried together in the joint plot Ernie had bought for them at the Mount Spinoza cemetery in Niskayuna. And nobody would give a damn.

There were no children. Not that they really ever wanted any. She had an incompetent cervix, and they had decided to get her tubes tied instead of risking problematic pregnancies. Her mother had never forgiven her.

They would be survived by a five-year-old Rottweiler, who would certainly not lose any sleep over her death.

Surely there was more to life than dying cuffed to your stove. It was so senseless—cut down at age thirty-eight—done in by a pair of handcuffs purchased mail-order from Santa Monica, California.

She could think of no way out of her predicament without the house burning down, and there were no matches within reach. All she had was the TV remote.

On the screen of the TV set across the kitchen they were advertising an electric carving knife for seventy-nine dollars. Perfect for Easter. Audrey already had one. It was in the bottom drawer beside the stove. She had bought it last Christmas for Ernie to carve the goose.

The knife, the woman on TV said, was not just for cutting fowl. You could use it for vegetables, frozen food, and a dozen other kitchen jobs. If you weren't 100 percent satisfied, your money would be refunded.

Stretching the handcuffs as far as she could and inching Ernie along with her, Audrey managed to reach the cabinet beside the stove. Her fingers pried the bottom drawer open and explored the contents. There was an assortment of seldom-used kitchen implements—an apple corer, a garlic press, a coffee grinder.

She felt the edge of the carving knife, in its protective sheath, underneath the pie-wedge slicer. Slowly, carefully, she coaxed it forward with her fingertips. It seemed to take forever before she had it in her grip.

As her fingers closed around the Sunbeam deluxe model 370 multi-purpose carving utensil, her eye went to the outlet above the stove. There was just enough electric cord to do the trick. Which was a good thing, because the nearest extension cord was in the basement.

Chapter 3

Emmanuel Longhouse had been drunk, off and on, for at least three days when he ran out of money. It was a miracle that he was able to find his car, let alone drive it twelve miles to Schenectady from the bar along Front Street in Albany, where he had been drinking Narragansett since a little past noon.

The bartender, a fat Polish guy named Kratowski, had made it perfectly clear that he wasn't going to run a tab for him. Carl Kratowski didn't run a tab for anyone, and he wasn't about to start with a six-foot-five-inch deaf-mute Indian with an earring and a ponytail.

Kratowski had drawn his hand across his own throat to indicate that Emmanuel Longhouse was being cut off. And that was that. The bartender kept a .38 snubnose under the bar beside the bromo-seltzer packets to discourage any sort of discussion he was not inclined to have.

It was past midnight, then, that Emmanuel Longhouse—15/16 Mohawk, who hadn't spoken or heard since age nine, when he came home from school to the apartment above the Chinese restaurant in Utica and found his mother with her head in the oven—walked out of the Front Street Tavern and headed off into the March night in search of funds.

Finding his car turned out to be more a question of stumbling upon it by chance than of tracking it down with his three functioning senses. He was walking aimlessly west along Front Street when he happened to catch sight of the tan '84 Ranchero with the parking ticket under the

wiper and the tattered bumpersticker that read: INDIANS DO IT WITH-
OUT RESERVATIONS.

When the key fit in the ignition, he assumed it was his car and drove
away. The gas-tank needle was between a half and a quarter, which gave
him approximately fifty miles' range. He decided on Schenectady. In
the past he had had good luck there, especially in the suburbs east of
the city with the curved streets with the funny Dutch names. People who
lived in those houses had nice things.

He turned the Ranchero left at the next light and headed west into
the night, thereby following in the steps of his ancestors, who were
driven out of their encampments on the banks of the Hudson and sent
west along the river that bore their name to find new hunting grounds.

Audrey had passed out soon after the blood started flowing. In spite
of the claims made by the manufacturer, it was not like going through
butter with a hot knife.

In the background the Home Shopping Network was selling patio
furniture in anticipation of the approaching spring. The six-piece
recliner-and-beach-chair set was discounted to $199.95. Audrey con-
centrated on the voices in an effort to distract herself from the job at
hand.

There was a feeling of great relief when she felt Ernie's body slide to
the ground. She let out a small cry of triumph. Then she looked down
and saw the blood, and she lost it completely.

She screamed at the top of her lungs, went dizzy, and passed out. The
next thing she remembered was Siggy barking. But she was afraid to
open her eyes. She stood there, chained to her stove, eyes tightly shut,
refusing to open them.

"Shut up, Siggy!" she screamed. Siggy didn't shut up. On the contrary, he barked louder.

"I didn't have any choice," she whimpered, her eyes still closed.

If he was a smart dog, like Lassie or Rin Tin Tin, he'd go get help.
He'd run down to the fire station on Vermeer and lead the firemen here.

Siggy was not as dumb as Audrey thought. He had heard a scratch-
ing sound at the patio door, seen a large, dark figure working at the lock,
and was trying to alert his master that someone was breaking into the
house.

They didn't need the firemen. They needed the police. Or, even better, the cavalry. Because at that very moment their house was being in-
vaded by Indians.

· · ·

Emmanuel Longhouse used dogs the way they used canaries in mine disasters. If the canary lived, there was no poison gas, and if the dog barked for two minutes and lights didn't go on, it meant there was no one home. Which always made his job a lot easier. Especially when he was drunk.

With the house empty he wouldn't have to tiptoe around gingerly disconnecting wires, unbolting wall mounts, rifling drawers in the thin beam of a flashlight. He could work at a leisurely pace, examine the merchandise more carefully before choosing what was worth taking.

His dog-neutralization method entailed lying flat on his back and completely motionless for several minutes, allowing the animal to approach and sniff and assure himself that the large man on the living-room rug was no threat to him or his family. Then he stared into the dog's eyes until the dog blinked and looked away, and from that moment on, the dog would go to the ends of the earth for him.

The Rottweiler had sour breath and rheumy eyes, but within five minutes the dog was licking his face, eager to take him on a tour of the house.

They started out in the den, which gave onto the patio in the rear. Beyond the patio was a small pool with debris floating in it. He turned on a floor lamp to check out the den. Twenty-four-inch Sony, Goldstar VCR, Hitachi five-disc CD player with dual five-hundred-watt speakers, Panasonic phone-answering machine.

The equipment was all bought recently, except for the answering machine, which wasn't worth taking anyway. They were selling them brand-new for forty-nine dollars. He calculated two trips for the TV, VCR, and CD player. He'd leave the speakers if there were better things in the rest of the house.

He followed the Rottweiler out of the den and down a long hallway toward the bedrooms. There were three of them, two of them empty. The third was the master bedroom, a large, overfurnished room with bronze wall sconces and heavy oak fixtures.

Women's clothes were spread out over the dark-green bedspread. The closet door was open, as were the dresser drawers. There was a pair of scissors on the bed beside some pantyhose, still in its package. Jewelry was scattered on the dressing table.

Some silver jade earrings, a 14-karat-gold-plated locket, a bracelet with what could be a ruby but probably wasn't. None of it worth his time.

Beside the scissors on the bed was a cut-out section of pantyhose. What the hell was that all about? It wasn't until he followed the Rottweiler back down the hallway to the kitchen that he found out.

The first thing he saw was the TV on the kitchen table. The Home Shopping Network was selling garage-door openers. There were Chinese-food cartons on the table and a bottle of sherry.

The next thing he saw was a naked woman handcuffed to the stove, a pair of spandex pants rolled down around her ankles, and her bra in shreds.

Then there was a guy in a skirt hiked up above his waist lying with his tomahawk chopped off.

Audrey opened her mouth to scream, but nothing came out. She was all screamed out. She squinted at the vision in her kitchen, convinced that it was speedy divine retribution. She had already died and gone to judgment, and this was it—she was going to be raped and mutilated by a six-foot-five-inch Indian with an earring.

Emmanuel Longhouse, for his part, had several somewhat conflicting sensations simultaneously. The first was a completely involuntary response to the sight of the naked woman—the whiteness of her skin against the deep-red enamel of the stove, the almond-shaded nipples, the swell of her stomach accentuated by the rolled-down tights. The second was the sight of the guy in the women's clothes lying there without his dipstick. Which tended to neutralize the first impression. And finally there was the sight of the Sunbeam deluxe model 370 multi-purpose carving utensil in her free hand. It was both portable and pawnable. He could unload it directly without going through Freddie the Fence and his exorbitant 40 percent cut.

Though he wasn't Catholic in spite of all those years with the nuns at St. Ursula's Home, Emmanuel Longhouse crossed himself before removing the carving knife from her hand. He would have apologized if he could have or left one of those deaf-mute cards he used to carry with him before he realized they only made matters worse.

Then he made the mistake of looking down at the guy. Which explained the business of the scissors and the pantyhose.

Audrey's teeth were chattering now and she was uttering little whimpering cries as she watched the Indian go over to the sink and wash the blood off the carving knife. He carefully dried the stainless-steel blade and put it back in the protective sheath that was lying on the floor.

As Emmanuel Longhouse turned back for a last look at her, she said, "Plllllease . . . The keeeeeey . . . Could you get me the . . . keeeeeey before you leave . . . It's . . . with the . . . soooooooy-sauce on the taaaaaable. . . ."

For emphasis she looked toward the breakfast-nook table. There was the bottle of Harveys Bristol Cream and the take-out Chinese containers. Then he saw the key lying in the dish of soy-sauce packets.

Emmanuel Longhouse took a hit off the sherry bottle and considered the problem. There wasn't much percentage in uncuffing her. She could have a gun stashed someplace. At the very least she'd call the cops as soon as he was out of there.

Meanwhile the dog marched to his dish and looked back at Emmanuel Longhouse. Even a deaf-mute understood what this meant.

Putting down the carving knife, he went over and opened the cupboard. A lot of junk, but no dog food. When he looked back at the woman, her lips were saying, "Under the . . . siiiiiink . . ."

In the cabinet under the sink he found a bag of dried dog food. He poured a generous amount into the Rottweiler's dish and filled the water bowl to the brim. Then, as he replaced the bag, he wondered what a woman in her condition would want to eat.

In the refrigerator he found a couple of cans of Diet Coke, some margarine, half a container of cottage cheese, a few eggs, and four bottles of different types of mineral water, all half empty.

He took out the Diet Coke, then opened the freezer compartment. A gallon of rocky road ice cream, a package of bagels, three frozen Señorita enchiladas, and a Birds Eye lasagna TV dinner.

He threw the lasagna in the microwave and went out to load the TV, VCR, and CD player into his car. By the time he had returned, the cheese had melted.

She wasn't interested in the lasagna when he put it on the stove next to her, along with a fork, knife, napkin, and a Diet Coke. All she did was look at him pleadingly and murmur, "Prooooooozaaaaaac . . . In the . . . beeeeeedrooooooom . . ."

What the hell was she talking about?

"Meeeeeediiiiiiiciiiiiine caaaaaabiiiiiineeeeeet . . ."

He shrugged, unable to read her lips. He collected the microwave and the bottle of sherry and walked out of the kitchen without looking back. He'd leave her the portable TV. It looked like she could use it.

He said good-bye to the Rottweiler and went out the patio door, carefully relocking it. He didn't want some fuckup following him in and making a mess of the place.

At four o'clock that morning Emmanuel Longhouse woke up abruptly in his room on South Ferry Street in Albany. He had been having frightening dreams. If he had been able to scream, he would have. The image of the tomahawk being sawed off by the carving knife was starkly vivid in his mind.

He wished he had never broken into that house in Schenectady and seen what he had seen. At that point he had still been drunk enough to absorb the impact of the vision. But now, hours later, stone sober in his room, there was no defense against it.

He got out of bed and went for the bottle of Harveys Bristol Cream. He felt the alcohol seep into his bloodstream, gradually absorbing the shock, and lay back down on his bed.

As he stared at the water-stained ceiling above him, he wondered what happened to the guy's wazoo. He hadn't see it anyplace in the kitchen. Where could it have been?

Then he thought about the Rottweiler and started to laugh.

Chapter 4

By noon the following day, Emmanuel Longhouse had already cashed out with Freddie the Fence, netting $175 for the whole load, and was sitting in the Front Street Tavern watching the NBA on the TV above the bar. The Knicks were getting their asses handed to them by a team with orange uniforms.

Emmanuel Longhouse didn't give a shit about the Knicks. All those black guys with bald heads and attitudes. They were all making two, three million a year, not to mention the money they got from the sneaker ads.

But the game was keeping his mind off the events of the previous night. Ever since he'd gotten up that morning, with a particularly nasty hangover from that sweet shit he drank on top of the beer, he had been bothered by troubling thoughts. They had nothing to do with breaking into someone's house and stealing things. It was his job, the only thing he was trained to do in life. He had been working at it from the age of fourteen, did thirty-six months in Elmira when he was nineteen, and hadn't been caught since.

What was bothering him was the woman cuffed to the stove. The guy without his peashooter—there was nothing to be done about him. The guy was dead and that was that. But the woman was still alive when he left. Even with the lasagna and the Diet Coke, there was no way of knowing how long she'd make it unless someone showed up. She could die. And if she died, it would be on Emmanuel Longhouse's head.

He had another beer and tried to figure out what to do. He could call the Schenectady police anonymously and tell them about the woman. Describe the location of the house and the situation and hang up. But he hadn't spoken in twenty-seven years and wasn't about to start now.

He could write the police a letter, explaining things. But a letter could take a couple of days. And by then she could have starved to death.

Halfway through the Narragansett, he came up with the solution. He settled his tab with Carl Kratowski and left the bar.

In the post office on State Street, he went to the table with the out-of-town phone books and found the one for Schenectady. Under the Schenectady Police Department, there was a long list of numbers: Auxiliary Police, Child Abuse, Collision Reporting, Community Services, Crimes in Progress, Divisions, Emergencies, Handicapped Hotline, Ride Share . . . And there, at the very bottom, just after Parades, was Public Relations and a fax number.

He memorized the number and walked out onto State Street to look for a copy store.

Pauline Haggis did not generally work Saturdays. The job was strictly nine-to-five, with the occasional evening devoted to explaining to community groups why the police were not to blame for the upsurge of crime in their neighborhood. Deputy public relations officer for the Schenectady Police Department was grade-four civil service, forty hours a week, dental and medical plan, and a pension. In another eight years she'd be out of there with thirty-nine five and an IRA.

On that particular Saturday, the twenty-eighth of March, she happened to be in the office upstairs from the department headquarters on Liberty Street availing herself of the Xerox machine to run off copies of her daughter Kitty's term paper. A fairly minor white-collar crime, as these things went. Alicia Xentas in Ride Share used the phone on weekends to call her sister in Manila.

Pauline Haggis was just about done making the five copies of the eighty-page term paper when she heard the sound of the office fax machine. She finished collating the copies, then went over to the fax machine.

The cover sheet said only GIVE TO POLEECE RITE AWAY. The second sheet read, in its entirety:

There iz a womman chaned to her stove with notting to eat in the green howse with wite shudders and pool in bakyard with brown dog in skenectity. Her husban is ded and has no dong. She will dye if you dont help her. Street has duch name like van somthing. I left lasanya and coke but it wont be enuff. If you dont help her itl be on yore conchinch not mine.

Pauline Haggis read this strange fax three times. It was obviously written by a madman.

She took her illegally duplicated term papers to her car, locked them in the trunk, then went around to the front of the building and entered division headquarters.

Her I.D. card pinned to her coat, she waved at the duty sergeant and walked down the hall past the empty holding cells into the detectives' bullpen, where a half dozen weekend-shift plainclothes cops were sitting around with their paperwork.

Barney Abelove, a heavy-set veteran homicide detective who had been on the force even longer than she had, growled at her over his hero sandwich, "Jesus, Pauline, isn't five days a week enough for you?"

He had a dark, jowly face and thinning hair and wore sports jackets at least a size too small for him. He had been through a nasty divorce a few years ago, and he didn't look like he took very good care of himself.

"This came over my department fax machine a few minutes ago."

She handed him the fax. He glanced at it quickly, his sandwich in one hand, a stray onion dripping from the corner of his mouth. Putting his sandwich down, he then reread the fax and shrugged. "Why do you think they faxed it to you?"

"Because our fax number is listed and yours isn't."

"Maybe we ought to list our fax number, too. Get all sorts of loony-tunes shit like this."

He went back to his sandwich, dismissing her. She stood there for a moment, then, unable to just let it end there, asked, "Are you going to follow it up?"

He looked back up at her, a faint expression of annoyance on his face. "Sure."

She waited for another moment, realized that there was nothing more to say, and walked off.

"Teach you to work on Saturdays," he said to her retreating back.

As she walked away, she was convinced that he knew about the illegal copying. So what? Everybody did it. Abelove probably gassed his personal car up at the department pump.

Next time, she'd walk out the door without checking the goddamn fax machine.

On this particular Saturday in late March, Barney Abelove was on the eight-to-four shift. He had hopes of getting out of there on time so that he could get home, shower and shave, and still pick Renata up in time to make the early-bird special dinner at Grazziani's, which closed out at 5:45.

He glanced at his watch: 2:20. Then he glanced back at the fax. Ten to one it was a fruitcake or a kid playing games with his father's fax machine. If he slid it into his drawer for an hour and a half or so, it would become the swing shift's problem.

Abelove put the fax in his drawer and opened the top case file on his stack of unsolved crimes. A murder and carjacking in Colonie. All they had was a make on the car, '93 Buick Riviera. No witnesses, no evidence, *nada*. He started making a list of chop shops, but soon his mind was back on the woman chained to her stove.

He took the fax back out of his drawer and reread it once more. It was the details that intrigued him. The lasagna, the Coke, the color of the house, the dog . . . Hallucinations usually weren't that specific.

The number on the top of the fax had an Albany prefix. He went down the hall to the file room, pulled the reverse directory for Albany, found that the fax had been sent from Kopy Kat Kopy Korner on South Hudson Street. Then he pulled the regular directory and got a number, went back to his desk, and dialed.

"Kopy Kat," a voice with an Asian accent responded.

"This is Detective Abelove from the Schenectady Police Department. I have a fax here that was sent from your place of business at two-eleven this afternoon. You happen to know who sent it?"

"Sorry."

"Sorry what?"

"You pay one dollar each page. We send fax. Lots people send fax."

"You don't remember someone in the last hour sending a fax to Schenectady?"

"Sorry."

"Sorry what?"

"Lots people."

"About how many people?"

"Ten. Seventeen. Lots."

"Yeah, right, thanks."

He hung up the phone, put the fax back in the desk drawer, checked his watch: 2:35. An hour and ten minutes, an hour and twenty tops, and he could walk out of there.

He opened up the next case file, an armed robbery and homicide in Scotia. There was an inventory of serial numbers he was going to have to run through the pawn shops. His eyes started to swim in all those numbers. Lots numbers.

Her husban is ded and has no dong. She will dye if you dont help her . . .

Closing the file, he leaned back in his swivel chair and thought about what he'd have to do if he decided to run this down. He could send a car through looking for a green house with white shutters and a pool. Or he could send a chopper up.

According to the latest department cost-cutting memo, putting a chopper in the air cost close to a grand an hour. It required authorization from the watch commander. Abelove looked over at the glassed-in office at the edge of the bullpen, where Lieutenant Dick Jeffries was playing Minesweeper on his desktop computer. Abelove didn't like Dick Jeffries. He was a sarcastic black guy with a big chip on his shoulder. If he got Jeffries to authorize a chopper and it turned out to be a blind alley, Abelove would never hear the end of it.

The woman was chained to the stove. How long could you live on lasagna?

A chopper could spot a dog, and then if there was a swimming pool, the pilot could bank down and verify the color of the house and the name of the street.

Taking the fax with him, Abelove walked across the bullpen in the direction of Dick Jeffries's office. It looked like he was going to have to spring for the full-price menu at Grazziani's.

Audrey had been dozing on and off for hours when she heard the noise of the helicopter. She had fallen asleep in the middle of an Ida Lupino movie, sitting on the floor, leaning against the stove, her left arm twisted around in the handcuffs and suspended at the level of her head.

At first she thought it was the TV. One of those news traffic people reporting tie-ups on the thruway. But as she opened her eyes and squinted at the screen, she saw what looked like *Little House on the Prairie*, and she knew they didn't have helicopters back then.

The noise got louder. It sounded as if the helicopter were going to land on the roof. The whirring of the chopper blades didn't help the dull, throbbing headache that had been getting steadily worse since dawn.

"Will you shut up, for godsakes!" she cried, hoping they would go away.

It took her a moment to realize that she didn't want them to go away. On the contrary. What she wanted to do was let them know she was in the house, chained to her stove.

"Help!" she screamed in a feeble, parched voice.

The helicopter noise got louder, drowning out her cry, as well as the sound of Michael Landon's horse as he rode across the prairie bringing a freshly cut Christmas tree back to the little house.

Abelove went east on Union Street, past the college, driving at moderate speed without the siren or the roof bubble. There was no point going Code 3. If the guy was dead, he wouldn't be going anywhere, nor would the woman chained to her stove.

A patrol car was waiting for him in front of 474 Van Schuyler Lane. He knew one of the uniforms, Doetz, from the bowling league. The other one was a short guy with a trim mustache named Gallagher.

Abelove pulled up across the street, got out, and walked slowly over to the patrol car.

Doetz rolled down the window. Abelove could hear the basketball game on the radio.

"We checked the perimeter. There's a dog in the backyard."

"Brown?"

Doetz looked at Gallagher, who nodded. "Yeah. Brown. A Rottweiler."

"We ought to get Animal Control down here," said Doetz. "Those things are trained to attack."

Abelove rubbed his eyes. More authorizations. More expenditure of funds. He'd be tied up here till midnight.

"We'll go in the front," he said.

"Without a warrant?"

"We got a fax."

Doetz and Gallagher looked at him funny. But it wasn't worth explaining.

The uniforms got out of the car. As they walked up to the front door, Abelove asked, "What's the score?"

"Forty-six to thirty-nine Duke."

"Shit," he muttered. "I gave ten points."

Siggy was way ahead of them. As soon as he heard voices in front of the house, he was in the doggy door, through the house, and on patrol in the entry foyer, barking himself into a frenzy.

"We can take out the Rottweiler," suggested Gallagher, pulling his weapon.

Abelove thought about the paperwork on a dog shooting and shook his head.

He tried the heavy front door with the Niskayuna neighborhood-watch decal and found it locked.

"You want to call in the battering ram?"

Abelove shook his head again. "Maybe there's an open door or window in back," he said without conviction.

As the three of them walked along the side of the house, Siggy followed them from the inside, keeping track of their progress, room by room. The Rottweiler went apoplectic each time they tried to force one of the windows open.

By the time they reached the backyard, Siggy was outside in the yard. There was a fence with an unlocked gate. The three policemen watched the dog dig in to defend his turf.

Abelove thought about the fettucini Alfredo at Grazziani's and about Renata's dark Sicilian eyes. He loved to watch her wrap pasta around her fork and then slide it over her tongue. And here he was in Niskayuna staring down a rabid Rottweiler with two trigger-happy uniforms ready to blow the dog away and bring in the battering ram.

"Fuck the dog," he said, pushing open the gate and walking right toward Siggy. Doetz and Gallagher watched in amazement as the Rottweiler made a brief stand, then turned and headed for the far end of the swimming pool, where he slunk down underneath a rusting aluminum recliner and whimpered.

Abelove's five-year stint in Burglary led his eyes immediately to the small, precisely cut hole made by the glass cutter, a hole just large enough for a hand to penetrate and slip the lock from the inside. Whoever had broken into this particular house had, for some reason, reclosed and relocked the sliding door.

As the uniforms looked on, the homicide detective slipped his hand through the glass hole carefully, concerned with preserving as clean a print base as possible. He opened the lock, withdrew his hand, and slid open the door.

Their weapons drawn, Doetz and Gallagher followed Abelove into a den. There were loose wires and empty spaces where a TV, VCR, and CD player presumably had been.

"Dollars to doughnuts they don't have the serial numbers," said Doetz.

But Abelove wasn't listening. He was heading toward the kitchen, from where he could swear he heard Michael Landon's voice.

This time Abelove, too, drew his service revolver. He entered the kitchen and saw a white high-heeled shoe lying on the floor beside a dead man in women's clothes with his dick cut off and a naked woman handcuffed to a stove, an empty plate of lasagna beside her.

Whatever appetite he'd had dissolved on the spot. He'd order the meat wagon, then call Renata and blow off Grazziani's.

Chapter 5

Barney Abelove and Assistant Medical Examiner Milton Zieff stood in the kitchen of the Dutch Colonial on Van Schuyler trying to remain professional in the presence of one of the more bizarre crime scenes that either of them had seen. Audrey, meanwhile, was permitted to lie down in the bedroom under the watch of Doetz, Abelove's initial attempt to question her having ended in paroxysms of sobbing. Gallagher had already tossed his cookies in the powder room.

Though Milton Zieff, in the course of performing autopsies, had taken all sorts of liberties with the human body, he, too, was shaken by the condition of the victim, who had been identified off the DMV database as Dr. Ernest Haas.

"You want to take a flyer on cause of death?" Abelove asked him as they watched the body-bag team do the corpse.

Zieff cleared his throat nervously before saying, "Well, if . . . it was in fact removal of the member which caused death . . . there would be more blood on the floor, wouldn't there?"

"Right." Abelove nodded, feeling his stomach churn.

"Of course, we have evaporation and absorption over the elapsed time period, so it's difficult to say exactly how much blood was lost."

"Can a guy survive losing his dick without immediate medical attention?" Part of Abelove did not want to know the answer.

"Problematic," uttered Zieff.

"Any speculation on weapon?" Once again, Abelove wasn't sure he wanted to know the answer.

"It would have to be something relatively sharp with a certain amount of torque, I should think. The penis is an organ with thick intertwined networks of membranes, arteries, and veins, which would make it somewhat . . . resistant . . . to amputation."

"That's good to know," quipped Abelove, but Zieff didn't even crack a small smile.

There was no weapon in sight and the woman had been found handcuffed to the stove. There was another, even more perplexing piece of the puzzle that neither of them wanted to consider, but since Abelove would have to question the wife, he needed to know the answer.

"What do you think happened to it?" he asked Zieff.

"Beg your pardon?"

"The guy's dick."

"Well, it appears as if it's missing, doesn't it?"

"Yeah. I suppose we'd have recognized it if it was lying around here somewhere?"

"Oh, yes," Zieff answered quickly. "It would have been hard to miss, wouldn't it have been?"

"You'd think so."

Abelove stood in the doorway of the bedroom, peering in at the woman asleep in the bed.

"She's been out cold for a half hour," Doetz said from his post in the hallway. "You think she cut it off?"

"The fuck do I know."

When Abelove had called in to explain what they found at the scene, Jeffries had asked him point blank, "You got a homicide?"

"Either that or a really hinky accident," he had replied.

"There a weapon?"

"Nope . . ."

There was silence on the other end of the phone. Abelove could tell that Jeffries was pissed. He, too, must have had Saturday-night plans that were in jeopardy now because of the goddamn fax.

"Should I read her her rights?"

"I'll talk to the D.A.'s office and get back to you."

Five minutes later, the phone rang and Jeffries told him to see if he could get her to consent to a medical examination.

"Why?"

"Check for semen traces."

If this was a rape case, Abelove decided, the guy certainly got what was coming to him. The vaginal exam would establish whether she cut it off before or after he shot his load. Another detail he wasn't entirely sure he wanted to know.

One of the forensic guys came down the hallway and told Abelove that he wanted to fingerprint the woman to get a set of eliminators on her.

Abelove sighed and nodded. He was going to have to wake up an exhausted, extremely traumatized woman, read her her rights, take a set of prints, and then get her to sign a consent form for a vaginal.

As he approached the bed and bent down over her, he could hear her labored breathing.

"Mrs. Haas?" he called softly, as if he were waking a sleeping child.

Raising his voice by degrees, he kept calling her name without result. Finally, he put his hand on her shoulder and pushed. She didn't flinch.

He turned around to Doetz. "Was she out of your sight at any time?"

"Just to go to the can."

Abelove saw the closed door of the master bathroom. He hurried inside and opened the medicine cabinet. There was a veritable drugstore in there.

"Get the doctor," he barked, as his eyes scanned the vials of prescription drugs marked AUDREY HAAS, TAKE ONLY AS DIRECTED.

There was one empty vial in the wastepaper basket. He fished it out and handed it to Zieff as he entered the bathroom.

"Prozac," Zieff said and hurried out of the bathroom to look at the sleeping woman. He sat down on the bed, took her pulse, and shined a pocket flashlight in her eyes.

"How many she take?"

"I don't know how many were left in the vial. But if we don't get her stomach pumped in the next hour, we can do the vaginal as part of the autopsy."

The second ambulance brought the neighbors out of their houses. As it roared away with Audrey's Prozac-saturated body, sirens blasting, people stood in little clusters watching the action.

Abelove had decided to stay at the crime scene, for the moment at least, instead of following the ambulance to the hospital. The paramedics told him that even if they managed to get enough out to save her, she wouldn't be in any shape to talk for a while.

He walked around the house trying to come up with some sort of vaguely logical scenario for the events that apparently took place there. He had a woman cuffed to her stove, her husband, in women's clothes, dead and dismembered three feet from her, no weapon, and no member.

There was a wild card in the whole mess. The fax. That and the glass cut out of the patio door indicated that someone had broken into the house. And if someone broke into the house that night, he could have been the dismemberer and/or the murderer and taken the weapon and/or the guy's dick with him.

Then there was the relocked patio door, the lasagna, and the Diet Coke can.

And the dog. What did *he* know?

When Abelove walked out into the backyard, the Rottweiler was pacing on a strip of dying grass between the pool and the fence. He looked back at Abelove with a detached look, as if to say, Don't look at me—I just live here. Then, as if making a definitive comment on the whole situation, he went into a crouch and took a dump.

Watching him, Abelove had one more unsettling thought in a day filled with a number of unsettling thoughts.

He went back inside and caught Zieff just as he was packing up his equipment.

"We got to leave no stone unturned here—you understand what I'm saying?"

Zieff nodded.

"I'm thinking about the missing member. We've been all over the house and the yard looking for it, right?"

"Right."

"What if the dog ate it?"

A pained expression came over the doctor's features, and he muttered, "You don't really think that . . . that would happen, do you?"

"Like I said, I'm turning over stones."

"Well, it's conceivable, I suppose . . . though I'm not a veterinarian."

"So let's say the dog ate it. Would it show up if he took a dump?"

Zieff didn't flinch. He merely stroked his chin and said, "Interesting question. It would depend, I would imagine, on how the dog's digestive system broke down the fatty tissue and cartilage . . . We would have to do a content analysis from the stool, I suppose, wouldn't we?"

Abelove nodded rhetorically. "So we have Forensics bag the dogshit, right?"

"Right."

• • •

By the time the first minicam unit showed up, they were already hanging tape. A tall strawberry blonde in a knockoff Burberry got out of the van, followed by a camera crew and a man with makeup and hairspray.

Carrie Castle, co-anchor of *WSCH Action News*, went over to work the tape hangers. The forensic team was under strict orders not to talk to the press, and Carrie Castle knew that, but she worked them over just the same, and had them leaning when the front door opened and Barney Abelove walked out.

"Barney. How about a quickie for the six o'clock?"

Abelove squinted into the lowering sun and made out the features of the WSCH anchorwoman. She was always the first one out of the box. Probably slept in the goddamn van.

Abelove didn't have time for this right now. He needed to get to the hospital in case Audrey Haas woke up and was ready to talk. He needed to confer with Jeffries and the department PR people on how to handle the situation, as well as with the district attorney's office to figure out if they were going to file on the woman and, if they were, what they were going to file. He needed to interview neighbors to find out if they'd seen or heard anything. He needed to push Forensics for prints. He needed to run burglary rap sheets. He needed to get serial numbers and put the TV, VCR, and CD player on the hot sheet. He needed to check out the fax. He needed to notify next of kin. He needed to sit on the lab and get them to run the dogshit. Just for starters.

"Sorry. I've got no time now."

Carrie Castle stayed right with him, walking alongside him as he headed for his car.

"Come on, Barney. I came all the way out here. You got to give me something."

Abelove stopped and saw that she had signaled the camera crew. One guy with a minicam on his shoulder, another guy with a boom mike were moving in on him. These people were like hit-and-run muggers. You stopped walking for a second, you were dead.

He knew that if he didn't give them something, they'd go up and down the street putting the neighbors on tape. You could always get someone to shoot their mouth off in front of a camera. Then the PR people would have to get into damage control, and they'd be all over Abelove.

"Give me two seconds, okay?" she said, as the camera guy shoved a light meter in his face.

In not much more than two seconds, the anchorwoman had positioned them so that they were backlit by the setting sun and was already vamping into the mike. "I'm here on Van Schuyler Lane, in Niskayuna, with Detective Barney Abelove of the Schenectady police, where a homicide has just occurred. Detective Abelove, can you tell us what happened here?"

Abelove stared straight into the camera for a moment, with no idea where to begin.

"There appears to have been some foul play here, though we're not yet prepared to say just what occurred."

"Do we have a dead body?" Carrie Castle persisted.

"Yes, we do."

"Can you identify the victim?"

"Not until notification of next of kin."

"Were there any survivors?"

"The victim's wife has been taken to the hospital."

"Was she attacked?"

"We believe so."

"Did the husband attack the wife?"

"Well, that would be pure speculation."

"Did the wife murder the husband?"

"I can't comment on that, pending forensic tests . . ." As soon as those words were out of his mouth, Abelove realized he had made a mistake. Carrie Castle could start a brush fire with them. He tried to go back and fill in hurriedly, "We really don't know exactly what happened there last night."

"But we do have a possible homicide involving a wife killing her husband?"

"Possible. Anything's possible. There's evidence of housebreaking, there's a dog involved—"

"A dog?"

He felt the quicksand starting to suck him in.

"It would be foolish to speculate any further until we know all the details. I'm sorry. I have to go."

And he yanked open his car door and got inside. As he rummaged for his car keys, he could hear Carrie Castle's voice, not missing a beat, saying, "The police are remaining extremely tight-lipped about what exactly did happen here in this quiet neighborhood of Dutch Colonial houses and green lawns . . ."

As Abelove drove away, he thought about all the things he could have told Carrie Castle. He would have loved to have seen the look on her face if he had said, "Well, Carrie, I just sent a Baggie full of dogshit to the lab to be analyzed for traces of Ernest Haas's penis. We're taking seriously the possibility that the dog ate it. As soon as we finish pumping the Prozac out of the wife's stomach, we'll try to find out if she cut it off or not. Then, there's the fax from a burglar we received on the Public Relations department fax machine this afternoon . . ."

Chapter 6

It took Audrey what seemed like days to swim to the surface. And when she finally broke the plane of the water and emerged into blinding sunlight, she wanted to go back down into the murky water and stay there.

There were strange voices and disturbing noises all around her. Her throat was full of bile, her head full of disconcerting memories. The details of the past twenty-four hours replayed themselves in reverse, like a film running backward, running all the way back to the moment she lined up the Sunbeam deluxe model 370 multi-purpose carving utensil . . .

Gallagher, who was standing guard outside her room, heard the scream. He threw open the door and saw his charge staring right at him.

"You okay?" he muttered.

Audrey said nothing, merely lay there, her eyes looking straight through Gallagher.

"You scream?"

She said nothing. Gallagher did a peremptory check of the bathroom, and then went to summon a nurse.

Phyllis Pascudny, RN and head nurse of the psychiatric emergency unit, into whose care Audrey had been entrusted after the stomach pump, verified Audrey's vital signs before asking if there was something the matter.

"Could I have my Prozac, please." These were Audrey's first words since being admitted to the emergency room of Mohawk Valley Community Hospital in Cohoes, where she had been since a little past six that evening.

"I'll need to talk to the doctor," Nurse Pascudny said.

"Zadek," Audrey mumbled. "Marvin Zadek. He's in the book."

While the psychiatric resident was being summoned, Gallagher went to find Abelove in the coffee shop, as he had been instructed to do as soon as Audrey was awake. The detective had been on the phone for the past hour trying to get a decision out of Jeffries and the D.A.'s office about whether they were going to arrest her and move her to a jail hospital facility.

After a half dozen phone calls back and forth, they decided to wait until Abelove questioned Audrey Haas. When Gallagher told Abelove that Audrey Haas was conscious and screaming, Abelove told Jeffries he'd get back to him.

The detective reached the room at the same time as the psychiatric resident, a kid named Wechsler with a gold stud earring and tinted glasses. Abelove was asked to wait until the resident examined the patient and determined whether she was up to being interrogated.

"You understand," said Abelove, "that we have a possible homicide here?"

"Yeah, well I have an attempted suicide," Wechsler responded, as if it were self-evident that suicides had priority over homicides.

Five minutes later, the resident emerged from the room and told Abelove that he would have to check with Audrey Haas's personal physician before permitting him to question her.

Abelove went back to the coffee shop, where he dialed Renata's number from the pay phone on the wall.

"I'm going to be here for a while," he told her.

"You know who just called? My brother-in-law Tony. He said you were on the six o'clock news. With Carrie Castle."

"Shit. I didn't say anything."

"That's what he said."

"Huh?"

"He said you didn't say anything. Maybe they'll replay it at eleven."

He hung up and walked back across the coffee shop, thinking, for some reason, about the way Renata got voraciously hungry after they made love. Abelove'd be lying there, barely able to move, and she'd be up and in the kitchen making herself a bologna-and-cheese sandwich.

Well, there were worse things a woman could do after you fucked her, right?

• • •

Marvin Zadek, M.D., was beeped in Monte's Steakhouse in Scotia, where he had been dining with his wife, Ellen. He sent Ellen home in a cab, with doggy bags for both of them, and drove to Mohawk Valley Community.

Zadek conferred briefly with Wechsler before seeing his patient. The resident told him they had pumped enough Prozac out of her stomach to wipe out a gorilla. Maybe even two gorillas.

"I don't think she was fucking around," he said.

"I see," Zadek said condescendingly, as if to imply that this guy with the earring had no business making a judgment about his patient.

"There's this detective here keeps trying to get in to talk to her. I told him it was your call."

"Do you know what she's done?"

"Nope. She's not talking, at least not to me. She just asked me for Prozac. I mean, we just pump a couple dozen pills out of her stomach and the first thing she asks for when she comes out of it is more. Can you beat that?"

As soon as Zadek entered the room, Audrey started to cry again. It was an automatic response, a sense memory of all those hours spent together in Zadek's office on Van Curler Street with the box of tissues on the table next to the armchair.

The doctor sat down on a straight chair beside the bed and waited for Audrey's sobbing to quiet. When it abated, he said, "Would you like to tell me what happened, Audrey?"

She shook her head like a stubborn three-year-old.

Zadek nodded, then said, without raising his voice, "I can't help you if I don't know what happened."

"Nothing happened," she said through her teeth.

"If nothing happened, Audrey, why did they have to pump your stomach?"

She didn't answer. Instead, she turned her head away from him. Zadek just sat there, his hands folded in his lap, watching her.

More silence, then he said, "Audrey, where's your husband?"

The mention of Ernie sent her into a paroxysm of sobbing so intense that Zadek considered getting the resident to give her a shot of Thorazine. He waited until she had calmed down before telling her that he would be right back and then left the room.

The uniformed cop at the door directed him to the coffee shop, where he found Abelove with a cup of coffee and a newspaper.

"Detective Abelove?"

The cop looked up at him through lidded eyes. He looked exhausted. There was a tomato-sauce stain on his sleeve.

"I'm Marvin Zadek, Audrey Haas's doctor. Could you tell me what happened?"

Abelove looked at the short, dapper-looking man in the bow tie and wondered just where to begin.

"Where's her husband?" Zadek asked.

"In the morgue. They're doing an autopsy."

"An autopsy?"

"Yeah," Abelove nodded. "They're trying to figure out what happened to his dick."

Sitting within earshot of Barney Abelove as he told Marvin Zadek what had apparently occurred the night before in Schenectady, ostensibly immersed in a book entitled *Intermediate Endocrinology*, was a second-year medical student at Albany State named Eugene Zukoff, who supplemented his meager income of student loans by working as a freelance stringer for Carrie Castle. The WSCH anchorwoman had called him earlier that evening and asked him to follow an ambulance.

Following ambulances was a specialty of Eugene Zukoff. In his white med-school lab jacket and scuffed Reeboks, he looked like a resident and, as such, was able to wander around hospitals without drawing attention to himself.

He had gotten the patient's name and room number from a nurse he knew in Admitting, and then went after the cop.

It hadn't taken Eugene Zukoff long to locate Barney Abelove. After seeing him confer with the uniformed cop in front of Audrey Haas's door, Zukoff followed Abelove to the coffee-shop pay phone and heard him say that they wouldn't let him talk to Audrey Haas until her shrink signed off on it.

So as soon as Zukoff had seen the short man in the bow tie enter the coffee shop, he'd figured it was Audrey Haas's shrink. The conversation between the cop and the shrink turned out to be a real earful. Sitting at the next table, Zukoff made notes on a yellow legal pad, underneath the names of the principal glands of the endocrine system.

By the time the shrink got up to go talk to the woman who had apparently cut off her husband's schlong and fed it to the dog, Zukoff had filled three pages with the details.

Carrie Castle led with the story, preempting film of the governor's visit to farmers in Endicott promising more state aid to agriculture and a live minicam of a three-alarm fire in Troy. They replayed the earlier interview with Abelove outside the Haas home on Van Schuyler and then had a mobile reporter do a stand-up in front of the hospital.

All this before Barney Abelove was able to question Audrey Haas, who, Zadek had declared, was still too traumatized to discuss the events with the police. Abelove sat in the coffee shop watching the news on the wall-mounted unit, along with a dozen visitors and nurses who had wandered in there at the sound of Carrie Castle's adrenalized voice.

Dumbfounded, Abelove listened as Carrie Castle described a plausible scenario for the events that no one but Audrey Haas and possibly the burglar had witnessed. She began the story with a disclaimer that the details were not fit for family viewing and suggested that children be asked to leave the room. When she got to the part about the dismemberment, she repeated the disclaimer before saying that, pending police corroboration, there seemed to be a strong indication that Audrey Haas had amputated her husband's penis and fed it to the dog.

How the fuck did she know *that*? Had they gotten to Zadek? If the man was so concerned with medical ethics that he was withholding his patient from police interrogation, would he have gotten on the phone and called Carrie Castle?

Would Renata Sbazio, his girlfriend of three years, have telephoned Channel 6 with the story?

Could Audrey Haas herself have picked up the bedside phone and, through her postsuicidal haze of tranquilizers, managed to get the number of the WSCH studio and get through to Carrie Castle?

It was a complete puzzlement to Barney Abelove. He waited for the shit to hit the fan.

It didn't take long.

Ralph D'Imbroglio, the Schenectady County district attorney, had been dozing off in bed watching the news between his toes when he heard Carrie Castle's report. A major homicide and scandal in Schenectady and he wasn't in the goddamn loop. Furious, D'Imbroglio grabbed the phone, called his deputy, and ordered him to convene a meeting at eight o'clock in the morning in his office with Dick Jeffries and the detective on the case.

Dick Jeffries had already fallen asleep, knocked out by a large anchovy pizza and two beers, when he was awakened at 11:15 P.M. by the deputy district attorney, Clint Wells, and told of the Sunday-morning meeting.

"This can't wait till Monday?" Jeffries asked. He had a 7:30 reservation to tee off at Rip Van Winkle with his chiropractor and a guy from Poughkeepsie who wanted to sell him a time share in Killington.

"Direct orders from Ralph."

Emmanuel Longhouse, for his part, had been sitting in the Eagle Bar and Grill on Front Street in Albany drinking Narragansett and staring absently at the TV. At eleven o'clock Carl Kratowski switched the TV to *Cheers*, but even if he hadn't, Emmanuel Longhouse wouldn't have paid attention. He rarely bothered to lip-read TV newspeople. It wasn't worth the effort.

Among the twenty to twenty-five thousand other people who, according to the local ratings, did watch the WSCH eleven o'clock news that night, was a feminist lawyer from Saratoga Springs named Susan Anthony Bremmer.

To Susan Bremmer, the image of Audrey Haas chained to her stove to satisfy the carnal desires of her husband was a powerful symbol of the systemic sexual abuse of women. And her reaction to it was heroic. Beyond heroic. It was mythic. By cutting the chains of bondage represented by her husband's penis, this woman had struck a blow for the freedom and dignity of women everywhere.

Audrey Haas had stormed the Bastille. Now it was up to the rest of them to close ranks behind her. *Aux armes, citoyennes.*

Chapter 7

Barney Abelove had barely slept when he arrived at Ralph D'Imbroglio's office in the county building on State Street Sunday morning. Only a few hours earlier, at 3 A.M., with Audrey Haas sound asleep and showing no signs of awakening in the near future, he had left Doetz and Gallagher to guard her door and driven home through a thin, cold rain.

He had managed a few fitful hours of sleep before being rousted out of bed by his alarm clock. On the way to the D.A.'s office, he drove through a McDonald's for a twelve-ounce cup of black coffee, which, he was hoping, would get him through the morning.

He was going to be asked a lot of questions to which he didn't have the answers. Instead of questioning Audrey Haas and trying to get the answers, he was going to have to waste god knows how many hours explaining to them why he didn't know the answers.

"Sorry about this," Clint Wells said as Abelove walked in the door at eight o'clock sharp, "but Ralph doesn't like hearing about this kind of shit on the news."

Abelove dozed on the couch until ten after, when Jeffries and D'Imbroglio entered the office together. The lieutenant was wearing a Jack Nicklaus all-weather golf jacket, the D.A. an extra-large emerald-green jogging suit.

"Get some coffee and bagels," D'Imbroglio told Clint Wells, then lowered his bulk into an executive desk chair behind a mahogany desk the size of an aircraft carrier. Jeffries took the other side of the leather couch, barely acknowledging Abelove's presence.

"Who the hell talked to the press?" D'Imbroglio growled.

"That's what I want to know," piped in Jeffries, clearly trying to put distance between himself and Abelove. "What the hell were you doing on TV, Barney?"

"I was blindsided by Carrie Castle at the scene. She must have gotten a Code Four off the radio. But I didn't give her any details. I don't know who her source was on the details."

"Jesus! His own wife. A man can't turn his back on anybody these days." D'Imbroglio shifted his weight uncomfortably in the chair before continuing. "All right, lay it out to me from the beginning."

"Well, yesterday afternoon, around two-fifteen, we got this fax—"

"A fax? You got a *fax* reporting a homicide?"

"It came over the PR department's machine. They've got a listed number."

"Who sent it?"

"We don't know."

"Let me get this straight. You got an anonymous fax reporting a guy with his dick cut off in Niskayuna?"

"Yeah . . ."

Unable to get through to Audrey Haas by telephone that morning, Susan Anthony Bremmer decided to drive down to Schenectady and go directly to the hospital. If Audrey Haas had already retained counsel, then the lawyer would offer assistance to the defense team *pro bono*.

Speeding along Route 50 in her green-and-rust 1978 Saab, she contemplated a national class-action lawsuit, a test case to publicize the issue of spousal abuse. She'd get millions of anonymous women to constitute a class of plaintiffs, challenging so-called sexual prerogatives within marriage as adherently coercive and in violation of the Thirteenth Amendment's prohibition against involuntary servitude.

For some time now, Susan Bremmer had been writing briefs and position papers to support the notion that certain sexual acts, ostensibly consensual, were in fact coercive, amounting to a denigration of the value of a woman's life, and thus a badge of slavery, forbidden by the Thirteenth Amendment to the Constitution. Accordingly, any act taken by a victim of such sexual abuse within or without marriage was not only a legitimate act of self-defense but also an expression of her inalienable right not to be subjected to involuntary servitude.

In an *amicus curiae* brief filed on behalf of a woman in Potsdam who had shot her drunk and abusive husband forty-one times with a twelve-gauge shotgun, Bremmer had argued that there was no such thing as an excessive or unwarranted expression of self-defense on the part of a woman whose body was being violated. One of the appellate judges in the case had written her a private letter saying that she was a dangerous woman and should be disbarred.

She wrote back that as far as she was concerned, abuse was not just in the eye of the beholder but in her vagina as well. The very notion of a jurist without a vagina holding forth on this issue was absurd. She respectfully suggested that the honorable judge arrange to get himself incarcerated in a state prison and rewrite his opinion after being sodomized by a couple of hardened criminals.

She crossed over the Mohawk and into Schenectady in the quiet of a Sunday morning. Church bells were sounding discordantly at odd intervals throughout the city. As she drove through the nearly deserted streets, she suddenly realized it was Palm Sunday. Not that it made a difference. Susan Bremmer was a lapsed Jew with a Lutheran ex-husband and an Irish setter named Margaret Sanger. She could never remember when Christ went up on the cross and when he came down. The only person who interested her in the whole business was Mary Magdalene, who, as far as Bremmer was concerned, was just a poster girl for Jesus.

It was heterodox views like this one that endeared her to her students at Skidmore while antagonizing the administration and the fundraisers. But Susan Bremmer had tenure and didn't care. Just let them come after her. She would take them to the Supreme Court and back again, and, by the time they were done, they'd have to pay her enough in damages to fund her retirement.

Bremmer parked the Saab in a handicapped space, put the sign on her dashboard that read ATTORNEY ON CALL, and entered the hospital. When she was told at the desk that there were no visitors allowed until 2 P.M., Bremmer cited boilerplate from the Sixth Amendment's right to counsel and was given directions to Audrey Haas's room.

The cop in front of the door, half asleep, looked at her and shook his head. "No visitors."

"I'm an attorney," Susan Bremmer said, as if those words alone would part the Red Sea.

"D.A.'s orders."

"Listen, the district attorney has no right to deny her access to counsel. You want me to go wake up a judge and get a writ of habeas corpus?"

Doetz blinked again. Abelove was meeting with the D.A. at this very moment. He better call him.

"Wait here. I have to make a call."

As soon as he turned the corner, Bremmer entered the room. Audrey Haas was lying on the bed, her eyes wide open, staring blankly at the ceiling.

"Hi," Susan Bremmer said. "How are you feeling?"

"You have any Prozac?"

The discussion in Ralph D'Imbroglio's office that morning centered around various legal distinctions involved in cutting penises off. If Ernest Haas had been alive at the time of the dismemberment and it could be proved that Audrey Haas knew it, then she could be charged with anything from aggravated battery to first-degree murder. But if she reasonably believed that he was dead, then they were looking at mutilation of human remains, a seldom-enforced Class E felony with a maximum of thirty-six months in prison. And if it turned out to have been, in fact, the burglar and/or the faxer who committed the crime, then there were no charges at all to file against Audrey Haas.

To make matters even more confusing, the police were faced with the absence of both the murder weapon and the mutilated member itself.

"You didn't find it?" Jeffries asked Abelove.

"No."

"You think we're looking at some sort of cult thing here?"

It was at this point that Abelove was summoned to the phone and told by Doetz at the hospital that a lawyer wanted to speak with Audrey Haas. When he told the district attorney, D'Imbroglio groaned, "If she's not well enough to speak to us, how can she be well enough to speak to a fucking lawyer?"

Clint Wells, trying to cover all the angles, as he had been taught that a good prosecutor should, said, "You don't think she'd try to slip the dick out with the lawyer, do you?"

The district attorney pushed the remains of his bagel away and muttered, "If she had the dick on her, don't you think it would have turned up when they put her in a hospital gown?"

"Just trying to be thorough," Clint Wells said in a small voice.

"When do we get the M.E.'s report?" D'Imbroglio asked.

"He promised it by six tonight."

"What about the dogshit analysis?"

"Tomorrow morning."

"Where *is* the dog, anyway?"

"County Animal Control in Albany."

D'Imbroglio leaned back in his large upholstered swivel chair and shook his head. "A dog wouldn't eat his master's dick. No matter how hungry he was."

Audrey Haas liked Susan Bremmer right from the start. Besides the fact that the lawyer was the first woman she had spoken to since it happened, Susan Bremmer did not bombard her with a lot of questions. She sat down, handed her a card, and explained that she was an attorney and wanted to help her. And when the cop came back and yelled at her for entering the room without permission, she told him that she had more right to be in this room than he did and that if he really wanted to be useful he could go get the doctor and have him prescribe the medication that Mrs. Haas was asking for.

When the cop tried to frisk her, she said that if he so much as laid a finger on her, she would have him up not only on sexual harassment and battery charges but also on violation of Title 18 of the federal Civil Rights Act.

"I'm supposed to frisk anybody in and out of here," Doetz protested.

"The constitutional test for a valid frisk is reasonable suspicion that the person may be armed and dangerous. Do I look armed and dangerous to you?"

He slunk out of the room with his tail between his legs. Susan Bremmer turned back to Audrey and said, "You can never find a cop when you need one, and they're always around when you don't."

Then she puffed up Audrey's pillow, poured her a glass of water, and sat down beside her bed.

"Nobody should have to go through what you went through, Audrey," she said. "You are a very brave woman—a heroine and role model for us all."

"Really?"

"Really."

Bremmer took out a yellow legal pad and a pen from her colorful hand-woven briefcase, a gift from a weaver in Schoharie for whom she had handled a sexual-harassment case.

"Now was this incident with the handcuffs and the women's clothes an isolated occurrence or typical of a pattern of behavior on the part of your late husband?"

• • •

When Abelove got out of the meeting in Ralph D'Imbroglio's office—a meeting at which nothing was resolved except that they would wait for the M.E.'s report before deciding what charges to file against Audrey Haas, if any—he drove to the hospital, where he found Doetz dozing in a chair outside Audrey Haas's room.

Not bothering to disturb the cop, Abelove walked past him into the room and found Susan Bremmer sitting beside the bed with a yellow pad. She looked up at him with a peremptory air and said in the tone of voice one uses for an intruder, "I beg your pardon . . ."

Abelove flashed his shield and said, "Barney Abelove, Schenectady Police Department."

The woman handed him a card with a Saratoga Springs phone number. Printed in raised blue letters was

SUSAN ANTHONY BREMMER
ATTORNEY-AT-LAW
PROFESSOR OF JURISPRUDENCE
WOMEN'S STUDIES

"I'll need to talk to your client," Abelove said, pocketing the card.

"Is there a charge filed against her?"

"Not as yet . . ."

"The Fifth Amendment protects individuals from being interrogated against their will by a police officer."

"Look, she happens to be the only witness in the possible homicide of her husband . . ."

"I hate to tell you this, Detective, but this is not a police state. The Constitution guarantees us protection against harassment from the government and its agents, of which you are one at the moment. If citizens could be hauled off the streets at any time, day or night, and made to answer to charges that have not been formally made against them, then we would be living in a police state."

"No kidding."

"Let me tell you something else, Detective. Women have been victims not only of crimes of violence perpetrated by society but also of prejudicial treatment on the part of the criminal-justice system. . . ."

Abelove looked at Audrey Haas, who was lying there in awe as her attorney went on at length about inadequate protection for women under the present laws. When Bremmer was finally finished ten minutes later, Abelove asked, "You bill by the hour or by the word?"

•   •   •

Abelove woke Doetz up and told him to let him know if anyone else, besides the lawyer, tried to get in. Then he beeped Jeffries off the golf course and told him what had gone down.

"Well . . . you better call Ralph on this," the lieutenant said predictably. Abelove left a message with Clint Wells and then drove out to Niskayuna to begin the painstaking job of ringing doorbells on Van Schuyler Lane.

Half the households on the street were in church, and the other half hadn't seen or heard anything unusual Friday night or Saturday morning. They all agreed that the Haases were quiet people and nice neighbors. Except for the Rottweiler. Nobody liked the Rottweiler.

The next-door neighbors, the Kitteridges, told Abelove that the Rottweiler was a hole digger. They said that the dog had gotten under the fence and into their yard and torn it all up. "God knows what he was burying. We found a piece of silverware once and a pot holder. Is it true what they said on TV?"

Abelove dodged the question and went back out to the car. He called the forensic lab to check on the possibility of sending a team out.

"For what?"

"The Rottweiler could have buried it in the neighbor's yard."

"Come on, Barney, it's Sunday. You really want me to send a team out on a long shot? What happens if we find it? Then what?"

"It's evidence."

"It wasn't the murder weapon. What are you going to learn from it that you don't already know?"

The idea of beeping Jeffries off the golf course again to authorize a forensic team to go through the Kitteridges' yard on a Sunday looking for Ernest Haas's penis did not appeal to Abelove. He decided, instead, to drive to Albany and check out the Kopy Kat Kopy Korner for a possible I.D. on the faxer.

It was a combination Xerox place and convenience store run by a family of Koreans on South Hudson Street, a dreary neighborhood down by the river. After speaking with all of them, he wound up with the same answer he had gotten over the phone: "Lots people. Lots fax."

He left and drove down Front Street, right past the Eagle Bar and Grill, where Emmanuel Longhouse was drinking. The Indian still had no idea that the Schenectady police were looking for him—or should have been looking for him. At the moment the Schenectady police didn't know anything at all about the six-foot-five-inch Indian who had stolen the Haases' appliances and left frozen lasagna and Diet Coke for the surviving spouse. In any event, Emmanuel Longhouse had already cleared his conscience by sending the fax. It was no longer his problem.

But it was very much Barney Abelove's. He drove back to Schenectady, grabbed two slices of pepperoni pizza, dropped a Rolaids, and headed for the lab.

Zieff was just finishing up when Abelove arrived at a few minutes past three. The assistant M.E. invited him into his cramped office, which smelled of formaldehyde and ammonia.

"Well, we have a cause of death," Zieff announced dramatically and then paused to make Abelove wait for the punch line. When it didn't come, Abelove barked, "What is it?"

"Cardiac arrest. Complete shutdown of the heart, leading to massive failure of the vascular system feeding the organs and causing fatal trauma to the brain."

"Yeah, but what *killed* him?"

"I just told you."

"Was he dead before or after he lost his dick?"

"I don't know."

"You don't *know*?"

"The removal of the penis, as I told you, was not, *ipso facto*, the cause of death. Cardiac arrest was. So it's equally feasible that the cardiac arrest was caused by the severing of the member and that it wasn't. There's no way to determine that without an eyewitness."

"Jesus Christ . . ."

"You'll just have to ask the wife."

"Her lawyer won't let us talk to her."

Zieff reached into his pocket, took out a small Neosynephrine, and sprayed his nostrils. Then he took a few deep inhalations and, his nasal passages momentarily cleared, said, "That could be a problem."

As he walked Abelove to the elevator, the assistant medical examiner reflected, "You'd think a woman having intercourse with a man would know if he was dead or not, wouldn't you?"

"You'd think so."

Chapter 8

When Herbert Haas, Ernest Haas's older brother, a medical-equipment salesman living in Costa Mesa, California, was notified that the Schenectady urologist had been found dead under suspicious circumstances, he said, "Oh, my."

"Would you happen to know if your brother had any enemies?" Abelove asked him, *pro forma*.

"Ernie? Why would Ernie have enemies? He was a doctor."

Abelove didn't go into the details of the death, except to say that it was a possible homicide perpetrated by a housebreaker and that Mrs. Haas was in the hospital being treated for shock and exhaustion.

"Is Siggy all right?" Herbert Haas asked.

"Siggy?"

"Their dog."

"Yeah, he's fine. He's being taken care of by the county at the moment."

"Beautiful dog, isn't he?"

"Uh-huh . . ."

"Very intelligent. You know, Rottweilers have an undeserved reputation for being vicious. They're really quite gentle. We have a schnauzer, three years old. Named Frasier. My wife loves that show."

Abelove then had called Denise Mezzogiorno, Ernest Haas's receptionist. Ms. Mezzogiorno sounded put off on the phone. He asked her

the same question he had asked Herbert Haas regarding possible enemies.

"Not that I know of."

"When was the last time you saw him?"

"Friday, around six-thirty, when he left the office. . . . What about
my benefits?"

"Benefits?"

"Dr. Haas had been paying into a Keogh for me. I don't even know
where that money is."

"I'm sure it'll turn up."

"He's supposed to do a trans-urethral subsection at seven o'clock
Monday morning . . ."

"Oh my."

Doltha, the Haases' cleaning lady, claimed she rarely ever saw Dr.
Haas. She merely ironed his underwear. Did Abelove know whether
Mrs. Haas wanted her to come on Wednesday? Abelove said he'd have
to get back to her.

And that was that. Ernest Haas was apparently a man with no other
family, close friends, or colleagues. Audrey Haas had parents in Phoenix
and no siblings. The two of them lived what appeared to be a quiet life
in their green-and-white Dutch Colonial on Van Schuyler Lane with
their Rottweiler, Siggy.

Except that Ernie occasionally liked to dress up in women's clothes,
handcuff his wife to the stove, and fuck her.

At six Sunday night, Abelove got a call from the forensic pathologist
telling him that tests on the dog fecal sample taken from the Hasses'
yard were inconclusive.

Before he could stop himself, he said, "No shit."

Dr. Lenore Yamamoto, a woman with no discernible sense of humor,
replied, "It may not have passed through the dog's digestive system yet.
Have you checked for subsequent bowel movements?"

He hung up and put his head in his hands, bone tired. He had been
on this miserable case since two o'clock Saturday afternoon and had had
only four hours of sleep and two slices of pizza.

D'Imbroglio seemed paralyzed with indecision. When Abelove had
called him earlier that afternoon to inform him about the lawyer, he had
merely cursed into the phone and told him to wait for the M.E.'s report. When Abelove phoned to tell him about his conversation with
Zieff, D'Imbroglio had said to wait for the forensic pathologist's report.
Now Abelove had to call and tell him what Dr. Yamamoto had said
about the inconclusiveness of Siggy's stool analysis.

"No shit . . ." D'Imbroglio muttered.

Abelove started to laugh. He couldn't help it.

He got in his car and drove back to the hospital, where he found that Audrey Haas was now guarded not only by her lawyer but also by her shrink. Dr. Marvin Zadek was there, conferring with the resident.

The question was whether or not Audrey Haas should be moved out of the emergency area and into the psychiatric ward. Abelove began to see the closed doors of a hospital psychiatric ward separating him from his witness. He went to try to call D'Imbroglio to tell him about this new complication, but found the coffee-shop phone occupied by a tall, thin resident in a white coat who was whispering into the phone.

Eugene Zukoff was filling Carrie Castle in on the latest development in the Audrey Haas business. He had found out from overhearing another phone call—this one made by a short, frizzy-haired woman carrying a briefcase that looked like a shower curtain—that Audrey Haas had retained counsel and that the counsel was concerned about a possible arrest.

Susan Bremmer had been talking to Tammy Stockpile, the chairperson of the Schenectady County Chapter of the National Organization for Women. Stockpile wanted to call a news conference in the event that the police decided to arrest Audrey Haas.

"Let them put cuffs on her," Bremmer had said to Tammy Stockpile. "I'd love to see that picture on the front page of every newspaper in this country. We couldn't buy that type of press."

The Mexican standoff that had developed between the police and the district attorney, on the one hand, and Audrey Haas and her lawyer and psychiatrist, on the other, continued through the early hours of Sunday evening.

Audrey herself, meanwhile, was insulated from it all by a Valium drip. After talking with her lawyer, she had a nice chat with Dr. Zadek, who refrained from asking her those dreadful questions he had asked her before. Instead they discussed her plans for remodeling the kitchen. He agreed that Santa Fe modern would be striking.

After he left, she lay there and thought about Ernie. She remembered the trip to Hawaii they had taken last summer for an American Association of Urologists convention. They had drunk mai tais and played miniature golf and gone on an authentic luau with dancing and drum music. In September they had joined a new bowling league at the Niskayuna Lanes along with another urologist, a periodontist, and an ear, nose, and throat man. At Christmas Ernie had bought her a new vicuña coat, which he had borrowed only once, in January, when he had taken her in the toolshed in the backyard during a snowstorm.

Susan had arranged to have a TV brought in. Audrey ran through the channels on the remote until she found a TV movie with Valerie Bertinelli starring as the mother of an adopted baby who turned out to have sickle-cell anemia.

As Audrey drifted on her gentle lapping sea of tranquilizers, she fantasized about Valerie Bertinelli playing her in her life's story. Or Meredith Baxter. Or Farrah Fawcett. Farrah would be terrific. She could see Farrah cuffed to the O'Keefe and Merritt staring down the Rottweiler and the Indian. She could see Farrah in court, beside Sigourney Weaver or Susan Sarandon as the lawyer, fighting for the rights of women victims everywhere.

Audrey fell asleep just before Valerie Bertinelli, tears in her eyes, told the district attorney that no amount of money in a legal settlement from the adoption agency could compensate her for the loss of her baby. Nevertheless, she would use the money to start a fund for sickle-cell-anemia babies. And she would get on with her life.

That same Sunday night, during a commercial break from *A Mother's Anguish: The Yvonne Shapiro Story*, Tammy Stockpile called the chairperson of the New York State Chapter of NOW. The state chairperson, Catherine Slevin, phoned their lobbyist in Albany, Millie Vandenberg, who managed to get Rhonda Eddy, head of the Governor's Task Force for Equal Opportunity for Minorities and Women, on the phone, and she phoned the state attorney general at his weekend place outside of Bennington, Vermont, and the attorney general phoned Ralph D'Imbroglio, who had just gotten into a warm sitz bath to relieve discomfort from an inflamed hemorrhoid.

"Ralph, what the hell's going on down there?"

"It's just a little domestic-violence case that this goddamn lawyer is trying to blow up into some women's rights issue."

"Well, according to the NOW people, you're harassing the victim."

"Harassing? We're just trying to question her. And her lawyer won't agree to let her be questioned."

"So file."

D'Imbroglio took the portable phone away from his mouth and sighed deeply. This guy was sitting around his four-hundred-acre farmhouse in Vermont drinking hot chocolate and telling him how to handle what was turning out to be a very tricky little case. He didn't need this. He had a plea bargain at nine the next morning and his hemorrhoid was killing him. The proctologist had recommended surgery. . . .

"Ralph, you're facing a writ of habeas corpus if you continue to hold her without a charge."

"We're not holding her. She's in the hospital."

"What if she tries to leave?"

"Then we have to either arrest her or let her leave."

"I see. . . . Well, carry on, then. . . . How's the weather there?"

"It's lousy."

"Same thing here. Nice talking to you, Ralph. Keep me posted."

And the attorney general hung up. D'Imbroglio sat in his tepid bathwater and considered the conversation he had just had with the chief law-enforcement officer of the State of New York, who had just neatly lobbed the ball back into his court.

Carry on? Carry on *how*?

If he filed against her, even just for aggravated assault, there would be an arraignment in front of a judge during which he would have to ask for bail to be posted. The lawyer would argue that Audrey Haas was in the hospital and not a flight risk, and she'd probably win that point. In the meantime the women's groups would be all over him, as would the goddamn media, from Carrie Castle on up.

They were sitting on heavy overtime already, what with the around-the-clock surveillance and the extra hours that Abelove was putting in. The county law-enforcement budget was already strained, a point that his opponent in November's election would not hesitate to stress.

It was, when you thought about it, a lose-lose situation. Even if they nailed the woman, they'd come under attack from every fucking women's rights group in the country.

The guy was dead. He wouldn't be needing his equipment, anyway. Fuck him.

D'Imbroglio called Abelove at the hospital and told him to send the uniforms home and clock out.

"Tomorrow you can run down the breaking-and-entering."

"The evidence is going to get cold."

"We don't have any evidence."

"Look, what if the dog buried it in the neighbor's backyard? If we sent a team out—"

"Abelove, I'm not spending any more county money trying to find this guy's dick. Go home. Get some sleep. Tomorrow, go to work, check out your other cases."

"Then what?"

"Carry on."

Abelove hung up the phone and looked wearily around the nearly deserted coffee shop. There was the same resident who had been on the phone earlier, sitting in the corner writing on a pad, and two maintenance workers speaking Spanish to each other.

He was sick of this coffee shop. He was sick of the whole goddamn case.

He walked down the hall to Audrey Haas's room, where Gallagher, who had replaced Doetz earlier that evening, was on duty outside the door.

"We're off the clock," Abelove told him. "D.A.'s orders."

"What if she tries to make a run for it?"

"Not our problem."

Abelove walked through the quiet hospital and out to the parking lot, where the rain had tapered off, leaving the funky smell of the approaching spring. It was an in-between season, the weather tentative and uncertain, the days imperceptibly getting longer.

He got into the light-brown Cutlass with the bad springs and started up the engine. In spite of the season, he did not feel a rebirth of energy. On the contrary. He felt older than his years, tired and depressed. He had just spent two days wading through a pile of dogshit and come up empty-handed with his shoes smelling.

As he turned the car onto Route 7, heading back to town, he thought of D'Imbroglio. *Carry on!* Easy for him to say. He hadn't been at the crime scene. He hadn't seen what Abelove had seen. He didn't have the image emblazoned in his mind of Ernest Haas, in a pair of tattered pantyhose lying in a pool of coagulated blood on his own kitchen floor.

With all his heart Abelove hoped it was the burglar who did it to the urologist and not the wife. He could live with the thought of the burglar. Breaking and entering, a struggle, housebreaker kills the homeowner, the guy's dick gets caught in the wringer . . .

But every time he floated this scenario, it went right to the bottom and lay there. As hard as he tried, Abelove couldn't buy the burglar.

His cop's sense told him that Audrey Haas had done it to her husband. Whether it was before or after he died did not seem terribly important at this point. It was just another forensic detail.

As far as Abelove was concerned, the guy had gotten whacked by his wife and eaten by his dog. Which was a pretty shitty way to buy it.

Chapter 9

Ernest Haas was buried in his prepaid plot at the Mount Spinoza cemetery in Niskayuna at 11 A.M. Monday morning, March 30. In attendance were Herbert Haas and his wife, Ceal, who had flown in late Sunday night from California; Ernest Haas's in-laws, Frances and Jack Myers, from Phoenix; Denise Mezzogiorno, Ernest Haas's receptionist; Doltha Toussaint, the cleaning lady; Dr. Yale Mittner, on behalf of the Schenectady County Board of Certified Urologists; Eugene Zukoff, on behalf of Carrie Castle; stringers from the *National Enquirer* and the *Star*; assorted funeral freaks, the kind who like to attend funerals of people they don't know; and a tearful woman dressed in a black hat with a veil, who would later be referred to in coverage of the burial as "the woman in the black veil."

Audrey Haas did not attend the funeral, it being deemed too stressful by her doctors. At the very moment that Ernie was being lowered into the still-frozen ground, Audrey was being transferred by ambulance to Cloverdale, a psychiatric facility in Troy with no bars on the windows, excellent food, and a cable-TV system that delivered sixty-four channels. She was given a private room with blue-and-white curtains and a view of the garden courtyard.

Barney Abelove did not attend Ernest Haas's funeral either. At eleven o'clock Monday morning he was sleeping soundly in his apartment on

Zeider Zee Crescent in South Schenectady, the ringer on his phone turned off.

There was no telling how long Abelove would have slept if he hadn't been woken by his girlfriend, Renata Sbazio, who, unable to rouse him by phone, had driven over to the apartment during her lunch break from Mitnick's, where she worked in the luggage and travel accessories department, and rung the doorbell until Abelove had staggered to the door to let her in.

"I was worried about you," she said to the haggard police detective standing at the door in his underwear and socks. "I've been calling since nine."

"Yeah, well, uh . . ."

"You disconnect the phone or what?"

"Yeah, well, uh . . ."

It wasn't long before Abelove found himself back in bed without his underpants and still half asleep, as Renata shed the lime-green slacks of her new spring pants suit, gave him a few affectionate strokes, and mounted him. In a matter of minutes he was back asleep.

So efficient was she that she had time to make herself a salami-and-Muenster-cheese sandwich in Abelove's kitchen and be back at the luggage counter at Mitnick's only seven minutes late.

It was all very subliminal, so much so, in fact, that when Abelove woke up again two hours later, he wasn't sure the episode had actually occurred. Then, in a sudden flash of terror, he quickly looked down to make sure he was intact. Reassured, he stumbled out of bed and headed for the bathroom, his heart beating like a tom-tom.

The tabloid coverage of Ernest Haas's death flared up and died down quickly. WOMAN EMASCULATES HUSBAND AND FEEDS IT TO DOG was a headline that even the hard-core supermarket-rag readers had trouble digesting. Unable to get an interview with Audrey Haas, Carrie Castle decided that the story was dying and, even if it wasn't, it was just too weird for the six o'clock news. She called Eugene Zukoff off, and the medical student returned to the endocrine system.

After an awkward visit with Audrey at the hospital, Herbert and Ceal Haas returned to California, taking Siggy, the only possible eyewitness, with them. Audrey's parents, Jack and Frances Myers, were quoted by the *Enquirer* as "standing by their daughter in her hour of need."

District Attorney D'Imbroglio came down with a particularly nasty cold and stayed out of work Monday, instructing Clint Wells not to disturb him unless the sky fell in. Clint Wells called Dick Jeffries and told him the D.A. didn't want to file, which was fine with the lieutenant, who didn't see much percentage in trying to make a collar.

Which left Barney Abelove pretty much alone in the conviction that Ernest Haas's death deserved some sort of investigation. But since no charges had been filed, he was left with only two options. He could pester Audrey Haas's attorney and her doctor for permission to talk to her in the hospital and wind up with nothing but a compromised case in the event that they got evidence down the line that they could make stick. Or he could pursue the burglar.

Rummaging around in his jacket pocket, he found the business card that the lawyer had given him and called her in Saratoga Springs.

"I am in the middle of a deposition here," Susan Bremmer said when she got on the phone.

"This won't take long. I need the brands and serial numbers of the Haas's electrical equipment and appliances."

"She's under sedation."

"C'mon. How traumatic can that be?"

Twenty minutes later Susan Bremmer called back with a list of brands for the TV, VCR, CD player, and microwave.

"How about serial numbers?"

"She said her late husband kept track of those things, and she had no idea where to find them."

"Would you agree to our entering to look for the serial numbers?"

"In your dreams."

"You're really going to make me go get a warrant?"

"That's the way we do it here in the United States of America." And she hung up.

Abelove looked down at the list. A Sony TV, a Goldstar VCR, a Hitachi CD player, and a JVC microwave. All standard brands without serial numbers. Your basic needle in a haystack.

He called Clint Wells to ask him to get a judge to write a warrant. Clint Wells told him that he couldn't do it without Ralph D'Imbroglio's say-so, and D'Imbroglio was out sick and had left instructions not to be disturbed unless the sky fell in. "The sky's not falling in, Barney."

"This is a fucking homicide, for chrissakes!"

"The serial numbers'll be there when Ralph gets back."

"When will that be?"

"A couple more days, a week . . ."

Abelove slammed down the phone.

Didn't anybody else want a piece of this fucking case?

. . .

Emmanuel Longhouse had unloaded the TV, the VCR, the CD player, and the microwave with Freddie the Fence Davis, a former semi-pro basketball star for the Elmira Eagles, who operated out of his station wagon and offered 30 percent of the resale value, if you were lucky. That's how tight-fisted Freddie the Fence was. He had operating costs, he would tell you, if you bothered to ask. Emmanuel Longhouse never bothered.

He had hoped to get close to fifty dollars for the carving knife by pawning it downtown, so he didn't even bother offering it to Freddie the Fence. Instead he went to Dave's Bait, Tackle, and Pledge Store on Beaver Street, and pocketed two twenties, letting Dave haggle him down ten bucks. Emmanuel Longhouse wrote the name GORGE A. CUSTARD on the pledge slip.

So Ernest and Audrey Haas's stolen merchandise was in fact in at least two places, if not more, within twenty-four hours of the theft. Had Abelove known this at the outset, he might not have bothered undertaking the search. Having done five years in Burglary before moving to Homicide, Abelove understood the futility of chasing hot merchandise.

He gave his list to Mike Medaroy in Burglary. Medaroy said to Abelove the same thing that Abelove would have said to a cop who came to him with a list of stolen merchandise and no serial numbers.

"C'mon, Barney, this cheap Japanese shit is all over the place. What happens if I find it? Without serial numbers I can't do a thing. You know that."

"I'll do the legwork, okay? Can you just run the list?"

Several hours later Medaroy handed him a list of five pawnshops and secondhand stores in the tri-cities area that had a Sony TV, a Goldstar VCR, a Hitachi CD player, and a JVC microwave.

Abelove spent the remainder of Monday driving from one to the next, trying to find out if any one individual had unloaded all four items. Pawnshop proprietors weren't the most forthright people. They were aware that a percentage of their merchandise was stolen, and if the police had proof that an item was hot, it could be confiscated without restitution. Some of them were known, in fact, to remove serial numbers for that very reason.

Even when Abelove promised to reimburse any loss on the items, none of the pawnshops had the same name on any of the pledge slips, and none of the secondhand-store owners could or would remember one individual selling those four exact items.

By nine that night he had drawn a complete zero, as he knew he would. He drove home with his lower back hurting from too many hours in the car.

He poured himself a Seagram's and water, got into the bathtub, and soaked. As the liquor and the hot water penetrated, he began to understand what he would have to do if he wanted to get to the bottom of this. He needed the serial numbers. And he needed them fast, before the items were resold.

Unfortunately, there was only one way to get them quickly, and it didn't involve a warrant.

Frances Myers sat with Audrey in the room at the Cloverdale psychiatric facility watching a rerun of a Joan Collins miniseries in which Joan plays a Russian chanteuse and Allied spy caught in Monte Carlo during the Second World War. Under the noses of the Gestapo, she sends radio signals to the RAF in London with information about Nazi shipping in the Mediterranean. In the last act she gets caught and is taken to prison, where she is tortured by the evil Gestapo colonel, while George Hamilton and a band of French Resistance fighters battle their way in to save her.

Audrey couldn't get over how good Joan Collins looked in 1940s clothes. Except for when she was in the Gestapo prison, where she was forced to wear the same outfit for almost a half hour, she was absolutely stunning. Audrey wondered how Joan Collins managed to smuggle her eye makeup into the Gestapo prison if they didn't let her change her clothes.

When it was finally over, after Joan Collins and George Hamilton flew off to England together in a plane provided by the French Resistance, Audrey's mother asked her how she was feeling.

"Fine," Audrey said.

"You know, you can always come to Phoenix and stay with your father and me."

"Uh-huh," Audrey replied absently. She didn't relish the thought of living in that stucco house with the minuscule swimming pool and the air-conditioning on so high you felt you were in a meat locker. At night they would go out to one of those restaurants with a $5.99 salad bar and Musak. And then eighteen holes of miniature golf.

"I suppose," Frances Myers said, clearing her throat loudly, as she always did when she was about to broach something uncomfortable, "that Ernie left provision for you."

"Provision?"

"Life insurance."

"Life insurance. Yes. I'm sure he did. I mean, he would. Ernie always thought of those things."

"Your father promised to look into it while you were in the hospital."

"That's nice."

"I don't suppose you know where Ernie kept that sort of stuff."

"What sort of stuff?"

"His will and his life-insurance policy. Did he keep them with his lawyer?"

"Oh, no. Ernie didn't like lawyers."

"Well, do you have a safe-deposit box?"

"I'm sure we do."

"Would you happen to know where the key is?"

"Around the house someplace."

"Do you think you could narrow that down just a little bit, Audrey?"

Joan Collins had managed to withhold information under Gestapo torture. But Joan Collins didn't have to deal with Audrey's mother.

"I think the key's in the drawer."

"What drawer?"

"Under the TV. With the spare batteries and Siggy's dog license. You think that was Joan Collins's real hair?"

From his years in Burglary, Barney Abelove knew that it is best to rob a house in broad daylight. Since there were fewer people around during the day, the chances of someone spotting you were less than at night; and if someone did spot you, there were a number of plausible reasons why you might be there. He also knew that prowler calls, especially during the day, were low priority for the police. Ninety-eight percent of them were from nosy neighbors calling to turn in the gas-company meter reader or the cable-TV installer.

Whatever Susan Bremmer might have thought, breaking back into a crime scene without a warrant to fish for evidence was a time-honored police method in the United States of America. If you got what you wanted, you went to the judge for the warrant and then went back in armed with the warrant to seize what you already knew was there.

The crime-scene tape was down on the house at 474 Van Schuyler Lane when Abelove drove up at a little before eleven on Tuesday morning, March 31. He pulled the Cutlass into the driveway, another burglary technique he had picked up over the years. If you park in someone's driveway, people assume you're a friend or a family member. He got out and, without hesitating, walked straight into the backyard, as if he were an insurance adjuster or a real-estate agent checking out the property.

He was relieved to see that the hole in the glass patio door had not been repaired. He had been counting on that. It reduced his potential exposure from breaking-and-entering to trespassing.

Abelove took a fast look through the house, then entered the kitchen. He studied the room, trying to intuit where Ernest Haas would have kept the instruction manuals, warranties, and serial numbers of his household appliances. Systematically, he went through every drawer and cabinet, impressed with the variety of kitchen implements that Audrey Haas possessed.

There was a drawer underneath the silverware drawer that contained a number of different-size knives. As he examined them, he remembered Zieff's words: *The penis is an organ with thick intertwined networks of membranes, arteries, and veins, which would make it somewhat resistant to amputation."*

Even if he found the weapon, the chain of evidence would be flimsy at best. Audrey Haas would have had to use it, rinse it off in the sink, and replace it in the drawer, all while still cuffed to the stove.

After he finished in the kitchen, he went back through the bedroom night tables and chest of drawers, checked the two spare bedrooms, and then went into the den.

He found what he was looking for in a drawer underneath where the TV had been. There were spare batteries, a safe-deposit-box key, a dog license for the Rottweiler, and a folder containing the instruction manuals and sales warranties for the Haases' household appliances and electronic equipment.

Abelove took out his notebook and copied the model and serial numbers for the Sony TV, the Goldstar VCR, the Hitachi CD player, and the JVC microwave oven. There were a number of other items for which Ernest Haas had kept the paperwork—an Interplak electric toothbrush, a Casio pocket organizer, a Rubbermaid heating pad, a Sharper Image exercise treadmill, a Sunbeam deluxe model 370 multi-purpose carving utensil . . .

Abelove had replaced the folder and was stretching, working the kinks out of his legs, and preparing to leave when it hit him. It was the word *multi-purpose* that did it.

He hurried back into the kitchen and spent ten minutes methodically rechecking every drawer and cabinet. It wasn't there. And Audrey Haas hadn't reported it. Of course she hadn't. Why would she?

Abelove examined the idea under a sharp light of skepticism. The absence of the carving knife was not prima-facie evidence that it was the murder weapon. Audrey could have thrown it out. She could have loaned it to a neighbor. She could have left it outside while barbecuing and Siggy could have buried it in the backyard . . .

Back in the den he checked the purchase date of the carving knife. December 18, not even four months ago. No way she throws it out. She keeps it in.

He returned to the kitchen and studied the distance between the stove and the drawer where Audrey Haas kept her other kitchen utensils. Pretending he was handcuffed to the oven door, he stretched and reached the drawer with his free hand.

So . . . Audrey Haas gets the carving knife, does Ernie, then leaves the knife on the floor, and the burglar takes it. The burglar, realizing that an electric carving knife is light, portable, and fast cash in a pawnshop, takes it with him, and, presto, the murder weapon disappears.

The scenario had seventy-one holes in it. It wouldn't have floated a paper boat. And yet Barney Abelove liked it. Of all the scenarios he had considered, it was the only one that explained how Audrey did it—*something relatively sharp with a certain amount of torque*—the role of the burglar, *and* the absence of the weapon.

The fact that she had omitted the carving knife from the list of appliances made sense. When she had seen the burglar take it right before her eyes, picking it up from the kitchen floor, she realized she was off the hook. There was no way to pin it on her.

Unless a very smart cop, someone like Barney Abelove, was able to find the carving knife, trace it to the burglar, get the burglar to testify to what he found in the kitchen that night . . .

These thoughts were interrupted by the sound of a key in the front door. Abelove's heart stood very still as he heard the tumbler disengage and the door swing open.

Chapter 10

After thirty-four years of selling insurance, Jack Myers figured he had things pretty well covered. He owned the house in Phoenix outright, held a second mortgage on a condo in Palm Springs, had a paid-off cash-value whole-life policy, and half a million in tax-free munis. Barring a major disaster in the bond market, he was good for the duration.

Of course, he hadn't been counting on his son-in-law cashing in his chips. He had been comforted by the fact that his only daughter was married to a doctor, knowing, actuarially at least, that doctors were a good bet to provide, even in difficult times. So when he learned that Audrey had become a widow, it threatened to throw a wrench into his plans for a peaceful retirement.

To make matters worse, Audrey had gone to pieces. They had her in a psych ward, drugged to the teeth, at god knows how much a day. Not that she would have been much help clearing up the financial details in any event. She had always been an airhead when it came to money.

Jack Myers had seen his son-in-law only a half dozen times since the wedding. The urologist was a pleasant enough sort of guy, although not much on the golf course. He couldn't hit the side of a barn with a nine iron. But he had been a good provider and, as far as Jack Myers knew, a good husband to his daughter.

As he drove his rented Mercury Sable out to Niskayuna, Jack Myers wondered why there was no lawyer handling the will. It made him nervous to think that Audrey knew so little about her husband's finances. And what if there was no insurance? All those speeches he had given couples over coffee around their kitchen table about the horror of being caught unprepared in their moment of need. Jesus, what if his own daughter . . .

The last thing he needed at his age was having a thirty-eight-year-old woman with a history of depression as a dependent.

The sight of a dirty gray Olds with a missing hubcap in the driveway of 474 Van Schuyler was not very reassuring. You'd think a successful doctor could afford a better car. This one looked like the type of car their cleaning lady in Phoenix drove.

Fishing for the key that Frances had found in Audrey's pocketbook at the hospital, he got out of the rental and approached the front door, stopping to gather the newspapers scattered over the walk. As he always told his homeowner-policy customers, uncollected newspapers were a sure invitation to burglars.

As soon as he put the key in the door, Jack Myers had a feeling that something was wrong. But it was too late. His momentum carried him through the open door and face-to-face with a man aiming a gun at his heart.

"Don't move," the man said in a tired, almost bored tone of voice.

Jack Myers couldn't have moved if he tried.

"Hands in front of you, away from your pockets." The man was wearing a corduroy sports jacket missing a button and a knit tie with a mustard stain on it. He moved around behind him and, the gun barrel in Myers's back, frisked him quickly, pulling his wallet from his back pocket.

"Take what you want," said Jack Myers in a cracked voice. He always told his customers never to resist a robber. Your life was worth more than your money.

But the man put the gun into a shoulder holster inside his sports jacket, took out his own wallet, and flashed a badge.

"Detective Abelove, Schenectady Police Department. You want to tell me what you're doing here, Mr. Myers?"

"Well, if you must know, I'm looking for my daughter Audrey's life-insurance policy. What are *you* doing here?"

As he drove to Albany with the list of serial numbers, Abelove tried to put in perspective the fact that he had been caught searching a suspect's house without a warrant. On a list of things that a cop didn't want to happen, this was right up there at the top.

In his best cop jargon, Abelove had explained to Jack Myers that he was securing the premises, protecting them from unlawful entry by criminals or reporters, that it was S.O.P. for the police to reenter a crime scene to safeguard the perimeter.

He tap-danced around with some more invented procedural bullshit, and, by the time he left, he and Jack Myers were chatting amiably about the weather in Schenectady and the early-bird special at Grazziani's. He told the retired insurance salesman to give him a ring if he could be of help and got the hell out of there.

Abelove had more important things to do at the moment than worry about Jack Myers. The existence of the warranty certificate didn't mean jack shit unless they could put the carving knife into Audrey Haas's hands on the night of March 27.

And the best way to do that was through the burglar. Find the carving knife, trace the burglar, get the burglar to cop, and then arrest Audrey Haas for murder.

It was dark by the time Abelove got to the last pawnshop on his list—Dave's Bait, Tackle, and Pledge Store on Beaver Street in Albany. It was a shitty neighborhood, full of the homeless and the soon-to-be. The local bars catered to the hard-core drunks, selling shots of watered liquor at a buck and a quarter. Hardly the part of town where someone would be in the market for an electric carving knife.

He got out of the car and walked across the street, convinced he was drawing to an inside straight. The store was dark and smelled of bait and motor oil. There were used fishing rods and tackle boxes in the window, along with the usual calculators, VCRs, and toaster ovens.

Dave was tall and thin with a reedy little mustache and ferret eyes. He didn't blink when Abelove flashed his badge. Abelove looked through the shelves—most of it fishing equipment—then asked to see the storeroom in back.

Dave led him down a dingy hallway to a back room, where shit was piled haphazardly into bins. Some of the stuff had pledge tags attached to it, but most of it was just collecting dust.

He waded through the bins, sifting through cordless telephones, car radios, portable tape players—most of it hot, he was sure.

Just as he was about to abandon the search, as he was about to go home and blow the whole fucking case off, he saw it. It was at the bottom of the last bin, underneath a pile of used CDs—a white enamel utensil with a vinyl protective sheath covering the blade. In red letters was written SUNBEAM DELUXE MODEL 370 MULTI-PURPOSE CARVING UTENSIL.

Abelove fumbled for his glasses to read the serial number off the list in his jacket pocket: 3G99852267 XA. Turning the knife over quickly, he found the same set of numbers in tiny letters just below the anti-shock plate.

Written on the pledge slip was the name GORGE A. CUSTARD. The address was LITTLE BIG HAWN, SOWTH DAKOTA.

Bingo.

The best Dave could do was a tall Indian with a ponytail and an earring. The guy had come in once or twice before with merchandise that he never redeemed. He never said anything at all, according to Dave, who didn't say a whole lot himself.

"He wasn't much of a speller either, was he?" said Abelove.

"Not so as you'd know it," replied Dave, deadpan. Abelove searched his face for irony. There was nothing there. This guy could do stand-up in the morgue.

When Abelove told him that he needed the carving knife as evidence, Dave, apparently familiar with this end of the business, asked him if he had an evidence warrant on the carving knife.

Abelove took out two twenties. Dave said he had loaned forty on it and would need fifty to cover his costs. When Abelove pointed out that the law required that he wait thirty days from the date of the pledge to recover his costs, Dave pointed out that the law also required that he retain the pledged item against redemption within those thirty days.

"The guy could show up, ask for his knife."

"Case you haven't heard, Dave, General Custer ran into some problems out there in South Dakota."

They settled on forty-five. Out of Abelove's pocket. He was now throwing good money after time on behalf of Ernest Haas. He told Dave not to leave town without calling, in case he wanted to send a sketch artist out.

Dave didn't look like he was going anywhere. Dave didn't look like he had ever gone anywhere outside this pawnshop and fishing-tackle store on Beaver Street in Albany.

Abelove got in the car and drove back out Route 5 toward Schenectady. He knew he should check in with the Albany police. If only as a courtesy. They might have the tall Indian with the earring in their mug book.

But Abelove was too impatient to play this one by the book. He was finally on a roll, and he didn't want to give the dice a chance to cool down. If they could find the Indian, they'd have two witnesses, not to mention two suspects. And then he could play them against each other until he got the truth out of them.

A little after seven, Abelove pulled up in front of Ralph D'Imbroglio's restored white Colonial on Grotius Lane down in the Stockade area by the Mohawk. He had been there once before, for a Fourth of July barbecue that the D.A. had thrown for the detective squad a couple of years back. D'Imbroglio had cooked hamburgers over an open barbecue pit, wearing a white chef's apron that said D.A.'S DO IT BETTER.

The carving knife in hand, Abelove rang the doorbell. Instead of a bell, he heard the theme from *Dragnet*. Dum-da-dum-dum. After a moment the door was opened by the district attorney himself, wearing a purple terry-cloth robe over silk pajamas.

He stared at Abelove, then at the carving knife.

"Sorry to bother you at home, sir, but I've got a crucial piece of evidence on the Haas homicide."

Ralph D'Imbroglio continued to stare blankly at the carving knife, wondering what Barney Abelove was doing on his doorstep with an electric carving knife.

"I'm confident that this was the weapon that she used," said Abelove, and then, by way of explanation, removed the leather cover to expose the blade.

D'Imbroglio looked extremely pissed off, standing there, his nose red from blowing, his eyes rheumy.

"Abelove, I'm not feeling very well . . ."

"I understand, sir, but if I could arrest her tonight, we could get a judge to write a search warrant tomorrow. And I could check the house for evidence. All I have to do is put the carving knife in reach of the stove Friday night, and we've got her."

"What the hell are you talking about?"

"The Ernest Haas case. The guy who got his dick sliced off. This is the weapon. It was pawned by the burglar in Albany—remember the burglar who broke in and then sent the fax? We arrest the wife, get her to describe the burglar, find the burglar, and then get him to roll over on her, and we could have a murder indictment. We could solve this fucker."

D'Imbroglio took a wad of used Kleenex out of his robe pocket and blew his nose. It sounded like a plumber's snake cleaning out a badly clogged drain.

"Where'd you get the knife?"

"Pawnshop in Albany."

"How do you get it in her hands?"

"Serial number."

"How do you get the serial number?"

"Search the house."

"What if there's no match?"

"There will be."

"Oh, Jesus . . . you went in empty?"

"Sorry, sir—it was the only way."

D'Imbroglio sighed deeply, shook his head. Then, just before closing the door in Abelove's face, he said, "We never had this conversation."

Chapter 11

Audrey was watching Joanna Kerns play a single woman trying to adopt an AIDS baby in *Home Is Where the Heart Is: The Karen Margolin Story* when there was a knock at the door. She hoped it wasn't her mother. They had spent the entire afternoon discussing her mother's ovarian cysts, and Audrey wasn't up to more.

"Yes," she said with just a bit of hostility in her voice, hoping that whoever it was would go away.

The door opened, and a man in a beige raincoat a size too small for him entered along with a tall woman with blond ringlets wearing a silver-and-red windbreaker over a shoulder holster. The man looked vaguely familiar to Audrey, like someone on TV or a relative she hadn't seen in a long time.

He took out his wallet, flashed a badge, and said, "Mrs. Haas, I'm Detective Abelove and this is Detective Kettner. You're under arrest on the charge of murdering your husband."

Audrey hit the mute button on the remote and said, "What?"

"We're arresting you for murder," he repeated.

It was his badge that made her remember. It was tarnished. And the raincoat needed to be cleaned. The last time she'd seen this man she had been handcuffed to her stove.

Still, his message didn't quite sink in. "What do you want?" she asked him, though she had heard what he said.

"Mrs. Haas, you have the right to remain silent. If you choose to speak, anything you say may be used against you at trial. You have a right to an attorney . . ."

On the screen Joanna Kerns was arguing with the director of the adoption agency, played by Barry Bostwick, her nostrils flaring in righteous anger. Audrey wished this man would go away so that she could turn the sound back on.

"There's an ambulance waiting to take you to police headquarters and then on to the county jail. You'll be permitted to make a phone call from the station house."

Audrey stared incredulously at the detective, refusing to believe that she was going to have to leave this lovely room with the blue-and-white curtains and go someplace with bars on the windows.

"Now? I have to go *now*?"

"I'm afraid so."

"Can't I at least see the end of this movie?"

"Sorry. Detective Kettner will help you if you'd like to change before leaving."

Abelove went to wait in the hallway. He wanted to make sure this collar went 100 percent by the book. Especially since he was now out there alone without a net. D'Imbroglio had closed the door in his face. Since the conversation on the steps of the D.A.'s house had never taken place, Abelove was going to have to hope that Clint Wells would back him up at the arraignment when they asked the judge for a warrant to search the premises for a murder weapon.

After leaving D'Imbroglio, he had gone to headquarters to pick up a female detective to accompany him on the collar. Carla Kettner was the only woman detective on four-to-midnight. On the drive out to the hospital, he ran down the background for her.

"You see," Abelove told her, "they don't know whether he was dead or alive when she cut it off. Zieff says it could go either way. Cause of death was cardiac arrest either preceding or following the amputation. What's interesting, see, is if she cut it off while it was still in her, then you gotta wonder how the guy keeps it up if he's dead. Of course, we don't even know if there was penetration because we didn't do a vaginal on her. We were going to, but she took a couple dozen Prozac, and the next thing we knew she was in an ambulance getting her stomach pumped."

Carla Kettner didn't reply, but merely stared out the window, a little pale around the gills. When they pulled up in front of the hospital,

Abelove turned to her and said, "Why would a woman do that to her husband?"

"I don't know. There could be a pattern of abuse going back years."

"So?"

"So she acts."

"Yeah. She walks out the door. She comes to us. She goes to her lawyer. There's got to be fifty things she can do short of taking a carving knife to it."

Susan Bremmer's answering service called her at home Tuesday night shortly before eleven o'clock to relay a message from Audrey Haas that she had been arrested. She immediately called the Schenectady police and was told that Audrey Haas was in transport to the county jail on Veeder Street.

Susan Bremmer phoned the head of the women's studies department at Skidmore and left a message on her voice mail that she wouldn't be meeting her 9 A.M. seminar, Misogyny and Menstruation. Then she changed into her bail-bond-and-arraignment outfit, a dark-green wool skirt-and-sweater set, put on socks and comfortable brown flats, chose a pair of nondangling earrings—she had found over the years that judges were put off by dangling earrings—and headed for the Saab.

Audrey Haas was still being admitted into the jail when her lawyer arrived. Susan Bremmer brandished her card, but she was no longer dealing with Schenectady patrolmen. She was dealing with New York State troopers, and they weren't intimidated by lawyers. She was made to wait in an ugly little green waiting room with uncomfortable chairs while Audrey was put through the complex formalities of being admitted simultaneously into both a hospital and a jail.

Twenty minutes later, a short, balding, heavy-set man wearing a god-awful tweed sports jacket and a bow tie showed up and identified himself as Audrey Haas's doctor. In spite of his protests, he, too, was made to wait.

Susan Bremmer introduced herself to Marvin Zadek. The doctor shook her hand and sat down beside her on a vinyl chair. "Is there anything to be done to get her out of here?" he asked her.

"As soon as I have a look at the charges, I'll get a judge on the phone for a writ of habeas corpus."

"In the middle of the night?"

"They're civil servants."

In her address book, Susan Bremmer had the home phone numbers of several judges whom she would not hesitate to call if she felt she could argue not only that there were insufficient grounds for incarceration but also that putting her client in jail would be irrevocably detrimental to her health.

"I'll need an affidavit from you," she told Zadek, "stating the irrevocable consequences to her health of her being locked up in here. The key word is *irrevocable.*"

They sat for a moment without speaking, the doctor and the lawyer, and then Zadek leaned over and asked her in a confidential tone, "I don't suppose you know exactly what happened, do you?"

"I really can't talk about that."

"I understand. Neither can I. But I thought that, seeing as I am her doctor, it would not be a violation of confidentiality to give me just the broad strokes."

"As soon as the police report comes out, I'll get you a copy."

"Thanks."

Another moment of silence, then the lawyer leaned back toward the doctor and said, "I take it she hasn't spoken to you about it either."

He shook his head, said, "A trauma of this dimension often causes temporary blockage."

"Uh-huh. So . . . she actually may not remember exactly what happened."

"That is often the case with trauma."

"I don't imagine she could be much help to the police, then, could she?"

"No."

"Not in these surroundings, in any case."

"Absolutely not."

Informed that both the lawyer and the doctor were outside in the waiting room, Abelove arranged for an interview room for his prisoner. While Audrey was being medicated and then accompanied to the interview room by a hospital orderly and Detective Kettner, he went out to confront Susan Bremmer and Marvin Zadek.

He found them huddled together, speaking in hushed tones. The lawyer got up when she saw him and said, "This was entirely uncalled for, Detective, and I'm going to make sure the district attorney hears about it."

"He already has," Abelove lied.

"Charges?"

"Suspicion of murder."

"You have anything beside your own lurid imagination?"

"Uh-huh."

"Would you care to disclose?"

"Tomorrow at the arraignment. Right now I would just like to ask her a few questions. In your presence, of course. And the doctor, too, if he'd like to attend. She's been both medicated and Miranda'd, so I think we're covered on all fronts here."

"Do you really think I'm going to permit you to question her?"

"There may be a simple explanation for all this."

"There may indeed be, but you're not going to hear it now."

Zadek turned to the lawyer and said, "Why not? We could just all sit down in a nonconfrontational atmosphere and discuss this."

Bremmer gave him a withering glance and said, "Doc, do me a favor, will you? Stick to the medical questions and let me handle the legal ones. All right?"

"Well, I just thought that if Audrey could explain what happened, we might be able to sort this out."

"Right. And any exculpatory evidence contained in her testimony becomes inadmissible."

"I beg your pardon?"

"It would be hearsay: a prior consistent statement made after a motive to falsity had arisen."

Abelove put his fist to his mouth, covering a yawn. They ought to put lawyers into concentration camps in the Gobi Desert without an opportunity for parole.

"Look," he said, "can't she just give us a description of the burglar? That way we can get a sketch out to the uniforms."

"No."

"Do you think that refusing to cooperate with the police is going to make her sympathetic to a grand jury?"

"Frankly, I don't give a damn what a grand jury thinks. You and I both know that any half-competent prosecutor, even Ralph D'Imbroglio, could get a grand jury to indict a lamb chop. Now would you be good enough to provide me access to your prisoner before you violate the Sixth Amendment as well as the Fifth?"

Abelove wondered what amendment he'd be violating if he took a punch at her. Feeling the bile rise in his throat, he decided it would be appropriate if these concentration camps in the Gobi Desert had cruel and unusual torture devices that slowly and excruciatingly bled the lawyers to within an inch of their lives and then revived them, only to start again and repeat the process indefinitely.

Chapter 12

In accordance with the law, notice of Audrey Haas's arrest was posted at the police station. The wife of the late Schenectady urologist was in the company of a group of other criminals—B&E's, D&D's, D.W.I.'s. But she was clearly the star, the only murder suspect in Schenectady at the moment.

Carrie Castle got wind of the arrest when the station's police-beat reporter woke her up at 8:30 A.M. with the news that the woman whose story she had broken several nights ago had been taken into custody.

"What time's the arraignment?"

"Three P.M. Section Ninety-six."

"Get a van and a crew and clear the time with Marco," she said, getting out of bed. She turned on the TV, switched her treadmill to low, and started to walk.

She had walked nearly three miles, channel-surfing with the remote, before she was reasonably sure that no one else was ahead of her on the story.

By ten she was at the station, working the phone. D'Imbroglio was out of the office. Clint Wells had no comment. She went to the file footage, stuck it in the three-quarter-inch, replayed her interview with Barney Abelove, then dialed the Schenectady police.

Abelove wasn't at his desk. She went to the classified Rolodex and found the detective's unlisted home number.

He picked up on the ninth ring.

"Good morning, Barney," she said sweetly.

"Who's this?"

"It's Carrie Castle."

"What do you want?"

"Can you tell me the charges you're filing against Audrey Haas?"

"Show up at the arraignment. You'll find out."

He leaned back on the pillow, holding the phone an inch from his mouth. If he stuck his tongue out, he could lick Carrie Castle's ear. He wondered how she'd react. Renata loved to have her ear licked. Among other things. As he began to feel the blood heading south, he exhaled loudly, coughed a few times, and said, "I don't suppose there's anything I can do to keep you from showing up at the arraignment with the cavalry?"

"You could give me an exclusive—a walk through the scene, something like that."

"Just the two of us?"

"Sure."

"All alone at the scene?"

"Yes."

"What would you be wearing?"

There was a moment of silence, then: "Abelove, am I going to have to file a sexual-harassment charge against you?"

"If anyone should file a fucking harassment charge, it's me. *You* called *me*, remember?"

"Listen, I have a good mind to call Pauline Haggis in PR and tell her how one of the department's senior detectives treats the press."

"Hey, why bother calling? Fax her. Their fax number is listed. And when you're finished, you can go fax yourself!"

And he hung up. As soon as he had gotten up and padded to the bathroom, he regretted what he had said. Antagonizing the press was not a good idea under any circumstances, and in these particular circumstances, it was especially ill advised. A lot of people listened to Carrie Castle on the six and the eleven o'clock news. She could crucify you with one of those cute little asides to her co-anchor, Cliff Nevins, just before they went to commercial. "It looks like the police have really mishandled this one, Cliff, doesn't it?" And Nevins would nod knowingly and reply, "That it does, Carrie. We'll be right back . . ."

It was bad enough that Jeffries didn't like him, that D'Imbroglio had closed the door in his face, and that he had gotten caught by Audrey Haas's father searching the premises without a warrant. But making war with the media was a no-win situation.

So why did he do it? Maybe he ought to go to a shrink and pay a hundred an hour to find out. While he was at it, he could find out why, at fifty-six, he had next to nothing in the bank, no children, was twenty-five pounds overweight, and had tomato-sauce stains on his sleeves.

And a sinkful of dishes and no coffee. Opening the refrigerator, he saw a collection of half-empty takeout cartons, two cans of beer, and a container of what at one point was probably grapefruit juice.

He sat at the cluttered counter, making a pass through five-day-old shrimp lo mein, and decided that he would call Carrie Castle up and apologize. Before the arraignment. Then he would put on his best sports jacket—the herringbone tweed—the fifty-dollar silk tie that Renata got him last Christmas, and his oxblood Florsheims, and smile for the cameras.

Audrey Haas was arraigned on a felony complaint before Judge Carmen Fenetre in Section 96 of the Schenectady County Courthouse on State Street in downtown Schenectady, not far, as it happened, from Ernest Haas's office.

Appearing for the people was deputy district attorney Clint Wells. For the defendant, Susan Anthony Bremmer, L.L.B., Ph.D. Also present were Gary Lindheim, the Channel 6 *Action News* police-beat day-shift guy, in cellular-phone contact with Carrie Castle, who was outside in the truck with her film crew, and Detective Barney Abelove.

Abelove sat in the back and watched what should have been a *pro forma* exercise to bind a felony suspect over for a grand jury. He had been to a couple of hundred of them. Judge Fenetre was a large, imposing, no-bullshit judge who ran proceedings like a train dispatcher. On a good day you could be in and out of there in fifteen minutes. Okay, next.

Abelove had met with Wells at the D.A.'s office to decide on a preliminary charge. The rule of thumb was to ask for the most you could get and then let the grand jury reduce it for you. And to disclose as little evidence as possible, so as not to tip your hand to the defense.

Abelove had told Wells about the carving knife but not about his run-in with Audrey Haas's father. The deputy D.A. had reacted in much the same way his boss had.

"You went in without a warrant?"

"You sound like it's never been done before."

"Why didn't you wait?"

"Because no one was paying any attention to this case, that's why. Ralph doesn't want to go near it."

"I suppose you want me to ask for a warrant."

"No, Clint, I went in there so that we could get the whole fucking case thrown out on procedure."

"You don't have to be sarcastic."

Abelove was not only pissing off the press these days, he was pissing off the district attorney's office. He apologized to Clint Wells, as he had to Carrie Castle, leaving a contrite message on her voice mail when she wouldn't take his call.

In the absence of D'Imbroglio's input, they decided on second-degree murder, which would do for the arraignment, though it might be hard to prove down the line. At the moment, all they needed to do was convince Fenetre that there was sufficient evidence to establish that Audrey Haas had cut off her husband's penis.

Wells presented the police report describing the scene at the time Abelove, Doetz, and Gallagher arrived, followed by the M.E.'s report, establishing the time and cause of death. There was no mention of the fax, the burglar, the lasagna, the carving knife, the dog, or the missing dick. Fenetre sat there with an impassive look on her face as if she were listening to the report of a run-of-the-mill convenience-store robbery.

Bremmer moved for summary dismissal based on the fact that the state's case was entirely circumstantial, notwithstanding the fact that her client's actions, should they be established beyond a reasonable doubt, were nonetheless well within the purview of her legitimate right of self-defense.

Fenetre peered over the top of her reading glasses and asked the defense attorney if an exculpatory right of self-defense was not, in fact, inconsistent with a motion for dismissal that argued that her client did not commit the offense in the first place.

"Not contradictory, Your Honor, although perhaps redundant. Given the gravity of the charges against my client, I would like to establish the broadest possible context for her defense. Because, Your Honor, I am not merely defending Audrey Haas here in this court, but I am defending all women who have been the victim of this kind of abuse. As you know, since the passage of the Fourteenth Amendment guaranteeing equal protection for all citizens under the law—"

Fenetre shut her down. She was not about to allow a simple arraignment on a felony complaint become a soapbox for this windbag lawyer from Saratoga Springs. She had a full calendar for the day. Let the grand jury deal with redundant defenses and the Fourteenth Amendment. Okay, next . . .

The judge ruled that Audrey Haas be bound over for a grand-jury hearing, her lawyer having waived the right for an immediate hearing upon the evidence, not wanting to disclose her tactics at this point, and certainly not to an empty courtroom.

Bremmer then asked that, given her client's character, her lack of any sort of criminal record, and her medical condition, she be released into her own recognizance pending grand-jury action, should there be any.

"My client has been under constant psychiatric care since the death of her husband, Your Honor. I have an affidavit here from her physician, Dr. Marvin Zadek, of Scotia, attesting to the fact that incarceration would cause irrevocable harm to her health and could even be fatal in view of the fact that there has been a recent suicide attempt."

The judge glanced at the affidavit, then looked down at Clint Wells and asked, "Does the State object to my releasing Mrs. Haas on her own recognizance?"

"We do, Your Honor."

"On what grounds?"

"On two grounds."

"Is this another redundant argument?"

"We believe, Your Honor, that the very gravity of the charge should preclude the defendant—"

"Objection."

Fenetre sighed, looked down at Bremmer, and said, "Yes?"

"Ms. Haas has not been formally charged yet and is therefore not a defendant."

"Sustained. Moving right along here . . ."

"And secondly, the . . . suspect is, in fact, suicidal, which could very well cause her to fail to appear."

"That's true, Mr. Wells, but if she failed to appear due to suicide she would be dead and this case would become moot, wouldn't it?"

"With all due respect, Your Honor, in this state a suspect's mental condition is considered a factor in setting bail. *People* versus *Karman*, 126 A.D. 2F 657."

Bremmer didn't let any grass grow under that argument. "Your Honor, *Karman* refers to a mental condition that could cause danger to others, not to the suspect herself. In 1988 the appellate court ruled, in *People* versus *Infante*, 144 A.D. 2D 896, that bail cannot be denied merely on the grounds of a threat of suicide. Here is the key sentence in the decision, and I quote, 'It could be argued that suicide is the surest "escape" from prosecution, but, in our view, a suicidal tendency cannot be equated with an attempt to abscond or flee in the context of a bail application.' "

Fenetre set bail at $50,000, a moderate amount considering the charge, and Audrey was taken back into custody while her lawyer went to arrange for a bail bond. Before crossing the street to Grossi's twenty-four-hour bail-bond service, however, Bremmer stopped on the court-house steps to say a few words for Carrie Castle's camera and a half dozen other local newspeople who had picked the arrest up from the police-station notice.

In essence, this is what Susan Bremmer said: that Audrey Haas was a victim of a consistent pattern of sexual abuse from her late husband. That the charges against her were no more than an attempt to discredit her legitimate and heroic resistance to this abuse. That women had been waiting for someone to lead them in their battle to preserve their con-stitutional right to the pursuit of happiness. That Audrey Haas was that person. That she, Susan Bremmer, intended not only to vindicate her client, but to ventilate the issue beyond Schenectady to the nation and world at large. That the first shot had been fired across the bow of the vessel of sexual abuse. And so on.

Among the reporters taking this in was a man named Darryl Den-dron, an AP stringer from Albany, who, instead of attending a state Con-servation Department hearing on the pollution of Lake Champlain, had decided to drive to Schenectady for a lunch-hour assignation with his ex-wife, who worked as a data processor at G.E. and with whom he was thinking of getting back together.

In the brushfire that was to follow Audrey Haas's arrest and trial, this story filed by the Albany stringer was the spark that ignited the blaze. Once the story went out on the national wire, there was no containing it. One can only wonder what would have happened had Darryl Den-dron not had an ex-wife in Schenectady for whom he still had feelings and instead had stayed in Albany to find out who was dumping what into Lake Champlain.

But Darryl Dendron filed his story when he returned to Albany after forty-five minutes of bliss with his ex-wife at the Ramada Inn on Nott Street. And the story was picked up on two out of the three networks in time for the eleven o'clock news that night.

By the following morning, a great many people in the country knew who Audrey Haas was, what had happened to her husband, and the rel-evance of the Fourteenth Amendment to sexual abuse and, by exten-sion, to Ernest Haas's penis.

Chapter 13

People magazine reporter Carl Furillo had been dozing through the eleven o'clock news when he caught the story out of Schenectady. At first he thought he had already fallen asleep and was only dreaming about a woman lawyer standing on the courthouse steps claiming to have fired the first shot across the bow of sexual abuse. The egregiousness of the metaphor alone was enough to wake him from his stupor.

He picked up the bedside phone and called a friend on the graveyard shift at the *New York Post* and asked him to read him the story off the AP ticker.

The graveyard-shift guy said, "It's Lorena Bobbitt all over again."

"Much better. The woman was chained to her stove. The victim's dead, not just missing his dick, and we got a lawyer claiming legitimate self-defense. This one's got legs."

He hung up and called his assignment editor at home, waking her up.

"Sharon, did you hear about the urologist who got his dick cut off in Schenectady?"

After a few seconds of silence, Sharon Marcuzzi muttered, "You want to run that by me again?"

"Guy puts on women's clothes, handcuffs his wife to the kitchen stove, and she cuts off his salami. They arrest her for murder, and the lawyer's claiming it's self-defense. It's a cover story."

"What's the hook?"

"The hook? How about feminine rage? Sexual abuse and self-defense. Sodom in Schenectady. The dickless urologist. Kinky sex in the suburbs. The wages of cross-dressing. Pick one."

"Furillo . . ."

"I could get a car as soon as Hertz opens, be up there by eleven A.M."

Sharon Marcuzzi digested this information for a moment, then: "I don't know—I have to clear this through Barry tomorrow morning," she said.

"You wait till tomorrow morning, I'm not in Schenectady till the afternoon. By then they've already got the *Hard Copy* camera crew up there, if not Ted Koppel and Connie Chung."

"Connie Chung was fired."

"That won't stop her. Hey, it's not like I'm asking for a Learjet. We're talking a Hertz car and the Holiday Inn."

"What happened to it?"

"To what?"

"His . . . thing. Did they find it and try to sew it back on like they did with Bobbitt?"

"I don't know. That's what I want to go up to Schenectady to find out. What do you say?"

"Okay," she said. "You got a car and two nights at the Holiday Inn."

"All right if I get a full-size?"

"No. I've only got budget for a compact."

He hung up, went into his den, and found the road atlas. Schenectady was 165 miles from the city, a straight shot up the thruway. If he got out of Hertz by 8:30, he could be there before noon. If he sped, he could make it by eleven. Stick the magazine with the speeding ticket. Serve them right. How much more expensive was a full-size? He had gotten a Taurus for O.J.

Carl Furillo set the alarm and went back to bed. He drifted off in the middle of Letterman's monologue. Just wait until Letterman got a hold of this baby. He'd take no prisoners.

In order to prove that the house on Van Schuyler Lane was community property and thus Audrey's to offer as collateral for the bail bond, Bremmer had to get the safe-deposit-box key from Jack Myers, go to the bank with an order from the judge to allow her access to the safe-deposit box, then drive back downtown to get Ernest Haas's death certificate in lieu of his signature on the promissory note.

Then she had to get the bond issued and run the paperwork. It was late before the lawyer was able to get her client released from the Schenectady County Jail. As Susan Bremmer drove Audrey Haas back to Van Schuyler Lane, she assured her that it was all going to work out fine. There was nothing to worry about. She was in good hands.

Audrey nodded, leaned back in the seat, and watched the traffic flow by. The arraignment had been like a tennis game to her. She had sat there watching them hit the ball back and forth across the net, as a large woman in black robes who looked like Ethel Merman sat in the umpire's chair and awarded points.

She was relieved to be out of jail. It was green and ugly with hard plastic seats and fluorescent lighting. They gave her a bologna sandwich and an apple for dinner. The women in there with her spent most of their time trying to get cigarettes from one another and from the guards, who all looked like female bodybuilders.

And so she allowed herself to be comforted by the assurances of her lawyer that she would never see the inside of a jail again. Sitting back in the passenger seat of the Saab, she made herself relax for the first time since she had been arrested. Susan Bremmer was a good lawyer. She would deal with everything. It would all be taken care of.

But as they turned off Poltroon Road onto Van Schuyler, this little bubble of placidity burst wide open. There, at the end of the street, in front of number 474, were a half dozen TV minivans. On both sidewalks neighbors were milling around, mingling with the reporters and the curious.

Bremmer slammed the brakes on hard, jarring Audrey out of her reverie.

"Shit," she muttered. "I should have realized this was going to happen."

Bremmer told Audrey to slide down in her seat. Then she sped right past the reporters. They managed to make the other end of Van Schuyler without Audrey being spotted, turned up Van Eyck Lane, and headed back toward the Northway.

"What are we going to do?" asked Audrey.

"You can spend the night at my place in Saratoga Springs."

"That's very nice of you."

"Don't worry. First thing in the morning, I'll get Fenetre to issue a restraining order to keep those vultures away. Anybody gets within two hundred yards of your house'll be arrested."

"Can you do that?"

"Sure."

Bremmer knew that there wasn't a chance in hell she'd get a restraining order barring the press from badgering Audrey Haas. But she didn't want her client to be any more distraught than she already was. She couldn't afford to have her become a complete basket case. At least not before she became the test case to rewrite the sexual-abuse laws in this country.

In spite of the eight ounces of Brazilian espresso and the two grams of vitamin C he had dropped before he left his apartment, Carl Furillo wasn't completely awake until he was past Poughkeepsie. He dial-surfed on the AM radio, looking for news out of Schenectady.

Two of the all-news stations had forty-five-second blurbs taken pretty much verbatim from the AP story. The same sketchy details: woman dismembers her physician husband after being chained to kitchen stove and forced to have sex with him.

Furillo wondered why they were assuming he forced her. Maybe it was her idea in the first place. Who knew what went on in the murky recesses of people's minds in Schenectady, New York?

This story not only had legs, it had angles. There were psychological angles, there were legal angles, there were kinky angles. He just hoped that the facts did not disappoint him, that there was not some banal and straightforward explanation to the chain of events that had led Audrey Haas to do what she had done.

Carl Furillo was going through a rough patch in his life. He was both restless and listless. Ever since he had gotten back from L.A. he had been at loose ends. O.J. had burnt him out badly. After sitting in that court-room day after day for nine months, he had stopped caring about the DNA and the gloves and the passport in the Bronco. He had started to drift in the courtroom, to the point where he actually fell asleep during the redirect of one of the fiber experts.

He had called New York and asked to be relieved, turned in his Tau-rus, and flown back to Manhattan, only to find his girlfriend involved with a Haitian taxi driver and his cat with terminal emphysema. He sent his girlfriend's Paul Simon CDs back, buried his cat in a pet cemetery in the Bronx, and tried to get on with his life.

At the magazine he felt as if he were merely phoning it in. He did the nineteenth profile on Donald, Marla, and the baby, covered a story of an ex-con with Tourette's syndrome who won $16 million in the New Jersey state lottery, wrote an in-depth piece about two baseball players who had been caught kissing in a changing stall in a Neiman-Marcus in Dallas. But nothing had really engaged him. Until he'd heard the Haases' story on the eleven o' clock news.

For the first time in nearly a year, he felt excited. He was onto something. He felt sure of it. The adrenaline was pumping again.

His father, Lawrence "Bud" Furillo, a reporter for the old *Brooklyn Eagle*, had named his only son "Carl" in honor of the great Dodger right fielder of the 1950s, who had wound up working as a hard hat on the construction of the World Trade Center.

When Furillo was a kid, his old man took him down to meet his namesake. They found the "Reading Rifle" screwing rivets into a girder. "Carl," the father said, "this is my kid, Carl. He's got the same name as you."

Furillo looked at him through dark scowling eyes and said, "Why'd you do that?"

"You were the best, Carl."

"So what am I doing here with a fucking rivet gun in my hand?"

Over the years Carl Furillo had often thought about the ex–Dodger right fielder standing in the shadows of that monolith with a three-day growth of beard and a yellow hard hat on his head. It was an object lesson in the perils of failure. It wasn't necessarily how you played the game. It was how you ended up. It was either Palm Springs with a golf-club membership and a three-bedroom condo on the back nine or the rivet gun.

His foot sank down harder on the gas pedal. The Ford Escort climbed with difficulty to seventy-five. With the Taurus he would've been on cruise control and already past Kingston. The Escort was the rivet gun reincarnated. If this story turned out as big as he thought it might, forget the Taurus. Next time it would be a Crown Victoria.

At ten o'clock that morning, a meeting was called in Ralph D'Imbroglio's office. The district attorney had returned from the dead to preside over the strategy session to decide what evidence to present to the grand jury. He could no longer ignore a case that had become national news.

He summoned the entire staff of attorneys into the conference room, and, sitting at the head of the large walnut table, he asked for an update on the events in the case. Since Barney Abelove's visit to him had never taken place, he was ostensibly in the dark about the burglar and the carving knife.

Clint Wells filled him in on the arraignment on arrest before Judge Fenetre, the warrant to search the premises for the serial number of the potential murder weapon, Barney Abelove's *ex post facto* obtaining of the match with a Sunbeam electric carving knife that had been pawned in Albany on the day after Ernest Haas was killed.

After expressing the appropriate amount of disapproval of the warrant maneuver, D'Imbroglio asked his staff for their take on the issues surrounding the case.

"The knife's not prima facie, in any case," said Jason Rappaport, a brilliant and unconventional New York lawyer in his forties, who had been confined to a wheelchair after the cab he was in hit a guardrail on the West Side Highway and careened across three lanes of traffic. He had made the most of his disability by first suing the cab company for a shitload, settling out of court for half a shitload, and then getting a disability scholarship to Columbia law school, where he discovered a talent for drilling into the soft gum tissue of other people's arguments. Ten years later he was the top gun in the Schenectady County district attorney's office.

"Yeah, but we put the carving knife in her hands, we've got weapon, opportunity, and motive," Clint Wells maintained.

"I don't see motive," Rappaport interrupted.

"Marriage."

"*Marriage* is a motive?"

"Why not? You got a fifty-percent divorce rate out there—people fucking around left and right . . . I mean, they were into handcuffs . . ."

"You ever try it, Clint?"

"Me? No . . ."

"Don't knock it if you haven't tried it."

"No, thank you . . ."

"All right, forget motive for the moment—you have any forensic evidence establishing the knife as the weapon?"

"No . . ."

"So we've got a carving knife, taken presumably by the burglar and pawned in Albany, but nothing to put the carving knife either in her hands or through the guy's penis."

D'Imbroglio winced. Every time the act was mentioned, he found himself wincing. So did the other men in the room. The sole woman on the staff, Martha Demerest—an African-American two-birds-with-one-stone affirmative-action appointment of D'Imbroglio—winced for entirely different reasons. She thought the case had already been badly mismanaged by Ralph D'Imbroglio, who seemed to be standing on the bridge waiting to see which way the torpedoes were headed before he chose a course.

"What's our criterion for second-degree murder?" she asked.

"Extreme recklessness," said Rappaport.

"How do we sell that?" Demerest challenged.

"Second-degree murder in this state is defined as taking a life either intentionally, knowingly with extreme recklessness, or during the commission of any other felony. Extreme recklessness can be defined as: with an abandoned and willful heart, with a depraved heart, with a wanton and malignant heart, with depraved indifference, or with extreme indifference to the value of human life. I particularly like depraved indifference."

"What if they argue that she thought he was dead?"

"That's the beauty of depraved indifference. It covers that base. We argue that she didn't exhaust all the remedies available to her to make that judgment. She was depraved and indifferent to his welfare."

"The guy tied her up."

"Presumptive. We don't know that for a fact."

D'Imbroglio asked Clint Wells to reread the forensic report to the attorneys. When he was finished, there was some more wincing in the room.

"Maybe we should go for first degree here," said Jason Rappaport. "I mean, if the guy is dead, he's got no blood flow, right? No blood flow, no erection. No erection, he falls out of her onto the floor, thereby making the act difficult for a woman with one hand cuffed to the stove."

"Could've been vaginismus."

The whole table turned and stared at Martha Demerest. Without lowering her eyes or looking away, she explained, "It's a spasm of the vaginal sphincter muscles that causes the vagina to become rigid. It generally occurs before penetration, effectively preventing it. In this case, it may have occurred after penetration."

"So he dies, then she clamps him?"

"Possibly."

"You mean it's, like, caught in a vise?"

D'Imbroglio decided this would be a good time to take five and went into his office to return calls. There was a stack of phone messages on his desk from two dozen reporters and from the state attorney general.

He dialed the attorney general's office in Albany and was put right through.

"How's it going, Ralph?"

"All right."

"You got a case?"

"I think so."

"The blood flow, right?"

Jesus. Was his office bugged?

"Man can't keep it up without blood. You should be able to nail that bitch."

"Right . . ."

"Carry on, Ralph."

Chapter 14

Barney Abelove was not worried about blood flow to the penis. He was worried about the *ex post facto* search warrant and the illegally obtained serial number for the carving knife. Even though he logged the knife into the evidence locker the day after the date on the warrant, Audrey Haas's father could come out of the woodwork and nail him. He would step around that dog turd if and when he had to. For the moment Abelove was trying to find a burglar.

The Albany police took him through the mug books. Of the three Indians they had, one was dead, one was in Elmira doing twenty-to-life, and the third had had a sex-change operation and was living now in Pompano Beach, Florida.

He had managed to get Dave of Dave's Bait, Tackle, and Pledge Store to open his mouth long enough for a sketch artist to produce a rough drawing of the Indian who had pawned the knife. It was basically a tall Indian with a ponytail and an earring. Could've been any Indian. Could've been Tonto.

He could publish the sketch and wait for leads. But the sketch was so generic, they would be inundated with calls. Every Indian from here to Little Big Horn would be dragged in for questioning. It would take a staff of twenty to process them all, open them up to racism charges, and undoubtedly get them nowhere in the end.

He would have to run this one down with legwork—start with the bars and flophouses within a mile radius of the convenience store from which the fax was sent and work from there. He would show the sketch to the people at the Kopy Kat Kopy Korner on South Hudson, but he already knew what they would tell him: Lots fax. Lots Indians.

There was a message on his voice mail from Clint Wells.

"Let me ask you a question," the deputy D.A. asked him when Abelove called back. "You were at the scene, right?"

"Right."

"How far was the body from the stove?"

"Couple of feet. It was in the police report."

"Was the chain on the cuff long enough for her to bend down and cut it off while the guy was on the floor?"

"Huh?"

"Supposing the guy goes soft. You know, loses it. So he falls out of her and onto the ground. Can she lean over and slice it off using one hand?"

"Beats me."

"She probably has to hold it with one hand while she slices it with the other, doesn't she? I mean, you ever try to slice salami with one hand?"

"No . . ."

"It's not easy. Think about it, will you? This whole case could be decided on that point."

Abelove hung up and chose not to think about it. He trudged out to the car to drive to Albany. If he found the Indian, he'd ask him about the salami. See what he said.

The first thing Carl Furillo did when he checked into the Schenectady Holiday Inn was call the court and get the name of the lawyer defending Audrey Haas. Susan Bremmer was on the phone with Tammy Stockpile in the office/den of her Saratoga Springs house when she was interrupted by Carl Furillo. She told Stockpile she would call her back and took the call.

Bremmer told Furillo that she had nothing to say publicly at the moment, but she was planning a joint news conference with NOW for later that afternoon in Schenectady. Furillo heard that as a soft "No comment" and persisted.

"Are you claiming she didn't do it, or that she did it but for justifiable reasons?"

"Audrey Haas is a victim. Period."

"What about Ernest Haas?"

"He stepped over the line."

"What line?"

"The line in the sand that all women have the right to draw when they are being violated."

"What is the difference between consensual sex and violation?"

"Handcuffs."

Bremmer hung up and called back Tammy Stockpile.

"Do you think I should have the state people there?" Tammy Stockpile asked.

"As far as I'm concerned, the more the better."

"What about Audrey? Are you going to let her speak?"

Bremmer looked out through the doorway of her den/office. Down the hall in the living room Audrey Haas was watching television. They'd had their heart-to-heart the previous night, when they arrived from Schenectady. Over a cup of peppermint tea, the lawyer asked her new client to tell her exactly what had happened on the night of March 27. She had prefaced this request by explaining that nothing Audrey said would in any way dampen her resolve to defend her, that there were issues of law and theory that transcended any issues of fact in this case.

It took Audrey a while to get going, but when she did, it all came pouring out—starting with the salad spinner, the Chinese food, the handcuffs, and the pantyhose, all the way to the Hallelujah chorus and the Indian. There was, however, a large gap in the middle of the story. From the Hallelujah chorus to the arrival of the Indian, Audrey claimed that things were very hazy. It was as if she had blacked out during the sex act and had reawakened afterward to find her husband dead at her feet and an Indian standing in her kitchen holding a carving knife.

The presence of someone else in the house on Van Schuyler Lane the night of Ernest Haas's death created another dimension. The closed-room aspect of the case did not apply: There was a second legitimate suspect.

This fact presented the opportunity for a reasonable-doubt defense. She might be able to get a jury to acquit even if they never found the Indian.

But if she pursued this tactic, the issues of spousal abuse and self-defense would become moot. The case would become largely a question of whom the jury believed, and the trial would degenerate into conflicting statements and character assessments.

Bremmer was convinced that her client would not present well to a jury. She was unstable, dippy, and inarticulate. There was a kind of nebulous sexuality about her: She looked like the type of woman who lay around the house all day in a negligee and wore perfume when she went to the mall. Women would instinctively dislike her.

It was this sense that a jury would not acquit Audrey Haas on reasonable doubt that enabled Bremmer to rationalize the tactics she would adopt. She would forget about the Indian. Let the prosecution find him, make him a suspect or a witness, cut a plea deal with him. She would ignore him.

And in so doing, Susan Bremmer would still be fulfilling her ethical obligation to provide her client with the best available defense. If, in the process, Audrey Haas also became the vehicle for publicizing a number of long-standing legal issues affecting women in this country, so much the better.

She was convinced, then, that keeping Audrey Haas not only off the witness stand but away from the press was ultimately in her client's own best interest. Audrey Haas was a loose cannon. She would have to rehearse the hell out of her before she let her speak in public.

"I'll have her read a prepared statement," Bremmer responded to Tammy Stockpile. "We'll say she's still too upset. Maybe we should have a nurse there. What do you think?"

"A nurse? What kind of nurse?"

"I don't know. Someone in a white uniform. Can't you rent them by the day?"

"I guess so."

"See if you can find one."

About fifty folding chairs were set up in the courtyard of the offices of the Schenectady Chapter of the National Organization for Women's headquarters on Erie Boulevard. But by 3:45, people were already standing in the aisles, and there was a dangerous confluence of cables and cameras competing for views of the rostrum, where Audrey Haas was set to appear with her attorney.

Carl Furillo had gotten there early and staked out a front-row seat. He had just settled in, looking back toward the entrance to watch the arrivals, when a voice said, in a tone that was more a command than a request, "Excuse me—would you mind moving over a few seats?"

Furillo turned back around and saw a blond woman wearing pancake makeup and enough hair spray to coagulate linguini.

"Yes, I would," he replied.

When he didn't move, she said, "I'm Carrie Castle, *WSCH Action News*. I need the space for my crew."

"I'm Carl Furillo, *People* magazine. And I'm not moving."

She glared at him for several seconds, then stalked off. A minute later, two men accompanied Carrie Castle back to the front row. They stepped pointedly over Furillo as they laid cable to the rostrum mike, then sat down, one on each side of him. Carrie Castle refused to look at him. She sat down and studied her notes, occasionally brushing an errant strand of linguini from her forehead.

By 4:15 the courtyard was overflowing, and when Audrey, her lawyer, and Tammy Stockpile finally arrived at 4:30, they had to fight their way to the rostrum. Cameras clicked furiously as they stepped over the cables and made their way to the front.

Audrey was wearing a peach cotton pants suit, with beige flats, a yellow blouse, and a lime-green silk scarf. Susan Bremmer was in a long denim skirt, a paisley shirt with a knitted vest, and work boots. Tammy Stockpile had on a blue linen suit and black suede shoes that must have cost at least $300. They were definitely not members of the same sorority.

Furillo studied Audrey Haas as she took one of the three folding chairs behind the rostrum. She was not unattractive in a sort of spaced-out Susan Hayward manner. Her eyes were dusted over with the glazed veneer of tranquilizers, her mouth slack. She looked both absent and exhausted.

Tammy Stockpile approached the rostrum, cleared her throat, and welcomed the assembled press on behalf of the Schenectady County Chapter of NOW. She informed them that Audrey Haas would read a short statement; then Susan Bremmer, her attorney, would expand upon it. After which they would answer questions as time permitted.

Tammy Stockpile turned and looked at Audrey, who looked at her lawyer for approval before getting up and walking a little unsteadily toward the rostrum.

It took Audrey a moment to locate the index cards that Susan Bremmer had prepared for her. She gazed down at the cards, keeping her eyes lowered, not looking at the audience.

"Good afternoon. Thank you for coming. My name is Audrey Haas. I have been unjustly arrested and charged with murder. I did not murder my husband. I am a victim of spousal abuse and media exploitation. Women have been victims for too long. It's time this violence and abuse stopped. Thank you very much."

Then she turned abruptly and went back to her seat. Susan Bremmer took the rostrum and introduced herself. "My name is Susan Anthony

Bremmer, and I am an attorney as well as the chairperson of the women's studies department at Skidmore College and the author of numerous books and articles on the subject of women and the law. Since the grand jury has not yet heard the evidence and returned an indictment, it would be both unwise and unethical for me to comment on the merits of any case that might be tried. However, I will comment on the issues surrounding the State of New York's arrest and charging of Audrey Haas with second-degree murder, for these issues concern the basic constitutional rights of all citizens in the United States. . . . As Dred Scott became the subject of a test case on slavery, so Audrey Haas will lend her name to a case that will establish, once and for all, that women are not chattel to be used in any manner that men, including their husbands, see fit, that marriage is not a license to abuse and rape, that the notion of self-defense extends beyond the protection of our bodies to our very sense of self-worth and dignity. . . ."

Susan Bremmer was only warming up. She went on for nearly an hour on the subject of abuse, rape, and the law. She talked about movies, television, and advertising objectifying and victimizing women through their innately violent imagery. She talked about the notion of consensual sex as an abstraction in a society that had been inundated with imagery of male domination and female submission. She quoted Susan B. Anthony, Margaret Sanger, Gloria Steinem, and Gandhi.

When it was over, Carrie Castle charged over the cables to try to get a stand-up with Audrey, but Tammy Stockpile cut in front of her and told her that Audrey had no further comment. Carrie Castle had to content herself with putting Bremmer on camera, while Tammy Stockpile hustled Audrey past the clicking cameras.

Furillo didn't follow the pack of reporters out to the car. He knew from experience that when you wanted to find out about a crime, the last person to ask was the person who was accused of committing the crime—or her lawyer. All you got was spin.

He went outside and asked one of the TV van drivers for directions to police headquarters.

When Barney Abelove got back to his desk on Liberty Street, he was tired and disgusted. He had spent the day in and out of bars and convenience stores in Albany and had wound up with nothing. A couple of drunks said they knew Indians, but the descriptions were so varied and imprecise as to be virtually worthless. An Indian mechanic at an Exxon station told him that most of the Mohawks around Albany had intermarried and moved west. A woman in a laundromat told him that she had a friend who was living with an Indian and gave him an address on South Huron, where Abelove found a one-eighth Algonquin named Jerry with a buzz cut, who thought Abelove was from the IRS and produced a bank book with no money in it.

So when Abelove was told that there was a *People* magazine reporter waiting for him at his desk, he almost turned around and walked back out. He was in no mood to talk to the press.

The guy was young, maybe thirty, in jeans, a T-shirt, sports jacket, and white tennis shoes. He was sitting at a chair beside Abelove's desk reading the *Gazette*.

Abelove sat down and said, "Look, you got to go through the PR department. They're handling this."

The young man extended his hand. "Hi. I'm Carl Furillo."

Abelove couldn't suppress a vagrant smile. "How're the Duke and Pee Wee?" he asked.

Furillo smiled back. "Not bad, but we lost Gil, Jackie, and Campy."

"So, Carl, what can I do for you?"

"I'm doing a story on Audrey Haas."

"Look, I'd really like to help you out, but I'm not supposed to talk to the press about pending cases."

"We'll do it on deep background. 'Sources in the Schenectady Police Department.' That's all. I won't use your name."

"I'm real tired . . ."

"There's a steakhouse I passed on the way down here. It looked kind of nice. What do you say?"

"You trying to buy a story with a steak?"

"Of course not. I'll let you pay."

Abelove started to shake his head again when Furillo said, "Listen, sooner or later they're going to write about you, whether you like it or not, and you'll have no control over what they write. Wouldn't it be better to talk to someone who's willing to sit down and take the time to hear it all?"

Furillo looked around the squad room, then added, in a confidential manner, "You want Carrie Castle telling your story or me?"

Abelove gave Furillo deep background on the Audrey Haas case over a couple of sixteen-ounce T-bones at Rodney's Steakhouse. He told him about the fax, the helicopter, the dog, the medical examiner, the Prozac, the stomach pump, the warrant, the carving knife, and the arrest. He did not tell him about the first trip to Van Schuyler Lane without the warrant, his meeting with Jack Myers, his reporting to Ralph D'Imbroglio and getting the door slammed in his face, or his present search for an Indian in a haystack, beyond the fact that they were checking leads on the burglar.

Furillo listened carefully, not taking notes and letting Abelove finish his story without interruption. Then he shook his head and said, "I don't get the fax. I mean, why doesn't he just pick up the phone?"

"His voice. Maybe there was something about his voice that would give him away—like an accent or a speech impediment or something."

"You think the burglar could've done it?"

Abelove hesitated before slowly shaking his head.

"How come?"

"Guy breaks into a house, sees a guy screwing his wife, kills him by cutting off his dick, and leaves the wife alive as a witness?"

"Maybe he's a headcase."

"Maybe, but not only does he not kill her, but he brings her something to eat and drink, then sends us a fax."

"You got an angle on the women's clothes?"

Abelove shook his head.

"No record as a cross-dresser?"

"He's got no sheet. Not even a parking ticket."

"What do the neighbors say?"

"The usual. He was a nice man and a good doctor. Went to the mall, mowed his lawn, washed his car on Sunday."

"What about Audrey?"

"Nobody knows much about Audrey. As far as I can tell, she stayed home all day and watched TV. No kids, no brothers or sisters. Parents live in Phoenix. She's been seeing a shrink, a guy named Zadek in Scotia, for some time. D.A.'ll probably subpoena the shrink, and the shrink'll claim confidentiality."

Abelove leaned back in his chair and folded his hands across his stomach reflectively. After a moment, he said, almost to himself, "Why couldn't she have just shot him?"

When he got back to his room, Furillo called Sharon Marcuzzi in New York and gave her the broad strokes. She told him to fax her eight hundred words and see if he could make a deal for photos locally. Otherwise they'd have to go with Ernest Haas's Cornell University medical-school graduation picture.

"Any chance of getting to Audrey?"

"You kidding? They've got her stashed away like she was Salman Rushdie."

"Guess what Geraldo's doing tomorrow."

"What?"

"Women who mutilate their lovers."

Chapter 15

On April 23 the Schenectady County grand jury handed up an indictment for murder in the second degree in re *The State of New York* v. *Audrey Roberta Haas*. The indictment referred to Statute 125.25 of the New York State Criminal Code, which stipulates that "a person is guilty of murder in the second degree when . . . under circumstances evincing a depraved indifference to human life, he recklessly engages in conduct which creates a grave risk to another person, and thereby causes the death of another person."

The *ex parte* proceedings took place without the presence of Audrey Haas, who was not called on to testify—not that Susan Bremmer would have permitted her to, in any event. Clint Wells, Jason Rappaport, and Martha Demerest simply read the police and medical examiner's reports and then asked for a second-degree-murder indictment. It was, in the words of Ralph D'Imbroglio, a slam dunk.

The formal arraignment on indictment took place the following afternoon before Judge Fenetre. This time Audrey was present to plead not guilty to the charge. Susan Bremmer, appearing for the defendant, moved for the indictment to be quashed on grounds that depraved indifference to human life could not possibly apply between spouses. The motion was summarily dismissed by Judge Fenetre.

The prosecution asked for bail to be increased because of the greater risk of flight due to the second-degree murder indictment. Fenetre denied that motion too.

All this, however, did not really interest the readers of *People* magazine. What they wanted to know was what Audrey Haas was wearing for the arraignment on indictment. *Time* reported her in a beige knock-off London Fog, dark-brown wool suit, orange faux-Gucci scarf, and sensible heels. *Women's Wear Daily* was less charitable. They said she looked as if she were going to work in the Motor Vehicle Bureau.

Also present in the courtroom that day, wearing a black silk dress and too much lipstick, was a woman named Janice Meckler, who actually did work in the Motor Vehicle Bureau. She was a clerk supervisor in charge of smog-inspection-sticker enforcement and lived in an apartment on Escher Avenue near the college. For anyone observant enough to notice, she was the only person in that courtroom who had also been present at Ernest Haas's funeral several weeks before and had, at the time, been referred to as "the woman in the black veil." No one, however, made the connection, and Janice Meckler's identity and connection with Ernest Haas would not be revealed until the urologist's will was made public.

At which time certain facts about Ernest Haas's life would be revealed that would make the trial even more sensational than it already was. For the moment, however, she was just an overdressed woman taking a day off from her job in the Motor Vehicle Bureau to attend an arraignment.

Furillo's *People* magazine piece on Audrey had had the headline MURDERESS OR ROLE MODEL? SCHENECTADY WOMAN STRIKES BACK AT ABUSIVE HUSBAND BY THE UNKINDEST CUT OF ALL. It was on page 34, between profiles of Joey Buttafuoco and the cast of *Friends*. Citing sources in the Schenectady Police Department, Furillo had referred to complications in the investigation regarding the existence of a possible second suspect, a burglar who may have been present at the scene of the crime on the night of March 27. He said that there was still no conclusive murder weapon and that the county medical examiner was being very tight-lipped about the investigation. He referred to the Haases as "a quiet couple living in a green-and-white Dutch Colonial house on a quiet street in middle America who, nevertheless, enjoyed cross-dressing and bondage in their knotty-pine kitchen."

He had reduced Susan Bremmer to "a defense attorney with a feminist agenda" and Judge Fenetre to a "no-nonsense magistrate." Ralph D'Imbroglio's office had had no comment other than saying that they were pursuing their mandate to prosecute all felons to the fullest extent of the law.

It was with the appearance of Carl Furillo's *People* magazine piece that the Audrey Haas case grew to be a worldwide story. It became the most discussed topic on call-in radio programs and afternoon TV talk shows. Magazines bumped stories to make space for it. Letterman and Leno couldn't keep their hands off it. Development deals for movies floated through Hollywood like smog, clogging the production pipeline with conflicting projects.

So even before the trial began, before a jury was empaneled and the case tried, the story was hot. What had started off as a little après-Chinese-food frolic in the kitchen of a home in suburban Schenectady became a cause célèbre that polarized the country and made the thirty-eight-year-old Schenectady housewife the biggest media star since Princess Di. Who, when asked her opinion of the case, replied, "Well, it is going to a bit of an extreme actually, isn't it?"

The first of what would eventually be a series of safe houses for Audrey Haas was a red-brick split-level on Erasmus Drive, not far, as it turned out, from Audrey's own house on Van Schuyler Lane. The house belonged to Cissy Weiner, a paralegal and single mother with two young children, who, besides being active in the Schenectady County Chapter of NOW, was a third-degree black belt.

Audrey was given Cissy Weiner's recently departed mother's bedroom, with her own TV and bathroom. She wasn't crazy about the arrangement. In addition to the young children, one of whom was hyperactive and kept coming into Audrey's room while she was watching television and jumping on her, the room had ugly patterned wallpaper and smelled of disinfectant. But going back to Van Schuyler Lane and living with the army of reporters on her front lawn was out of the question.

The house functioned not only as a safe house but also as the command center for Audrey's defense team. Aside from Susan Bremmer and Tammy Stockpile, a number of prominent lawyers had volunteered to be a part of the legal team that would defend Audrey Haas. The legal bills would be substantial.

When Bremmer asked Audrey if she had the resources to finance her own defense, Audrey had responded that she thought there was a life-insurance policy somewhere but she didn't know exactly how much it was for.

After Judge Fenetre had authorized her to go through the Haases' safe-deposit box to get the deed to the house for the bail bond, Bremmer had discovered a life-insurance policy with a $500,000 death benefit. Though Audrey Haas was the beneficiary of the policy, the insurance company would not pay out the benefit until she was acquitted of the murder charge.

"Oh," Audrey had said when Bremmer explained the problem to her.

Bremmer asked Audrey how much was owed on the house. Audrey said she didn't know that either. Ernie handled the finances. Bremmer explained that if there was not enough equity left in the house, after the amount that was needed as collateral for the bail bond was subtracted, she would be unable to borrow against it.

"Oh," Audrey repeated.

Asked about money in bank accounts, all Audrey could come up with was the checkbook she carried in her pocketbook.

It began to dawn on Bremmer that not only was Audrey Haas a bimbo but she was a broke bimbo. She would get the judge to issue an order to search for bank accounts and other assets in Ernest Haas's office, but for the moment it was all strictly *pro bono*.

At the first meeting of the Audrey Haas Ad-Hoc Defense Team, Bremmer explained the money situation.

"I don't know what the big deal is," said Lizzie Vaught, a high-profile New York criminal attorney, whose usual fee was $500 an hour. "This case'll be worth its weight in publicity alone."

Lizzie Vaught was rich, blond, blue-eyed, and sexy. She wore Donna Karan suits, Italian shoes, and real jewelry.

"In any event, we don't have a choice at the moment," Bremmer responded. "So anyone who wants to start billing hours might as well leave."

Bremmer proceeded to outline the facts of the case as she had been told them by Audrey. When she was finished, Lizzie Vaught asked, "Do you believe her about the blackout?"

Bremmer turned toward the open doorway. Audrey was resting in the guest room with the door closed. She had told Cissy Weiner she wasn't feeling well and asked that the meeting proceed in her absence.

"I don't see that we have much of a choice but to believe her," Bremmer replied.

"You understand," Lizzie Vaught continued, "that the determination of fact as to whether she was or was not conscious during the dismemberment is the pivot of the entire case. If she claims no memory, then we have a straightforward reasonable-doubt argument."

"We can still argue a history of abuse, spousal rape, legitimate self-defense . . ." Bremmer said.

"We can argue it all we want, but it all becomes moot once she claims she doesn't know what happened to her husband's penis. Whatever he did or didn't do to her is immaterial if she doesn't claim to have acted as a result of it. Then there's no provocation, no grounds for self-defense, no lesser-evil justification—in fact, the entire argument dissolves."

"What about the burglar?" Cissy Weiner asked.

"Until the police find him, if they ever do, we have to proceed as if he doesn't exist," Bremmer said.

"Uh-uh," said Lizzie Vaught. "The existence of a burglar or of some other presence in the house the night of the crime has already been established. Somebody sent that fax to the police, and it wasn't Audrey. So to that extent the burglar is real, whether or not they ever find him, and he becomes key in the reasonable-doubt defense. He's another plausible suspect. If we've got nothing but Audrey in that house and a dismembered penis, then either she cut it off, he cut it off himself, or it fell off."

Lizzie Vaught paused for a moment, like Lana Turner, to brush an errant strand of blond hair from her forehead. Bremmer imagined Vaught in front of an all-male jury. She could have gotten Attila the Hun off.

"At the end of the day," the blond lawyer summed up, "the problem we're facing is that at this point our client's best shot is a narrow defense based on facts and not on law. We make no inroads in Thirteenth or Fourteenth Amendment areas, in criteria of abuse, spousal rape, legitimate self-defense, et cetera. We wind up arguing that the state cannot prove that Audrey Haas dismembered her husband beyond a reasonable doubt. Meanwhile the prosecution parades coroners, pathologists, urologists, and god knows who else in front of the jury, and we sit there taking pot shots at them. I don't know about you, but it sounds like a big yawn to me."

There was a convincing finality to Lizzie Vaught's assertion. The other women in the room began to see the dilemma that confronted them. And they didn't like it.

"Well, if she doesn't remember, I don't see what we can do about it," Bremmer said finally.

"We can help her remember," Lizzie Vaught said.

"What do you mean?"

"Get her a therapist."

"She already has one."

"Let's put him on the team."

"That's unethical."

"So is failing to provide a defendant with the best possible defense. Anyway, here's the way I see it—either Audrey admits to doing it and we go from there, or we get out our tap shoes and do a song and dance for the jury."

So the day after the strategy meeting in Cissy Weiner's den, Marvin Zadek became an unofficial member of the defense team. Bremmer called him to explain the dilemma facing the lawyers and her own conviction that Audrey was blocking her memory of what had occurred in her kitchen the night that Ernest Haas died.

After pointing out various conflict-of-interest and confidentiality issues and reiterating that he would not testify or be deposed in any manner whatsoever, Zadek agreed to see Audrey and try to help her go back and confront the events of March 27. But, he insisted, she herself would have to communicate these revelations directly to her lawyers. His lips were sealed.

"Fine with me," said Bremmer. "Just see if you can get her past the block."

Zadek said that he would do his best, then cleared his throat several times, as if he had something stuck in his esophagus, and asked, "By the way . . . what are the lawyers doing about . . . fees?"

"We're working *pro bono* pending discovery of assets."

"I see," said Zadek. "Are there any assets . . . to be discovered?"

"I think we're getting into my area of confidentiality here, Doc. Tell you what, though, as soon as we find some assets, I'll let you know."

After she hung up with Zadek, Bremmer called Clint Wells to find out whether the prosecution was opposing her motion for discovery of assets.

"We have no reason to do that," Clint Wells replied.

"Have you already been in his office?"

"I'm not at liberty to disclose that."

"Listen, everything in that office is community property and belongs to my client, with or without a will."

"You'll get everything, whatever there is, as soon as we dust and copy any documents."

"You're right on the edge of unlawful seizure here."

"The state has an overriding right to any evidence in a homicide."

"I don't know where you went to law school, Clint, but they probably didn't have a copy of the Constitution around."

That afternoon Bremmer received by messenger an envelope from the district attorney's office containing two items—a passbook for a savings account in a bank in Troy and Ernest Haas's last will and testament. After she had looked at both documents, she understood why the urologist had kept them in his office and not in his home. Ernest Haas was not only a cross-dresser, he was also a two-timer. The bank book contained over $400,000 and was not enumerated in the accounting of assets in the will. More significant, it was a joint account. The other name on the account, however, was not Audrey Haas. It was Janice Meckler.

Chapter 16

By the time Susan Bremmer learned of the existence of Janice Meckler and of the joint-bank-account passbook in Ernest Haas's office safe, the Motor Vehicle Bureau smog-inspection-sticker-compliance supervisor had already been interviewed by Clint Wells and Barney Abelove.

Abelove called her at the Motor Vehicle Bureau on State Street to ask her to stop off at the district attorney's office after work to answer some questions. At 5:20 that afternoon she arrived at Clint Wells's office wearing a black sheath dress and carrying a black patent-leather purse. They went down the hall to a small interview room, her perfume trailing behind them.

She opened her purse, checked her makeup, then blinked several times, as if her contact lenses were bothering her. She spoke with a brittle, overaspirated voice, and knocked back three cups of black coffee during the hour they spent with her. Abelove got the feeling that this woman, like Audrey, did not necessarily have a full set of lug nuts.

When Clint Wells asked what her relationship to Ernest Haas had been, she blinked several times before blurting out, "Ernie and I were lovers."

"I see," said the deputy D.A., making notes on a yellow legal pad in the small, anal handwriting that Abelove was beginning to hate.

"How long had this affair been going on?"

"Four and a half years."

"Did his wife know about it?"

"Audrey? Audrey barely knows her own name."

"When was the last time you saw Dr. Haas alive?"

"March twenty-fifth, five forty-five in the afternoon. On the steps of my apartment on Escher Avenue. The sun was setting. Ernie was wearing his tan wool sports jacket and brown loafers. If I had only known it was the last time I would see him alive, I would never have let him leave."

With that she took out a wad of Kleenex from her purse and dabbed her eyes.

"Where were you on Friday, March twenty-seventh, between eight P.M. and two A.M.?"

She took the Kleenex from her eyes and looked suspiciously at Clint Wells.

"Am I a suspect?"

"Not necessarily."

Jesus, Abelove thought. The guy had no bedside manner. In two seconds she was going to clam up entirely, and the next time they'd get to talk to her would be on the witness stand.

"Listen, if you think for one minute that I would have *ever* done *anything* to hurt Ernie, you're out of your goddamn mind. I adored that man. I weep for that man every day since he's been gone. I will have to take salt tablets to compensate for my body's loss from the tears I shed. And you, you have the *nerve* to ask me for an *alibi*?"

Janice Meckler chugged what was left of her coffee, leaned back in her chair, and glared at Clint Wells, who looked down at his legal pad, at a loss for words.

"I'm sorry. We didn't mean to upset you, Miss Meckler," Abelove jumped in, playing good cop to Wells's bad cop—or in this case smart cop to Wells's dumb cop. "We're just trying to have you help us find Dr. Haas's murderer."

"Find? You found her. Standing over the body. She cut it off. With a carving knife. Just the way they said in *People* magazine. She couldn't bear the thought that Ernie was happy with another woman. The only reason he didn't divorce her was that he didn't think she could take care of herself. She's a zombie, that woman. A vicious zombie. I hope they give her the chair."

"May I ask you about something a little delicate?" Abelove offered in a tone of voice that was mollifying and confidential—as if he were a priest in a confessional trying to ease her into a difficult admission of sin. She looked at him for a moment, then nodded.

"Dr. Haas was discovered wearing women's clothes. Presumably belonging to his wife. Did he . . . practice cross-dressing with you as well?"

She took out her compact, opened it, checked her lipstick. Then in a small, almost coy voice, she said, "When you love someone, you love that person totally, uncritically, irrevocably."

"Did you and he share clothes?"

"Yes." She nodded. "Ernie was a size eight. Just like me."

And just like Audrey, Abelove thought, wondering how many other size eights in Schenectady the doctor had been banging.

"What about handcuffs?"

"I beg your pardon?"

"Did you and Dr. Haas use handcuffs?"

She pushed her hair back from her forehead, shook her head, and said in her breathy whisper, "We used silk. Sashes from bathrobes and dresses. They don't leave marks."

At Susan Bremmer's suggestion, Audrey resumed her therapy sessions with Dr. Zadek. She was driven to her appointment by a volunteer from the NOW office, who waited for her and then drove her back to the safe house.

Audrey and Zadek sat in his knotty-pine office, Audrey on the faux-leather couch with the homey throw pillows, Zadek on a bentwood rocker ten feet away. The conversation drifted aimlessly for several sessions, with Zadek allowing Audrey to ramble with little direction, hoping that she would eventually want to talk about the events of the night of March 27.

It soon became clear to Zadek, however, that she didn't want to go anywhere near that evening. Either she had completely blocked it or she was consciously refusing to deal with it.

So Zadek began to nudge her gently in what he hoped was the right direction. Audrey was talking about a movie on TV she had seen with Tori Spelling playing a victim of sexual abuse when the doctor suddenly interrupted and asked her if she'd felt abused.

"What?"

"Do you feel that Ernie ever abused you?"

"I don't understand what you mean."

"Like in the movie, Tori Spelling is abused by the man in her office. How did you feel about your husband? Did he abuse you?"

"We were married. In the movie, the guy in the office was trying to come on to Tori Spelling—"

"Husbands sometimes abuse wives."

"So what are you trying to say?"

"I'm not trying to say anything, Audrey. I'm trying to help you remember some painful things, which I don't think you want to remember."

"Ernie's dead. What difference does it make?"

"Just because someone's dead doesn't mean they stop affecting our feelings."

So they started talking about Ernie. It took another session before she told him about the shopping for clothes together, the wardrobe, and, finally, the sex in out-of-the-way places—the backyard barbecue pit, the garage, the basement beside the water heater.

"How did you feel about it?" Zadek asked.

"I don't know. It was a little weird but it meant so much to Ernie, I figured okay, if that's what he liked."

"Did you ever tell him you didn't want to do it?"

"Well, it wasn't that I didn't want to do it—it was that I would have preferred doing it in bed."

Zadek leaned back in his chair, stroked his chin. The door was open just a crack. He stepped forward and gently put his foot in it.

"What about March twenty-seventh? What did you want to do that night?"

"There was this movie I wanted to see. With Meredith Baxter. And I was tired. Ernie had brought Chinese food home. Chinese food makes me tired. They say they don't put MSG in it, but I think they do anyway. . . ."

Zadek pushed the foot a little deeper into the doorway. "How did you feel about the handcuffs?"

"What handcuffs?"

"The ones he used to attach you to the stove."

"Oh *those* handcuffs. Well, I didn't particularly like those handcuffs even though they were padded inside. I don't know what they were padded with—some sort of quilted material, you know, like they use for potholders."

"But wasn't it these handcuffs that prevented you from getting to a phone to call the police after Ernie died?"

"Well, yes. And I couldn't reach the refrigerator either. I got hungry. Very hungry. If it wasn't for the fact that he left me the lasagna—"

She stopped abruptly, like a car skidding to a halt just before it went over a cliff.

"He?"

She avoided his eyes, turning quickly away.

"Let's talk a little about him," Zadek suggested in his most therapeutic voice.

Instead of answering, Audrey grabbed the Kleenex box and started pulling out tissues one after another and rolling them into tight little balls, which she then stuffed into the pockets of her slacks.

Zadek let the silence fill the room. It was a pivotal moment. She could slam the door and run for cover, or she could open it and let the light shine in.

They must have sat there for a solid minute without talking. Then Audrey said in a very quiet, but very clear voice, "The Indian. He broke into the house. While we were doing it. He attacked Ernie. With my electric carving knife. He went into the drawer next to the stove, got the knife, and . . . and he killed Ernie. That's what he did."

The first thing that Bremmer did after receiving the will and the bank book was to file a motion to freeze the assets of the joint bank account in order to preserve funds to cover Audrey's legal expenses. By the time the paperwork cleared, however, the account had a balance of $14.25, the remainder having been withdrawn, presumably by Janice Meckler. Bremmer filed a new motion for a temporary restraining order to prevent Meckler from spending the $400,000 that she had allegedly withdrawn, and that motion was pending when Janice Meckler's existence was discovered by the press.

Carrie Castle's courthouse stringer reported the motion for the temporary restraining order, and it didn't take long for the WSCH anchorwoman to track down Janice Meckler. She was on the Motor Vehicle Bureau smog-inspection-sticker-compliance supervisor's doorstep with a camera and a soundman waiting for her to come home from work.

When Ernest Haas's former lover got out of her light-green Mazda and walked across Escher Avenue to her condo, she found Carrie Castle lying in ambush.

"Are you Janice Meckler?"

"Yes . . ."

"Did you have a joint bank account with Ernest Haas?"

Janice Meckler looked quickly up the stairs to her front door. Thirty feet and she could be in the safety of her condo. But they would film her dodging the cameras, fleeing from reporters. It would be on TV that night. Her makeup needed retouching. There was a run in her stocking.

"How about we go inside and have a chat?" Carrie added quickly.

"Just the two of us. You can tell me your whole story. Just the way you want to. What do you say?"

Janice Meckler considered her options. If she agreed to the interview, she could go upstairs and put on her mourning clothes, the same black dress she wore to the interrogation at the district attorney's office. They could sit in the corner of the den, beside the walnut étagère with the pictures of Ernie and her in Atlantic City. She could tell the world what they had meant to each other. On TV.

"All right," Janice Meckler said finally.

"Let's do it then." Carrie Castle signaled the van for the makeup and hair people.

At nine that night, the phone rang. Susan Bremmer was working on a brief in support of her motion to seize the assets that Janice Meckler had withdrawn from the joint bank account that she'd shared with Ernest Haas.

The soft, uninflected voice of Dr. Marvin Zadek greeted her. "Good evening. I'm sorry to disturb you, but something has come up."

"What?"

"As you know, I really can't discuss that."

"So why are you calling me?"

"To alert you to the possibility that Audrey has something important to tell you."

"Is she going to tell me?"

"I don't know. I suggested that she do so. But, as you know, Audrey doesn't always do what you suggest."

"Look, can we cut through this? My relationship with her is privileged, too. So whatever you tell me will remain confidential."

"We've already discussed this. I can't tell you anything substantive. Audrey herself has to tell you."

Bremmer sighed deeply. Not only did she have a bimbo for a client—she had an imbecile as an expert witness.

"All right. Here's what we'll do. I'll say something, and if it's true, you hang up. All right?"

"I'm not sure I understand."

"It's very simple. Like Woodward and Bernstein in *All the President's Men*. Robert Redford got someone on the phone—I think it was Colson or Segretti or someone—and he said something about the slush fund for the Watergate burglars and told him he was going to count to ten and if he was still on the line after that, then he'd assume it was true. Remember?"

"Wasn't it Dustin Hoffman who said that, not Redford?"

"Huh?"

"Bernstein made the phone call. And he was talking to Hugh Sloan."

"What?"

"On the phone. Sloan was the treasurer. He reported directly to Stans."

"Look, can we just do this?"

"Am I supposed to hang up or stay on the line if it's true?"

"If it's true, you hang up. If it's false you stay on the line. Got it?"

"True I hang up. False I stay on the line . . ."

"Right. Here we go. Ready?"

"Is this ethical?"

"Of course it is. You're not saying anything. You're just hanging up the phone or not hanging up the phone."

"But isn't that just a way of answering?"

"Zadek, we're on the same team here. I can't give Audrey the best possible defense if I don't know the truth, can I?"

There was a moment of silence, then Zadek said, "All right."

"Okay. Here it is. Ready? Audrey confessed to cutting her husband's penis off."

Bremmer listened for the click of the line going dead. When she didn't hear it, she asked, "You still there?"

"Yes. I'm still here."

"So that means she didn't confess . . ."

Marvin Zadek hung up. It took Bremmer a moment to figure out what he was trying to tell her. He didn't hang up the first time, which meant that it was false that Audrey confessed to cutting her husband's penis off. Then he hung up when she said she didn't confess, which means it was true that she didn't confess.

So she didn't confess. What did that mean? Did he mean that she claimed that she was innocent? Did it mean that she was just not talking about it?

She called him back and said, "Help me out here. All I know is that she didn't confess. I don't know what she *did* say."

"Sorry. I can't tell you that."

"Did she say someone else did it?"

"Was it Magruder?"

"What?"

"The guy on the phone when Dustin Hoffman counted to ten."

"I don't know, all right? Now did you hear what I asked?"

"You asked, 'Did she say someone else did it?' "

"Right."

There was a pause, then the phone line went dead. What did *that* mean? Was it true if he hung up, or false? Were they still playing the game, or was he just pissed off? Was it Magruder?

As she got up to stretch her legs, she realized that it wasn't Magruder. It wasn't Sloan either. Or Segretti. It was some guy in the Justice Department. They never gave his name.

Two hours later, Carrie Castle's exclusive interview with Janice Meckler led off the WSCH eleven o'clock news. It ran for six minutes, preempting news from Bosnia and limiting coverage of a four-car collision on the thruway to fifteen seconds.

Barney Abelove was dozing over his nightly ESPN beach-volleyball match when Clint Wells called him and told him to tune into Channel 6. Abelove grabbed the remote and zapped the bikinis in favor of Janice Meckler. Ernest Haas's former lover was sitting on an expensive beige leather couch, beside a glass-and-wicker étagère that displayed a number of framed photographs of her and the dead urologist in vacation attire on the Atlantic City boardwalk.

She was wearing the same severe black dress that she had worn for their interview. And she spoke in the same overaspirated stage whisper. Carrie Castle sat opposite Meckler, her well-above-average legs crossed in front of her at a flattering angle for the cutaways.

The Motor Vehicle Bureau smog-inspection-sticker-compliance supervisor spoke candidly and at length about her affair with Ernest Haas. She described it as an escape from a loveless marriage. She said that the doctor stayed married to his wife only out of pity for her. She claimed that Audrey Haas was a manic-depressive and had killed her husband in a fit of jealous rage. She said that Audrey should be given the death penalty for what she did. She said that she'd like to push the button herself.

Fortunately, Audrey herself did not see the newscast. Susan Bremmer caught the last few minutes when Tammy Stockpile called her. After it was over, the lawyer called back the chairperson of the Schenectady County Chapter of NOW and suggested that NOW organize a boycott of WSCH. She would draft a letter first thing in the morning and fax it to the station manager, strongly protesting the interview. Then she would file a motion with Judge Fenetre requesting a change of venue.

"We'll get the trial moved to Albany," Bremmer said and hung up.

She thought about the publicity this trial was already generating. If things continued like this, you wouldn't be able to find an untainted jury anywhere. They'd wind up trying this case on Neptune.

Though Carl Furillo wasn't on Neptune, it wasn't until the next morning, as he was sitting in his office trying to cut fifty words out of a piece he had written about Sharon Stone's gynecologist, that he heard about Janice Meckler's interview with Carrie Castle.

Sharon Marcuzzi stuck her head in the doorway and said, "The other woman in Ernest Haas's life just showed up. And she's claiming Audrey did it."

"No shit."

"You want to go back to Schenectady?"

"Can I have a Taurus?"

"Get her before *Hard Copy* gets her and you can have a Ferrari."

Chapter 17

At five o'clock on a humid Friday in June, Barney Abelove sat in the Riviera Lounge on Front Street in Albany watching the ice cubes slowly melt in his glass of ginger ale. He had been off the clock since four, but he might as well have been off the clock for the last two months. He had hit every shithole bar, hotel, and convenience store within walking distance of the Kopy Kat Kopy Korner with his rapidly deteriorating composite of the Indian and a copy of the fax. He had tracked down every false lead and bullshit tip given him by the lowlifes that frequented this area of town, and by now he was convinced that if there actually was an Indian fitting Dave's description, he had either skipped town long ago or had radical plastic surgery.

As the Audrey Haas story started to heat up, the crazies came out of the woodwork. The police were deluged with false leads. Jeffries had to give Abelove clerical help to sort the mail and another detective to run down leads.

"Boy, you really started a shit storm, Abelove," the lieutenant said, as if Abelove himself were responsible for the Ernest Haas murder and all the attendant work it had brought to the Schenectady Police Department.

The help Jeffries gave him on the case was a twenty-eight-year-old detective named Preniszni out of Auto Theft, who had had his detective's shield for less than three months and complained if Abelove wanted to smoke in the car. He was on some sort of fruit diet and brought his lunch of fresh watermelon and apricots, which he ate in the car, spitting the seeds out the window.

Meanwhile, Renata was making noises about moving in together. She wanted them to get a two-bedroom condo in Scotia with a health club downstairs so that Abelove could improve his cardiovascular conditioning. At his last department physical he had been borderline on weight and blood pressure. His cholesterol was above 220. He had four months before the next physical.

So these were difficult days for Barney Abelove. And it was only going to get worse as the trial approached. Carl Furillo was back in town and leaving messages for him. Along with those messages were messages from other reporters, talk-show bookers, and a publisher from New York who wanted him to write a book about the Audrey Haas case.

Barney Abelove didn't want to write a book. And he didn't want to live in a condo in Scotia. He just wanted to nail whoever it was who had taken the carving knife to Ernest Haas. Then he could get through his last few years on the force, retire, and let his cholesterol go over 220. But in order to do that he had to solve this case. And to solve this case he had to find the Indian.

Preniszni walked into the bar and sat down next to him. His breath stank from apricots.

"I checked the laundromat over on Capital. There's a guy there who thinks he remembers an Indian coming in about two weeks ago."

"Did you show him the picture?"

"Yeah."

"What'd he say?"

"He said that his Indian had blond hair. And blue eyes."

"You ever hear of a blond, blue-eyed Indian?"

Preniszni shook his head, asked the bartender for a glass of water with ice. Then he turned to Abelove and said, "Could be recessive genes. You never know."

As it turned out, Furillo was behind *Hard Copy* by an hour. They had gotten him a four o'clock with Janice Meckler, with a photographer right behind him at five. But as he pulled up to the condo on Escher Avenue in his loaded red Taurus, he saw the *Hard Copy* van already parked in front.

They'd have the story in the can and turned around in twenty-four hours. It was brutal. You had to be mobile, hit fast, and keep moving. You slowed down for a second, you were dead. They ran on you, took the extra base, and before you knew it you were at the World Trade Center with a rivet gun in your hand.

Furillo got there just as the *Hard Copy* crew was yanking the cable. The door to the condo was open, and inside he saw a woman dressed entirely in black beside an Asian woman talking on a cell phone.

The Asian woman nodded to the woman in black, then said something into the cell phone before folding it up, turning back to Janice Meckler, and shaking her hand.

As she moved through the doorway, her eyes caught Furillo's. For a split second they locked glances. There was a sense of instant recognition. Two predators around the same carcass. But she had gotten there first, and she couldn't suppress a little smile of triumph as she nodded and walked past him out to the van.

Furillo caught a whiff of lilac hair conditioner in her wake. He turned and watched her walk down the stairs. She was wearing a tailored jacket, wool skirt, and fabulous shoes. There was a very slight sway to her hips, so slight that it was nearly subliminal. But it accentuated the muscles in her calves. She had phenomenal calves.

He stood there for a moment, trying to clear his brain of lilac before turning back and knocking on the open door to the condo. The woman in black came across the living room to greet him.

"Hi. Are you from ABC?"

"No. *People.*"

"Oh, sorry. Please come in."

She ushered him to a chair in the living room and then picked up a phone. "Would you excuse me just a moment," she said to him in her breathy whisper. "I've got to call Barbara Walters."

She dialed seven numbers, then, after a moment, "Barbara? Hi . . . It's Janice Meckler. Listen, I'm running a little late . . ."

With the publicizing of Janice Meckler's story, there was pressure brought on both the prosecution and the defense to accelerate their preparation in order to empanel and sequester a jury before Audrey Haas was tried in the press. Both sides objected, claiming they needed more time to interview witnesses and prepare their cases. Judge Fenetre told them to get moving. She was starting the trial before the end of July. With or without them.

Though Clint Wells had done most of the spadework in the case,

Ralph D'Imbroglio appointed Jason Rappaport and Martha Demerest to head the prosecution team. It was nothing personal, he explained to Wells. He just figured they had a better chance with a gimp and a woman.

It was Jason Rappaport's opinion that the case was far from the slam dunk that Ralph D'Imbroglio was telling people it was.

"We've got a victim whose girlfriend has been on TV every day telling the world how he liked to put on her size-eight cocktail dresses, tie her to the bannister with silk bathrobe sashes, and fuck her brains out," he said to Martha Demerest and Clint Wells.

"We could get character affidavits from his patients," Clint Wells suggested.

"Forget the character argument," Martha Demerest argued. "It's a nonstarter. We push Audrey's motivation, the jealousy angle, vis-à-vis Janice Meckler."

"You don't pitch a guy cheating on his wife to a jury with women on it," replied Jason Rappaport.

"What else do we have besides opportunity and motive?"

"Erections."

In addition to opportunity and motive, the prosecution had the urological argument, or, as D'Imbroglio referred to it, the hard-on theory. They could argue that in order for Ernest Haas's penis to be cut off, it had to be erect, and if it was erect, blood was flowing through it and therefore he had to be alive. And if Ernest Haas was alive, Audrey Haas showed depraved indifference to his well-being by severing his penis.

With this in mind, they had interviewed a number of urologists to find the one who would present the best on the stand and hold up under cross-examination. They sat in the conference room and listened as a parade of doctors lectured them on the physiology of the penis. Though most of the doctors confirmed that it was impossible to be dead and maintain an erection, a few referred to the possibility of some sort of stroke or seizure, which they referred to as a chronic persistent vegetative state. In such a condition Ernest Haas could appear dead but continue to function in a limited capacity. A kind of "diesel effect," said one of them, explaining that it was similar to the phenomenon of your car motor still running after you turned the ignition off.

They settled on Dr. Jaakko Karjalainen, the eminent Finnish head of the University of Rochester medical school's Department of Urology. He was a tall, laconic man with a salt-and-pepper beard who answered questions dryly and with just a trace of an accent.

They had tested his composure by simulating a cross-examination and throwing at him the same type of questions that the defense would during cross.

"Isn't it true, Doctor, that a man could technically be dead and still maintain an erection?" Jason Rappaport asked him during the dry run.

"In order to maintain an erection, the intracavernous blood pressure must rise above the diastolic blood pressure, a condition which can occur only in the systolic phase. At death, the systolic heart rate flat-lines, thereby making it impossible to create any type of compression in the venous channels of the penis that cause tumescence," the doctor replied.

"Still, can't a penis possibly remain erect for a limited time after death?" Rappaport continued.

"Only the time it takes to detumesce."

"And how much time is that?"

"A few seconds, at most. The time for the arterial flow to compress the venous channels to below levels required to maintain a rigidity in the pudential artery, which, as you know, is the major carrier of the blood supply to the penis . . ."

It was the *as you know* that endeared Jaakko Karjalainen to Jason Rappaport. When the doctor was gone, Rappaport said, "Book him."

"You think so?"

"Absolutely. The jury'll love him. Finns don't lie."

Meanwhile the defense was interviewing its own group of forensic urologists. Though Lizzie Vaught argued against their calling a urologist at all—"the less said about penises in this trial, the better," she maintained—it was decided that they needed someone available for the prosecution's claim that Ernie was alive and Audrey knew it.

They wound up with Murray Tartar, a vice president of the American Board of Certified Urologists, who would testify in court that the existence or nonexistence of an erection was not *ipso facto* proof that someone was alive or dead. Dr. Tartar had done some seminal research on necrophilia, which he was prepared to share with the jury in order to defuse testimony by the prosecution's expert witness.

"Look, we can call this guy if you want," argued Lizzie Vaught, "but the whole erection debate is a canard."

"A what?" asked Cissy Weiner.

"It's spurious. As soon as they bring it up, we argue that it's irrelevant. It makes no difference whether he was actually dead or alive when his penis was removed. All that matters is the *perception* of whether he was dead or alive. How does a reasonable person, under great stress, make that call? More to the point, how does a woman chained to a stove against her will, spouse-raped by a man in a dress and high heels with his dick coming out of his pantyhose make a medical judgment?"

Lizzie Vaught was pushing a variation of a diminished-capacity defense based on a psychoneurological disorder. This line of argument would enable them to retain the spousal-abuse elements of the case without having to admit that Audrey simply cut it off in full consciousness of what she was doing. They would argue that Audrey was not suffering from simple temporary amnesia but instead from a psychomotor epileptic seizure, brought on by the trauma of being chained to her stove and raped by her husband. And whatever actions she may have taken were the result of an altered state of consciousness and, therefore, without criminal intent or depraved indifference.

Lizzie Vaught cited a case in which the wife of a Lutheran pastor in Spokane suddenly took off her clothes in the middle of a crowded shopping mall and started to offer herself sexually to total strangers. When the seizure was over, she had no memory of the event.

The psychomotor-epileptic-seizure argument had two other advantages, she said. Unlike with an insanity defense, the burden of proof was on the prosecution, and if the jury found that a seizure did in fact take place, the defendant went home instead of to a mental hospital.

"Of course, juries don't always buy it," Lizzie Vaught conceded, with a slight shrug of her shoulders. "Jack Ruby tried it and he got shot."

Carl Furillo was sitting alone in a corner booth in the bar at the Van Twiller—an old and stately hotel near the river that had seen better days but was nonetheless an upgrade from the Holiday Inn—working on a follow-up to his Janice Meckler piece, an update of the legal maneuvering, which Sharon Marcuzzi wanted to run that week to keep the story hot for the trial. He had done phoners with lawyers on both sides and was trying to condense the issues into five hundred words.

Furillo liked working in bars. It wasn't the booze so much as the darkness and the sodden atmosphere of fractured lives that he found soothing. People who hung out in bars had stories to tell, and stories were Carl Furillo's bread and butter.

At the moment, 10:45 P.M. on a Friday in late July three days before jury selection was scheduled to begin, the bar was empty except for Furillo and a couple of salesmen drinking alone and watching *Homicide* on the bar TV.

Furillo was having trouble concentrating on his story. Instead of cutting the fat from the piece, he found himself thinking about the Asian *Hard Copy* reporter he had crossed at Janice Meckler's condo. He had seen her interview with Ernest Haas's lover. By the time she was done with her, she had turned the Motor Vehicle Bureau smog-inspection-sticker-compliance supervisor into Wallis Simpson.

Her name was Lilian Wong, and she was an up-and-coming star in the tabloid-TV business. She had the ability to say something completely outrageous without cheapening herself. She seemed to go right to the core of the people she interviewed, right to whatever dark and shameful secret they were hiding.

So when he heard her voice there in the bar, he was convinced it was a hallucination. He looked up and saw her standing over him with a bottle of Perrier and a glass.

"If you're working . . ." she said.

"No, no, of course not," he mumbled, hastily moving his yellow legal pad out of the way and making room for her to sit down. She crossed her legs gracefully and sat beside him in the large booth.

Furillo took a sip of his draft beer and said, "I didn't think you'd be back here till the trial began."

"This is a hot story."

"You think so?"

"If it isn't, I don't know what you and I are doing in Schenectady," she said. "You talk to Susan Bremmer?"

"Uh-huh."

"You think she's going to get Audrey off?"

"I don't know. She might bore the jury to death first."

Lilian Wong let just a shade of a smile curl her small, exquisitely shaped mouth. It was so unexpected that it disarmed Furillo.

So much so that he began to talk about the case, sharing his ideas and theories with her. And as he was doing it, he realized that it was dumb to be opening up to the competition. Yet he couldn't stop. She had him talking, just the way she'd had Janice Meckler talking.

So he talked, and she listened. And he sat there inhaling her lilac hair conditioner, trying not to think about the future of this night and of the other nights they would be spending together in Schenectady.

Just as he had segued to sightseeing in Schenectady, she pleaded an early appointment, excused herself, and walked out of the bar. Just like that. She was up and at the door before Furillo even knew what had hit him.

He watched her exit, staring dumbly after her calves. She had fucking *interviewed* him!

And he had been dumb enough to let her do it. She had walked in, had her way with him, and left. And he was sitting there, two more draft beers to the wind, high and dry, with nothing but the lingering smell of lilac.

Chapter 18

Charlie Berns had to leave three messages for Barney Abelove before he got the cop on the phone. The Hollywood producer finally got through to him as Abelove was wolfing down a liverwurst-and-Muenster hero, on his way out the door to the D.A.'s office.

"You must be a very busy guy," Charlie Berns said.

"Yeah. What can I do for you?"

"I'd like to acquire the rights to your story."

"What story?"

There was a moment of silence on the other end, then, "You jerking my chain?"

"Listen, I don't even have the time to jerk my own chain, let alone yours. So you want to tell me what you want?"

"Okay. I've got a deal with NBC to do a two-hour television movie called *Flight from Abuse: The Audrey Haas Story*. I'd like to use you as a resource, send a writer out there to talk to you . . ."

"Sorry. It's against department policy."

"You ever hear of the First Amendment?"

Abelove shoved some liverwurst in his mouth and suppressed a belch. This guy was beginning to sound like Susan Bremmer, with the fucking amendments.

"I've done two dozen fact-based television movies," Charlie Berns went on. "I did Amy Fisher. I did Tonya Harding. I'm doing Marcia Clark. There's no way they can keep you from talking to me."

"That so?"

"Absolutely. There's serious interest from Heather Locklear."

"No kidding."

"Uh-huh. And what do you think about Dennehy to play you? Or, better, we go with Dennis Franz . . ."

"Listen, Mr. Bernstein—"

"It's Berns."

"I got to go."

"I'm talking about serious money here—a five-figure option against mid-six—"

"Can you do anything about my cholesterol?"

"What?"

"You get it down below two hundred, call me back."

Barney Abelove hung up the phone disgustedly. Jesus. They were really coming out of the fucking woodwork. Fruitcakes from Hollywood offering him money to tell his story. What story? On a Saturday afternoon a couple of months ago he had run down a fax and wandered into a hinky homicide. Since then he'd been spending most of his time looking for a nonexistent Indian. What kind of story was that?

With the trial starting Monday, Abelove was spending his afternoons at the D.A.'s office being coached by the prosecutors. Seated at the head of the conference table, Martha Demerest took him through simulated testimony.

"Where was the location of the body with respect to the defendant, Detective?"

"Would you describe the condition of the corpse, Detective?"

"Did the defendant make any statement to you about there being anybody else in the house at any time that evening, Detective?"

"In your professional opinion, Detective Abelove, did Audrey Haas sever her husband's penis?"

"Objection," Jason Rappaport said. "She'll never give that to you. It's conclusory."

"I can try it, can't I?"

"You don't want to piss Fenetre off this early or she'll sustain everything that comes down the pike."

Then Rappaport went to work on him to prepare him for cross-examination. Sitting in his wheelchair, the little prosecutor with the permanent scowl fired questions at him, barely giving him a chance to catch his breath.

"Tell me, Detective, how short were the handcuffs?"

"Wouldn't you say, Detective, that it would be difficult, if not impossible, for anyone shackled to a stove to have found a weapon and manipulated that weapon with her free hand?"

"From the evidence at the scene, Detective, would you infer that someone else, besides Dr. and Mrs. Haas, had been in that house the night of March twenty-seventh?"

In the middle of the rehearsal Abelove was beeped by Preniszni at the station. "There's a guy on the phone from Hollywood, wants to buy my story," Preniszni told him.

"Congratulations."

"There's no department rule against it, is there?"

"As long as you don't compromise the prosecution."

"Hey, don't worry, I won't do that. They're offering high–five figures against mid–six figures plus a point in the movie. You know what a point is?"

"Yeah. It's what you roll in craps coming out if you don't roll a seven."

Susan Bremmer was able to convince Karyn Lusskin, a $1,000-an-hour jury consultant from New Jersey, to give the Audrey Haas defense a couple of hours on the cuff in the name of sisterhood. On the Sunday before jury selection began, they had a conference call with Lusskin from her home in Secaucus.

"What are we looking for?" Lizzie Vaught asked over the speakerphone in Susan Bremmer's office.

"I'll tell you what you're *not* looking for," said Karyn Lusskin. "You're not looking for minorities, veterans, men who've been recently divorced, women with very young children, Jews, substance abusers, or born-again Christians."

There was brief silence in the office, then Bremmer said, "What does that leave?"

"Plenty."

"You can't be more specific?"

"This is not an exact science."

"Neither is this," said Susan Bremmer. "Just out of curiosity, what's wrong with Jews?"

"They tend to get a little Talmudic."

"Talmudic?"

"How-many-angels-on-the-head-of-a-pin–type thing. The last thing you need is a juror who sees the larger picture. You want to keep it focused. She didn't do it, she's a victim, the husband's a kinky sex freak. That's all she wrote."

"Thanks. Anything else?"

"Yes. When you run out of your peremptory challenges, use cultural bias."

"What do you mean?"

"The candidate's education and background, whatever it happens to be, have conditioned him to be biased in matters of sexual relations. If he's black, it's black rage. If he's Latino, it's machismo. If he's Asian, it's affirmative action."

"What if it's a white female?"

"Deficient self-esteem."

On Sunday night, July 26, Emmanuel Longhouse was sitting in the Thunderbird bar on East Third Street in Utica, staring bleary-eyed at the TV. On the screen, Utica's version of Carrie Castle was standing in front of the Schenectady County Courthouse and saying that it was here, at ten o'clock the next morning, that the Audrey Haas trial would open. It would, she said, become the focus of worldwide media attention. Reporters from as far away as Sri Lanka were expected to attend, and she would be there to provide her viewers with gavel-to-gavel coverage.

Emmanuel Longhouse didn't bother to lip-read the cupcake. It was just another one of those crime stories that happened every night of the year. He wished they would change the channel.

He had left Albany in mid-April on a tip from a guy about a blood bank in Utica that paid good money. When he had spent the blood-bank money, he had done a few jobs and, at the moment, was sitting on $450 hard cash and thinking of staying in Utica for a while.

So Emmanuel Longhouse wasn't thinking about Audrey Haas or her trial that Sunday night at the Thunderbird bar in Utica. Once he had sent his fax, his conscience was clear. And since Emmanuel Longhouse did not read newspapers or magazines, he wasn't aware of the attention the case had been getting or the fact that a Schenectady cop named Barney Abelove had been scouring Albany for him.

Emmanuel Longhouse wasn't in Albany. He was ninety-five miles west, in Utica, down a couple of quarts, but otherwise doing pretty well.

But now, when Longhouse suddenly saw the green-and-white Dutch Colonial house flash on the screen, he had a vague feeling of déjà vu.

Since the cupcake was doing voice-over file footage, there was no way for Emmanuel Longhouse to identify the house as the one he had broken into in Schenectady in March.

But when they flashed a picture of a woman on the screen, the wires finally connected. It was the woman who had been chained to the stove, the one who had cut off her husband's dipstick. Then there was a picture of a wimpy-looking guy with thin hair and glasses. It took Emmanuel Longhouse a moment to recognize this guy because he wasn't lying on the floor in women's clothes without his tomahawk.

Holy shit, Emmanuel Longhouse said to himself. These people were on TV. The woman and the guy.

What if the woman tried to pin it on him? Maybe they could trace him through the shit he stole. Maybe they were going to say that he was the one who cut it off. And the carving knife. He had hocked that at Dave's in Albany for forty dollars. Dave could finger him.

Emmanuel Longhouse settled his tab and headed for the door without looking back. It took him a moment to spot the Ranchero, parked in a loading zone with the usual ticket on the windshield.

He got into the Ranchero without bothering to remove the ticket, started up the engine, and headed west along Third Street. By midnight he was in Buffalo.

Chapter 19

Even though it was just jury selection, Monday, July 27, the opening day of the Audrey Haas trial, was SRO. It was a very hot ticket. Press credentials were carefully scrutinized, hotel rooms were at a premium, flights to the Albany County airport had been overbooked for weeks.

Right from the beginning, Judge Fenetre vowed to do everything in her power to keep the trial from becoming a media circus. She refused a request to knock down the wall between her courtroom and the neighboring one to produce a room large enough to sit all the press comfortably, as well as to accommodate long-angle shots from the TV cameras.

"Let them squeeze in," she said. "This is a trial, not a peep show."

When the BBC complained of being limited to only one seat, she said, "What do they think this is—the opening of Parliament?"

In chambers before the beginning of jury selection, Judge Fenetre issued warnings to both sides about posturing for the press. "I will not permit this trial to be argued in the media. I am cautioning you here and now against making any public statements that could further inflame the atmosphere surrounding this case. If in doubt, keep your mouth shut."

"Only *she*'s allowed to posture for the press," muttered Jason Rappaport in an aside to Martha Demerest, as he wheeled himself out of the judge's chambers and toward the packed courtroom. "You read her

Time interview? 'Issues of constitutional law'—the only issue of constitutional law in this trial is the inalienable right of a man not to have his penis cut off. I think that falls under the Eighth Amendment's proscription against cruel and unusual punishment, don't you?"

Carl Furillo watched the lawyers approach their respective tables in the front of the courtroom with their stacks of files and yellow legal pads, Martha Demerest and Jason Rappaport on one side of the aisle, Susan Bremmer and Lizzie Vaught on the other side.

It was like a wedding, he thought. The bride's family and the groom's family on either side of the aisle waiting for Mendelssohn. In the front rows were the family and close friends—Jack and Frances Myers, the bride's parents, who had returned from Phoenix for the trial; Herbert and Ceal Haas, the groom's brother and sister-in-law; Janice Meckler, the groom's mistress; Marvin Zadek, the bride's psychotherapist; Denise Mezzogiorno, the groom's receptionist; Doltha Toussaint, the bride and groom's cleaning lady.

Slightly farther back were seated the distinguished guests—Tammy Stockpile, chairperson of the Schenectady County Chapter of NOW; Chet Isakaya, executive justice of the New York State Court of Appeals; Yale Mittner, chairman of the Schenectady County Board of Certified Urologists; Rhonda Eddy, head of the Governor's Task Force for Equal Opportunity for Minorities and Women; Nita Nickerson, president of ACTEAH—the Ad-Hoc Committee to Exonerate Audrey Haas.

Behind them were the members of the Fourth Estate. Furillo recognized Carrie Castle, the gonzo blonde from the local TV station; Phil Marzo, from *Newsweek*; Charles McClure, from *The New York Times*; Ted Sartorius, from *Rolling Stone*; Casey Caminitti, from *Vanity Fair*; and, sitting studying his notes and trying hard to look like a working journalist, Dan Rather from CBS.

Sitting right beside Rather, wearing a smart dark-gray tailored suit, was Lilian Wong. She had gotten the best press seat in the house, the one next to Dan. Furillo watched as she chatted with him, wrapping her equivocal gaze around his words in such a manner as to anoint them with great import.

Furillo felt a little frisson of jealousy as he watched Lilian Wong fellate Dan Rather's opinions. He wouldn't be surprised if she rode this trial to a co-anchor job on the *Evening News*. Once Dan got a good look at her calves, he was finished.

When Audrey finally arrived, all heads turned toward the rear of the courtroom. There was the usual collective sucking in of breath at the sight of the bride. She was wearing a simple beige skirt-and-sweater ensemble, loosely fitting and off the rack. Audrey walked toward the defense table, her eyes straight ahead—not down—as she had been coached to do by her defense team.

She took a seat between Susan Bremmer and Lizzie Vaught. Bremmer gave her a legal pad and a pen and whispered into her ear a reminder not to doodle. Audrey nodded and folded her hands in front of her.

Laptops were opened, and soon the courtroom was filled with the sound of reporters typing descriptions of Audrey Haas's uninspired wardrobe. They were interrupted by the arrival of Judge Fenetre, an imposing figure in her black robe.

"All rise," the bailiff called, and the courtroom rose to its feet for the judge. Fenetre took her place, adjusted her microphone, and gaveled the proceedings open.

What followed was a succession of prospective jurors being sworn in and asked questions by the lawyers from both sides. The jury questionnaires they had filled out were designed to weed out those who were obviously unfit to serve, but within two hours the lawyers on both sides had already rejected fifty-three potential jurors.

At noon, with only two jurors empaneled, Judge Fenetre called a lunch recess. She ordered the lawyers into her chambers and told them to get their act together.

"I'm not about to spend an entire week just to empanel a jury," she said, looking straight at Susan Bremmer.

"Your Honor, given the publicity surrounding this case . . ." Bremmer began, but Fenetre cut her off.

"Given nothing, Ms. Bremmer. I don't want to have to postpone the trial in order to examine more prospective jurors. The people are spending a great deal of public money on this trial. Your client is under a murder indictment. We owe both the people and your client a speedy trial, don't you think?"

"Yes, Your Honor."

"Empaneling a jury is like buying a house. There will always be something you don't like. There may be a powder room in the wrong place or a shake roof when you wanted composition. And there will always be a juror or two whom you won't be happy with. But then, there will be a juror or two whom the prosecution isn't crazy about either. Am I right, Mr. Rappaport?"

"Absolutely, Your Honor."

"So let's get a jury seated and get on with it, all right?"

The lawyers nodded and filed out. As they walked down the corridor together toward the cafeteria, Jason Rappaport said to Susan Bremmer, "Refreshingly candid, isn't she?"

"She's not going to push me around," said Bremmer. "I've gotten better judges than her reversed on appeal."

"Already planning our appeal, are we?"

Bremmer glared down at him as he wheeled his chair alongside her. She didn't like Jason Rappaport. Just because he was in a wheelchair he thought he could say anything he wanted. If he was such a hotshot lawyer, what was he doing working for the county? Sixty-five grand a year and a caseload large enough for three lawyers.

"Excuse me," she said, turning abruptly and heading for the ladies' room.

"Hey, why go for a reversal?" he called after her. "Why not go all the way and impeach her? Procedural malfeasance during jury selection. You can call me as a witness . . ."

The door to the ladies' room closed, and Jason Rappaport allowed a rare smile. He had the first taste of blood in his mouth and was ready for more. At the very least he was going to enjoy this.

Furillo spotted Lilian Wong alone at a corner table with her cell phone and her laptop. She was typing and talking at the same time, a liter of Evian in front of her. He navigated through the crowded cafeteria to her table, and then stood there with his Saran-wrapped chef's salad and iced tea until she nodded in his direction.

He took a seat and unwrapped the salad as she said into the cell phone, "Uh-huh. Uh-huh. Uh-huh . . . uh-huh."

Five seconds of silence, then a final *uh-huh* and she folded the phone, looked across at Furillo, and said, "I wouldn't eat that salad if I were you. They wash it in hydrogen peroxide to get rid of the pesticide."

Furillo put his plastic fork down and said, "Uh-huh."

"You think we'll have a jury by Labor Day?"

"Not at this rate. You have incredible calves."

"Thank you."

"So is there any hope for me, or am I just sexually harassing you?"

She almost smiled. At the last minute, she caught her lip and straightened it out. "You think she's gay?"

"Who?"

"Fenetre. She's fifty-six. Never been married. She spent a month on Mykonos last summer . . ."

Jesus, Furillo thought, this woman kept the meter running nonstop.

As he was sitting there trying to picture her bouncing up and down on a StairMaster in spandex, his eye suddenly caught sight of a muscular man in a tight T-shirt signing autographs across the cafeteria.

". . . she'll probably never come out of the closet. Just like Janet Reno. You'll never get a thing on her."

"Holy shit," Furillo muttered.

"You got something on Reno?"

"What?"

"Janet Reno, the attorney general."

"You know who that is across the cafeteria?"

Lilian Wong looked across, squinting just slightly, then said, "Is that Arnold?"

"I think so."

"What's he doing here?"

"Beats me."

Furillo stared across the room as Lilian Wong fingered her cell phone. "The courteous thing to do, Lilian, would be to wait till I'm gone," he said.

"I was just going to confirm some plane reservations."

"No you weren't. You were going to call your assignment editor."

"You think there's a movie deal?"

"Who would he play?"

"Barney Abelove?"

"You see Arnold playing Abelove?"

"Uh-uh. What about Ernest Haas?"

"The guy dies in the first scene. Besides, I don't see Arnold playing a guy who gets his dick cut off, do you?"

She shook her head.

"Not unless he blows Audrey away after she cuts it off and then grows it back."

The story that Arnold Schwarzenegger was attending the Audrey Haas trial with an interest in making a movie about it was phoned in by Lilian Wong to her producer in New York and made its way out across the wires almost before Carl Furillo, or anybody else, was able to ascertain whether or not it was true.

The following morning Arnold shared the headlines with Audrey Haas in several newspapers around the world. The *Daily Express* in London went with ARNOLD SPOTTED AT NEW YORK SEX TRIAL. The New York *Daily News*, not ordinarily known for its restraint, ran JURY SELECTION IN THE HAAS TRIAL: ARNOLD IN ATTENDANCE?

Furillo got a phone call from Sharon Marcuzzi asking him to run with the movie story.

"There's no story," he told her.

"What do you mean no story?"

"I think he was just here on a lark, Sharon. I mean, I don't see this as his type of material."

"He's been talking about doing more sensitive-type material."

"This'd really be a stretch."

"Check it out."

He managed to get Sharon Marcuzzi off the phone with a promise of checking out the story. Furillo lay down on his bed, put his hands beneath his head, and closed his eyes. Forget Arnold. The person he really wanted to check out was Lilian Wong. Furillo was convinced she was wired differently from any other woman he had ever met. Her circuitry was plugged into a twenty-four-hour satellite feed. Everything went directly to videotape.

Furillo drifted off into a troubled sleep. Soon he was dreaming that he was standing behind Lilian Wong on a StairMaster built for two. They were watching Dan on the *Evening News*. He was winking at them. Furillo kept shaking his head, trying to tell Dan that he didn't know what he was winking about. But Dan kept talking and winking, and Lilian Wong turned up the StairMaster another notch, to expert level. Furillo grabbed for the spandex to keep from falling. It disintegrated in his hands, and as he looked down at Lilian Wong's calves, he woke up screaming.

Chapter 20

Opening statements in *The State of New York* v. *Audrey Roberta Haas* were delivered on Monday morning, August 3, before a jury of nine women and three men. Although there were no recently divorced men, substance abusers, or born-again Christians empaneled, the defense had to settle for two African-Americans, a pregnant woman, and someone who was half Jewish. As Fenetre had said, you've got to take a powder room in the wrong place or a shake roof when you wanted composition.

The prosecution wasn't thrilled with the jury either. Rappaport was particularly unhappy with the pregnant woman. "There's not much you can do in the face of hormones," he said. "She's going to fixate on the handcuffs."

"At least she isn't lactating yet," said Martha Demerest.

"With Susan Bremmer arguing, she could be before we're finished."

It was decided to let Martha Demerest make the opening statement, to soften up the jury. Rappaport would close, to nail it down.

Martha Demerest, wearing a conservative navy-blue linen suit, Gucci scarf, and low heels, kept her eyes on the jury and not on the TV cameras as she spoke.

She began by stating that the prosecution's case would be straight-forward. They would establish what had occurred in the kitchen of the house on Van Schuyler Lane on the night of March 27 and then let the jury reach its own conclusion as to the guilt or innocence of Audrey

Haas. They would not attempt to distract the jury with extraneous arguments or irrelevant issues, as the defense was sure to do.

This was not a case, she maintained, about sexual abuse or women's rights. This was a case about whether a woman took a carving knife to her husband with depraved indifference to his life, which, she reiterated, was one of the criteria for second-degree murder in the State of New York.

Everything else, she said, was window dressing. Everything else was an attempt to distract the jury, to make it forget that there was a thirty-nine-year-old doctor lying dead in the cemetery many years before his time due to the actions of the defendant.

Demerest's performance was lauded in the press as a triumph of understatement and a tactical success. Susan Bremmer, who followed her, got mixed reviews. By planting in the jury's mind the idea that the sexual-abuse argument was irrelevant, Demerest had taken a lot of wind out of the defense's sails.

Bremmer was wearing one of her long peasant skirts, a cashmere vest over a white paisley shirt, and a pair of reading glasses suspended by a macramé chain. She looked, in the words of the reporter from *GQ*, "like she had a charge account at Eddie Bauer."

Bremmer spoke for nearly three hours about cultural stereotypes, subliminal symbols of bondage, violence toward women.

By the time she reached her summation, everyone in the courtroom had been edified about the sociological and political history of violence against women. The entire courtroom, especially the jury, looked exhausted. Heads were throbbing, bladders distended, stomachs rumbling.

Bremmer looked at the jury box, letting her gaze pan slowly across each face, before turning back to the TV cameras and saying with great solemnity, "Audrey Haas is on trial in this courtroom merely for exercising her inalienable right not to be abused. As you listen to the evidence, picture yourself handcuffed to your stove with a deranged man raping you in high heels and a pair of torn pantyhose. Ask yourself, 'What would I do in such a situation?' If you look deep enough into your conscience, you'll find the answer."

Fenetre proclaimed a recess, and people ran for the phones and the facilities. Carl Furillo sat there, his ass nailed to the seat, reeling from Bremmer's dissertation on sexual abuse. As far as he was concerned, Audrey Haas couldn't possibly be as depraved as her lawyer.

He looked around for Arnold but didn't see him. He must have decided to fly his F-14 back to the Coast the night before without waiting for opening statements. He'd call Sharon, tell her that Arnold was over Kansas in his jet fighter. She'd send out a squadron of reporters in Ajax missiles. They'd nail Arnold before he cleared the Rockies.

"State your name and occupation, please."

"Pauline Haggis. Deputy public relations officer, Schenectady Police Department."

"And how long have you been doing this?"

"Eleven years."

"Could you please describe the events of Saturday, March twenty-eighth."

Pauline Haggis sat primly in the witness box replying to the questions put to her by Martha Demerest. She was the lead-off witness, called by the prosecution merely to establish the chain of events leading to Audrey Haas's arrest. Martha Demerest led her through a recounting of how she had received the fax and brought it downstairs to the detectives. Her testimony was considered *pro forma*, a warm-up for Barney Abelove, and so when Demerest said to Bremmer, "Your witness," she fully expected Bremmer to waive cross-examination.

But, as the prosecution and the world were soon to learn, Susan Bremmer waived nothing. She never met a witness she didn't like, wrote Dominick Dunne in his piece on the trial for *Vanity Fair*.

Bremmer rose and approached Pauline Haggis, who squirmed in her seat. Not having expected this, the prosecution had not prepped her. Demerest looked at Rappaport, who shrugged, as if to say, "Who knew?"

"Do you normally work Saturdays, Ms. Haggis?"

"Well, no . . ."

"Then could you tell us why you were working on that particular Saturday?"

Pauline Haggis blanched. Did they check the Xerox machine's copy counter? She should have gotten immunity before she had agreed to testify. She was under oath. Perjury was worse than illegal copying.

"I was using the Xerox machine."

"To do what?" Bremmer asked.

Demerest rose. "Objection, Your Honor. This line of questioning is completely irrelevant."

"Could you give me an idea where you're going with this, Ms. Bremmer?" Fenetre asked.

"The question goes to the witness's credibility," Bremmer replied.

Fenetre nodded, sighed, then said, "I'll allow it, but please remember that the witness is not on trial here." She turned to Haggis and said, "Please answer the question."

"I was using the Xerox machine."

"What were you using it for?" Bremmer persisted.

This time Pauline Haggis went completely white. All the blood left her features and traveled directly to her ankles. She was tongue-tied, a look of terror on her face.

"Would the witness please answer the question," Fenetre directed.

Taking a deep breath, Pauline Haggis announced, "I was making copies of my daughter's term paper."

"You were using the police department Xerox machine to do copying for your personal use?"

There was nothing to do but nod. Pauline Haggis did so, a bit too demonstratively. But it wasn't enough.

"Would you please answer 'yes' or 'no'?"

"Yes."

"Did you reimburse the department for the cost of the photocopying?"

"Objection, Your Honor," interjected Demerest. "I don't see what any of this has to do with the guilt or innocence of Audrey Haas."

"Ms. Bremmer, can we move forward here?"

"I'm almost finished, Your Honor." Bremmer turned back to the witness stand and asked, "Ms. Haggis, isn't it true that you've signed a contract to write a book about your involvement in this case?"

Pauline Haggis nodded again and was instructed to reply verbally by the judge.

"Yes."

"One final question. How much of an advance did you receive?"

"A hundred thousand dollars."

"I have nothing more for this witness."

Jason Rappaport wheeled himself up to the microphone, had the bailiff lower it to accommodate his disability, and, in a voice of surprising resonance, asked Barney Abelove to state his name and occupation for the record.

For the first hour, Rappaport took the Schenectady police detective over the procedural minutiae—the receipt of the fax, the decision to investigate, the sending up of the helicopter, the location of the house in Niskayuna. Abelove answered dryly and narrowly, offering the bare minimum in a quiet, uninflected tone of voice.

The courtroom, and the nation, sat spellbound as Barney Abelove recounted his entering the green-and-white Dutch Colonial on Van Schuyler and discovering Audrey Haas chained to her stove, and her husband dead at her feet.

"In what condition did you find Dr. Haas?"

"He was lying face-up in a pool of coagulated blood, his eyes open, not breathing."

"How did you ascertain that he was dead?"

"I checked for pulse and heartbeat."

"Was there anything unusual about the victim's condition?"

"His penis had been severed."

Even now, after all that had been written about Ernest Haas's death, the simple descriptive phrase *his penis had been severed* sent a chill through the courtroom. And Rappaport, wanting to make sure that the chill stayed with the jury, led Abelove through a thorough description of the urologist's condition.

"By looking at Dr. Haas, were you able to ascertain how his penis had been severed?"

"Objection," Bremmer said. "Calls for a conclusion."

"I'm merely asking the witness to recount his observations at the scene," rejoined Rappaport.

"The witness is not a forensic expert."

"The witness is a homicide detective with twenty-eight years' experience on the Schenectady police force."

"Overruled. You may answer the question, Detective."

"It seemed to me that it had been severed with a sharp instrument. Something with a serrated edge."

Serrated edge was another phrase that Rappaport wanted bouncing around the courtroom. There wasn't a man anywhere who could think of the words *serrated edge* in the proximity of his penis without wincing.

"What sort of serrated edge?"

"The kind that you would have on a carving knife."

"Was there a carving knife anywhere in the vicinity of Dr. Haas's body?"

"No, there wasn't."

"Did Audrey Haas own a carving knife?"

"Objection. Leading. There's no way the witness could have made this determination on March twenty-eighth." Bremmer had a small smirk of triumph on her face, anticipating being sustained.

Instead, Fenetre asked both attorneys to approach the bench.

"Look, Counselor," she said to Bremmer, "you know he's going to get there soon enough, so why don't you just let him get there directly and save us all a lot of time?"

"With all due respect, Your Honor, I would prefer not to."

"Suit yourself," Fenetre sighed. "I hope you haven't made any travel plans for Christmas."

". . . after lunch."

"How long do you think it'll go?"

"With Bremmer? Could be weeks, maybe months. This is their big cross. Their whole case, apart from the abuse and violence shit, is police incompetence. They're going to try to make Abelove look like an idiot."

Furillo was in the Taurus in the underground parking lot talking to Sharon Marcuzzi on a cell phone and trying to put down a tuna hero at the same time. The reception was lousy, and strands of the sandwich kept falling in his lap.

"What?"

"They're going to go after Abelove with their bazookas."

"Their what?"

"Bazookas. Bad metaphor."

"Is Abelove's girlfriend there?"

"Haven't seen her."

"What have you got on her?"

"Her name's Renata Sbazio, she's forty-five and works in the luggage department at a place called Mitnick's in the mall."

"Got a picture?"

"Not yet."

"Any connection with Audrey?"

"Uh-uh."

"What?"

"You're fading on me. I'll call you tonight from the hotel."

"What?"

"Tonight. From the hotel. I'll call you."

Furillo tossed what was left of the sandwich, got out of the car, and was almost at the elevator when he caught sight of Lilian Wong sitting in a parked Crown Victoria on her cell phone.

Their eyes met through the windshield. She looked up at him from her Perrier bottle—that provocative look that promised absolutely nothing. It made him think of the language of the second-degree-murder indictment—depraved indifference. It summed up Lilian Wong perfectly. She was going to murder him with depraved indifference.

Furillo turned quickly back toward the elevator and pressed the up button. Jesus, he muttered to himself, pissed off. *Hard Copy* sprang for a Crown Victoria. What was he—chopped liver?

As Barney Abelove watched the intense woman with the colorful skirt rise and approach the microphone, his body tensed. Jason Rappaport had been lobbing softballs at him. Susan Bremmer was going to come with the heat.

"Detective Abelove," Bremmer began, "this morning Ms. Haggis testified that she received the fax from the so-called burglar at two-eleven P.M. the afternoon of March twenty-eighth and that she brought it directly down to you at approximately two-fifteen P.M. Is that correct?"

"As far as I can remember."

"You don't remember the time you received the fax?"

"Not exactly. But it would have been sometime after lunch and before I went off shift at four."

"Do you have any reason to doubt Ms. Haggis's recollection of the time?"

"No."

"Then since the fax is marked two-eleven P.M., we may assume that Ms. Haggis's recollection that she handed you the fax at two-fifteen P.M. is correct. In which case, Detective, how is it that you didn't act on this until after three P.M., according to the deposition of your superior officer, Lieutenant Richard Jeffries?"

"We get lots of phony tips, you know, people calling up and saying there's a crime going down somewhere, and I wasn't sure this was real."

"You get a fax describing a woman chained to her stove and you decided this may not be real?"

"You never know."

"What if it had been a *man* chained to a stove. Would you have responded more quickly?"

"Objection," said Rappaport. "Badgering the witness."

"I'm trying to establish a pattern here, Your Honor."

"A pattern of what, Counselor?" Fenetre looked down at her imperiously.

"A pattern of deliberate insensitivity on the part of the police to women as victims of domestic violence."

"All right, Counselor. You may proceed, but if you are going to allege conspiracy, you'd better get concrete pretty quickly. The witness is directed to respond."

"What was the question?" Abelove asked.

The court stenographer read, "What if it had been a man chained to a stove. Would you have responded more quickly?"

"No," Abelove responded without hesitation.

Hit the fastball right back up the middle. Okay, sweetheart, throw me another one. I'm ready.

"In your police report, Detective, as well as in this morning's testimony, you said that you immediately noticed that Ernest Haas was missing his penis. Is that correct?"

"Yes."

"Did you observe the missing organ anyplace in the kitchen?"

"No."

"Did you immediately institute a search for it?"

"No."

"How come?"

"I attended to Mrs. Haas first."

"And why, may I ask, did you do that?"

"Because of my sensitivity to women as victims of domestic violence."

Abelove delivered the line with a perfectly straight face. It went over big. The courtroom erupted in titters. Judge Fenetre gaveled hard and said, "I'm cautioning the spectators to refrain from outbursts and the witness to refrain from sarcasm."

"After you dealt with Mrs. Haas, what did you do?"

"I called in the medical examiner."

"And after that?"

"I attempted to interrogate Mrs. Haas in order to find out what had happened to her husband."

"And did she speak to you?"

"No."

"Do you know why she didn't speak to you?"

"She was apparently too upset."

"So at what point, then, did you institute a search for the missing penis?"

"Immediately after Mrs. Haas went to lie down."

"Where did you look?"

"In the house."

"Did you look outside the house?"

"Not immediately."

"How come?"

"It didn't occur to me that it could be outside. I mean, how would it get there?"

A few semi-titters, immediately squashed by Fenetre's stern look.

"In your estimation, Detective, could Mrs. Haas have possibly disposed of her husband's missing penis in such a way as to have made it invisible to you?"

"Yes."

"And how is that?"

"She could have swallowed it."

This time there were no titters. Instead a collective shiver ran through the courtroom as this new, and even more grisly, possibility floated through the air. Only Jason Rappaport was tempted to laugh. He was rapidly falling in love with Barney Abelove.

"Are you implying, Detective, that Mrs. Haas committed that act?"

"No, I was merely responding to your question."

Bremmer glared at her witness. Then she grabbed the ball, turned her back to the plate, picked up the resin bag, and took a deep breath.

In the dugout Lizzie Vaught shook her head and wrote down on her legal pad, "Get him off the stand!"

Chapter 21

Barney Abelove's performance during Susan Bremmer's cross-examination made him an overnight celebrity. The public loved him. The press wrote about his offhand wit, quoting some of his responses as if they were one-line gags in a comedy routine. His phone rang off the hook. The talk-show bookers and reporters were coming after him, now joined by a new collection of Hollywood types with more propositions.

Charlie Berns sent him a fax escalating his offer to "mid–six figures against high–six figures with meaningful back-end participation." Abelove put it on Preniszni's desk, next to the piles of mug shots of Indians and burglars.

He took refuge at Renata's apartment on Van Gogh Boulevard. Renata had taped his testimony off Court TV, but Abelove refused to watch. It had been bad enough having to sit through it the first time.

So they sat there and watched *SportsCenter* and were one of the few households in Schenectady not tuned to those channels replaying excerpts from the trial. On WSCH Carrie Castle moderated a panel of legal experts evaluating the effect of Abelove's testimony on the prosecution's case.

"Sooner or later the defense is going to have to make a decision," said Arnold Kantrow, an Albany State law professor. "Are they going to admit that Audrey did it and argue that it was justified self-defense, or are they going to argue that the prosecution can't prove she did it beyond a reasonable doubt? They're beginning to resemble a truck speeding toward a fork in the road, and if they don't take one turn or the other, they're going to crash."

Diana Di Meori, a legal reporter for the *Schenectady Times Union*, disagreed. "What Susan Bremmer is trying to do is undermine the state's case by demonstrating procedural errors and police incompetence and, at the same time, plant in the jury's mind the image of Audrey as the victim of a historical pattern of abuse. It may be redundant, but when that jury goes into that room to deliberate, there's no telling what they're going to remember."

"Do you think the defense is going to cut short its cross-examination of Barney Abelove?" Carrie Castle asked.

"They should. He's killing them," argued Philip Verger, a retired judge from Watervliet.

"I disagree," said Di Meori. "I thought Bremmer scored some points on the dog business. He looked bad when he admitted that he didn't order a forensic search of the neighbor's yard."

"Finding the penis is completely immaterial," interjected Kantrow. "The fact that it was missing is more than sufficient."

"Yes, but it goes to establishing a pattern of sloppy police work."

"Searching the neighbor's yard for *dog excrement* . . . ?"

Ralph D'Imbroglio, sitting on the mohair couch in front of the TV in his house on Grotius Lane, reached for the phone and dialed Jason Rappaport at his home.

"Let's go after the dogshit on redirect."

"I don't see much percentage in that."

"The dick's not in the house, not in the dogshit. That leaves only one place for it to be, right?"

"I really don't think this is a productive line of argument."

"You kidding? She swallows the guy's dick after cutting it off? No jury in the world, not even in New Guinea, is going to acquit after that."

"We have no way of establishing that except circumstantially."

"Just toss it out there and let her object. They'll strike it, but who the fuck cares?"

"I don't think it'll work."

"Bullshit. Nobody likes a cannibal."

At the same time, Barney Abelove's testimony was causing dissension within the defense team. Lizzie Vaught was convinced that the phlegmatic cop was not going to trip over himself on the witness stand. No matter how hard Bremmer pushed him, she argued, he wasn't going to become unglued.

But Bremmer was confident that with enough time she could impugn his credibility. Besides showing the incompetence of the police and attacking the chain of evidence, she wanted to demonstrate the absurdity of the notion that a woman, raped and handcuffed to her stove, having somehow found the strength and wherewithal to cut off her rapist's penis, could have managed to dispose of it at the same time.

"I'm telling you," argued Lizzie Vaught, "get off the penis. You'll lose every male vote on that jury."

"We've still got nine women."

Undeterred by her co-counsel's arguments, Bremmer continued her cross-examination of Barney Abelove when court resumed the next morning. The homicide detective was wearing an olive-green sports jacket with a brown tie, light-gray slacks, and an off-white shirt, which Renata had bought at Mitnick's to reduce the glare from the TV cameras.

The cameras kept him under surveillance, pushing in for close-ups and revealing a shaving cut and some recent dental work. Abelove tried to ignore the cameras as he watched Bremmer open her plaid briefcase and approach the microphone.

"Detective Abelove, you mentioned in your testimony yesterday that you believe that the weapon used in the dismemberment was a Sunbeam deluxe model three-seventy multi-purpose carving utensil, which, you say, you located in a pawnshop in Albany called Dave's Bait, Tackle, and Pledge Store. Is that correct?"

"Yes."

"And you said that this utensil had a serial number that matched the serial number on a warranty certificate located in a drawer in the Haas house at 474 Van Schuyler Lane. Is that correct?"

"Yes."

"Before you were a homicide detective, you were a burglary detective. Is that correct?"

"Yes."

"From your experience as a burglary detective, would you speculate how Ms. Haas's carving knife may have gotten to Dave's Bait, Tackle, and Pledge Store in Albany?"

"Objection. Calls for a conclusion."

"The witness is expert in this area, Your Honor."

"Overruled. You may respond, Detective."

"It was either sold to a fence by the burglar and the fence hocked it, or it was hocked directly by the burglar or by someone else."

"Which of these two scenarios do you consider the more likely?"

"For fifty bucks you probably don't go through a fence. There's not enough profit."

"So the carving utensil, according to you, was most probably hocked by the burglar."

"Unless it was hocked by someone else."

"Someone else? Who could this someone else have been?"

"Could have been anyone."

There was a sudden hush in the courtroom. The reporters, sensing something dramatic, leaned forward in their seats. The TV cameras panned the defense table, lingering on Audrey, as she sat there trying very hard not to doodle on her legal pad.

"In any event, Detective, this *someone else* could not have been Ms. Haas, could it?"

"Yes."

"Yes, it could have been?"

"Yes. That's right."

"Would you explain how that could have been?"

"Mrs. Haas could have driven to Albany and hocked it."

"Wasn't she under guard at the hospital?"

"Yes."

"So how could she have gotten out of the hospital unnoticed?"

"She could have hocked the knife after being released from the hospital."

"According to hospital records, Ms. Haas was transferred directly to another psychiatric facility in Troy. From there, she was arrested, incarcerated, and eventually released on bail on Tuesday, March thirty-first. So it wouldn't have been until the thirty-first of March—during which time she was with me, I might add—that Ms. Haas would have been able to drive to Albany to hock her own carving knife. Now, according to the pledge slip you entered into evidence, the article was pledged on Saturday, March twenty-eighth. Is that correct?"

"Yes."

"So, Detective, how could Ms. Haas have possibly hocked the knife?"

"Pawnshop owners often falsify the dates on pledge slips in order to expedite the thirty-day waiting period so that they can sell the item."

"Are you saying, therefore, that Dave . . . Briggs—is it?—falsified the date on the pledge slip?"

"No."

"Then the date is legitimate?"

"No."

Bremmer stopped, put her hands on her hips, and glared up at Abelove. Then she turned to Fenetre and said, "Your Honor, the witness is responding frivolously."

"The witness, Ms. Bremmer," Fenetre shot back, "is responding literally, not frivolously. You have asked him in his capacity as an expert witness on burglary to speculate among various possible explanations for a fact, which is precisely what he is doing. He is speculating. If he is not an expert witness, then his speculation is of no value and you should abandon this line of interrogation and concentrate on questions to which he, as a nonexpert witness, having witnessed the events in question, can respond in a nonspeculative manner."

There was a long silence after Fenetre's expostulation. She had nailed Bremmer to the wall and was banging the head of the nail in with a heavy hammer.

Watching on TV from the sunporch of his house in the Beverly Hills flats, Charlie Berns turned a fresh page of his pad and opposite the name of Judge Carmen Fenetre wrote OLYMPIA DUKAKIS.

The London *Daily Mail* ran with the headline AUDREY'S LOVER MAY HAVE PAWNED CARVING KNIFE. Closer to home, the *Enquirer* led with AUDREY'S COHORT USED CARVING KNIFE ON DOG AFTER USING IT ON DOCTOR. *The New York Times*, in a two-column headline on page 4, wrote POLICE DETECTIVE'S TESTIMONY RAISES NEW QUESTIONS IN HAAS CASE.

The *Times* went on in the article to say:

Homicide Detective Barney Abelove's second day on the witness stand raised speculation regarding the possibility of a new suspect in the Audrey Haas murder trial. During a frequently contentious cross-examination conducted by defense lead counsel Susan Bremmer, the Schenectady police officer suggested that someone else beside the burglar could have pawned the Sunbeam carving knife, alleged to have been used in the removal of Dr. Haas's penis, and that it was within the realm of possibility that Mrs. Haas herself was that person. Though no evidence was presented in support of that theory, it was clearly a setback for the defense, which had been hoping to use the cross-examination of Detective Abelove to impugn both his credibility and the chain of evidence that the prosecution is in the midst of presenting. In the opinion of most legal experts, Ms. Bremmer's cross-examination of Detective Abelove has done neither.

Carl Furillo marveled that an institution as prestigious as *The New York Times* was reduced to running this type of story. In contrast, *People* was a model of restraint.

In Furillo's piece about Judge Fenetre, he had managed to avoid even the slightest innuendo regarding the judge's sexual orientation, in spite of Sharon Marcuzzi's attempt to get him to make an allusion to it.

"What if we just say that her personal life is shrouded in mystery?" the editor had suggested.

"What the hell does that mean?"

"Our readers know what that means."

"So . . . we imply she's gay. So what?"

"Lesbians don't like penises."

"Is that scientific, Sharon, or anecdotal?"

Furillo had prevailed with the copy for the article entitled NO-NONSENSE JUDGE KEEPS HAAS TRIAL ON TRACK. He had written only that the judge lived quietly by herself in a ranch house in Scotia with her two Siamese cats, Eudora and Virginia. There were graduation photos of her from the Syracuse University law school, a shot of the judge showing Eudora at the Saratoga cat show, and a fortuitously blurry shot of her in shorts on Mykonos, to which Furillo had written the simple caption JUDGE FENETRE ON VACATION IN EUROPE.

Sharon Marcuzzi said the story was a dud. She wanted him to redeem himself with a no-holds-barred piece on Barney Abelove, who was now the hot story. Furillo had already written a piece on Abelove during the pretrial period and didn't think there was anything to add.

"What about the ex-wife? There's been nothing on the ex-wife," Sharon Marcuzzi persisted.

"You want me to look up Barney Abelove's *ex-wife*?"

"Ex-wives love to talk. See if you can get her talking about the divorce. Maybe there was a drinking thing, abuse, maybe they had problems in bed . . ."

There were so many different stories going in so many different directions at the same time that Schenectady was beginning to resemble Dodge City, with reporters roaming around town like bored gunslingers looking for action. Anybody vaguely connected to the Haases became fair game.

Along with the reporters came the book publishers and agents, with fat advances for book contracts in their pockets. In addition to Janice Meckler and Pauline Haggis, Ernest Haas's receptionist, Denise Mezzogiorno, was writing a book about the Haases, which was entitled *Ernie and Audrey: Beyond the Veil.* So was the Haases' cleaning lady,

Doltha Toussaint. Her book, *Out of the Closet,* was rumored to discuss the closet full of size-8 clothes that the Haases shared and purported to contain never-before-seen photographs of Ernest Haas's collection of mutilated pantyhose.

Late on the second day of Susan Bremmer's cross-examination of Barney Abelove, she had begun a line of questioning that made him very nervous.

"Detective Abelove," Bremmer had asked, "could you tell us what made you ask for a search warrant to return to the Haases' house on April first, five days after the events under examination here?"

"I wanted to obtain the serial numbers of the stolen merchandise."

"What was the date you actually conducted your search?"

"April first."

"The same day?"

"Yes."

Abelove felt the perspiration start to trickle down from his armpits. He kept his eyes straight ahead, not daring to look at Jack Myers, who was sitting with his wife in the first row behind the defense table.

Abelove saw his future flash in front of him: drummed off the force to face a barrage of civil lawsuits that would deplete his meager savings and drive him into poverty, having to spend the rest of what life remained for him in the company of lawyers . . .

"Detective Abelove, have you ever heard of the practice of the police conducting an illegal search and then going and getting a warrant after the fact?"

"No."

"In your entire twenty-eight years on the police force, have you ever done that yourself or heard of someone else doing that?"

"Your Honor," Rappaport interjected, "counsel is asking the witness to reply to a question that could be self-incriminating. If she insists on pursuing this line, he should be advised of his rights, under the Fifth Amendment, not to reply."

"I'll rephrase," Bremmer said.

"Did you, Detective, reenter the premises of the Haas house at any time prior to the date on the warrant, that is, April first?"

"No," he replied, a little too quickly. He felt his entire body respond to the lie. If they had put a polygraph on him, he would have gone off the meter.

"You are aware that you're under oath here, Detective?"

"Yes."

Abelove was convinced that she knew and that she was deriving sadistic pleasure by dragging it out.

But it turned out that Bremmer was merely throwing a piece of pasta against the wall to see if it stuck. It didn't. It slid down the wall and onto the floor. And as she moved on to question him about the search of pawnshops, he breathed a quiet but enormous sigh of relief.

He had emerged from the valley of the shadow of perjury. His rod and his staff were still in one piece. His armpits had run over. He would live in the house of the lord forever. Or at least for another twenty-four hours, as it turned out.

At 11:30 that night, Jack Myers was lying in bed beside his sleeping wife watching *Nightline* with lidded eyes. He and Frances had moved into the house on Van Schuyler Lane for the trial, spending all day long at the courthouse and, in the evening, visiting with Audrey at one of the secret houses they had her hidden in.

In order to see her, they had to drive to an underground parking garage in downtown Schenectady, leave their rental car there, and be driven, each time in a different car, to the house where Audrey was being kept.

On this particular evening, Jack and Frances had gotten home in time for the eleven o'clock news. Frances had dozed off during sports. Jack stayed up to watch *Nightline*. He had stopped watching Letterman because of the tasteless jokes. Last week Letterman had recited a list of the top ten things to do with an electric carving knife.

Koppel had a panel of legal experts discussing Susan Bremmer's cross-examination of Barney Abelove. Jack Myers was nodding off, just about ready to hit the off button on the remote when he heard one of the lawyers say, "Of course, if she could put him in that house *before* the date on the warrant, she could blow him right out of the water . . ."

He moved his thumb from the off button to the volume control, turning up the sound. The noise woke Frances, and he had to shush her to hear what was being said.

"Are you saying that there could be an illegal search here by the police?"

"It wouldn't be the first time it's been done. The police go in without a warrant, find what they're looking for, then go and get a warrant and simply use the warrant date as the date on which they obtained the evidence."

"How do you prove that?"

"You need someone observing the police officer in the house before the date on the warrant."

"Well, if that were the case here, someone would have already come out of the woodwork to testify to that effect, wouldn't they?"

"Not necessarily. People forget. Or they're intimidated by the police. Or they simply don't make the connection."

Lying there in his daughter's house watching *Nightline*, Jack Myers made the connection.

"The insurance policy," he whispered loudly.

"Jack," Frances said, now fully awake, "what are you talking about?"

"Ernie's insurance policy. Do you remember when I went to the house to look for it?"

"Yeah . . . so . . ."

"I ran into the cop."

"What cop?"

"Abelove. The guy on the stand. What day was it?"

"It was months ago. Who remembers?"

"He pulled a gun on me and frisked me. I told you about it. I said I felt like I was on *NYPD Blue*."

"So?"

"So we were watching *NYPD Blue* when I told you. Remember?"

"Yeah . . . so?"

"*NYPD Blue*'s on Tuesday night . . ."

Jack Myers got out of bed and went to get his wallet off the dresser. Inside he kept insurance cards with little calendars on the back. As he dug out a card and fumbled for his reading glasses, he muttered, "He said he was just checking to see that the premises were secure . . ."

Frances sat up in bed, removing the mask from her eyes. "What was he doing there?"

"Looking for evidence. . . . Here it is . . . Tuesday, March thirty-first . . . March thirty-first was a *Tuesday*, Frances . . . do you know what that means?"

"What?"

"We got the cop on perjury."

He went over to the bedside phone and dialed information.

"Saratoga Springs," he said. "I want the number of an attorney named Bremmer. Susan Anthony Bremmer . . ."

Chapter 22

When Ralph D'Imbroglio's bedside phone rang at ten minutes after midnight, the last person he was expecting to hear on the other end of the line was the lead counsel for the defense in the Audrey Haas case.

"D'Imbroglio," she said, getting right to the point, "I want to talk deal."

"What?" The Schenectady County district attorney was still half asleep.

"I have a proposition to make."

"A proposition. What kind of proposition?"

"I'm not prepared to discuss that over the telephone. Meet me tomorrow morning at seven."

"Jesus, seven. That's awfully early."

"There has to be enough time to get a recess."

D'Imbroglio hesitated for a moment. Seven o'clock was early for a meeting. What the fuck did she want?

"All right," he said finally. "My office at seven?"

"Sorry. It can't be a public place. We'll meet in my car."

"Your car?"

"It's a 1978 Saab. Green. I'll be parked down by the Mohawk, across from Lock Five."

"Are you going to be alone?"

"Absolutely. And you better be, too."

The phone clicked in his ear. He stared dumbly at the receiver. What the hell was *that* all about?

He got out of bed, went downstairs to the den, and poured himself two fingers of Chivas straight up. Then he went into the game room and took the cover off the pool table. He set up a tight rack of nine ball. He broke clean and got a good spread. As he ran the table, his mind raced like a badly tuned car.

It had to be a plea deal. But plea deals almost always followed the revelation of some sort of dramatic new evidence. What the hell could they have gotten?

Fuck it. He'd wear a wire. Get himself fixed up by one of their investigators. He put the nine ball squarely in the corner, then went to the red wall phone behind the bar and dialed Clint Wells's home number. It took ten rings for the deputy district attorney to pick up.

"Hello . . ." His voice sounded far away, as if he were underwater.

"Call Warshaw from Investigations," D'Imbroglio said. "Tell him to meet me at six-thirty tomorrow morning in my office with a wire."

"Huh?"

"I don't want one of those tooth-cap wires. They hurt. I want a tie pin."

"A tie pin?"

"Right."

"Six-thirty. My office. Bring bagels."

Susan Bremmer did not discuss the Jack Myers phone call or her meeting with D'Imbroglio with the rest of her legal team. Nor did she mention it to her client, Audrey Haas, on whose behalf she was about to initiate a plea-bargain discussion. It was a clear violation of ethics to present a deal without the client's approval, not to mention knowledge, but she knew that there was no point bringing anything up with Audrey until it was concrete. Hypotheticals only bewildered her. If Bremmer got what she wanted from D'Imbroglio, she could go back and sell it to Audrey and the rest of the team.

It was barely light as she drove down Union Street toward the Stockade. The city was quiet except for the early-morning joggers and the day-shift factory workers. Beside her on the front seat was a thermos of eucalyptus tea and a corduroy attaché case. Inside the attaché case was a very tiny Panasonic battery-operated tape recorder. She would set up the tape recorder in the glove compartment and run the minuscule mike out through the empty cigarette-lighter opening.

The sun was climbing between the birches on the far side of the river when Bremmer pulled up in the clearing opposite Lock 5. She parked the Saab with her back to the river, then hooked up the tape recorder and waited.

D'Imbroglio arrived at ten after seven driving a dark-blue Seville with tinted glass. In his glove compartment was a .45 automatic and a box of suppositories. Beside him on the seat was his attaché case and the remains of a poppyseed bagel.

He shut off the motor, reached into his pocket, and hit the on switch. Then he coughed into his tie pin, got out of the car, and walked the thirty feet to the Saab.

"You're late," she said, as he slid his bulk into the passenger seat and closed the door.

"Sorry. I had to stop by the office first."

"You're not wearing a wire, are you?"

"Why would I do that?"

"Beats me. It's inadmissible. Unless, of course, you want to formally advise me of the fact that this conversation is being recorded . . ."

"Look, can we get going here?"

"All right. Here's what I got. I got Abelove on the premises twenty-four hours before the warrant."

"What?"

D'Imbroglio did his best to keep his voice steady and not to look away as she elucidated.

"I've got an eyewitness prepared to testify that a police officer entered the Haas residence on March thirty-first, the day before he applied for the warrant."

"Who's the eyewitness?"

"Her father. Jack Myers. Do you deny it?"

"Deny what?"

"Knowing that Abelove went fishing without a license."

"Of course I deny it."

"I don't blame you. The district attorney of Schenectady County wouldn't want to countenance that type of police misconduct. Anyway, I figure I got a very good case for suppression of evidence. At the very least."

"How's that?"

"The jury's been given tainted evidence. It's a mistrial."

"Only if it's material evidence."

"When you have a police officer putting a murder weapon in the hands of the defendant in front of the jury, and that murder weapon is inadmissible, how does she get a fair trial? Come on, Ralph, you know that's a mistrial."

He knew that was a mistrial. Jesus H. Christ. Fucking Abelove and the goddamn carving knife . . .

"We not only have perjury, we have prosecutorial misconduct, don't we?" she said, twisting the knife another turn.

He looked at her and regretted not having brought the .45 with him. He would have liked to squeeze off a few rounds into her mouth and dump the body into the Mohawk.

"All right, so what's the deal?"

"We plead guilty to involuntary manslaughter. Audrey gets two years suspended."

"No way I can sell that. There're a lot of people very incensed about this case. Woman cuts off her husband's penis—"

"*Allegedly* cuts it off. You haven't proved she did it yet, and with the knife excluded, you may never be able to prove it. You could wind up with an acquittal instead of a mistrial. Think about that."

"I'll get back to you," he said, his hand on the door handle.

"You got twenty-four hours. If I don't hear from you by this time tomorrow, I'm going to make a motion to suppress the knife, and then I'm going to move for a mistrial."

"You'll hear from me."

"You know, even if I can't prove that you knew about Abelove up front, I can put enough doubt in the minds of the voters of this county to run you out of office in November."

He just glared at her, then turned and got out of the car. As he slammed the door, he heard her say, "Have a nice day."

D'Imbroglio got Fenetre's clerk on the phone at 8:05 to request a recess. Then he called Clint Wells, Jason Rappaport, and Martha Demerest and told them to get their asses down to his office by 9:00. They had a crisis on their hands.

The anxiety in his voice was palpable enough to get all three of them in his office by a quarter to nine. There were bagels left over from earlier that morning, when Warshaw had wired him, but the district attorney did not offer them to his staff. Instead he briefed them on his seven o'clock conference with opposing counsel.

When he was finished, there was a heavy silence in the room. The lawyers looked as if someone had just landed a punch to their collective solar plexus.

"Well, what if we impeached the witness? I mean, it *is* her father," Clint Wells said, breaking the silence. "We could send somebody out to Arizona, dig something up on him . . ."

"He's a Lutheran married to the same woman for thirty-nine years, a retired State Farm salesman with a condo and an eight-stroke golf handicap," Rappaport replied, wheeling himself over to the sideboard and helping himself to a bagel.

"All right, so we lose the knife," said Martha Demerest. "We don't need the knife."

"It's not the knife. It's the tainting of the jury. If Fenetre grants the mistrial, we'll have to empanel a new jury and start over again without Abelove. That leaves us the M.E., the forensic urologist, and the girlfriend, which could blow up right in our faces."

"What about the other two cops, Doetz and Gallagher?"

Rappaport shook his head. "Forget it. They're complete loxes. We might as well just enter the police report and go straight to the Finn."

"The goddamn fucking warrant," muttered D'Imbroglio. "Who knew about the goddamn fucking warrant? I didn't know about the goddamn fucking warrant . . ."

Clint Wells averted his eyes from the acid glare of his boss. He knew that Ralph D'Imbroglio knew that he knew about the warrant. What was the point of bringing it up, except to humiliate him?

The truth was that D'Imbroglio had treated him like shit ever since he'd taken the job—sending him for bagels like he was some sort of errand boy. And now that the ship was going down, Ralph D'Imbroglio was heading for the lifeboats.

There was another extended silence in the room. Clint Wells could feel the sense of despair.

"What about first-degree manslaughter instead of involuntary?" Martha Demerest suggested.

"It won't fly."

"Well, let's float it and see what happens," Ralph D'Imbroglio suggested. "Meanwhile, maybe something'll break."

"Like what?"

"Maybe the burglar will surface."

"You mean, maybe the police'll trip over the burglar while we're dicking around with the deal?"

"Hey, you never know," Ralph D'Imbroglio said. "They tripped over Patty Hearst, didn't they?"

"She was robbing a bank."

"So maybe the burglar gets caught on a hidden surveillance camera trying to hock another carving knife."

They all looked at D'Imbroglio, wondering whether he was being facetious.

He wasn't. His face was red with anger. He was going to have to play ball with Susan Bremmer, and he hated the idea.

"I just don't want to give that c——" He looked at Martha Demerest and stopped himself in time. "I don't want to give that woman the fucking satisfaction."

"You presented a *plea bargain* without telling me?" exclaimed Lizzie Vaught, confronting Susan Bremmer at the offices of the Audrey Haas Legal Defense Fund.

"Relax. I just floated a balloon. We can negotiate up from there."

"Based on what?"

Bremmer told her about the 11:45 P.M. phone call from Jack Myers and her subsequent call to D'Imbroglio.

"And you think that's enough for a mistrial?"

"Absolutely. Fruit of the poisonous tree. *Nardone* versus *United States*. 'Once the roots of a tree are nourished by poisonous ground, any fruit thereof is poisoned.' "

"She can throw out the knife without declaring a mistrial. All she throws out is the serial-number match."

"Yes, but Abelove is completely compromised. Anything he says about anything comes from the mouth of a perjurer."

"Still, you should have discussed this with us, not to mention Audrey. It's a major decision."

Susan Bremmer walked over and closed the door to the office.

"Look, can I be frank with you?" she said, her voice lowered.

"Why stop now?"

"I think we've got a nonstarter here."

"What do you mean a nonstarter?"

"Audrey Haas is a clinically depressed woman addicted to TV and Prozac. She is inarticulate and shallow. She looks like a slut even when you put her in Kmart clothes. I can tell already that the jury doesn't like her. And not just the women. If we get a mistrial, there's no telling they won't retry the case. So we've got to go back through jury selection, start all over again, which gives the police time to find the burglar . . ."

"You really think she's guilty, don't you?" Lizzie Vaught interrupted.

Bremmer didn't answer immediately. She sat down on the desk, flexed the muscles of her mouth in a gesture that Lizzie Vaught had grown to recognize as a sign of stress. Then she said, in a measured, almost clinical tone of voice: "I don't care whether she's guilty or not."

"Well, that's comforting."

"I took this case to publicize the issue of sexual abuse, and frankly I don't see that happening. What I see is months of testimony about penises and erections. And at the end of that a good chance of a conviction on second-degree-murder charges."

"So we bail out."

"No. We get our client the best deal she's ever going to get. And while we're doing it we take the moral high ground by saying we're doing it to spare Audrey and the county the expense of an extended trial."

"What about spousal rape and sexual abuse?"

"We find another horse."

Lilian Wong was lying on her bed in her room at the Hotel Van Twiller with a cold washcloth over her eyes. She had woken with a migraine so bad that she could barely see. Fortunately, the trial was recessed for the day, and she was able to lie in the darkened room and ride the migraine out.

Thank god for that. The medical examiner was due to testify after the redirect of Barney Abelove, and from what she had heard, the guy was a complete yawn.

The prospect of several more months of trial did not make her happy. She was stuck in Schenectady, living in a hotel that didn't have a health club—or even an Exercycle—and eating badly. She had put on three and a half pounds and was badly constipated. She needed to rent a StairMaster, put it in the room. Charge it to the show . . .

The phone rang. It was as if the ringer were wired directly to her migraine. She nearly went through the roof. She groped for the receiver.

"Lilian Wong," she whispered.

A man's voice on the other end said, "I have a story for you on the Audrey Haas case."

"Who is this?"

"A source in the district attorney's office."

Lilian Wong threw the washcloth off her eyes, swiveled around, and dangled her legs over the side of the bed. She made a mental note to shave them as she asked, "Can you give me your name?"

"No."

"What's the story?"

She heard him clear his throat and then say in a tentative voice, "We're offering a plea deal."

"What kind of deal?" She grabbed the laptop from under the bed, and booted it up.

"She cops to involuntary manslaughter and she gets two years suspended."

"How come?"

"They got us on a major procedural error."

"What kind of error?"

"Tainted evidence."

"What kind of tainted evidence?"

"The knife."

"How is it tainted?"

"I can't tell you that."

"I won't quote you directly."

"I'm sorry. That's all I can say about that."

"Can't you be just a little more specific?"

"The fruit of the poisonous tree . . ."

"Excuse me?"

"Felix Frankfurter."

"Who?"

"*Nardone* versus *United States.*"

"What are you talking about?"

There was a pause on the other end of the line, then the voice said, "D'Imbroglio knew all the time."

"Knew what?"

"That the fruit was poisoned . . ."

The line went dead. Lilian Wong hit the interrupter. "Hello? Hello?" He was gone.

The fruit of the poisonous tree? Felix Frankfurter?

She glanced down at the screen, saw the words *D'Imbroglio knew all the time.* Her migraine suddenly got better. She picked up the phone and dialed New York. When she got her producer on the line, she said, "Clear some time for me tonight. I've got a bombshell."

Clint Wells walked rapidly away from the phone booth on the corner of Maastricht and Einthoven streets in South Schenectady. As he walked, he felt his heartbeat gradually begin to slow down. He had actually done it—pulled the trigger. And the bullet was aimed right for Ralph D'Imbroglio's heart.

Now he had to make sure that he, Clint Wells, was the only one in the lifeboat. He'd wait a respectable amount of time before starting to explore offers in the private sector. Maybe he'd even throw his hat in the ring for district attorney of Schenectady County. Why not?

At the very least, he wouldn't have to fetch bagels for that fat slob anymore.

Chapter 23

Emmanuel Longhouse was sitting in the Maple Leaf Bar and Grill in St. Catharines, Ontario, drinking Molson and watching TV. A good-looking Oriental woman was standing with a microphone in front of some building in Schenectady talking about the Audrey Haas trial. He had been lip-reading her ever since they flashed on the screen the words LIVE FROM SCHENECTADY, NEW YORK.

Though he had crossed the border into Canada, it was as if the dead doctor without his tomahawk and his wife chained to the stove with the pants around her ankles had followed him. Every time you turned on the TV, they were either showing the trial or talking about it.

Sometimes it was hard to follow. When they had the cop on the stand, the camera would occasionally wander away from him—to the woman or to the lawyers—and Emmanuel Longhouse couldn't read lips if he couldn't see them.

But this time they weren't in the courtroom. The Oriental woman was standing in front of the courthouse looking straight into the camera. He concentrated hard on what she was saying. There was some shit about trees and poisonous roots, and then something about a deal.

The guy on the next bar stool turned to him, and Emmanuel Longhouse read on his lips: "Can you fucking believe that! She cuts off his dick and she's going to walk!"

Walk? How the hell was she going to *walk?* She sliced off the guy's tomahawk. How could a woman do that and get away with it?

He had gone to the trouble of giving her the lasagna and sending the fax so that she could live to face the music. And now they were saying she wasn't going to face any music at all. The carving knife was poisoned. The fruit was bad.

She was going to cop a plea and walk.

Fuck that.

Emmanuel Longhouse downed what was left of the Molson and left the bar. He walked along Queen Street toward the Lester Pearson Mall. Down on the first floor, beside the Burger King, was a copy place. There was a sign in the window that said FAX.

Barney Abelove was lying on his bed watching the Budweiser Open bowling semifinals live from St. Louis when Renata called him and told him to turn on *Hard Copy*.

"Why?"

"Quick, turn it on. Channel Five. They're going to announce a major development in the case."

He hit the remote just in time to discover Lilian Wong, her long black hair flowing down her back, standing in front of the courthouse on State Street with a microphone in her hand.

"A source within the district attorney's office," she began, "has reported that secret plea-bargain negotiations are in progress in the Audrey Haas case. The defense has apparently obtained proof of illegally obtained evidence that could seriously undermine the prosecution's case. The source further indicated that the illegally obtained evidence was the electric carving knife, alleged to be the weapon used by Audrey Haas in removing her husband's penis . . ."

Abelove's mouth went slack, and he felt the air begin slowly to seep out of him.

"Is that true?" Renata asked.

Abelove didn't answer. Instead he put the phone down and turned up the volume on the TV.

"If the defense can prove that the carving knife was obtained illegally by the police," Lilian Wong went on, looking back through the camera as if she were talking directly to him, "then they can move for a mistrial based on the fact that the jury has been exposed to tainted evidence. This development could not only prove fatal to the prosecution's case against Audrey Haas but seriously damage the political career of Schenectady County District Attorney Ralph D'Imbroglio, who is up for re-election in November, as well as the future of Detective Barney Abelove of the Schenectady Police Department, who, it is being speculated, obtained the evidence illegally. Abelove has testified under oath that he entered the premises to search for serial numbers of the stolen merchandise on April first, after applying for and receiving a search warrant signed by Judge Carmen Fenetre. If it can be proved, however, that he entered the premises earlier, then Abelove could be guilty of perjury."

Abelove lay there, feeling the splinters of his house coming down upon him, as Lilian Wong went on to conclude, "The United States Supreme Court has held that if the roots of a tree lie in poisonous soil, then all the fruit thereof is poisoned. Those words, written by Justice Felix Frankfurter, have formed the basis of the exclusionary rule in criminal law, which forbids the state from introducing any evidence that has not been obtained properly."

"Barney? Are you there? Barney?"

Renata's voice rose from the phone receiver lying beside him on the bed. He reached for the phone and muttered, "Yeah?"

"Is it . . . true . . . what they said?"

"Yeah. It's true," he answered.

She didn't say anything for a moment, then, "Why?"

Because nobody gave a fuck about this guy's dick but me. That's why.

But all he said was, "It's a long story."

Another pause, then she said, "I just want you to know, Barney, that I still love you."

"Thanks."

"No matter what happens."

"I appreciate that."

He hung up the phone and lay back, staring up at the ceiling. So there it was. Just when he thought he was in the clear, the border in sight, he stepped on a fucking land mine.

One thing was sure. They would throw him to the wolves. D'Imbroglio would claim he never knew, deny that Abelove had told him about the knife up front. Clint Wells would take the fall for D'Imbroglio unless, of course, Clint Wells covered his own ass.

It was going to be an ugly spectacle—people running to their lawyers and to the press with their stories of deniability. Fuck them. He might not have a lawyer but he had something better.

Abelove picked up the phone and dialed 411 for the number of the

Hotel Van Twiller. When he got it, he dialed and asked for Carl Furillo.

Carl Furillo was not in his room when Barney Abelove called him. He was sitting downstairs in the Henry Hudson Room knocking back vodka shooters and trying to figure out who the hell Lilian Wong was fucking to be getting that kind of scoop. It certainly wasn't him.

Sitting in his favorite booth in the corner of the dark room lined with faux Van Eycks, he had watched her over the bar TV as she broke the story of the plea deal. If it was even remotely true, it was the biggest story since they found Ernie Haas in high heels with his dick chopped off.

She had looked terrific on TV in a pair of studded jeans with boots and a tailored leather jacket.

The fact was she was driving him crazy. In court he found himself indulging in extravagant daydreams in which Lilian Wong and he trashed hotel rooms together, hanging from chandeliers suspended only by silk sheets scented with ointments from exotic Far Eastern cities, licking Dom Pérignon off each other's skin. All this in the middle of testimony about search warrants.

It was starting to interfere seriously with his work. He was less than twenty-four hours to deadline on a five-hundred-word sidebar about Preniszni, the cop they had working with Abelove, and he hadn't written a word yet. As soon as he got back from the courthouse, he repaired to the Henry Hudson Room with his yellow pad and sat in his booth, doodling, watching TV, and drinking vodka shooters.

William, the bartender—a tall, silver-haired man in his sixties with the steadiest shot-pouring hand this side of the Mohawk—suggested in that noncommittal manner of the best bartenders that perhaps he ought to consider winding down with the vodka shooters. Furillo decided to test his equilibrium by stepping carefully off the bar stool.

As he did that, he slowly rotated his eyes 180 degrees, checking his peripheral vision, always the first system to kick out on him when he drank too much, and received clearance from the tower to attempt to walk. He threw a ten on the bar to thank William for his forbearance and walked steadily but slowly toward the exit.

The elevator was old and slow. Built by the Dutch, undoubtedly, in the seventeenth century. As Furillo got in and heard the door slide shut with a heavy clanking sound, it hit him. Right between the nostrils. The scent of lilac.

Oh, Jesus. He was in no condition for lilac right now. He squinted at the floor buttons and pressed 9. Then, as the elevator slowly started to rise and the lights went on opposite each button, his hand reached out and pressed 7.

She was in room 723. He knew this because, like any good reporter, he had a mind for details. And this was one detail he had checked out early.

Furillo emerged from the elevator on the seventh floor, blinked at the atrocious pattern of the wallpaper, looked left, then right, as if he were crossing the street, and then headed off tentatively to the left. He walked very slowly, mindful of his condition, watching the room numbers get progressively higher.

Stopping abruptly in front of room 723, he took several deep breaths, stuck his hands in his pockets looking for a breath mint that he knew he didn't have, wondered what he was doing there, remembered, and knocked on the door.

There was no answer. He knocked again, louder. Then he heard her voice. "Who is it?"

"Me," he replied.

He had no idea whether she knew who "me" was, but she opened the door. She looked at him a little strangely and said, "Furillo?"

She was still wearing her jeans, but had taken off the boots. Without heels she couldn't have been more than five-two. She had on a gray cashmere sweater, top two buttons opened. Furillo did his best not to stare at the exposed tops of her breasts emerging from the push-up bra.

He concentrated on looking her straight in the eyes and said cheerfully, "How you doing?"

"I was just about to get into the bathtub."

"How about a drink?" Furillo said cheerfully, walking past her into the room, doing his best not to stumble in the wake of the vodka shooters. He got three steps into the room when it started to come apart on him.

As he pivoted toward the chair, his peripheral vision went out. He started back in the other direction and his knees hit the edge of the bed. Like a running back seeing the hole fill up, he cut back and lost his footing, tumbling over onto the bed.

As soon as his nose hit the bedspread, he knew he wasn't getting up right away. He sank down into the lilac and lay there motionless.

Lilian Wong looked down at the drunk reporter sprawled across her bed and wondered what she had done to deserve this. She had just a few more phone calls to return before she got into the bathtub. And now this.

She prodded him in the ribs with a finger but got only a few moans in response. Then she reached over for the bedside phone and dialed the concierge.

When the bellhop arrived at the door, she asked him if he would be kind enough to move Mr. Furillo back to his room. Eddie Lepelletier looked down at the snoring man on the bed and said, "No problem."

He gathered up Furillo, threw him over his shoulder in a fireman's carry, and headed for the door.

"Thank you," said Lilian Wong, closing the door behind them. When they were gone, she went into the bathroom to draw her bath.

She poured in two capfuls of the special lilac-scented bubble bath she was never without and wondered what Carl Furillo had wanted to talk about. He must have gotten drunk when he realized she had scooped him—and every other reporter covering the trial. Well, too bad. This particular race was definitely to the swift.

She looked at herself in the mirror. God, she looked awful. It had been a grueling day. And tomorrow would be no better. She'd have to find out if the deal was going to go down. They would call a press conference, make some sort of statement. D'Imbroglio was probably up in his office right now with his staff discussing damage control.

As she went back into the bedroom to get her cell phone, she saw something on the bed, partially covered by a crease in the bedspread. Pulling the spread taut, she discovered a wallet and a room key.

She looked back at the phone and decided she didn't want to get Eddie up here again. It would take her only two minutes to do it herself. She could use the exercise. Buttoning her top two buttons, she grabbed her own key, and headed out the door and up to the ninth floor.

She knocked on the door to 923, got no answer. She knocked again, louder, called, "Furillo? You in there?"

When she got no response, she put his key in the door and entered. Lying flat across his bed, in much the same manner that he had lain across her bed, was Carl Furillo. Snoring like a lumber mill.

She placed the wallet on his dresser and was about to exit when she saw the message light flashing on the phone. She stopped in her tracks, looked back at the sleeping reporter, and wondered what leads Carl Furillo had that she didn't have.

Lilian Wong had been a tabloid reporter long enough to be unable to resist this type of invasion of privacy.

She walked quietly over to the desk phone, sat down, looked back at the sleeping Furillo for a moment, then picked it up and dialed the message-retrieval number and listened for the voice mail.

"You have five messages," intoned the computer-generated voice. To hear them, please press one."

Lilian Wong pressed 1. A woman called Sharon asked him to please call her as soon as he got the message. Then there were three further variations of the same message, each one expressing greater urgency. The final message, recorded only a half hour before, was from Barney Abelove.

"Furillo, I know all about the plea deal. Call me."

Then the computer voice said, "If you want to replay your messages, press one. If you want to save your messages, press two. If you want to erase them, press three."

Lilian Wong didn't hesitate for a moment. She pressed 3.

Chapter 24

When Pauline Haggis arrived at her office on Friday, August 7, she was exhausted. She had been up late working on her book, and she was beginning to wonder how long she could continue burning the candle at both ends.

This book-writing business was much more difficult than she had thought. Her publisher wanted the manuscript by September 1—to beat the other books into the bookstores. She didn't know if she could deliver on time. Or deliver at all.

How much was there to write about the morning of March 28 and the fax from the burglar? She had pretty much covered it all in the first 30 pages, and she still had 170 pages to go. Her editor urged her to write about how discovering the fax had affected her life.

The truth was that, apart from the first half of the advance, which she had invested in fiber-optics stock, it hadn't affected her life all that much. After the interviews and her testimony in court, things had quieted down considerably.

She closed the lid of the coffee machine, flipped the switch, and headed for her desk, stopping at the fax machine to pick up whatever had come in yesterday after she'd left. There were fifteen letters from reporters asking for interviews with Barney Abelove. She was sifting through them when she came upon one that was not from a reporter asking for an interview. It was handwritten and barely legible.

I saw awdrey with the nife in her hand. She cut it awf. I was there and I no. Dont make no deel and let her wawk. Its not rite.

Barney Abelove had just gotten out of the can with the sports section when he saw Pauline Haggis heading for his desk. By the time Abelove got there, she was waving a piece of paper and talking a mile a minute.

"I don't believe it. It's from the same guy. I swear. I don't know why he sends these things to me."

She handed him the piece of paper. He read it twice. Then he saw the return fax number. There was a 905 area code.

"It's the same guy, isn't it?"

Abelove didn't answer. His mind was already spinning at 2,000 RPMs.

"What're you going to do?"

"Find him," he muttered, going for the phone book. Abelove turned to the area codes to check 905. It was Ontario. Canada. It ran from Toronto east to the border.

"Should I tell anybody else about this?"

"Not necessary. I'm on top of this, Pauline."

"You think I can put this in my book?"

"Why not?"

Abelove went to his Rolodex and leafed through it until he found the number of Constable Scott Cooper, RCMP. He had helped Cooper extradite an armed robber who had fled to Schenectady about ten years ago. The guy had sent him Christmas cards for a couple of years after that.

As he dialed the number in Ottawa, he silently prayed that Constable Cooper hadn't moved.

Carl Furillo was still deep in lilac and vodka fumes when the phone rang in his room at the Van Twiller. With a reporter's survival instinct, he managed to get to the phone just before it stopped ringing. He mumbled something unintelligible and heard the voice of Barney Abelove on the other end.

"I got a fax from the Indian."

"Huh?"

"The burglar. The guy who broke into the house and stole the knife. He says Audrey did it. She had the knife in her hand. He saw it. Why didn't you call me back last night?"

Last night. The vodka shooters and the late-night visit to Lilian Wong. What had happened? He had no recollection of getting to his room . . .

"I need to talk to you. Right away."

"Right away . . ."

"I'm going to try to find the Indian. He's in Canada."

Furillo pulled himself together as the smell of the story wafted over the phone line. He sat up in bed and said, "Right. Absolutely."

"You know someplace quiet where we can meet?"

Furillo thought of the dark, empty recesses of the Henry Hudson Room. "The bar at the Van Twiller."

"I'll be there in fifteen minutes," Abelove said and hung up.

Furillo swallowed four extra-strength Tylenol, dragged himself into the shower, did three minutes under as cold a spray as he could stand, threw some clothes on, and got down to the bar in twelve minutes flat.

The place was deserted except for a man vacuuming the carpet. The whirr of the vacuum cleaner set off a sympathetic vibration in his head, and as he gritted his teeth and waited for the Tylenol to kick in, he tried to remember what had happened with Lilian Wong last night.

All he could recall was the sight of her breasts emerging from the top of the sweater. The rest was drowned in vodka. He had woken up in his clothes, which usually meant that he was at least three sheets to the wind, if not four, when he went down.

He was thinking about how to approach Lilian Wong and inquire discreetly what had happened, when Barney Abelove walked into the bar like a guy looking for the men's room and slid into the booth beside Furillo.

"The reason I'm talking to you," he said, not even bothering to say good morning, "is in case they come after me. I know where the bodies are buried."

Furillo wondered if the guy hadn't lost it entirely. He sounded like a raving paranoid.

"I'm leaving in an hour for St. Catharines, Ontario. I have a lead on the burglar. If I find him, I'm bringing him back to testify. This'll blow off the plea deal, which is going to piss off some people in high places, which means my ass could become very expendable. I'm going to tell you the real story. If anything happens to me, I want you to print it, okay?"

"Sure," said Furillo. He took out his pocket tape recorder and set it up on the table.

"But only if I'm killed. Otherwise, it's off the record."

Upstairs in room 723, Lilian Wong was working the phones, trying to find out if there was going to be a breakthrough in the plea-bargain negotiations that were going on during the recess. She was getting nothing but "No comment," unable to confirm that they were even having negotiations.

Disgusted, she hung up with Martha Demerest's office, realizing she'd have to go down there herself and work the corridors. Getting out of bed, she went over to the closet to check her wardrobe. It was growing thin. She had brought only six outfits with mix-and-match possibilities.

She settled on the brown knit Anne Klein suit, with a peach blouse and green silk scarf. She slipped into it, went with the tan Alexis Misrali shoes, and called down to the desk and asked to have her car brought around.

Then she sat down for a fast makeup job and thought about last night—Furillo drunk on her doorstep, Eddie the bellhop, the phone message from Barney Abelove. Furillo was apparently wired to the Schenectady cop, who was feeding him the story on the plea deal.

She'd have to work Barney Abelove, try to get the story before Furillo took it and ran with it. Or she could work Furillo. The guy got a bulge in his pants every time he looked at her. He wasn't unattractive, just put together in a peculiar way. He had prominent ears and thin lips, with dark hair that fell over his forehead like an English schoolboy's. And this little cowlick that stuck up at a funny angle and made him look like he had slept on his hair.

She found him attractive in an odd sort of way. Though she had no idea why, he appealed to feelings inside her that she had deep-sixed years ago and hadn't heard from since. Now and then, after a few glasses of wine or a sudden rainstorm, these feelings wafted up through the bedrock, threatened to disinter themselves.

But whatever feelings she might or might not have for Carl Furillo, she reminded herself, he was the competition. He was the only reporter in town who could keep up with her and with the story, which was moving now like a brushfire across a dry canyon. If the deal went down, that would become the story. Audrey would be shunted to the side, and they'd all be chasing Abelove. And Carl Furillo looked like he had Abelove in his pocket.

Fifteen minutes later, she exited the elevator, and, as she headed for the front door of the hotel, she walked past the entrance to the bar. Out of the corner of her eye, she caught a glimpse of two men sitting in a booth on the other side of the bar.

Lilian Wong walked five steps past the bar and stopped in her tracks. The man facing the door had a cowlick sticking up at an odd angle.

Retracing her steps, she peeked inside the bar. Carl Furillo was sitting in the booth opposite a heavyset man, his back to the door. Between them was a small cassette recorder. The heavyset man was wearing a god-awful brown herringbone tweed sports jacket.

She could think of only one person in Schenectady who dressed that badly.

At 10 A.M. Ralph D'Imbroglio was sitting in the bathtub soaking his hemorrhoid and thinking hard. At 10:30 last night he had called Bremmer and asked for an eight-hour extension on the deadline. She had chiseled him down to four hours, making the new deadline noon. Which gave him two hours to make the decision.

His spin guy told him it was probably a push. He'd lose the hard-core male vote but win the feminists. If he delivered a clever enough speech for the news conference, he might even come out ahead. The spin guy suggested he say something along the lines of he was accepting the deal in an effort to begin healing the deep wounds that this case had created in the psyche of the American people. It was time for the nation to put this behind it. Nothing they could do would bring back Ernest Haas. Let us join together—prosecution and defense, man and woman, chauvinist and feminist . . . And so on.

On the other hand . . .

He hated the fact that Bremmer was extorting a deal from him simply because of a goddamn procedural error. Going in cold was no big thing. It actually saved the taxpayers money. If there was nothing in there, they didn't have to go through the expense of filing for a warrant. It's not like they couldn't have gotten the fucking warrant in the first place.

In any case, he'd have to maintain deniability right to the end. The police acted prematurely. He didn't know. There was no way he would have authorized a search without a warrant. It was unconstitutional. The Fourth Amendment. This was America and not fucking Libya . . .

His train of thought was interrupted by the ringing phone. He had told Rappaport to call him if Fenetre threatened to curtail the recess and order them back into court. Grabbing the portable phone, he growled, "Rappaport?"

"It's Barney Abelove."

What the fuck did *he* want? D'Imbroglio moved the phone to his other ear, lowered his voice even though no one could hear him in the bathroom.

"Yeah?"

"Don't take the deal."

"What're you talking about?"

"I have a lead on the burglar. He's in St. Catharines, Ontario—just over the border from Buffalo. If I can get him back here to testify, it'll cancel out the warrant problem."

"You bullshitting me?"

"I got a fax from the guy."

"A fax?"

"That's right. He says he saw her with the knife in her hand. We don't need the serial-number match anymore. You give him immunity on the B and E, we may be able to get him to testify."

"Look, Abelove, you already fucked me over once. How do I know you won't do it again?"

"I didn't fuck you over. You knew about the knife and the warrant even though you're going to lie through your teeth—"

"Who the hell do you think you are?"

"A cop who committed perjury to make you look good. Now if you want to get up there in front of the TV cameras and tell the world that you're letting Audrey Haas cop to involuntary manslaughter because the case was compromised, I can't stop you. But if you give me till Monday to bring the burglar back I can save everybody's ass, including yours."

For a long moment, D'Imbroglio did not say anything. Then, in a very low voice, he said, "Monday?"

"Monday. All you have to do is stall Bremmer today and give me the weekend to find the guy."

When D'Imbroglio didn't reply, Abelove said, "Look, you do what you want. But you're going to look even dumber than you already do if you sign a plea deal on Friday and I bring an eyewitness back on Monday."

Abelove walked out of the phone booth in front of Piece of Pizza across from the Van Twiller and got into the Cutlass. It was 320 miles to Buffalo, but he decided not to gas up at the department pump. They could confiscate the car, take his shield away, or, even worse, read him his rights.

He was going to have to do this one solo. With only a little help from the RCMP. Constable Cooper had been excessively genial when Abelove called for the reverse directory listing on the fax number. It was all Abelove could do to get off the phone without winding up with a contingent of Mounties to help him track the Indian.

He figured if he pushed it he could be in St. Catharines in five hours.

There was no telling how long it would take from there. All he had was a starting point—Wise's Stationery and Copy Store, Ltd., in the Lester Pearson Mall. He'd work within a radius of the copy store. Either he'd find the Indian or it'd be Monday and the clock would have run out.

He stopped at an Exxon station on Rensselaer Street, filled up the tank, and dialed Renata's number at Mitnick's.

"Luggage and accessories," she answered.

"I have to go to Canada for the weekend."

"What're you going to do in Canada?"

"It's complicated. I'll tell you when I get back."

"Barney, they said on *Good Morning America* that they may file perjury charges against you."

"Yeah, well, that's why I'm going to Canada."

"You're not running away, are you?"

"No. Look, I can't explain now. I'll talk to you on Monday, okay?"

"Okay. Be careful. . . . Barney?"

"What?"

"Could you bring me back some of those coconut mint cookies they sell in Niagara Falls?"

"Sure."

He hung up, stopped in the convenience store, and stocked up on munchies for the trip. Then he headed down Rensselaer toward Erie Boulevard and the entrance to the thruway.

As he swung the Cutlass onto the westbound on-ramp, past the sign that said NEW YORK THRUWAY WEST: UTICA AND BUFFALO, he didn't notice a rented Ford Crown Victoria two cars behind him. At the wheel was an attractive Asian woman in a brown knit Anne Klein suit. Two cars behind her was a red Ford Taurus driven by a man with prominent ears and a bad hangover.

Chapter 25

"What does involuntary manslaughter mean?"

Audrey was sitting on a brown knockoff Mies van der Rohe leather chair in the den of the penthouse condo in the Mohawk Towers that had been rented for her by the Audrey Haas Legal Defense Fund (1–800–4AUDREY) after the last of the safe houses had been compromised. Opposite her were Susan Bremmer, Lizzie Vaught, and Cissy Weiner.

"In the statute books," explained Bremmer, "it is defined as recklessly causing the death of another person."

"Recklessly?"

"That's just the word they use. Otherwise, it would be an accident, like if you were driving a car within the speed limit and somebody else hit you, it wouldn't be reckless on your part, but on the part of the driver of the other car—"

"What it means," interjected Lizzie Vaught, "is that you did it but you didn't mean to do it."

"Oh," said Audrey, nodding. They had explained to her that the deal would mean she would get a two-year suspended sentence and wouldn't have to go to jail at all, but still she wasn't sure she liked the idea of *recklessly*.

"The point is, Audrey, if we don't make the deal, then the trial continues. We'd move for a mistrial based on tainted evidence, and then we'd have to empanel a new jury and start all over again, and . . . we might not win."

Audrey looked at Bremmer. This was the first time since she had met her lawyer that the idea of not winning had come up. Up until now it had been total victory, breakthrough decision, protection of abused women, and so forth. They had gone from that to recklessly causing the death of another person.

"What about the Thirteenth Amendment?"

"We've made great inroads, Audrey. After this case no man is ever going to handcuff his wife to a stove again. That's a great accomplishment. And it's all thanks to you."

"That's right," Cissy Weiner joined in. "We're planning to open an Audrey Haas Hospice for Abused Women in Albany. We already have half the funding . . ."

Audrey looked past them out the window to the Mohawk, as it wound lazily around the old Stockade section and headed west toward Rotterdam. There was a haze rising off the river. The woman on the Weather Channel last night had said there was a low front over Lake Ontario that would bring ground fog in the morning. She had been wearing a light-orange blazer with a black straight skirt and beige shoes. Audrey wondered whether you were allowed to keep the wardrobe or if they took it back after you wore it.

"Audrey?" Susan Bremmer's voice punctured her reverie.

"I'm sorry. What is it?"

"We were discussing the plea bargain."

"Right . . . if I take this deal, does it mean that they can make a movie about me?"

"No one can stop them from making a movie about you, but this way, you can participate in it."

"You mean, I could talk to the Hollywood people?"

"Sure . . ."

"The only exposure you'd have," said Lizzie Vaught, "would be a possible civil action to attach proceeds brought by the estate of your late husband. They could argue that you were profiting from his wrongful death."

"But if it was *involuntary* manslaughter?"

"Makes no difference. But I really think that's a long shot. It's a very hard case to win."

"So do you think I could start talking to the movie people?"

"I don't see why not."

"I read in *People* that they were talking about Michelle Pfeiffer. What do you think?"

"She'd be terrific," said Cissy Weiner. "Though personally I like Julia Roberts."

"Julia's good."

Ralph D'Imbroglio had two phone calls to make. He waited until five minutes before noon before making the first one. Susan Bremmer picked up the phone and said, "Boy, you really believe in pushing deadlines, don't you? I've got thirty seconds before the hour."

"Something's come up," D'Imbroglio said.

"Is that so? What?"

"We may have a new witness."

"A new witness. At the eleventh hour, the state comes up with a mystery witness. Where have I heard that before?"

"This is not a mystery witness. We may have the burglar."

"Oh, come on, Ralph, spare me the Perry Mason routine. You're just trying to throw some more chips on the table. We're not modifying the deal."

"I'm not asking for a modification of the deal. I'm asking for an extension of the deadline. Until Monday at ten A.M."

"You going to spend your weekend combing the bars of Albany? Like Detective Abelove?"

"Look," he said, "today's half gone, anyway. Monday morning. One way or another. You have my word."

"All right, but by Monday morning either I have a deal or I'm going in *ex parte* and moving for a mistrial. And Monday afternoon I'm calling a press conference to discuss prosecutorial misconduct."

D'Imbroglio hung up quickly, dialed the judge's chambers, and asked to be put through to Fenetre.

"Mr. D'Imbroglio," Judge Fenetre said, "how are the plea negotiations going?"

"They're going well . . . actually."

"Can I expect something this afternoon?"

"Monday, ten A.M."

"Mr. D'Imbroglio, I have a jury and alternates sequestered in hotel rooms, away from their families. I'd like them to hear the evidence so we could get a verdict before their children grow up and go off to college."

"I promise that by Monday either we'll have a deal to present or we'll proceed with trying the case."

"Monday morning. Ten A.M. My chambers, Mr. D'Imbroglio. With or without a deal."

"We'll be there, Your Honor."

Ten miles west of Rotterdam, Furillo spotted the Crown Victoria in the fast lane. He had the Taurus on cruise control at seventy-five, and he was barely keeping up with her. Lilian Wong drove the way she delivered the news—fast and loose.

She was maybe a quarter of a mile behind Abelove in the Cutlass, far enough behind not to be easily spotted but not too far to lose him. Tailing a car was an invaluable skill for an investigative journalist, and Furillo got the impression that Lilian Wong knew what she was doing.

He picked up the cell phone and dialed New York.

Sharon Marcuzzi was livid. "Where the hell are you?"

"About ten miles west of Rotterdam."

"Rotterdam? Are you in *Holland*?"

"No. I'm on the New York State Thruway."

"What? What about the plea deal?"

"I'm chasing the plea deal right now. It's about a half mile ahead of me."

"Furillo, what're you talking about?"

"Abelove's going after the burglar. And I'm following him."

"Where?"

"To St. Catharines, Ontario."

"Where the hell is that?"

"Just over the border. Look, I need you to do me a favor."

"You want a photographer to meet you there?"

"No. I do *not* want a photographer. Repeat *do not*. I just want you to get a phone number for me."

"Why not film the arrest?"

"There's not going to be an arrest. They're going to try to get him to testify. Sharon, I'll call you tonight. As soon as I have something. I promise. Now can you just call *Hard Copy* and get Lilian Wong's cellphone number."

"Why do you want that?"

"I want to talk to her."

"Isn't she in Schenectady?"

"No. She's two car lengths in front of me, in the fast lane."

As soon as she had hit the thruway, Lilian Wong realized she could be in for a long drive. She foraged through the glove compartment of the Crown Victoria for one of her motivational tapes.

She emerged with *Accessing the Warrior Within You: Strategies for Winning in a Dysfunctional World.* Snapping the tape into the cassette deck, she kicked up the cruise control to seventy-seven, leaned back into the contours of the orthopedic driver's seat, and kept a bead on the rear end of the dirty light-brown Cutlass ahead of her.

Where the hell was Abelove going? When she'd picked him up outside the Van Twiller, she thought she'd tail him to a secret meeting with D'Imbroglio. But he had taken a turn onto the thruway heading west, and here she was driving at nearly eighty miles an hour trying to keep up with him.

As she reached for the cell phone to call New York and tell them where she was, the voice on the tape told her that all great journeys were undertaken alone. "Stick your flag on the top of the mountain. Gaze down into the valley at all the others scrambling to get to where you've already been . . ."

She put the cell phone back down on the passenger seat. They'd get crazy, insist on her calling in every hour with updates. She'd have to drag them up the mountain with her. There'd be plenty of time later, after she put her flag in the ground, to call in for backup.

A few minutes later, the cell phone buzzed. She turned down the cassette-deck volume, unfolded the phone.

"Hello?"

"Nice scenery, huh?" said a familiar male voice. It took her a moment to place it.

"Furillo?"

"What do you figure he's doing—seventy-eight . . . eighty?"

"Excuse me?"

"Abelove. In the Cutlass. I got him at seventy-nine on my cruise control. How about you?"

"Where are you?"

"Right behind you. In a red Taurus."

She looked in the rearview mirror and saw a red Taurus directly in back of her. Behind the wheel was a man with very prominent ears waving at her.

"What are you doing here?"

"What are *you* doing here? He's my source."

"This is ridiculous."

"It sure is. We could have car-pooled, saved the gas."

"Do you know where we're going?"

"Uh-huh."

"Where?"

"That's on a need-to-know basis, Lilian, and I'm not sure you need to know. Yet. How much gas you got in your tank?"

She looked down at the gas gauge and saw the needle between a quarter and a half, as he continued, "Barney and I gassed up before we left Schenectady. If you have to stop for gas, you'll never find us again. Especially since you don't know where we're going."

She heard the voice on the tape say, "If you have enough leverage, you can move the world. Find your fulcrum and cultivate it . . ."

At the moment, Furillo had the fulcrum. And she had a dwindling gas tank.

"All right, Furillo, what do you want?"

"Lilian, I don't want this to be extortion. I want it to be collaboration—between colleagues. Do you think you could see your way to a cooperative venture between us? After all, we're really not in direct competition. I'm print, and you're TV. We can share the story."

"So what are you proposing?"

"Pull into the next service area. You leave your car, get into mine."

"What if he gets off the thruway in the meantime?"

"He won't. He's still got a lot of miles to cover to his destination."

"How do I know you're going to stop, Furillo?"

"Sooner or later you've got to trust somebody."

"This is strictly business, right?"

"Lilian, if it ever turns out not to be business, it'll be your call."

She suddenly realized what it was about Carl Furillo that she responded to. He reminded her of a man she had been in love with once, a long time ago, in Washington. A foreign correspondent on the Asian desk at the *Post*. They met at a sushi bar in Georgetown. He told her she looked like Susie Wong. They lived together for three months before he went off to Bangkok, where he was gunned down by a Thai drug lord.

She hadn't thought about him for a long time, and here she was, doing eighty on the New York State Thruway, with tears suddenly in her eyes.

"Lilian? You still there?"

She swallowed hard, then said, "All right."

They drove in silence for a while, their ears to their cell phones until Furillo said, "The next service area's in twelve miles. Signal if you're getting off."

Lilian Wong folded the cell phone, put it down on the passenger seat beside her makeup case.

The voice on the motivational tape said, "A sea voyage is not only measured in nautical miles but in fathoms. If your ship hasn't plumbed the depths, then it can't ascend the heights. There is no port that is completely duty free . . ."

Reaching back to the passenger seat, she picked up her makeup case. One hand on the wheel, she took out her eyeliner and went carefully to work.

Chapter 26

Abelove was past Syracuse before he made the red Taurus. Since the possibility of being followed had not occurred to him, he hadn't been paying much attention to the traffic behind him, but as he got bored with the local radio stations that kept fading in and out on him, his eyes wandered reflexively to the rearview mirror, where he saw a car maintaining a constant distance behind him.

He slowed down to seventy and watched the Taurus slow down with him. He sped up to eighty-five and watched the Taurus speed up. He repeated this series of maneuvers several times before he was certain that the red Taurus was tailing him.

Squinting into the rearview mirror, he was able to make out two figures in the front seat of the Taurus, but the car stayed far enough behind him so he couldn't get a good look at them.

There was an exit two miles ahead for Waterloo. A great place to make a stand if it came to that. His .38 service revolver was in the shoulder holster underneath his sports jacket.

It had to be at least ten years, maybe longer, since he had last fired his weapon. He had caught a kid ripping off a house on Van de Velde. The kid went out the window, and Abelove followed him around the back. When the kid grabbed a tire iron and came at him, Abelove fired. He hit him in the shin, shattered the shin bone.

When the shooting squad investigated, they told him that if you were going to fire your weapon you didn't fire at the legs. You fired at the chest. Abelove *had* been aiming at the chest.

As the exit sign for Waterloo appeared, Abelove moved the Cutlass into the right lane. Fifty yards back, the Taurus did the same. He slowed to forty-five, moved onto the exit ramp, and watched as the Taurus's right-hand signal light lit up.

Abelove handed the toll taker a ten, got his change, and took off heading south along Route 96 toward Waterloo. The Taurus was behind him in the slow lane, keeping the same fifty yards back.

When he saw a sign to Route 312A, he took it. It was a two-lane black-top with very little traffic. Reaching into his jacket, he removed the .38 from the holster. He slipped the safety and put the weapon beside him on the passenger seat.

The road curved along a small stream, before stretching out straight beside pastures with fat black-and-white cows grazing. Abelove looked ahead, saw there was at least a mile and a half, maybe two miles of empty road.

He pulled the wheel to the right, then jammed it sharply back to the left, causing the car to fishtail perpendicularly across the road. Jumping out of the car, he knelt behind the open door, weapon at the ready, in accordance with correct police procedure for stopping a vehicle containing unknown and potentially hostile passengers.

The element of surprise prevented the Taurus from adjusting. All the driver was able to do was jam on the brakes and skid to a stop twenty yards from the Cutlass. Keeping the car door in front of him for protection, Abelove raised the .38 and yelled, "Get out of the car, put your hands up, and don't fucking move."

The three of them sat in a Dairy Queen outside of Waterloo drinking coffee. The conversation had been tense ever since Abelove identified the two people in the red Taurus as Carl Furillo and Lilian Wong. The fact that he knew them didn't prevent him from going through the formality of frisking them before putting his weapon back into the holster.

"I'm really sorry, Barney, but if I told you, you'd have never agreed to let me come along."

"I understand that you're upset, Detective, but look at it this way—sooner or later we'd find out, and this way at least we get the story right," Lilian Wong added.

Abelove looked from one to the other, trying to decide what the hell to do with them. He could take them out to the pasture and shoot them both in the back of the head. It'd take a day or two before the bodies were discovered in the cowshit. By then he'd could be in St. Catharines and back . . .

"Look," said Furillo, "you're going to need a hand finding the Indian, aren't you? You don't have a sworn warrant in your pocket, so you're not going to be able to ask the local police for help."

"You could deputize us," Lilian Wong volunteered.

"Right. We could split up and fan out from the mall . . ."

"A dragnet . . ."

Abelove finished his coffee, took a toothpick from his pocket, and started to pick his teeth. There were onion-roll seeds stuck between his molars. They had a point. He had never been to St. Catharines, Ontario. He knew nothing about the city. He was one man, all alone, trying to find an Indian.

He stuck the toothpick between his lips, Dirty Harry–style, and thought about the alternatives. Lately, all his choices seemed to be very narrow. He checked his watch. It was already after two. They were losing time.

Abelove threw a couple of dollars on the table, got up, and said, "We'll take both cars. Just in case."

"Just in case what?"

"Just in case," he repeated and walked out of the Dairy Queen.

The Lester Pearson Mall was in downtown St. Catharines, between the business district and the Welland Canal. It was built with provincial urban-renewal funds in an unsuccessful attempt to revive the seedy area down by the artificial waterway that connected Lake Ontario with Lake Erie.

The streets from the mall to the Welland Canal were full of bars, fleabag hotels, and transients. In short, it was just the type of neighborhood that Emmanuel Longhouse felt at home in.

Since he had crossed over the border from Buffalo, Emmanuel Longhouse had been giving a couple of pints a week at a local blood bank and supplementing that by rifling parking meters, a sideline that he had perfected over the years. He found a sixty-five-dollar-a-week room at the Wellington Arms, basically a bed and a hot plate, and had become enough of a regular at the Maple Leaf Bar and Grill on Dominion Street that they let him run a small tab.

Emmanuel Longhouse had no way of knowing that on this August afternoon, as he sat in the Maple Leaf watching *Geraldo*, a cop and two reporters were on their way to Saint Catharines to find him.

If he had known about it, he might have gotten off his bar stool and headed west. To Saskatchewan. He'd always liked the name. *Saskatchewan*. It sounded like the kind of place where Indians got a good deal.

Maybe they even had one of those welfare operations for hearing-impaired Native Americans, or Native Canadians, or whatever they were called up here. You couldn't always count on blood banks and parking meters. You weren't careful, you could wind up standing by the side of the road selling blankets.

The nuns in Utica had told him that the white people had sold the Indians blankets with smallpox germs to try to kill them off. They should've known you couldn't kill off Indians that easy. No way. They were going to rise up and take the land back. One of these days.

Geraldo was interviewing men who had been beaten up on by their wives. Jesus. What a bunch of pussies. There was a guy with a black eye, another guy with his foot in a cast. One of the guys was saying that he forgave his wife because she couldn't help herself. It was a sickness. She was in a program.

Emmanuel Longhouse wondered if the woman who sliced off the guy's tomahawk in Schenectady was in a program, too. They had programs for everything these days. Maybe he ought to get in a program.

He signaled for another beer and decided that tomorrow he would look in the papers for a program. Maybe they had something for deaf-mute Indian burglars. He'd sign up, check it out.

It was after five by the time Abelove and his two newly appointed deputies pulled into the subterranean parking garage of the mall in downtown St. Catharines. They had driven in convoy from Waterloo without stopping, and as Abelove got out of the Cutlass, he could feel every joint in his body complain. The goddamn springs were so bad he was practically scraping the highway with his ass.

The two reporters who got out of the Taurus looked much less the worse for wear than he did.

"We get a map," said Carl Furillo, "draw concentric circles, using the copy place as center, then choose sectors and divide up, keeping radio contact with the cell phones . . ."

"Can we get something to eat first?" Lilian Wong suggested.

"We don't have time."

"How long could it take us to grab a taco?" she persisted. "You ever hear of a mall without a taco place?"

"This is Canada," Furillo pointed out.

"They have tacos in Canada."

Abelove turned his back and started walking toward the mall entrance. Furillo and Wong hurried after him.

"Where're we going?" Furillo asked.

Abelove didn't answer. He pushed open the door that led to the elevators. The mall was nearly empty. And the air-conditioning was arctic. The place was both desolate and freezing. It was like a trek to the North Pole through a terrain filled with brightly lit store windows.

They found Wise's Stationery and Copy Store on the ground floor next to the Burger King.

It, too, was empty and freezing. There was a girl with bright-green hair and wearing a Glenn Gould T-shirt sitting behind a counter reading a book. Abelove flashed his Schenectady Police Department shield.

"Wonder if I could ask you some questions," he said.

She glanced up from her copy of *Women Who Run With the Wolves* and looked him over, then examined Furillo and Lilian Wong. She put her finger in the book to keep her place and nodded as Abelove took the fax out of his jacket pocket and showed it to her.

"We're trying to find the person who sent this. The date on the fax is yesterday, and the time is eight-fifteen P.M. We're you working here yesterday at eight-fifteen?"

She shook her head. "I don't work Thursdays."

"Who does?"

"That'd be Sean."

"You know where we can reach Sean?"

"He went to Windsor."

"You have a number for him there?"

"Uh-uh. He went to see his girlfriend. She's on kidney dialysis. Sean's trying to raise the money for a new kidney . . ."

"Does a tall Indian ever come in here to use the fax machine?" Abelove cut her off.

"We don't call them Indians. We call them Natives."

"Very tall. About six foot five with an earring in his left ear?"

"You with the O.P.P.?"

"No, I'm an American police officer . . ."

"From Schenectady," Furillo volunteered.

"Schenectady?" She looked back quickly at the fax and saw the word *awdry*. The girl's face suddenly lit up. "Is this about *Audrey*?"

Abelove shook his head, but Furillo and Wong nodded.

"I heard she's going to walk."

"You sure you haven't seen an Indian in here?" Abelove persisted.

"I think she did it. I mean, they got her with the carving knife. Who else would've done it?"

"We don't know," said Lilian Wong. "Is there a taco place in the mall?"

The girl's face lit up again, and she said, "Hey . . . is this guy the burglar you're looking for?"

"We're not sure," Abelove mumbled, hoping to either end this conversation or move it in a more profitable direction.

"*Here?* In St. *Catharines?* The burglar is here in St. Catharines? He sent a fax from *the mall?*"

"You happen to have Sean's parents' number?"

"Uh-uh. He doesn't live with his parents."

"You know what his last name is?"

"Uh-uh." Then she looked straight at Abelove and said almost gleefully, "Hey, are you the cop that lied on the stand?"

Disgusted, Abelove turned and walked away.

"In the flesh," replied Furillo as he and Lilian Wong followed Abelove out the door.

"Cool," the girl said, reaching for the telephone.

They found a map of St. Catharines in a bookstore on the third floor and retired to the Burger King to figure out their next move. The map wasn't much help. It was designed for tourists and highlighted the sights of St. Catharines—the canal, Brock University, the Cannery, the Jacques Cartier house. There were no Indian reservations, bars, or blood banks listed.

Abelove, who knew just how difficult it was to find transients in a city you knew well, sat there trying to find the energy to face the job of hunting down a guy in a place he'd never been to before. In Schenectady, he had uniforms at his disposal, cars, choppers. Here, all he had were two amateurs and a tourist's map.

"So," Furillo said, "we draw a circle with a one-mile radius from the copy store, here." He pointed to an approximation of where the copy store was within the mall. "Then we divide the three hundred sixty degrees into three sectors of one hundred twenty degrees, each of us taking one—"

"What if one sector has lots of bars and restaurants and another sector has nothing but office buildings?" Lilian Wong said as she tongued a cherry tomato off her plastic fork.

Abelove sucked up the remainder of his chocolate shake through the straw, grabbed the map from Furillo, and said, "Your best bet for bars and cheap hotels is the area near the river. So we try here to the canal first."

He took out a ballpoint from his pocket, drew three lines from the mall to the canal. "I'll take Cartier to MacMurray. One of you take east of Cartier, the other take west of MacMurray . . ."

"What happens if we find him?" asked Lilian Wong.

"You call me."

"You don't have a cell phone."

"You give me one of yours."

"That leaves one person without a cell phone. What if that person finds him?"

"He uses a pay phone. Give me yours, Furillo," Abelove demanded. Furillo reached into his pocket and reluctantly handed Abelove his phone.

"Make sure she has the number," Abelove said, and then as he picked up his tray to dump the food wrappers, he said, "If you find him, first thing you do, you call me on this phone. No interviews. Right?"

They nodded, more or less in unison, and watched Barney Abelove walk out of the Burger King. Carl Furillo and Lilian Wong sat silently for a moment. Then he looked at her and said, "Fifty-fifty on the film rights?"

She considered the proposition for a moment as she finished the last of her low-cal dinner salad.

"Deal," she responded.

Chapter 27

While Barney Abelove, Carl Furillo, and Lilian Wong were combing the mean streets of St. Catharines, Ontario, looking for Emmanuel Longhouse, a dinner party was taking place on Manhattan's Upper East Side. The dinner party was hostessed by Binky Blayberg, a petrochemical widow of bottomless wealth, who had invited a cross section of New York's literary and publishing mafia to dine on *moules marinière* and *paella*. The conversation, as it so often did lately at dinner parties everywhere, turned to Audrey.

". . . I'll tell you what I think," opined Barry Pinolis, an editor at *Vanity Fair*, sponging up the white-wine-and-garlic sauce with a piece of sourdough baguette. "Our culture is so devoid of values that a woman like Audrey Haas has become a cultural archetype, not to mention a role model. O.J. at least could play football."

"Yes, but look what she's done for sexual equality," retorted Diana Ravello, an art historian. "All a woman needs is an electric carving knife in her kitchen to negotiate from strength."

There was general laughter, though less general on the part of the men at the table. Binky Blayberg turned to Charles McClure, the legal editor at the *Times*, and asked, "Well, Charles, is she going to walk?"

"I'm afraid Abelove's perjury may have sunk the ship. The prosecution has no independently obtained evidence except the fax, and that looks like a blind alley unless they find the burglar."

It was at this point that Jackie Leitmotov, the owner of a boutique publishing house that serendipitously happened to have bought the rights to Pauline Haggis's quickie book, *The Right Place at the Right Time: How I Blew the Whistle on Audrey*, made a calculated decision.

Pauline Haggis had phoned her that morning to tell her about receiving the second fax and giving it to the police. Leitmotov had told her to tell nobody else about it so that they could promote the book as containing never-before-revealed facts about the case. But as she sat there listening to the discussion, Jackie Leitmotov realized that this was the perfect forum for launching the publicity campaign for the upcoming book.

So Jackie Leitmotov one-upped everybody else at the table by telling them, confidentially, of course, about the receipt of the second fax that morning by her writer, Pauline Haggis, whose book, incidentally, was due in the bookstores by October, if not earlier.

A sudden silence came over the table. The *paella* lay untouched as the diners considered this bombshell casually dropped by Jackie Leitmotov.

"But what did the fax *say*?" Binky Blayberg broke the silence.

"Well, I'm not at liberty to tell you exactly what it said except that it's not good news for Audrey."

"Really?" There was a collective sucking-in of air around the table.

"Where was it from?" Barry Pinolis asked.

"I'm afraid I can't tell you that, either. It'll all be in Pauline's book."

Later on, during the tiramisù, Charles McClure excused himself to go to the bathroom, where he called the national-desk night editor on his cell phone. Over McClure's byline, exclusive to *The New York Times*, they'd run the headline POSSIBLE SECOND FAX FROM BURGLAR. The subhead would be: WITNESS COULD FORESTALL MISTRIAL MOTION EXPECTED MONDAY.

Unaware of all the excitement building up around him, Emmanuel Longhouse sat in the Maple Leaf Bar and Grill, staring bleary-eyed at the TV, and thought about calling it a night. He had reached the point of diminishing returns. Any more beer and he would be up half the night.

When Apaches had to get up early for a battle, they drank a lot of water before going to sleep. It was the only completely reliable alarm clock. Emmanuel Longhouse had to get up early to do some parking meters, so he got off the bar stool, nodded in the direction of Ian, the bartender, and headed off into the night.

A light drizzle had begun to fall, and he put up the collar of his flannel shirt as he walked the two blocks to the Wellington Arms. He was crossing the street, his mind on parking meters, when a cab came around the corner. The driver hit the brakes and pulled the wheel sharply, missing Emmanuel Longhouse by a few inches.

"Fucking Native," cursed the cab driver, then, looking in the rearview mirror at Lilian Wong, said, "Excuse the language."

Lilian Wong, who had been cruising the streets for three hours, stopping into bars and cheap hotels, going from cab to cab, sat up straight in her seat and said, "Did you say fucking *Native*?"

"Yeah, sorry. The guy's walking in the middle of the street, not looking where he's going."

"Stop!" she cried.

"What?"

"Stop the cab. Right here."

The cab stopped, and Lilian Wong got out just in time to see Emmanuel Longhouse's six-foot-five-inch frame disappear into the doorway of the Wellington Arms.

"Hey," she cried, but even if Emmanuel Longhouse had been stone sober he wouldn't have heard her. She went running across the street as best she could in her Alexis Misrali shoes.

By the time she reached the lobby of the Wellington Arms, such that it was, Emmanuel Longhouse was already on his way up the narrow stairway to his room on the fourth floor. She looked around her at the peeling furniture and the faded rug, saw a man sitting behind a caged window reading a newspaper.

"Excuse me," she called. "Did a tall Indian just come in here?"

The man put down his paper and glanced at the attractive Asian woman in the brown knit Anne Klein suit and said, "We call them Natives."

"Sorry. . . . Was there a Native who just came in here?"

"You must be talking about Speak No Evil."

"Beg your pardon?"

"That's what I call him. He don't talk or hear."

"Can you tell me what room he's in?"

"Four-oh-eight. Fourth floor, end of the hall. There's no elevator."

He pointed at the stairs, and as Lilian Wong headed off in that direction, she considered calling for backup and decided not to. Better make sure it's not a false alarm before she bothered them. She'd ask him a couple of questions first, just to be sure . . .

· · ·

Emmanuel Longhouse was sitting on his bed, removing his shit-kickers, when there was a knock at his door. He didn't hear the knock, of course, but he did notice a slight trembling of the rickety chest of drawers on the wall beside the door. Undoubtedly a truck passing in the street or a plumbing backup, he said to himself, and continued with his second shitkicker.

Outside his door, meanwhile, Lilian Wong knocked harder. "Hello! Anybody there?" she called.

After a moment, the door across the hallway opened, and a very old, very short, very hairy man in a maroon bathrobe looked her up and down and said hopefully, "You looking for a little action?"

She turned around and said, "Do you know if he's in there?"

"The Native?"

"Yes."

"Beats me. But he don't hear anything, so there's no point in knocking. I, on the other hand, got twenty-twenty hearing. And a quart of Labatt's . . ."

She turned back around from the little man, took a breath to calm herself.

"You want to come in and sit on my face it's okay with me," the little man said. She reached into her pocketbook and fished for her can of pepper spray. Behind her, she heard the high-pitched voice say, " 'Course, you want to put it in your twat and rotate, that's okay with me, too . . ."

Suddenly a little dizzy, she reached for the doorknob to steady herself and felt it turn in her hand. The door gave with her weight and slid open with a creaky whine. Sitting on the bed facing her, wearing nothing but a pair of Jockey shorts, was a very tall Indian with an earring in his left ear.

Instinctively, she closed the door behind her. The man looked at her with boozy eyes. He did not seem to be surprised that a strange woman had entered his room at midnight.

"I'm sorry to bother you," she said, and then, remembering that he was deaf, she repeated the words slowly with exaggerated lip motions.

He got up off the bed, and she backed up against the door, her hand on the pepper spray. In the small, low-ceilinged room, he looked enormous.

"Can you understand me?" she asked, once more with the exaggerated gestures.

He nodded, then reached over to the end of the bed for a pair of pants hanging over the bedpost. He sat back down holding his pants in his lap. Beside his feet were the biggest pair of boots she had ever seen in her life.

"My name is Lilian Wong. W . . . O . . . N . . . G. I'm here to talk to you about the fax. F . . . A . . . X . . ."

He nodded again, his face impassive. She stood with her back against the door, unsure how to proceed, as he got up again and, carrying his pants, walked over to a table and chair by the window, took the chair, turned it around, and offered it to her. Then he made a writing gesture, as if he had a pen and a piece of paper in his hands.

She fished a pad and ballpoint out of her pocketbook and handed them to him. He took them, walked back across to the bed, still carrying the pants, sat down, and started to write. He wrote laboriously. When he was finished, he tore the page off and handed it to her.

She read: I SORE U ON TV. She looked back at him and nodded. "Yes. I'm on TV. *Hard Copy.*" She searched for gestures to express her thoughts, but came up blank.

"What is your name?" she asked.

Again it seemed to take forever for him to write whatever it was he was writing. She read: IZ AWDRY GOIN TO WAWK?

"Not if you testify," she replied, then repeated it very slowly and very clearly.

He started to write again. As she sat there watching him, she thought about Abelove and Furillo and her promise to call them when she found the Indian. Just a few more questions, she decided, as he handed her the pad, upon which he had written: U LOOK LIK CONNEE CHUNK.

Abelove stood on the edge of the Welland Canal in a fine drizzle and looked at his watch. After three and a half hours of dragging the streets, he had come up empty. He was tired, wet, and disgusted. He should have stayed in Schenectady, ridden out the storm, taken the Fifth, and fuck the Indian and Audrey and St. Catharines, Ontario.

What's the worst they could do to him? Dismissal from the force with loss of benefits? Perjury charges? Five-to-ten in Elmira . . . ? His cholesterol would probably get him before then, anyway. Probably keel over chasing a crackhead up the stairs to some shithole apartment.

Abelove rummaged in his pocket for the number he had written down on the inside of a matchbook. He found it, squinted at it in the light, opened the phone, and dialed.

"Where are you?" he asked when she answered.

There was a silence, then, in a low voice, she said, "I don't know."

"You don't know?"

"I'm in a residential hotel called the Wellington Arms."

"Why are you whispering?"

"I found him."

"You *found* him?"

"Yeah."

"Is he talking?"

"He doesn't talk. He writes. He's been deaf and dumb since he was nine years old and came home from school and found his mother with her head in the oven."

"I thought I said no interviews."

"It's only deep background."

At one-thirty in the morning, Barney Abelove and Carl Furillo had joined Lilian Wong in Emmanuel Longhouse's small room on the fourth floor of the Wellington Arms. The Indian had put on his pants and had gone across the hallway to borrow a quart of Labatt's and two more chairs from his neighbor.

Though hospitable and polite, Emmanuel Longhouse was not forthcoming when it came to questions about whether or not he was at the Haases' house in Schenectady the night of March 27.

Barney Abelove did his best to enunciate promises of immunity from prosecution, but Emmanuel Longhouse didn't seem to respond to these overtures. He just nodded amiably, sipped his beer, and wrote notes to Lilian Wong about how it was growing up in an orphanage run by nuns in Utica. It was getting late. The rain had picked up. They were all getting tired and edgy.

"Just ask him if he wants to come to Schenectady with you, Lilian," Furillo suggested. "He seems to be quite taken with you."

"Then what?"

"We'll worry about it then."

She turned to Emmanuel Longhouse and said, "How would you like to take a trip with us?"

"With *you*, not with us," Furillo said.

She repeated the question, slowly and distinctly, changing *us* to *me*. He wrote for a long time, puzzling over the letters, then handed her the pad.

THANK U. I HAF TO GO TO WERK SOON. MAYBEE TOMORRO. OK?

She read it to the others.

"What kind of work?" Abelove asked. When he didn't reply, he asked Lilian Wong to repeat the question. Emmanuel Longhouse didn't nod or shake his head or write anything on the pad. Instead he got up and walked to the door. He opened it and made a gesture for them to leave.

The three of them looked at one another hopelessly, then got up and walked to the door. Lilian Wong said good night and smiled at him. He smiled back. It was the first time they had seen his smile—a broad, open, disarming smile that changed the entire configuration of his face, from sullen and menacing to gentle and beatific.

"What time tomorrow?" she asked him.

He reached out and took her hand, pointed to her Philippe Patek, his large finger covering the twelve.

"Noon?" she articulated.

He nodded again.

"See you then," she said and followed Abelove and Furillo out.

As the three of them headed for the stairs, the door opened across the hallway, and the little man stood in the doorway with an impressive erection.

He called after them, "Check this out, ay?"

But they were already in the stairwell. "Your loss," he muttered and closed the door.

Chapter 28

Charles McClure's story made the front page of Saturday's *New York Times*, above the fold. Shortly after the morning edition hit newsstands and doorsteps across the country, the story was on the wires, setting off a new chain of events that would keep the world's attention, to the extent that it wasn't already, riveted on Audrey.

Pauline Haggis was woken up by a phone call from Carrie Castle asking if she could confirm the *New York Times* story. As Jackie Leitmotov had told her to do, Pauline Haggis seized the opportunity to talk about her crucial role in the Audrey Haas affair and about the book she was writing. She invited Carrie down to her office to show her the fax machine that had received the two messages from the burglar.

From there, it didn't take long to trace the fax number to Wise's Stationery and Copy Store in St. Catharines, Ontario. By noon, most of the world knew that the second fax was sent from St. Catharines, Ontario, by the spelling-challenged burglar, and that Barney Abelove had presumably gone there to find him and bring him back to Schenectady to testify.

Ralph D'Imbroglio's phone was ringing off the hook. He issued a blanket "No comment" to the press while he tried to figure out how to play the story. His spin guy suggested that he issue a statement disavowing the Abelove mission and claiming that the district attorney's

office was standing by its attempt to bring the case to a successful res-
olution.

Susan Bremmer, on the other hand, was talking to anybody who
bothered to call. She claimed that Abelove's trip to Canada was a last-
ditch effort on the part of the prosecution to save a compromised case.

"What else do you do when you're caught perjuring yourself? You
tap-dance. Detective Abelove is tap-dancing all the way to a mistrial."

COP TAP-DANCING TO A MISTRIAL? was the front-page of the afternoon edition of the *New York Post*. By that time, there were reporters
on their way to St. Catharines with no clear idea where the story was
except at the copy store in the Lester Pearson Mall.

Not far away from that same mall, at 4 A.M. Saturday morning, several hours before the *Times* hit the streets, Barney Abelove was dozing
in his car parked across from the Wellington Arms, staking out the Indian's room. His two deputies were not with him.

Confident that the Indian wasn't going anywhere without Lilian
Wong, Furillo saw no reason to spend what was left of the night sitting
in a car in the rain watching the doorway of a fleabag hotel. On the contrary. He thought this might be the perfect moment to get to know Lilian Wong a little better.

The stress of combat, two lost souls thrown together in improbable
surroundings . . . *A Farewell to Arms* in St. Catharines, Ontario.

In the elevator of the Ramada Inn, as they stood there, each with a
room key, Furillo suggested a nightcap in his room. She looked at him
with a certain amount of intensity, if not tenderness, and slowly shook
her head.

"Too tired?" he said.

"Not tired enough."

Furillo let the line pass. It was too late for repartee. The elevator arrived at their floor, and they walked down the hallway in silence to their
adjoining rooms. She put her key card in the slot, and the green light
went on. She turned back to him and said, "I'm sorry. I didn't mean
that."

Furillo saw an exhausted woman, small and vulnerable in the aque-
ous fluorescent lighting of the Ramada Inn hallway. She stood on one
leg and unconsciously scratched the other with the tip of her $400
shoes. It was this type of intimate gesture that tended to endear a woman
to Furillo.

"I'm a badly fortified castle at the moment, Furillo. The drawbridge
may be down, but the moat is dry. It hasn't rained in a while. You understand what I'm saying?"

He looked her in the eyes, drinking up her exhaustion.

"Good night," she said and, blowing a little kiss in his direction, entered her room.

Furillo stood there for a moment and listened to his horse snort in the cold night air. He felt his lips forming to return the kiss, then replaced his sword in the scabbard and rode on.

Shortly after 4 A.M. Emmanuel Longhouse's beer alarm clock went off. As he staggered to the can in the hall, he considered blowing off the parking meters. He had been up late with the people from Schenectady and was dead tired. The parking meters weren't going to go away. Tomorrow night there'd be even more money in them.

But then he thought about Lilian Wong and decided he'd better have some funds in case they went out for a drink. She looked like she was accustomed to being entertained in style.

He put on his flannel shirt and shitkickers, got his work tool from the bottom of the duffel bag, and headed for the stairs. The tool, a modified ignition church key that he had bought off a car thief in Albany, was your basic one-size-fits-all lockpick. You could do just about anything with it, from cars to houses to parking meters.

Abelove was dozing with his eyes open when the tall Indian walked out of the Wellington Arms and headed south toward the canal. He waited for him to round the corner before starting the ignition of the Cutlass and rolling slowly toward the corner without his headlights.

The streets were deserted at this hour, making it difficult for Abelove to maintain surveillance without being spotted. Staying two blocks behind, Abelove managed to keep his target in sight as he turned east along the edge of the canal and headed toward a large outdoor parking lot beside the railroad station.

When the Indian entered the deserted parking lot, Abelove pulled over and got out of the car. His footsteps resonated through the empty pre-dawn streets. He was less than a block away before he was able to make out the looming figure of Emmanuel Longhouse going from parking space to parking space in the empty lot.

When Abelove realized what Emmanuel Longhouse was doing, he almost laughed out loud.

He went back to his car, waited ten more minutes as the Indian hit every meter on the lot, then followed him back to the Wellington Arms, where Longhouse disappeared inside.

Abelove sat in his car, exhausted, muttering to himself. You had to be pretty hard up to do parking meters. For fucking quarters. Canadian quarters, no less.

There was a sharp rapping on the window of the Cutlass. Abelove jerked himself awake and saw Carl Furillo and Lilian Wong standing beside his car in the noonday sun. He squinted at the light, realized he had overslept, unlocked the door, and got out of the car.

"What time is it?"

"A quarter to twelve," Lilian Wong said.

Furillo handed him a copy of that morning's *New York Times* with the three-column headline above the fold. Abelove glanced at the story briefly, then muttered, "Shit."

"You're a star, Barney," Furillo said. "You pull this off, you're going to be on Letterman."

Abelove grimaced as he felt his entire body complain from a night of sleeping in the car.

"Maybe you should get a cup of coffee," Lilian Wong suggested.

"I'm all right," he groaned. "Let's go." He started walking toward the Wellington Arms.

"I think we should let Lilian go up there alone," Furillo said.

Abelove stopped walking, turned around, shook his head.

"We want to get him back to Schenectady," Furillo insisted, "the best shot we have is Lilian. She goes up there alone, does what she can to get him to go back to Schenectady in the Taurus. We follow in your car. As soon as we cross the border, you can put the cuffs on him."

"I don't like it."

"Listen, in a couple of hours this city is going to be crawling with reporters, not to mention cops. All of them looking for him. If we can get out of here fast, we can get him to Schenectady before the shit hits the fan."

Abelove's mouth was dry and his head ached. His bladder was on overload. He needed a cup of coffee and a leak in the worst way.

"Why don't you go freshen up?" Lilian Wong suggested sweetly. "There's a place across the street."

He turned and saw a faded brick building with a flickering neon sign that said THE PRINCE OF WALES TAVERN.

"Go get an Irish coffee. It'll blow out the cobwebs," said Furillo.

Emmanuel Longhouse invited Lilian Wong for a drink at the Maple Leaf Bar and Grill. They sat in a booth and drank Labatt's while Emmanuel Longhouse wrote slowly and painstakingly on Lilian Wong's pad about his childhood with the nuns in Utica and his plans to go to Saskatchewan.

She told him that she admired him for having a strong vision of his life's journey. Too many people floundered around with no real purpose, but he seemed to know where he was heading. A sea voyage is not only measured in nautical miles but in fathoms, she expounded.

After a few more beers, Emmanuel Longhouse wondered if Lilian Wong would be interested in going to Saskatchewan with him. There must be great opportunities for an attractive Oriental woman in western Canada.

Lilian Wong thanked him and explained about duty-free ports. Before you were able to arrive safely on your voyage you had to deal with your baggage. You had to face up to the customs official and declare what you were carrying. Sooner or later you had to make a clean breast of it; otherwise you'd just be drifting aimlessly from port to port laden down with cargo.

"Emmanuel," she said, looking him directly in the eye, "you have to go back to Schenectady and pay your duty. You know that, don't you?"

He looked away for a moment, suddenly ashamed. She was a very smart woman. She made beautiful shapes with her lips when she spoke to him. He could almost taste the sound of her words.

"I'll go back with you and help you face things," she said. "I'll tell your story to the world so that people will know that you are a man of integrity and courage. Together, Emmanuel, we can reach port and make a clean declaration to the customs officials."

He was stunned by the simple truth of her words. She was right. He was carrying this baggage with him. It was weighing him down. Audrey and the man without his tomahawk. They were ghosts following him west through the night. They would follow him to Saskatchewan, just as they had followed him to St. Catharines.

He took the pad and started to write. It took him a while to write what he meant because he didn't know all the words. Finally, he handed the pad across the table to her, and she read: I PLAYCE MY TRUSS IN YOR HANS.

And so, less than twenty-four hours after the convoy crossed into Canada, it headed back toward the border. Lilian Wong drove the red Taurus, Emmanuel Longhouse beside her. Following them in the Oldsmobile Cutlass were Barney Abelove and Carl Furillo.

As they headed east toward the border, reporters began to arrive from the west in rented cars from Toronto. They were all racing to get the lead on the story, unaware that the story had already left town.

The networks would preempt regularly scheduled programming to carry live coverage of their reporters interviewing the green-haired clerk at Wise's Stationery and Copy Store, the cab driver who had picked up Lilian Wong, the night-desk man at the Wellington Arms, even the exhibitionist across the hallway.

In Schenectady Ralph D'Imbroglio was lying on the couch watching all of this on his forty-eight-inch television when Barney Abelove, heading east on Queen Elizabeth Way in the Cutlass, called him on Carl Furillo's cell phone.

"Jesus. What's going on? It's all over the goddamn news . . . Where are you? You got the Indian?" He blurted all this while hitting the mute button on the television.

"Uh-huh."

"Where are you?"

"Couple of miles from the border."

"Is he cuffed?"

"Nope."

"You got him in the backseat?"

"No. He's in the car in front of me."

"He's driving *his own fucking car*?"

"No. He's in Lilian Wong's car."

"Lilian *Wong*? What the fuck is he doing in her car?"

"Look, he's coming to testify of his own free will. I'm not putting cuffs on him. Just prepare immunity papers for him, and get him a lawyer."

"A lawyer?"

"Yeah. You don't want him signing immunity papers without a lawyer."

"Where am I going to find a lawyer?"

"You're the district attorney, and you can't find a lawyer?"

"It's Saturday."

"Trust me. Somebody on your staff knows a lawyer who works on Saturday."

"Should I get him an Indian lawyer?"

Abelove closed the cell phone without replying and kept his eyes focused on the red Taurus in front of him. They were approaching Niagara Falls. Unfortunately, there wasn't time to stop for Renata's coconut mint cookies. Not on this trip. When it was all over he'd take Renata to the Falls for a weekend. Provided he wasn't in jail.

Chapter 29

The Honorable Carmen Fenetre was in the knotty-pine-and-wicker den of her ranch house on Delft Drive in Niskayuna watching *Ben and Bill*, an old Best-Picture winner starring Jeremy Ikon and Jacqueline Fortier, on the Academy Award Movie Channel, when her clerk, Valerie, called to tell her that Lilian Wong was doing a live standup in front of Ralph D'Imbroglio's office.

Fenetre zapped the movie and found Lilian Wong on several channels at once standing in front of the district attorney's office on State Street. The reporter, wearing the same brown-knit Anne Klein suit that Fenetre had already seen in court more than once, announced that an eyewitness had suddenly surfaced in the Audrey Haas case—a 15/16 Mohawk Native American named Emmanuel Longhouse, who, at this moment, was inside with his attorney discussing the terms under which he would testify that he observed Audrey Haas with the electric carving knife in her hand on the night of March 27.

Fenetre reached out for a handful of microwave popcorn and turned up the sound.

Mr. Longhouse, Lilian Wong went on, turned himself over to authorities a half hour ago, after Schenectady Police detective Barney Abelove tracked him to a St. Catharines, Ontario, residential hotel, one of the places he had been living since leaving Albany in April. Mr. Longhouse had agreed to return to Schenectady and speak out because his sense of honor would no longer allow him to remain silent—a supreme irony, given the fact that Emmanuel Longhouse has been both deaf and dumb following a trauma at the age of nine, when he came home from school to discover his mother with her head in the oven of the family's apartment. Brought up by nuns in an orphans' home in Utica . . .

Fenetre grabbed the phone. When she got her clerk, she said, "I want D'Imbroglio's direct line at his office. Right away."

"I'm sorry, Your Honor, but I don't have it at home. It's at the courthouse."

"Well, then go to the courthouse and get it."

"I'm expecting people for dinner—"

"Valerie, what's more important—your dinner party or the American criminal justice system?"

Fenetre hung up the phone and paced back and forth across her den. The Lilian Wong standup had gone to sound bites over file footage of the trial. There were pictures of Audrey, of Abelove, of the lawyers, of her in court, as Lilian Wong explained the significance of Emmanuel Longhouse's testimony.

Both sides were allowing this case to become a public spectacle. In direct contradiction to her explicit orders. Perjury, eleventh-hour plea-bargain negotiations, witnesses coming out of the woodwork, immunity deals . . .

She would put a stop to it. Right away. She would issue a strong censure to both sides. Read them the riot act, make sure that they knew that this type of bullshit was unacceptable in Judge Carmen Fenetre's courtroom.

Feeling her heart begin to palpitate, she stopped pacing and sat back down on the couch, sinking into the puff cushions and taking deep, cleansing breaths. The trial, the lawyers, Audrey Haas—it was all starting to get to her.

She zapped back to the Academy Award Channel and watched the young Benjamin Disraeli sporting with a delectable young thing in a Maltese brothel.

It transported her to last August on Mykonos. The bittersweet taste of Metaxa, the stark white sand, the olive trees, the perfumed nights. The feel of a ripe fig on the edge of her tongue . . .

She had been on the bench too long, presiding over spectacles of human perversity and greed. She was fed up with the lawyers, the TV cameras, the soporific stares of the jury, the vacuous eyes of Audrey Haas. On Mykonos, life was clean and simple. She didn't have to worry about being reversed. As far as she was concerned, they could reverse the hell out of her there. They could nail her to the courthouse door.

She opened her eyes and watched the naked Maltese whore run out after the departing Disraeli into the beautifully photographed Mediterranean twilight, and she felt a deep sadness. Life was slipping away from her, minute by minute. And as the sun bled over the sea above Malta, Judge Carmen Fenetre curled up on her couch and wept.

Stanley Bluefinch, Mohawk tribal attorney, sat next to his new client in a conference room in the county building on State Street and watched him painstakingly write on a legal pad. He had been on this case since a little past six o'clock that evening, when he'd picked up his phone and had been virtually ordered by Ralph D'Imbroglio to represent a Native American in an immunity deal.

It was unheard of for a district attorney to assign specific counsel for a witness. Moreover, a lawyer who was principally involved in representing the Mohawk Nation in various land claims would not seem to be the ideal choice for the job.

But when Stanley Bluefinch had explained to Ralph D'Imbroglio that he wasn't a criminal attorney, the district attorney assured him that it was strictly *pro forma*—the granting of immunity from prosecution in exchange for an agreement to testify. All he had to do was draft a short document and advise his client to sign. He'd be in and out of there in an hour.

D'Imbroglio hadn't mentioned on the phone that it involved the Audrey Haas case. Nor did he mention that Emmanuel Longhouse was not only deaf and dumb, but indigent. It was not only *pro forma*, it was *pro bono*.

For several hours now, Emmanuel Longhouse had been writing long rambling paragraphs about sailing to duty-free ports and declaring his baggage. The spelling amounted to some sort of phonetic rendering of what he was able to lip-read.

Unsure of what all this had to do with his testimony, Stanley Bluefinch tried to guide him back to the specifics of the deal—what he had done for which he required immunity from prosecution. If he hadn't been told by the district attorney what the charges were, he would have thought that Emmanuel Longhouse had been arrested by customs officials for smuggling narcotics across the border.

Every fifteen minutes the phone rang and D'Imbroglio asked him if they were ready to draft the document. Stanley Bluefinch had to tell him that they were still discussing the issues.

"Are you billing by the goddamn hour?"

"It doesn't look like I'm billing at all," Stanley Bluefinch replied.

"Look," D'Imbroglio said, "I'll grant him blanket immunity for everything he's done in my jurisdiction in his whole goddamn life. From picking his nose to jerking off. You name it, he's got it. What more does he want?"

"Tell you the truth, it looks to me like he wants absolution more than immunity."

"I'm the district attorney, not the fucking archbishop."

"Do you suppose you can get a woman named Connee Chunk up here? He wants to talk to her."

"Who?"

"He's written a name that looks to me like Connee Chunk. Maybe he means Connie Chung."

"Connie Chung? She's off the air, isn't she?"

"That's what I thought."

"Why does he want to talk to *her*?"

"I don't know, but he seems intent on it. Maybe you ought to see if you can get her on the phone."

D'Imbroglio hung up and turned to Clint Wells.

"You know how I can get in touch with Connie Chung?"

"Connie Chung? The one who used to be co-anchor with Dan Rather on *CBS News*?"

"Yeah. The Indian wants to talk to her."

Susan Bremmer found out about the new witness from her paralegal, who beeped her in a Thai restaurant where she and Lizzie Vaught were sitting over pad thai noodles working on the text of the mistrial motion they were planning to file Monday morning if they didn't have a deal.

Bremmer barged into the kitchen, commandeered the owner's TV, and watched in horror as Lilian Wong explained the miraculous appearance of Emmanuel Longhouse. She stood there among the diced vegetables and woks, shaking her head in consternation at Lizzie Vaught beside her.

"Great," Lizzie Vaught murmured. "It's bad enough impeaching a cop. Now we have to impeach an Indian. A deaf-and-dumb Indian."

Stunned, they listened to Lilian Wong talk about Emmanuel Longhouse's past.

"A deaf, dumb Indian *orphan*, no less," Lizzie Vaught added.

"Who's going to get immunity on the burglary."

"If he doesn't have the dumbest lawyer on the planet," Lizzie Vaught said.

"So what do we go after?"

"I don't know. What can you go after with Indians these days?"

"God, I hate this case," Bremmer muttered, mangling a stray scallion with her hands, as Lizzie Vaught shook her head.

"If the guy has a record, you might as well forget it. And a drinking problem—there's no way you could touch that even if he was the town drunk . . ."

"Red rage . . ."

"Huh?"

"We can go with red rage."

"What are you talking about?"

Bremmer looked at her with a strange, almost demented expression on her face and whispered, "Cultural bias."

Lizzie Vaught stared at her blankly as Bremmer explained. "Remember what the jury profiler said about minorities? They have unconscious hostility toward majority cultures. So here we have a Native American, whose ancestors were forced off the land, harboring deep feelings of anger against Audrey Haas's ancestors. So he acts. He breaks into a house—"

"We can't bring that up."

"Sure we can. He just can't be prosecuted for it, but we can mention it. We mention the hell out of it."

"You want to try crucifying an Indian?"

"You betcha. By the time we're finished with him, we may have an immune burglar but we'll have a homicidal maniac. In the jury's mind Audrey's going to become the good schoolmarm kidnapped and raped by the Comanches. It'll be Little Big Horn all over again, except this time the white guys win."

They were still trying to track down Connie Chung's home phone number when Carmen Fenetre got Ralph D'Imbroglio on the phone.

"What the hell is going on, Mr. D'Imbroglio?"

"We have located a new witness, Your Honor. And we're in the process of interviewing him right now."

"So I gather. From the TV. I'm finding that the best way to keep abreast of developments in this case is to watch television."

"As you know, the First Amendment—"

"The First Amendment does not apply to attorneys in a criminal case."

"You're absolutely right, Your Honor—"

"All this time I have been led to believe that we were recessed to permit plea-bargain negotiations and not to provide an opportunity for the prosecution to produce a new witness. What type of immunity deal are you making with him?"

"A rather comprehensive one, I'm afraid."

"As soon as the deal is cut I want the full terms. You call me at home. Tonight. Tomorrow. Whenever."

"Certainly . . ."

"Monday morning, Mr. D'Imbroglio. Ten A.M. My chambers."

"I'll be there, Your Honor."

"Try not to give away the entire ranch, Ralph." And she hung up.

D'Imbroglio put the receiver down slowly and leaned back in his swivel chair. He looked at his watch: 10:30. It was getting late.

He looked across at Clint Wells, who was at the sideboard with the bagels, and asked, "Can we subpoena Connie Chung?"

"As a witness?"

"No. To talk to the Indian."

"I don't think you can use a subpoena to get someone to talk to a witness."

"What if we call her for obstruction of justice?"

"Beg your pardon?"

"We can argue that she's obstructing the prosecution by refusing to cooperate with the immunity deal."

"I suppose we could give it a try," Clint Wells said, doing his best not to gag on the bagel.

"Meanwhile, see if you can find her, so we know where the fuck to serve it."

"I'll get right on it," said Clint Wells. He gathered his things and went down the hall to his own office. Closing the door behind him, he walked to his desk and flipped his Rolodex to *C*. But it wasn't for Connie Chung's home number, which wasn't there in any event. It was for another anchorwoman's home number, an anchorwoman whose initials, coincidentally, also happened to be C.C.

Carl Furillo was in his customary booth in the Henry Hudson Room at the Hotel Van Twiller writing furiously against deadline. He was working on the cover story for Monday's edition of *People*—AUDREY'S SILENT ACCUSER SURFACES. The cover art was a silhouette of a vaguely Native American–looking man behind a superimposed question mark. The initial print run was 5 million.

When he finished the story he would modem it directly to the composing room, where Sharon Marcuzzi and a fact-checker were standing by. It was all a frantic rush to beat the dailies at their own game. And to be able to do this, they needed Furillo's copy by midnight.

The story he was writing was essentially a narrative of the mad jaunt to St. Catharines to find and bring back Emmanuel Longhouse. Lilian Wong had already delivered the headlines. Now he had a chance to get the texture.

Though he had no word limit—they would have given him the whole issue if he'd had the time to fill it—the deadline constraints were such that he was confined pretty much to the facts of how and where they had found Emmanuel Longhouse. There was no time to tell the full story, starting from Lilian Wong's lilac and the vodka shooters, all the way to the weenie waver and the parking meters.

Someday he would write *that* story. A long article, maybe even a novel. He would evoke the rain-slickened streets of St. Catharines, the smell of the Welland Canal, the little, overheated room on the fourth floor of the fleabag hotel where Emmanuel Longhouse stared at Lilian Wong's legs and scribbled his story on a memo pad. It was big. It was romantic. It was fucking Dostoyevsky . . .

He closed his eyes and saw Grushenka dancing in the roadside inn while Dmitri, driven mad by passion, called for more vodka, flinging the empty glasses into the fireplace as he frittered away the family fortune. While Grushenka danced, the snow fell outside in the endless Russian night. Inside there was the smell of Gypsy must and oranges, perfume, and vodka. And lilac . . .

His head jerked up, and he saw her standing over his booth in the Henry Hudson Room holding two glasses of champagne, one in each small, exquisitely fine hand. She was wearing jeans and a silk blouse tucked in at the waist, with high, polished leather boots. Her hair was combed, shining, with a flowered barrette in it. There was just a hint of makeup, an accent to the eyes, a touch of blush.

"I thought we deserved a little celebration," she said, offering him one of the glasses.

Jesus. Ninety minutes to deadline and Grushenka shows up with champagne.

"You're working," she said, sitting down beside him and squinting at the screen of the laptop.

He nodded.

"Oh, gee, I'm sorry. I should probably go, huh?"

He looked at her, unable to bring himself to tell her to leave. Here she finally was, the drawbridge down, the moat starting to fill up with champagne.

Dance for me, Grushenka. Put an olive between your teeth and dance on the table. Outside is my sleigh. We'll bundle up in furs and ride off over the tundra in the moonlight to my father's mortgaged estate . . .

"Boy, that's a tight deadline. Monday's *People*. Wow. What are you writing?"

"You mean, what am I *not* writing?"

"Sorry. I'll leave."

She started to edge out of the booth, but his hand reached out and grabbed hers. They sat there side by side, their hands entwined. Furillo downed his champagne as if it were a shot of vodka. She did the same. Then he threw his champagne glass against the faux Van Eyck behind the bar. She did the same.

He leaned over and kissed her. Lightly, letting his lips dance playfully over hers. It lasted longer than he had intended. And was interrupted by a loud voice from the TV. They broke away and looked over toward the bar.

Carrie Castle was sitting at her anchor desk, shuffling papers. As the camera zoomed in tight on her, she flexed her lipstick-smeared mouth, and, fixing her relentless gaze on the TV audience, announced, "Following today's dramatic revelation of an eyewitness in the Audrey Haas case, there has been another major development this evening. WSCH News has learned exclusively that the district attorney's office has been trying to get in touch with Connie Chung. Though it is not known whether the former *CBS News* co-anchor is directly involved in the case, there is speculation that she may have some relationship with Emmanuel Longhouse, the Native American burglary suspect now in custody who is said to have been present in the Haas house in Niskayuna the night of March twenty-seventh. Mr. Longhouse has been demanding to talk to Connie Chung since early this evening, when he voluntarily met with members of the prosecution team . . ."

As it happened, Carrie Castle's TV bulletin saved Carl Furillo's story. Actually it was Clint Wells's having called the local anchorwoman to leak the story that got it on the news and Lilian Wong out of Carl Furillo's arms to hurry to the district attorney's office to try to clear things up before things got completely out of hand.

As he watched Grushenka run out of the inn, Carl Furillo turned back to his laptop and went at the story with fury. Her lilac still in his nostrils, he used every bit of discipline he could muster to get the story written and modemed to New York by midnight.

He beat the deadline by seven minutes. They didn't even say thank you. They just downloaded it and fed it to the computer-generated type-setting programs that would digest it and work through the night to spew out 5 million copies.

Depleted, he unplugged his modem and sprawled across the chintz bedspread. As he lay there, snow began to fall against the wooden timbers of the roadside inn where Grushenka had danced for him. She was gone now, leaving him with a mouth full of stale vodka and an empty purse. All that was left were a few kopecks for the musicians. In the distance, far across the frozen tundra, he could hear the sound of sleigh bells getting fainter.

Chapter 30

By the time Lilian Wong showed up, everybody at the district attorney's office was irritable. Everybody except Emmanuel Longhouse, who had just polished off a large pepperoni pizza and was scribbling away on his legal pad and smoking unfiltered Camels.

Though it was a nonsmoking office, Ralph D'Imbroglio had granted an exception in the interest of expediting matters. While Clint Wells was next door trying to run down Connie Chung's home phone number, the district attorney was in his office with Jason Rappaport and Martha Demerest arguing over the new order of witnesses they would call. *If* they ever got the fucking immunity deal cut with their star witness.

They were debating whether to blow off the forensic urologist and go straight to the Indian, when Velma, the secretary, already heavy into gold time at county expense, stuck her head in the door to say that there was a reporter there to see the witness.

"Tell him to take a fucking hike," snapped Ralph D'Imbroglio.

"It's Lilian Wong."

"Fuck her. She's caused enough trouble already."

"She says that the witness doesn't want to talk to Connie Chung. He wants to talk to *her*."

Ralph D'Imbroglio got up out of his leather swivel seat and followed Velma into the reception area.

"Ms. Wong. Nice of you to stop in," he said, offering his hand.

She got up, took his hand, and said, "It's a confusion in his mind. He somehow has me crossed with Connie Chung."

D'Imbroglio thought about this briefly, then said, "You want to excuse me a moment?"

D'Imbroglio went down the hallway and knocked on the door of the conference room. When Stanley Bluefinch opened it, the district attorney whispered, "I got a reporter out here name of Lilian Wong. She says that your client wants to talk to her, not Connie Chung. Some sort of confusion of Asians."

"You don't have to whisper," Stanley Bluefinch replied. "He can't hear."

His back to the door, Emmanuel Longhouse continued to write furiously on the legal pad. There was a stack of papers beside him filled with his scrawlings and an overflowing ashtray.

"So what do you think? Should we let her talk to him or not?"

"At this point, I don't see that it could do any harm. I'm certainly making no headway here."

D'Imbroglio went back down the hallway and returned with Lilian Wong.

"Ms. Wong, this is Stanley Bluefinch of the Mohawk people. He's representing Mr. Longhouse."

"How do you do, Mr. Bluefinch. I think I may be able to help here."

"Be my guest. He's been writing for hours now. About customs officials and borders. I have no idea what he's talking about."

She sat down opposite Emmanuel Longhouse and reached out and touched his hand. Looking up, he offered her his big, disarming smile.

She looked back to Stanley Bluefinch and Ralph D'Imbroglio and said, "Do you think you could leave us alone for a moment?"

When the lawyers were gone, Lilian Wong lowered her eyes to him and said, "You know, Emmanuel, that I'm not Connie Chung. I'm Lilian Wong."

He took the legal pad and pencil and wrote: I NO.

"Do you still want to see her?"

He shook his head and wrote, U LUK NICE.

"Thank you. Emmanuel, do you understand what an immunity deal is?"

He nodded.

"Are you sure?"

He wrote, THEY CANT REST ME FOR NUTHIN.

"That's right," she said. "Whatever you say in testimony in the Audrey Haas case cannot be used to prosecute you for anything else."

He wrote, NO BRAKING ENTRING.

"So how come you don't want to sign the deal?"

His face positively beamed. I HAV NO BAGGUDG, he wrote.

"Yes. But you don't want to be arrested for burglary, do you?"

He smiled again and wrote, NO BAGGUDG. NUTHIN TO DEKLAR.

"Emmanuel, if you don't sign the deal, then whatever you say at the trial can be used against you. You might have to go to jail."

He turned over a new page and wrote for a long time. Lilian Wong watched him painstakingly draw the letters, like a child with a set of blocks. When she finally made out what he wrote, her eyes watered.

MY HART IS KLEEN. I SPEEK THE TREWT. NO MAN CAN HERT ME.

On Sunday morning, after being up half the night, Ralph D'Imbroglio had to call Judge Fenetre to explain that they still didn't have an immunity deal with the witness.

"Why?" she asked.

"Because he doesn't want one."

"I beg your pardon?"

"He's claiming he doesn't need one."

"What about the B and E?"

"He says that he has a clean heart and wants to speak the truth. Quote unquote."

"What does his counsel say?"

"His counsel has asked to be relieved. Your Honor, do you see grounds for contempt here?"

"For refusing to accept immunity from prosecution?"

"He's obstructing justice."

"No he isn't. He's obstructing the prosecution. What I see grounds for here is psychiatric evaluation, not contempt."

"You mean impeach our own witness?"

"If you don't, they will."

D'Imbroglio got off the phone with the judge and went into the bathroom for a suppository. Lilian Wong would run with the story. The spin would be that they were harassing the witness. He'd be up against it again. This time from the Indians. He'd already lost the women's vote. Now he'd lose the colored vote, not to mention the hearing-impaired. He'd wind up with the cops, the cross-dressers, and the dickless.

He called Clint Wells to ask him to find a Native American shrink.

"What for?"

"We need someone to testify that our witness isn't loony tunes."

"You want to introduce psychiatric testimony *before* he takes the stand?"

"Yeah. A preemptive attack. Like Pearl Harbor."

"What about Connie Chung? I think I have the number of her pediatrician . . ."

"Forget Connie Chung. Just get me an Indian with a psychiatry degree."

". . . there is no justice in this country for people of color."

"Why do you say that, Zachary?"

"We live in a country where police officers break into people's houses, lie about it in court, then travel to a foreign country to bring an innocent man back in handcuffs."

"According to the stories in the papers yesterday, Emmanuel Longhouse returned voluntarily."

"Who publishes the papers?"

"Are you saying that there is a conspiracy against Native Americans?"

"I am simply reporting the truth, the truth that every red man, woman, and child knows in his heart."

"Well, Zachary, you are certainly entitled to your opinion . . . Let's go to our next caller. Hi, you're on with Barry Belcher. Who's this?"

"Hi, Barry, it's Agnes from Cohoes. I'll tell you what I think. I think the police have completely mishandled the investigation. It's not just the cop who broke into the house and planted the evidence—"

"Wait a second, Agnes. Detective Abelove did not plant evidence, as far as we know. He just went in without a search warrant."

"That's what they want you to think. But how did he know the serial numbers for the knife would be in the drawer? Audrey didn't report the knife stolen, did she?"

"Well, no, but—"

"Because there never *was* a knife. The police planted the knife, then invented the Indian, and now Audrey's going to walk on account of falsification of evidence and illegal extradition. . . ."

Abelove shut off the car radio. There was no point changing the station. It was on every station. You couldn't listen to the radio, watch TV, pick up a newspaper, or even take a dump without hearing about it.

He had spent the night at Renata's, to elude the reporters that would be camped out in front of his apartment on Zeider Zee Crescent. She had made risotto and played gin rummy with him until he fell asleep in the chair at nine-thirty.

At four in the morning, he was wide awake. He got up and drove to the station, where he ran Emmanuel Longhouse on the computer to see if he had a sheet and came up with thirty-six months in Elmira for grand-theft burglary in 1978.

He waited until seven before calling the print guy in Forensics at home to ask him to run a match between the prints taken off the stolen merchandise and the prints on the rap sheet. When the guy complained that it was Sunday morning, Abelove said he would download the print card off the computer and bring it along with the print card in the evidence locker.

Yves Foucault greeted him in his bathrobe, and they went downstairs to his home office, where he had a small laboratory set up. He put the print cards under the microscope, focused, and grunted several times.

"You got a match?" Abelove asked.

"Ninety-nine point nine percent."

"What about the other one tenth of a percent?"

"That's for random statistical error."

"What the hell is that?"

"It's covering our ass. Now, can I go back to bed, please?"

Abelove drove back toward town. He took State Street, a ghost town of closed banks and office buildings, hooked a left on Nott Street, went past the college and out Route 7. It was, he realized, the same route he had taken that Saturday afternoon months ago when he had decided not to leave the fax for the swing shift.

Before then he was just a homicide detective three and a half years from retirement with a clean record and a pension. Now he was an international celebrity, a perjurer, and a harasser of Indians. There were reporters camped in front of his house. People spewed hate at him on the radio and TV.

It was only a matter of time before they brought him in front of an I.A. board of inquiry. They'd roast him in public for the sake of the department. They'd take his shield and pull his benefits. All because he ran into Audrey's father five minutes before he was out the door . . .

He made a left on Poltroon Road and a right on Van Schuyler. Pulling over across the street from 474, he killed the motor and stared at the green-and-white Dutch Colonial. There was a FOR SALE sign stuck in the lawn, looking brown and parched from lack of water.

Abelove had little doubt that Ernie Haas took better care of his lawn.

His lawn and his Rottweiler. After spending a day sticking litmus paper into people's urine, the guy came home at night and watered his lawn before cutting a hole in a pair of pantyhose, putting on a dress, and inviting his wife into the kitchen for a little handcuff dance.

It was as if he had never existed. Ernie Haas, the cause of it all, had vanished from public consciousness. Nobody talked about him anymore. Once Janice Meckler and her story faded into the woodwork, Ernie was cooked. He was just a guy who got his dick caught in the wringer.

Audrey was the star now. Audrey and Emmanuel Longhouse—a depressed housewife and an Indian petty thief. Ernie was no longer in the picture. Ernie was dead.

And Ernie's lawn, his legacy, was dying along with him. When you thought about it, what else did a man really leave in this world besides his lawn?

Barney Abelove sat in his car staring at Ernie Haas's lawn for a long time. Then he drove to Renata's and went back to sleep.

Susan Bremmer and Lizzie Vaught showed up in Audrey's condo in the Mohawk Towers a little after four on Sunday afternoon. Her ear pressed to the portable phone, Audrey told them she was just finishing up a telephone conversation with the Coast and she'd be right with them.

"No. I don't think Keanu Reeves is too young," she said into the phone.

Bremmer and Vaught exchanged a worried look, in view of what they had come to tell their client. There was some more silence, then Audrey said, "Listen, Charlie, I've got to go. My lawyers are here. Fax me his résumé, okay?"

She clicked the phone off, turned to them, and said, "That was Charlie Berns. He's producing the movie. What do you think about Keanu Reeves to play the Indian?"

"Great. Listen, Audrey, we have to talk," said Susan Bremmer.

"Sure. Sit down. You want a kir?"

"No thanks."

Audrey ushered them to the den with the 270-degree view of the Mohawk. The two lawyers sat down on the couch opposite Audrey.

"Audrey, I'm afraid we're going to have to adjust to these new developments," Bremmer began.

"You mean the Indian?"

"Yes. This puts a whole new light on things. As you know, we were going to make a deal with the district attorney for you to plead guilty to involuntary manslaughter."

"Two years suspended. No time."

"Right."

"So what's wrong?"

"What's wrong is that they now have a witness who can establish you in the kitchen with the carving knife. They no longer need Abelove's testimony, so the judge could rule against the mistrial motion, which effectively removes any leverage we had for a deal."

"What about the Fourth Amendment to the Constitution? Illegal search and seizure?"

"There's something called the 'independent source doctrine,' " Lizzie Vaught explained. "It allows the prosecution to argue that they would have had the same evidence inevitably from the legitimate source that they got from the illegitimate source. Which makes the illegal search moot."

"Moot?"

"Moot."

"What if I just . . . say it's the wrong Indian?"

"You don't get to testify until we present our case. So you can't say anything."

"I could go on *Larry King*, couldn't I?"

"You could, but the jury's sequestered."

"Sequestered?"

"Yes. It means that they're not permitted to watch TV or listen to the radio."

Audrey slumped in her chair. She was suddenly feeling very sad. The new medication that Zadek had her on wasn't working very well. She would have to call him in the morning and ask him to put her back on Prozac.

"Audrey? Are you okay?" Bremmer asked after a long silence.

Audrey nodded, fighting back the tears. Keeping her jaw muscles firm, as she had seen Victoria Principal do when confronted by the doctor with the news of her terminal uterine cancer last night in a TV movie called *Miracle of Love: The Marilyn Kantorian Story*, she asked, "So what are we going to do?"

"I think we're going to have to punt," said Lizzie Vaught.

"Punt?"

"That's what you do when you're deep in your own territory and it's fourth down. You give them the ball. See what *they* can do with it."

"Oh," said Audrey.

"Who knows? Maybe they'll fumble it back to us."

Audrey nodded and finally let the tears come. She couldn't hold them back any longer, unlike Victoria Principal, who, growing thinner and thinner, her hair falling out from the chemotherapy, never shed a tear in public as she went on to find homes for her four children. One by one she kissed them good-bye from her bed in the hospice. At her funeral the children planted a tree and read a poem about eternal life and love. Nobody fumbled the ball.

Chapter 31

At ten o'clock Monday morning, August 10, the follow-ing people were present in Judge Carmen Fenetre's chambers at the Schenectady County Courthouse: Susan Bremmer, Lizzie Vaught, Ralph D'Imbroglio, Clint Wells, Jason Rappaport, and Martha Demerest. At 10:05 the judge en-tered with a stack of newspapers under her arm.

Without saying good morning, she sat down at her desk and, one by one, tossed the newspapers face-up on the floor at the feet of the as-sembled lawyers, starting with *The New York Times*, whose headline read: IMMUNITY DEAL WITH WITNESS TO HAAS MURDER GOING SOUR, and finishing with the *Daily News*, whose front page had EMMANUEL SAYS AUDREY HAD THE KNIFE IN HER HAND smeared across it.

The judge leaned back in her swivel chair, crossed her arms, and looked from one to the other of them before saying, "You know, we can save ourselves a lot of trouble and the state a lot of money by just let-ting the jurors read the newspapers. It's all there, every move, coun-termove, argument, and motion. Why bother trying this case in the courtroom when it's being tried in the press?"

"Your Honor," said Bremmer, "we had reached a tentative plea bar-gain on Thursday, then on Friday the district attorney called me to ask for more time to locate a witness. When I granted it to him, I had no idea he was going to invite two reporters to accompany the police to Canada to apprehend the witness."

"Invite?" protested D'Imbroglio. "Are you accusing us of *inviting* Lilian Wong and Carl Furillo to accompany Detective Abelove?"

"How else did they get there?"

D'Imbroglio turned to Fenetre and said, "It is my understanding, Judge, that the two reporters in question used espionage tactics to follow Detective Abelove to St. Catharines. Once there, I believe that the detective needed help transporting the witness and so he enlisted their assistance."

Fenetre got up and walked over to the newspapers still lying on the carpet in front of the lawyers. She bent down and picked one up.

"Page one of this morning's *Albany Times Union*, and I quote: 'According to his attorney, Stanley Bluefinch, Mr. Longhouse returned to Schenectady of his own free will in order to testify in the Haas trial. He is anxious, Mr. Bluefinch said, to set the record straight.' Unquote."

She returned to her desk, refolded her arms, and said, "Ms. Bremmer, are you planning on filing for a mistrial based on tainted evidence?"

"I was, Your Honor, before the plea bargain was presented to me by the prosecution."

"Mr. D'Imbroglio," Fenetre said, "are you planning on invoking the independent source doctrine?"

"Absolutely."

"All right, what we appear to have here is your basic Mexican standoff, if you'll pardon the expression. Both sides have loaded guns pointed at each other. I see no clear winner here except the tabloid newspapers. So let's make a deal."

The judge took off her reading glasses and laid them on the desk.

"The defense will drop its mistrial motion. In return, the prosecution will allow full impeachment of the witness within the strictures of his Fifth Amendment protection against self-incrimination should the defense care either to cross-examine him or to call him as a hostile witness. And, having agreed to these conditions, we will, god willing, get on with this trial."

The judge looked around her and said, "Well?"

There was a good deal of hemming and hawing and exchanging of worried looks among the lawyers on each side.

"You've got a half hour to caucus among yourselves." Fenetre looked at her watch. "If we don't have a deal by eleven o'clock, I'm going to call a press conference to say, among other things, that in my sixteen years on the bench, I have never seen such ineptitude on the part of lawyers on both sides of a case. If it were possible to cite both sides for contempt on the grounds of incompetence, believe me, I wouldn't hesitate to do it. Any questions?"

There were none.

The deal closed before eleven o'clock. Jason Rappaport said it was the first time he had ever seen a judge effectively hold a gun to two heads at the same time, when the two heads were on different sides of the room. He did not, however, say it for attribution.

Judge Fenetre threatened that if word of the deal leaked, she would go through with her press conference, booking prime time on national TV. As of next Monday, she informed them, the trial was no longer adjourned. They were to be in court at 10 A.M. sharp on the seventeenth to proceed with testimony.

Fenetre's ruling caused frantic scrambling on both sides. Emmanuel Longhouse's immunity deal still not being closed, the prosecution had not begun to prep him. They would have to skip over him and go on to the next scheduled witness, the Finnish urologist, Jaakko Karjalainen.

Accordingly, the defense would have to run down Murray Tartar so that he could be present during Karjalainen's testimony and help Bremmer prepare for cross. And so all that week, both sides prepped their urologists, while Stanley Bluefinch continued unsuccessfully to get Emmanuel Longhouse to agree to the immunity deal being offered to him.

Ralph D'Imbroglio wondered whether they shouldn't arrest Emmanuel Longhouse on breaking and entering in order to prevent him from fleeing again.

"The guy's perfectly capable of taking another powder," he said. "This time he could go to Paraguay."

"He says he's not going anywhere. He wants to speak the truth," Clint Wells replied.

"Maybe he's on drugs. You know those magic mushrooms Indians get loaded on? Let's get him tested."

"I don't know if you can test for mushrooms."

"Call someone over at Controlled Substances and see if there's some sort of mushroom test."

At 10:15 A.M. on Monday, August 17, Dr. Jaakko Karjalainen stood behind an overhead projector with a set of colored pencils, making marks on a diagram projected in the front of the courtroom. There were side-by-side schematic drawings of the flaccid and the erect penis. Using his pencils to trace the flow of blood through the intricate system of veins and arteries, the Finnish urologist explained the basic hydraulics of the male sexual organ.

Jason Rappaport led him through the exposition methodically.

"So, Professor," Rappaport said, "it is true, then, that upon sexual stimulation the arterial flow passes through the entire sinusoidal system, producing tumescence?"

"Yes, sir. That is, until a new systolic equilibrium is produced at about one hundred HG. At that point only threshold amounts of blood flow through the corpora to maintain erection . . ."

"At the point of death, then, this systolic equilibrium would be severely disturbed, would it not?"

"Quite. There would be a complete drainage of the corpora cavernosa, as well as the distal shaft. And the dorsal vein, which connects to the preprostatic plexus, would be compromised . . ."

"Tell me, Professor—how difficult is it to amputate a flaccid penis?"

"Extremely difficult," Dr. Karjalainen said with little change of expression. "In the absence of erection, the arterioles and sinusoids are contracted, thereby presenting soft and malleable targets, well enmeshed within the cartilage and smooth muscle walls of the shaft."

"So that these arterioles would be difficult to sever even with . . . say . . . an electric carving knife?"

"Objection, Your Honor—leading," Susan Bremmer interrupted.

"It may be leading, Counselor, but at least it's leading somewhere. I'll allow it in the interests of saving time." Judge Fenetre leaned over her reading glasses and said to the witness. "You may proceed, Doctor."

"Quite difficult. Unless, of course, the penis were clamped in such a manner as to present an angle to the amputating instrument, which would provide sufficient torque to permit the blade to sever the enmeshed arteries."

"Conversely, Doctor, how much easier would it be to amputate an erect penis?"

"A great deal easier. In tumescence you have not only the prominence of the arterioles and sinusoids close to the surface of the skin, but the organ itself presents an angle that would naturally provide the knife with sufficient torque to sever the organ."

"In your opinion, then, Doctor, it is significantly easier to sever an erect penis than a flaccid penis. Am I correct?"

"Yes."

"Is the existence of an erection *ipso facto* evidence that a man is alive?"

"In the absence of persistent vegetative state, which does not appear likely on the part of a man engaged in sexual intercourse."

There were a few titters in the courtroom. Fenetre banged the gavel down hard.

"So, Doctor, to conclude: Given the fact that the penis was severed by an electric carving knife and given the fact that Dr. Haas had been engaged in sexual intercourse with the defendant immediately preceding the murder, would you conclude that he was in all probability alive at the time his penis was severed?"

"Yes, I would."

"Thank you, Doctor." Rappaport turned toward the defense table and said, with as straight a face as he could muster, "Your witness."

Susan Bremmer approached the lectern with a pad full of notes she had taken during Dr. Karjalainen's testimony.

"Mr. Karjalainen—"

"It's Dr. Karjalainen," the Finn corrected her.

Bremmer turned to Fenetre and said, "Your Honor, would you please instruct the witness to respond only to the questions asked him?"

"Certainly, Counselor, though I would also instruct you to accord the witness the proper respect due him by his credentials."

Bremmer decided to avoid the issue.

"Could the witness please state whether he has any experience as a pathologist?"

"Yes."

"And where was that?"

"In medical school in Helsinki."

"And how long ago was that?"

"Thirty-six years ago."

"While you were in medical school in Helsinki thirty-six years ago, did you study epilepsy? Near-death syndrome? Chronic persistent vegetative state? Coma?"

"Yes."

"Do you have occasion to see any of these conditions in your urology practice?"

"Not often."

"Can you tell us when the last time was that you treated a patient in a coma?"

"I don't recall."

"A person suffering from an epileptic fit?"

"I don't recall."

"A person diagnosed as chronic vegetative?"

"I don't recall."

"So would it be safe to say, *Doctor*, that you really have little practical experience with patients who are in near-death situations?"

"I suppose so."

"And yet you feel comfortable making a judgment about the cause of death of Ernest Haas based on the physiology of the penis?"

"I merely replied to the questions asked me."

"How about replying to this one, then? If a learned physician from Helsinki is unable to clearly establish whether at a given moment a person is dead or alive, how does a traumatized rape victim make that call?"

"Objection! There has been no finding of rape."

"Sustained."

"All right. How does a traumatized abuse victim make that call?"

"I wouldn't know."

"And isn't it the *perception* of whether the rapist—sorry, the abuser—was dead or alive that is material here, not the fact?"

"Objection!" Jason Rappaport's voice rang through the courtroom. "Counsel is trying to make her summation in the guise of cross-examination."

"Sustained." Fenetre looked down admonishingly at Bremmer and said, "Please refrain from posing questions of law to the witness."

But Bremmer had already paraded the question through the courtroom, and she merely said, "No further questions for this witness." As she headed back to the defense table, Susan Bremmer couldn't resist a little smile in the direction of Jason Rappaport.

Carl Furillo scored the round even.

That evening the six o'clock newscasts once again issued disclaimers warning their viewers that there would be material unsuitable for children before broadcasting the day's accounts of the Audrey Haas trial. Newscasters stared back stonily at the TelePrompTer and read words such as *flaccid* and *tumescent* in a tone of voice usually reserved for *inflation* and *Bosnia*. There were more charts and arrows and discussions of arteries, veins, and torque.

But as far as trial watchers were concerned, the forensic urologists were only the warm-up for the main event—the testimony of Emmanuel Longhouse. What he would say and when he would say it were subjects of intense speculation.

The media's attention was squarely on Emmanuel Longhouse. Reporters were sent to Utica to track down anyone who might have known him. Of the nuns who had brought him up, only one was still alive—Sister Ursula Alexandra, a desiccated woman in her nineties, living out her life in an old-age home.

Sister Ursula had very little to say about the young boy she and her fellow nuns had taken in twenty-seven years before.

"He ate a lot," she told ABC's Barbara Walters, in an exclusive interview held on the porch of the nursing home. "He particularly liked creamed spinach. He could eat bowls of it."

That was pretty much the extent of what anybody could find out about Emmanuel Longhouse's past. The media had drawn a blank—with the exception of Lilian Wong, who had become Emmanuel Longhouse's confidante.

It was Lilian Wong who convinced him to cooperate with the district attorney in preparation for his testimony. She explained that he had gotten all the way to the customs booth. There was no point in refusing to open his suitcase now. He was about to be a free man, completely unencumbered by anything but the truth, which was a light burden to carry with one through life.

In spite of the fact that it was emphasized in the news that Emmanuel Longhouse was a witness and not a suspect, there was a general perception that he was being held against his will. The district attorney's office became the site for demonstrations on the part of Native Americans and other disgruntled groups.

FREE EMMANUEL LONGHOUSE signs began to appear outside the courthouse. Keanu Reeves's house was picketed by Native American actors protesting his allegedly being cast in the movie. The Mohawk Nation's public relations coordinator, Gerald Oswego, gave a press conference to call the world's attention to the plight of the Mohawk people—evicted from their land, forced into a diaspora that too often led to poverty, alcoholism, and crime.

As far as Emmanuel Longhouse was concerned, however, his personal diaspora was over. He had arrived in port. At the end of this voyage that had taken him so far, he had found safe harbor.

He would speak out. He would stand baggageless over the dead body of the man without a tomahawk and proclaim his spirit avenged. It was, strangely enough, in this avenging of the stranger whose house he had robbed that Emmanuel Longhouse had found his salvation. No ship's course is truly straight. The race is not to the straight but to the unencumbered.

Chapter 32

"State your name and occupation," the bailiff requested, facing Emmanuel Longhouse and enunciating clearly in spite of the presence of a sign-language interpreter. Even though Emmanuel Longhouse claimed he didn't sign, the nuns in Utica not having deemed it necessary to teach him, D'Imbroglio thought it would be a good idea to have one in court, just to cover all the bases.

In addition to the sign-language interpreter, they had hired Dr. Annette Zaner, an eminent graphologist from New York, to read what Emmanuel Longhouse wrote on his pad.

Accordingly, Dr. Zaner read, "Emmanuel Longhouse. Burglar."

Ralph D'Imbroglio winced, but Emmanuel Longhouse sat straight in the witness chair and looked directly at the bailiff. Now that he had come this far, he wasn't going to backpedal in front of a low-level customs official.

The courtroom was packed to overflow, press passes having been issued to Native American media groups, who claimed priority in the wake of recent events surrounding the trial. Stanley Bluefinch was unable to convince Gerald Oswego that Emmanuel Longhouse was not the best spokesman for Native American rights. The public relations coordinator replied that, on the contrary, the 15/16 Mohawk burglar was a perfect example of what the white culture had wrought in America: a deaf-and-dumb thief.

"We couldn't have a better exemplar of the cultural genocide perpetrated upon us," he told the attorney.

Gerald Oswego sat among the reporters in his buckskins as Jason Rappaport wheeled himself in front of the microphone, lowered it to his level, and began his interrogation.

"Can you tell the court, Mr. Longhouse, how long you have been hearing- and speech-impaired?" Rappaport began, taking care to look directly at the witness and to speak slowly and clearly.

Emmanuel Longhouse took his pen and started to write in his laborious manner. It seemed to take forever for him to finish, tear off the page, and give it to the graphologist.

"Since I came home from school and found my mother breathing gas in the oven," Dr. Zaner read.

"And when was that?"

The process was agonizingly slow. The jury, used to the repartee-like cadence of question-and-answer testimony, were now stuck in the tedious, almost glacial progression of question, writing, verification, response.

Jason Rappaport took Emmanuel Longhouse through a leisurely exposition of his disadvantaged youth, highlighting the Dickensian aspects, before bringing him around to the night he broke into the Haas house.

The prosecution's strategy involved no attempt to hide or even minimize the fact that their witness was an unconvicted felon. It was, according to Jason Rappaport, a judo technique. Use your opponent's strength against him. If they, and not Bremmer, guided Emmanuel Longhouse through the details of the breaking and entering, they would be able not only to control the spin but also to force Bremmer into a repetitiveness that would alienate the jury.

And so Rappaport questioned Emmanuel Longhouse in detail about how he broke and entered—about the choice of the house, the cutting of the glass, the pacifying of Siggy, the trip through the bedroom.

Emmanuel Longhouse wrote and wrote and wrote. The spectators and the jury fidgeted, looked at their watches, looked at Audrey sitting at the defense table in a white sleeveless dress and dangling earrings. In spite of her lawyers' admonitions not to dress alluringly, Audrey had taken to dressing more fashionably. She told them she was tired of seeing herself on TV every night looking like a frump.

When Emmanuel Longhouse got to describing the scene he encountered upon entering the kitchen of the Haases' house, the entire courtroom moved forward in their seats.

As Emmanuel Longhouse handed the pages to the graphologist, the courtroom was dead quiet. Dr. Zaner read them in a loud, clear voice.

"I came into the kitchen. I saw Audrey at the stove. She had a knife in her hand. Then I looked down and saw the man without his dick. He was deader than I've ever seen a man be dead. I looked but couldn't see his dick. I took the carving knife because I could pawn it without Freddie the Fence. Then I gave her some lasagna and Diet Coke. I took the microwave, too. I left and locked the door again so that no one else would break in. I don't know what happened to his dick. The dog was very unhappy."

This disjointed series of sentences had a powerful effect. As is the case with children's testimony in molestation cases, it seemed too specific to have been fabricated. When the graphologist was finished reading, Rappaport waited a moment to let the effect sink in before wheeling himself to the evidence table and picking up the carving knife.

"People's exhibit eight-B," Rappaport announced as he wheeled himself back over to the bailiff and asked him to hand the knife to the witness.

"Can you tell us, Mr. Longhouse, if this is the carving knife that you found in the defendant's hand and that you took and subsequently pawned at Dave's Bait, Tackle, and Pledge Store in Albany the following day?"

Emmanuel Longhouse took the Sunbeam deluxe model 370 multi-purpose carving utensil in his large hands and examined it, then nodded.

"I'm afraid you'll have to answer by writing, not just by nodding, Mr. Longhouse," Rappaport said.

When Dr. Zaner read the word *yes*, it resonated through the courtroom.

The mute eyewitness had spoken. He had put the knife into Audrey's hands. He had pointed his finger squarely at her.

J'accuse!

Emmanuel Longhouse was a hit. The jury was visibly moved by his mute eloquence, his painstaking re-creation of the image of Audrey with the knife, his complete candor in the face of his own guilt. In fact, it was the very inarticulateness of his testimony that made Emmanuel Longhouse so convincing. He was innocent, childlike—a mute and beneficent giant, a hunchback of Notre Dame—in the imagination of people who saw him on the witness stand.

By the time Bremmer got to cross-examine him, he was impervious to her attempts at impeaching him. He had already impeached himself.

Openly, completely, and with dignity. He stood before the court as a repentant sinner who only wanted to tell the truth.

She flailed away at him for two hours—about the burglary, about his drinking, about his flight to Canada—and listened, along with the rest of the courtroom, and the worldwide TV audience, as Dr. Zaner read his simple and disarming responses.

Lizzie Vaught nearly had to drag Bremmer away from the microphone. It was obvious to everybody in the courtroom, with the exception of Susan Bremmer, that she was only sinking deeper into the quicksand.

And so a star was born. That night on TV and the following morning in the press, Emmanuel Longhouse was extolled as a speaker of truth, a man without an agenda, an atavism in a world full of self-interest. Much was made of his refusal to accept an immunity deal and the simple eloquence of his testimony. This deaf-and-dumb transient burglar became the voice of our nation's lost innocence.

So, Emmanuel Longhouse, the end result of four hundred years of cultural genocide, had become not just an exemplar. He had become a role model.

Carl Furillo stood on the courthouse steps and watched Emmanuel Longhouse, flanked by Stanley Bluefinch and Gerald Oswego, emerge into the adulation of the throngs outside on State Street. Reporters shouted questions at him, but Emmanuel Longhouse, as usual, had no comment.

Gerald Oswego had arranged for him to appear at a Native American rights rally on the ceremonial Mohawk burial grounds by the river immediately following his testimony. But Emmanuel Longhouse said he'd just as soon have a beer. And so everyone followed him down to the Endicott Tavern on South Broadway, leaving the reporters and news crews to scramble after them.

Furillo passed on the trek to the Endicott Tavern. He already knew more about Emmanuel Longhouse than he would ever need to know. Sharon Marcuzzi had sent him on a foray to Utica, where he had poked around and come up with nothing. Barbara Walters had already sucked Sister Ursula Alexandra dry. The ex–Mother Superior had tried to hit him up for $500, but when Furillo demanded a taste up front, she fell asleep, snoring in her wheelchair.

He turned around and reentered the building, walking across the rotunda and down the hallway toward the press room. As he rounded the corner, he saw her getting into the elevator, the light bouncing off her calves. By the time he got there, the doors had closed. His eyes followed the floor marker down to P2.

He ran to the stairway and took the stairs, two at a time, to the lower parking level. Swinging the door open, he looked both ways for her.

He listened for the click of her heels against the cement. But all he could hear was the dull hum of the ventilation unit and then the sound of a car ignition. He moved toward the sound, walking down the middle of the exit ramp and around a blind curve.

Suddenly there was a squeal of tires and a flash of headlights. But he didn't give ground. The car braked sharply and came to a stop, its hood ornament six inches from his belly button.

He looked into the headlights and saw her gripping the wheel, fear on her face. He didn't move, just stood there staring at her.

She stuck her head out the window and said, "Jesus, Furillo, I almost hit you."

You already have, Grushenka. You have smitten me with your lilac. I have swum through your dry moat and scaled the walls of your castle. What more can you do to me? Impale me with your hood ornament?

"Are you all right?" she said.

He walked over to her, bent down, and said, "I will be a lot better after two margaritas. There's the world's worst Mexican restaurant on Erie Boulevard. What do you say?"

"I was going to go work out."

"Work out?"

"I had a StairMaster moved into my room. I do three miles a day."

"We need to talk."

"Do we?"

"Well, maybe not *talk.*"

She looked at him, standing by her window amid the car-exhaust fumes, a little boy's grin behind the reporter's noncommittal expression. There were a few strands of hair hanging down over his forehead. She had an urge to reach out and brush them away.

"Where is this dive?"

"I'll show you."

He walked around and got into the passenger seat.

They talked shop and ate nachos through the first two margaritas, sitting in a booth in the dark recesses of the nearly empty restaurant. The waiter kept trying to take their order, but they shooed him away, and he had given up and gone back to watching the day's coverage of the trial.

"Emmanuel was wonderful, wasn't he?" she said.

"He capsized their canoe."

"Rappaport'll eat Audrey for breakfast."

"Eating Audrey is like eating a loose cannon. You may get gunpowder stuck in your teeth."

She drained her margarita, and Furillo called for more. And they drank them, too. The walls of Pablo's Cantina began to undulate gently. She began to hear the creaking of the drawbridge going down.

"You got a girlfriend, Furillo?"

"Nope."

"So you're unattached?"

"Utterly. You, too?"

She nodded.

"I'm sociopathic," he said. "What's your excuse?"

"I don't have the time."

"Hey, why waste time falling in love when you can run around the country chasing Indians?"

"Have you ever been in love, Furillo?"

"Why do you think I'm sociopathic?"

"Don't you ever answer anything seriously?"

"Okay. Here's a serious answer to an unasked question. The margaritas notwithstanding, I may be falling in love with you."

She did not avert her eyes, but looked right back at him, searching for flecks of irony in his dark-brown pupils.

Neither of them spoke for a very long moment. Carl Furillo had just made a declaration of love, and now, in the aftermath, they were wondering where to go from there.

The ball, if there was one, was in her court. It was lying on the table, beside the bowl of nachos. She either picked it up and put it between those beautiful lips or let it die from neglect.

It was one of those moments when the future of two people teeters in the balance. It would have been nicer in a field of lilac or standing on the Pont Neuf watching the sun sink over the Seine. But, as it happened, their moment occurred in a dreadful Mexican restaurant in Schenectady, New York, over a bowl of nachos.

Into this moment came the sound of Lilian Wong's cell phone. It was the wrong sound. His eyes said, Don't answer it.

His fingers found hers across the table. They stared into each other's margarita. The phone kept ringing. She reached into her pocketbook with her free hand, grabbed the phone.

"Yeah?"

A silence, then, "Uh-huh."

More silence, then more uh-huhs.

She refolded the phone, put it back in her pocketbook, looked up at him, and said, "Audrey's taken off."

"What?"

"There were receipts for three thousand dollars' worth of traveler's checks and a passport application in her condo."

"Where'd she go?"

"Mazatlán."

"Mazatlán?"

"They found a Club Med brochure on her coffee table, along with sales receipts for five bathing suits and a straw hat."

Chapter 33

Susan Bremmer had scheduled a meeting Friday evening at Audrey's condo to discuss whether she was prepared to testify in her own behalf when they presented their case Monday morning. She had arrived at 7:30, rung the buzzer several times, then knocked. Concerned about Audrey's mental health, she got the building manager to let her in. When Bremmer saw the brochure and the sales receipts, she knew they were in big trouble.

By the time the lawyer got in her car to race to the Albany County airport in the hope of heading off her client, the building manager had already gone downstairs to call Carrie Castle with the details.

From there it was a race between Audrey and the reporters, as airline route schedules were scrutinized to determine all possible routes from Schenectady, New York, to Mazatlán, Mexico. Every commercial airline that had a flight that could connect, no matter how remotely, to Mazatlán checked its reservations. Credit-card companies scanned their data banks for airline-ticket purchases.

All this was accomplished within hours of Audrey's condo manager's phone call to Carrie Castle. As it turned out, it was a little too late. Audrey's flight arrived at Dallas–Fort Worth Airport about ten minutes before reporters descended upon the arrival gate.

Audrey walked through the terminal in her dark glasses, Hawaiian sundress, and straw hat, oblivious to all this activity going on around her. She had an hour to kill before her flight to Mazatlán, and, thinking she might have a Harveys Bristol Cream on the rocks, she stopped into one of the bars along the concourse. But before she could order the drink, she saw her lawyer looking down at her from a TV monitor suspended from the ceiling.

The attention of everybody in the bar was riveted to the TV screen. Susan Bremmer, wearing one of her peasant skirts and hand-sewn blouses, was avoiding questions shouted at her as she left the Albany County airport.

The screen switched to the CNN anchor desk in Atlanta, where Bernard Shaw reported that Audrey Haas was apparently heading to Mazatlán, Mexico, for a vacation at the Club Med. She was, he said, in violation of her bail agreement not to leave the state, and if she failed to appear in court on Monday, she could be considered a fugitive from justice.

Doing a quick about-face, Audrey left the bar and found a ladies' room. She went into a toilet stall and locked the door. Sitting on the closed toilet seat, her hand luggage at her feet, she let it rip.

After a good cry, Audrey dried her eyes with toilet paper and considered her situation. They were probably watching the baggage claim. She had a suitcase full of tropical dresses, but she would have to do without them now.

There was no way she'd get to Mazatlán without everybody and his brother following her. They'd arrest her in Mexico for bail violation and throw her into one of those adobe prisons, where she'd be gang-raped by the guards.

She decided to make the best of the situation—check into a hotel, spend the night, then do some shopping in the morning before flying home. Opening her bag, she touched up her makeup. God, she looked awful. She hoped they didn't find her tonight.

The press was on red alert all Friday night. As deadlines approached, reporters swarmed around the wire-service tickers hoping for news of Audrey before they had to file their stories. But deadlines came and went, and all they had were the bare bones out of Schenectady.

For sidebars, the networks sent their Mexico City stringers to the Club Med in Mazatlán, where the manager confirmed that he had indeed made a weekend reservation for one person from Schenectady, New York. The name given over the phone was Jane Smith. The ticket clerk at USAir in Albany said a one-way first-class ticket to Chicago, with through-flights to Dallas and Mazatlán on American Airlines, had been booked in the name of Joan Smith and paid for in cash.

And so it went, the flotsam and jetsam of a story that, for the moment, was stalled in sidebars while the story itself was somewhere between Schenectady and Mazatlán.

Furillo sat in the Mexican restaurant, refusing to join in the feeding frenzy. Besides being several margaritas to the wind, he was in no mood for Audrey. Once again she had surfaced at an inopportune moment, barging into the inn just when Grushenka had been on the verge of getting into the sleigh and heading off for his rooms above the railroad station.

Furillo had been left abandoned in Pablo's Cantina with nothing but nacho crumbs and the beginnings of a headache. She had kissed him good-bye and promised to resume their conversation at the first available opportunity.

What conversation? They were beyond conversation. He had declared his love to her. She hadn't said no. They were about to get in the sleigh . . .

His cell phone rang. His heart leapt. She had changed her mind. She would meet him after all in the room above the railroad station . . .

He ripped the phone from his pocket and whispered, "I will hire Gypsies to play all night for us . . ."

"Furillo?"

Sharon Marcuzzi's flat voice bludgeoned his reverie. "I've got you booked on the seven forty-five tomorrow morning out of Kennedy to Mexico City."

He listened as she told him to drive directly to Kennedy, grab a few hours' sleep at the airport Ramada. He would be in Mazatlán by early afternoon local time. She'd hold the deadline for the Monday edition until noon Sunday.

"Sharon," he said, when she finally stopped talking. "I am not going to Mazatlán. I am going to have dinner. Then I'm going to go to sleep."

And he clicked off the phone, opened the battery compartment, and disconnected the power. Then he called the waiter and ordered the *ropa vieja* special and a Dos Equis to chase the margaritas. If he lived till morning, he would no doubt regret it.

Audrey checked into The Four Seasons under the name Jean Smith, paying cash in advance for her $375 suite with a Jacuzzi tub, minibar, large-screen entertainment center, and view of downtown Dallas. She took a bubble bath, ordered a jumbo shrimp cocktail and a Harveys Bristol Cream from room service, and settled in front of the twenty-seven-inch TV screen for the evening.

In the *TV Guide* she found *Anguish of the Heart: The Marla Ginsberg Story*, a TV movie starring Shannen Doherty playing a thoracic surgeon who has to decide whether to pull the life support from her terminally ill eight-year-old daughter. But when she flicked the TV on, instead of getting Shannen Doherty, she got Susan Bremmer standing in front of a bank of microphones.

". . . this trial has been hijacked by the prosecution," Bremmer read from a prepared statement. "The attention of the world has been focused on the plight of Native Americans instead of on the plight of battered women. Judge Fenetre has stood by and allowed the prosecution to present the life story of an admitted burglar, as if he were the downtrodden victim of an unjust world, while all this time sitting at the defense table is the real victim—a woman who has been battered and abused not only by her former husband but by the judicial system and the media. Who can blame her for being unable to shoulder the burden?

"Wherever you are, Audrey, I am appealing to you to come home. On Monday we will begin to present our case and let the jury, not the press, decide who is really guilty here. Women all around the world are with you, Audrey. Don't fail us."

Questions were shouted at Susan Bremmer, but she ignored them and walked away from the podium. In New York, Dan sat at his anchor desk, tieless, his Brooks Brothers blazer unbuttoned.

"That was Susan Bremmer, Audrey Haas's lawyer, live from Schenectady, in a dramatic appeal to Audrey to come back home. Earlier today it was discovered that Audrey Haas had left Schenectady, apparently en route to a Club Med resort in Mazatlán, Mexico.

"It is believed that Audrey may be in Dallas, having flown there from Albany, with a stop in Chicago, and that she decided to abort her trip to Mexico when she learned that the Mazatlán airport was besieged by reporters. She may also be in New York, Mexico City, or Miami.

"Schenectady County District Attorney Ralph D'Imbroglio said earlier this evening that he believes Audrey Haas's one-way airline ticket is a de facto admission that she is planning on jumping bail. At a news conference just before Susan Bremmer's, he said, quote, 'As far as I'm aware, Mexicans don't take any more kindly to dismemberers than Americans do,' end quote. Mr. D'Imbroglio, who is up for reelection in November, has been extremely vocal in his criticism of Susan Bremmer's defense tactics, calling them knee-jerk vigilante feminism . . ."

Audrey hit the remote, surfing the channels until she found a port in the storm.

A black woman, wearing a gray knit dress with a simple gold locket, stood in front of a map of Texas and said that a low-pressure system was drifting east from the panhandle, bringing scattered showers with it.

She was a light-skinned black woman with straightened hair and thin lips. The Weather Channel was apparently an equal-opportunity employer. Audrey thought the dress was a bit severe and needed a touch of color, but she liked the locket.

After the widely publicized videotaping of two well-known baseball players kissing while trying on trousers, the Dallas Neiman-Marcus had decided to put a warning in their changing booths that they were under videotape surveillance.

Upstairs in the security office, two separate banks of monitors, one for the women's changing rooms and one for the men's, were in operation during store hours to make sure the clientele were not putting clothes on under their own and walking out of the store.

At 11:45 Saturday morning, the head of security, H.A.L. "Hal" Porter, was working at his desk, glancing from time to time at the monitors, when Louanne Frizzoner, who worked the women's changing room, popped her head in to say she was going to lunch early.

"Now, don't you go peeking at the girls, Hal," she admonished.

H.A.L. Porter waited till the elevator doors closed before lifting his ass out of the chair and walking down to Louanne's cubicle to peek at the girls. It was one of the few perks of his job, and he wasn't about to pass it up.

As soon as the head of security sat down in front of the monitor, his eye was caught by a woman in changing room 4 trying on a pair of studded Keri Hanover jeans.

"Goddamn . . ." he muttered. He picked up Louanne Frizzoner's phone and dialed the store's assistant manager, Bib Jeeter, and said, "Bib, you ain't going to believe who we got down in Women's Wear."

"Who?"

"Audrey."

"Audrey? We got *Audrey* in the store?"

"Trying on jeans over in Ralph Lauren."

"No shit?"

"I got her right here on the monitor in changing room four."

Bib Jeeter called Debbi Decateur in public relations, who made a fast phone call to Kermit Bracko in Catalogues, and told him to grab his camera and get down to Ralph Lauren ASAP.

By the time Audrey finished trying on the jeans, there was a welcoming committee waiting for her in front of changing room 4. She stepped out into the explosion of flashbulbs and a big Texas smile from Bib Jeeter.

"Welcome to Neiman-Marcus, ma'am," the assistant manager said, as Kermit Bracko fired away and H.A.L. Porter doffed his Stetson. Surrounding them were several salespeople and customers taking advantage of the photo opportunity.

Audrey stood with a half dozen pairs of jeans over her arm, caught up in the clicking of cameras. She managed a smile and looked down at the jeans in her arms. They were just a bit tight in the waist. She handed them to Bib Jeeter.

"Would you happen to have these in a ten?"

Susan Bremmer and Lizzie Vaught were waiting for Audrey at the Albany County airport, surrounded by several hundred reporters and cameras, as Audrey's flight from Dallas, via Chicago, arrived late Saturday night. They hustled her through the madhouse and into Bremmer's Saab.

As they drove along Route 5 toward Schenectady, cars with photographers hanging out of them kept passing on the left and snapping pictures. Audrey pulled her sun hat down low over her eyes to avoid the flashbulbs that went off around her like shrapnel.

They drove in silence for a while, Audrey looking sullenly out the windshield. Finally, Susan Bremmer said, "Audrey, what in god's name possessed you to go to Mexico now? Of all times. Just before we begin to present our case to the jury. Do you know how bad this looks?"

"I'm sorry."

"Didn't I explain to you that the terms of your bail forbid you from leaving the state?"

"Yes."

"Let alone the country."

"It was just Mexico. And I was planning on coming back tomorrow, anyway."

Bremmer caught Lizzie Vaught's eye in the rearview mirror, as if to say, "Go ahead. *You* ask her."

"Audrey," Lizzie Vaught said, "if you were planning on coming back tomorrow, how come you only got a one-way ticket?"

Audrey took her sunglasses off and rubbed her eyes. She was exhausted. The trip to the airport, the flight, the connection at O'Hare, had been an ordeal. Everywhere she turned there were cameras pointed at her. Even in the first-class section of the American Airlines flight from Dallas she caught the hostesses snapping pictures of her.

"The reason we're asking you this, Audrey," Bremmer said, "is that they're probably going to move to have your bail revoked. And it would be helpful if we could tell them you were planning on coming back to appear in court on Monday morning."

"I just needed a vacation, okay?"

"This is hardly the time for a vacation—"

"Can't I even take a simple vacation without people asking me questions? I'm tired of people following me around with cameras. I'm tired of this stupid case. And this stupid judge. And I'm tired of you!"

Chapter 34

While Audrey was still in Dallas, Ralph D'Imbroglio filed a motion to have her bail revoked. And so on the Sunday morning after her return from Dallas, both sides were in Judge Fenetre's chambers to argue the motion. The judge, dressed casually in a mauve muu-muu that helped camouflage her girth, had ordered a deli platter of sandwiches and soft drinks for everyone. She sat behind her big mahogany desk, a pastrami sandwich in her hand, listening as Ralph D'Imbroglio made his case.

"I maintain, Your Honor, that the defendant's going to Mexico without any advance notice to anyone—including, I gather, her own attorneys—is a clear indication that she was attempting to escape the jurisdiction of this court, and that she should be considered, therefore, a flight risk."

Audrey sat there stony-faced between her attorneys as the district attorney elaborated.

"In the absence of her being able to produce a round-trip airline ticket, which I don't believe she can, her behavior is clearly that of a person fleeing from justice. Moreover, I believe that a second criterion for the revocation of bail adheres here—a substantial change in the circumstances of the trial. The fact that recent events have been detrimental to her case, to wit, the testimony of Emmanuel Longhouse, provides additional motivation for flight."

D'Imbroglio concluded, "Your Honor, here it is in a nutshell: We have a defendant clearly going south, along with her case."

Jason Rappaport did his best not to flinch visibly. D'Imbroglio's metaphors often skirted the edge of incoherence. Earlier he had tried to talk him out of moving to revoke Audrey's bail, arguing that it would only create sympathy for her.

"I'm not about to go on record as being soft on bail jumpers," D'Imbroglio had responded.

When Rappaport had pointed out that Audrey Haas was not technically a bail jumper until she failed to appear Monday, D'Imbroglio replied, "Yeah, and Oswald wasn't an assassin until he pulled the trigger."

Fenetre now turned to Susan Bremmer and said, "Counselor, what do you have to say to that?"

"Plenty," Bremmer replied. "I don't believe anyone has the right to infer someone's intentions based solely on circumstantial evidence. Until such time as a defendant actually fails to appear, she cannot be in violation of bail. And my client has never failed to appear in court.

"As far as the district attorney's assertion that there has been a turn of circumstances in the trial unfavorable to my client, I can only say that Mr. D'Imbroglio is not a member of the jury hearing this case but the prosecutor, and that his judgments should be regarded accordingly. The Eighth Amendment, Your Honor," Bremmer concluded, "clearly establishes the right to reasonable bail, and any withdrawal of that bail, based on speculative argument, would constitute cruel and unusual punishment."

Fenetre turned back to Ralph D'Imbroglio. "Any rebuttal, Mr. D'Imbroglio?"

"Just that when the Founding Fathers drafted the Eighth Amendment to the Constitution, Your Honor, I don't think they had a trip to the Club Med in Mazatlán in mind."

Judge Fenetre poured herself a glass of Dr. Brown's cream soda and leaned forward in her chair.

"Mrs. Haas," she asked Audrey, "was this trip to Mazatlán a spur-of-the-moment type of thing?"

"Well, sort of."

"Could you do a little better than *sort of*?"

"I saw this brochure for the Club Med in *Cosmo*. And it looked awfully nice. I'd never been. Ernie didn't like vacations very much. We'd go to urology conventions in, like, St. Louis or Seattle. Anyway, there was an 800 number. So I called, and they sent me a brochure. They had this special weekend promotion—three days, two nights . . . so I called the airlines—"

"When did you call the airlines, Mrs. Haas?" the judge interrupted.

"Let's see . . . today is Sunday. I got back last night. I left on Friday . . . bought the bathing suits and sun hat on Thursday after I got the brochure on . . . Wednesday . . ."

"Wednesday. Two days before you left?"

"Yes. That's why the ticket was so expensive. They really soak you if you travel on short notice."

"How come you didn't buy a return ticket?"

Rappaport watched Audrey's face closely. This was the question upon which the whole argument rested. It went directly to intent.

"Well, I thought about that. But then I thought what if the weather was bad there or what if I didn't like the food. Or what if my attorney told me not to go . . ."

"Did you ask your attorney?"

"No."

"Why not?"

"She would have said no. She's very strict. Anyway, since I was paying full price in any case, I figured it'd give me more flexibility to be able to buy a ticket there when I wanted to come back, you know what I mean?"

Judge Fenetre found herself nodding rhetorically along with Audrey. She took another sip of her cream soda. Then: "Just between us girls, how'd you manage to get to the airport without the reporters spotting you?"

Audrey smiled and then actually blushed.

"You promise you won't tell?"

"Word of honor."

"I took a bus."

"A bus? To the airport?"

"Uh-huh. I went out the service entrance in back, took Vandermeer to State, got on the number sixteen bus to Albany, and got off at the airport."

"With your luggage?"

"It was very light. All I had in it were bathing suits and sundresses."

Judge Fenetre's decision to continue Audrey Haas's bail led off the eleven o'clock news Sunday night. Barney Abelove lay in bed, Renata beside him, watching Carrie Castle standing in front of the Mohawk Towers, where, she explained, Audrey was in residence after an unsuccessful prosecution motion to revoke her bail.

After the standup, they cut away to footage of Susan Bremmer leaving the courthouse with Audrey and Lizzie Vaught. The defense lawyer, in her Sunday flannel shirt and denim skirt, held up her fingers in a Churchillian victory sign before getting into the Saab.

Over this was Carrie Castle's voice saying, "The prosecution's failure to get Audrey's bail revoked could be the first indication of a turnaround in the trial, which has been going badly for Audrey lately. Tomorrow morning the defense begins its case, starting with a forensic rebuttal to the prosecution's argument that the presence of an erection at the time Dr. Haas's penis was severed was *ipso facto* a sign that he was alive."

Abelove lay there, living proof of the contrary. Earlier Renata and he had gone up and down for close to an hour, and he hadn't been entirely there. He hadn't been entirely there for much of anything lately. Renata had suggested a vacation—a trip to Lake George or a weekend in Atlantic City—but Abelove couldn't bring himself to leave Schenectady while the trial was going on.

"Tell you what I think," Renata said. "I think she was planning on going from Mexico to Argentina. Did you know that we don't have an extradition treaty with Argentina?"

Abelove shook his head.

"They said so on *Nightline*. That's why all those old Nazis went there."

"Yeah, maybe she'll cut off Martin Bormann's dick."

"Isn't he dead?"

"You heard what the guy said in court. A guy isn't dead till he loses his hard-on, right?"

Abelove got out of bed and headed for the bathroom.

"You want to know if Martin Bormann's dead," he said, "you got to dig him up and see if he's still at attention."

On Monday the defense's expert forensic witness was called to rebut Dr. Karjalainen's testimony that dead men don't have erections. Dr. Murray Tartar testified that it was possible for a man to maintain an erection for a certain period of time after death. Armed with his own charts showing blood-flow movement to the organ, Dr. Tartar maintained that brain death preceded complete cardiac atrophy and that there were numerous recorded cases of men staying erect long after they were clinically dead.

Rigor-mortis jokes passed through the press corps all day long and into the evening. On Tuesday, in a further attempt to discredit the prosecution's case, the defense called Milton Zieff as a hostile witness and asked the assistant medical examiner a number of pointed questions about the disposition of forensic evidence, principally Ernest Haas's penis.

The jury and spectators listened to Dr. Zieff recount the conversations he'd had with Barney Abelove, the decision to have the dog's fecal matter examined, and the results of those tests.

"So, Mr. Zieff, what was your conclusion as to the disposition of Ernest Haas's penis?"

"I have none."

"Did it vanish into plain air?"

"It may have."

"Is it possible that it could have been removed by the burglar, Emmanuel Longhouse?"

"I suppose so."

"So, to conclude, Mr. Zieff, we have a missing genital organ and inconclusive laboratory test results for traces of the organ in the dog's fecal matter. This leaves us with two additional hypotheses. One, that it vanished into plain air. Or two, that Emmanuel Longhouse took it. Am I correct?"

"Why would he take it?" Milton Zieff said, articulating the question that was on the minds of just about everyone else in the courtroom.

"I suspect that only one person on this earth knows the answer to that question."

And Bremmer turned around and looked pointedly at Emmanuel Longhouse, who was sitting among the spectators. The 15/16 Mohawk Native American hadn't missed a day of the trial since he testified. The prosecution was putting him up at the Holiday Inn in the event that they would need to recall him, and he was running a tab at the Endicott Tavern on South Broadway, where business had never been better.

As it happened, Bremmer's innuendo went right past Emmanuel Longhouse because the lawyer had been facing the witness stand, her back toward the spectators, when she made it, and the deaf-mute did not lip-read backs.

Emmanuel Longhouse met Susan Bremmer's eyes squarely and did not look away. He had no reason to avoid any man or woman's look.

He had already opened his suitcase. They had seen everything. All that was left was the lining.

That moment of visual confrontation between Susan Bremmer and Emmanuel Longhouse provided the drama in the courtroom for the day. It was seen as a showdown, a duel between two conflicting versions of the truth. And once again Emmanuel Longhouse emerged victorious. He had withstood the hot glare of accusation. He was not a dick stealer.

Driving back after adjournment, Lizzie Vaught said to Susan Bremmer, "We're dying up there."

"What do you mean 'dying'? I thought the urologist was pretty convincing."

"The jury's sick to death of penises, erections, arteries, blood vessels . . . I think we should blow off the rest of the forensic case and call Audrey. As soon as possible. Tomorrow."

"There's no telling what she'll say up there."

"We'll coach her."

"She doesn't listen."

"Bremmer, we're not winning on reasonable doubt. We're not winning on the Indian. We're not winning on hard-ons. We only got one shot left."

"Diminished capacity?"

"Self-defense."

"Self-defense? We've just spent two days trying to establish he was dead. How can you kill a dead man in self-defense?"

"The same way you kill a live man—you go for the weapon."

Carl Furillo was in the Henry Hudson Room watching *Wheel of Fortune* on the bar TV when the news that Audrey was going to testify in her own behalf was announced. They cut away from Vanna White to the newsroom, where a breathless Carrie Castle reported that the defense was going to call Audrey Haas to the witness stand.

"Fuck," he muttered. Audrey had done it to him again. Maintaining that one day more or less of forensic evidence about dogshit was not essential to the story, he had convinced Lilian Wong to go on a picnic and rowboat ride on the Mohawk with him. He had arranged for a picnic basket of pâté, cheese, and grapes, along with a cooler containing several bottles of pinot grigio.

So much for a blissful afternoon on the banks of the Mohawk. He reached into his pocket for the cell phone and dialed her room.

"Lilian Wong," she answered.

"She's taking the stand tomorrow."

"When did this break?"

"Thirty seconds ago. Turn on the TV."

"I'm in the bathtub."

"What are you wearing?"

Lilian Wong swam right past that one. "What do you think she's going to say?" she asked.

"Who?"

"Audrey. Is she going to admit she did it?"

Furillo could hear the sloshing of the water as she moved the cell phone from one ear to the other. He could almost smell the lilac bath oil.

"You want some company in the tub?"

"Furillo . . ."

"I could scrub your back."

"I've got to call New York."

"Book time for tomorrow night, right?"

"Right."

"What about the banks of the Mohawk?"

"They'll still be there."

"Think so?"

"Uh-huh. We'll do it while the jury's out."

Furillo began to imagine scaffolding on the side of the castle. And ivy growing through the scaffolding as the years passed and the stone grew colder and grayer.

"God knows when that'll be," he murmured.

She didn't say anything for a moment, then: "Timing is everything, Furillo."

He took a long hit off the beer bottle and turned back toward Carrie Castle. She was wearing a plaid jacket with a Mary Jane collar and a silk scarf. She looked like a born-again Christian bank teller. Furillo wondered just how far down the talent chain you had to be to work as a wardrober on a Schenectady, New York, TV station.

". . . just what Audrey is going to say on the witness stand is anybody's guess," Carrie Castle continued, articulating her diphthongs the way they teach you in broadcaster's school.

"Reached at his home about a half hour ago, District Attorney Ralph D'Imbroglio said, "This is no more than a last-gasp attempt of the defense to obliterate the facts of this case with a fireworks show. And just like fireworks, after they explode, there's nothing there. That's what you'll see in court tomorrow. A lot of flash and a lot of nothing."

Ralph D'Imbroglio could give Yogi Berra a run for his money, Furillo thought, as Carrie Castle, promising details at eleven, returned them to *Wheel of Fortune*.

He knew he should call Sharon Marcuzzi and clear the deadline for Monday's edition. He knew he should have something to eat and then go upstairs and prep the story. Tomorrow was going to be a big day. The entire case was resting in Audrey Haas's shaky hands.

But instead of thinking about Audrey, he was thinking about Lilian Wong. By now she'd be out of the bathtub, powdered and perfumed, working the phones. He saw her sitting on the bed wrapped in a towel, her hair up, the cell phone at her ear, calling in the artillery.

The drawbridge was up again, the moat dry. He stared up at the tower for a moment, then, jerking the reins and digging in his spurs, he rode on to pitch his tent in the cold meadow.

Chapter 35

There was a sudden breathless silence when Audrey Haas entered the courtroom a little before ten o'clock on Wednesday morning, September 9. Every eye and every camera followed her as, flanked by her lawyers, she walked to the defense table.

She was wearing a light beige Ellen Tracy suit, a powder-blue silk blouse, a tan Gucci scarf, and a pair of off-white Joan Ryan shoes. At midnight, after nearly six hours of reviewing every question they would ask and every answer she would give, Susan Bremmer and Lizzie Vaught had made the wardrobe selection.

Audrey had wanted to wear a blue tweed Calvin Klein jacket with padded shoulders. "It was one of Ernie's favorites," she said. "He wore it with a white mini and black spiked heels."

But the lawyers had prevailed on her to wear something less evocative of her late husband.

"Ernie would have wanted you to wear the Ellen Tracy," Lizzie Vaught had assured her.

The reviews were mixed. *Women's Wear Daily* reported that it was one of the few times during the trial that Audrey was well dressed, though they thought that the Joan Ryan shoes were a little too light in color for the outfit. *Madame Figaro* pronounced the ensemble *"Un peu fade et mal conçu étant donné les circonstances."*

Audrey sat down at the table, looked over the jammed courtroom, and nodded to her parents, who were sitting, as always, in the first row, directly in front of Janice Meckler, who hadn't missed a day of the trial, either. The Motor Vehicle Bureau smog-inspection-sticker-compliance supervisor was wearing a burgundy linen suit and pink sweater—another outfit, as it happened, that Ernest Haas had enjoyed wearing.

Judge Fenetre was in one of her extra-large judicial robes, which she ordered from a mail-order place that specialized in larger women's professional uniforms. The judge gaveled the court to order and recognized Susan Bremmer, who got up and approached the microphone.

Lizzie Vaught had been working on Susan Bremmer's wardrobe as well, trying to get her out of her folksy feminist statements and into something a bit more attractive—in this case, a pale-green shirtwaist dress with a large tortoiseshell belt.

Bremmer cleared her throat and announced in her most dramatic voice, "The defense calls Audrey Haas."

As Audrey walked to the witness stand, she kept her shoulders square and her head as high as she could. She stood stiffly as the bailiff swore her in, then sat down. She started to cross her legs, but remembered Bremmer told her she shouldn't, and quickly uncrossed them.

"Ms. Haas," Bremmer began, "would you state your name and occupation?"

"Audrey Roberta Haas," she said. "Homemaker."

"How long had you been married to Ernest Haas?"

"Eleven years."

"And would you consider it to have been a happy marriage?"

"Yes, until about five years ago."

"What happened five years ago that had such a negative impact on your marriage?"

"My husband started to wear women's clothes."

"Did he wear women's clothes all the time?"

"No. Only when we had sex."

"How often did this occur?"

"A couple of times a month."

"So several times a month, Ernest Haas would force himself on you—"

"Objection. Counsel is putting words in the witness's mouth," Jason Rappaport said, firing his first volley of the day.

"Sustained."

"Was this sex consensual?"

"Well, not always."

"So sometimes you didn't want to have sex with him?"

"Right. Sometimes I was tired or I didn't want to go out to the garage for sex."

"So several times a month Ernest Haas would come home, put on women's clothes, and . . . have sex with you in inappropriate places against your will?"

"Yes."

"In other words, he raped you—"

"Objection. Conclusory."

"Your Honor, rape is any form of involuntary sexual activity—"

"Would counsel approach the bench," Fenetre ordered.

Rapport wheeled himself forward and sat there beside Bremmer as Fenetre asked her, "Where are you going with this, Ms. Bremmer?"

"I'm trying to show a consistent pattern of sexual abuse."

"Then use the word *abuse* and not *rape*. Unless you're prepared to offer unequivocal testimony that Ernest Haas was a rapist. I don't like impeaching dead people in my courtroom. They can't fight back."

Bremmer returned to her microphone and was passed a note from Lizzie Vaught, which read, GET TO MARCH 27.

"Moving to the night of March twenty-seventh, did Ernest Haas dress up in women's clothes that night?"

"Yes."

"Did he ask you whether you wanted to have sex that night?"

"No."

"What did he say?"

"Nothing. He just disappeared into the bedroom after dinner and came out wearing the clothes."

"Did he have anything special with him, besides the clothes?"

"Yes. A pair of handcuffs."

Susan Bremmer went over to the evidence table, where the handcuffs the police found in the Haases' kitchen were.

"Defense exhibit thirteen," she announced, before bringing the handcuffs over and handing them to Audrey.

"Are these the handcuffs he used that night?"

"Yes."

"Are these handcuffs specially designed for use in sadomasochistic sex acts?"

"Yes. He got them in the mail from a sex-novelty place in Santa Monica, California."

"What did he do with the handcuffs?"

"He put one end on my wrist and the other on the handle of the stove. It's an O'Keefe and Merritt antique stove that we had specially refinished—"

"Did you object?"

"Yes. I mean, I didn't see any reason why we had to . . . do it standing up in the kitchen. We had a perfectly good bed in the bedroom."

"So Ernest Haas shackled you to the kitchen stove with handcuffs he got from a sadomasochistic mail-order house in California and forced you to have nonconsensual sex with him while he was dressed in women's clothes. Is that correct?"

"Yes."

"And did you proceed with this humiliating and abusive activity?"

"Yes, I did."

"Until what point?"

"Well, until Ernie . . . until he . . . got off . . ."

"Ejaculated?"

"Yes."

Bremmer paused for a moment to allow her client to collect herself. They were about to enter the minefield. Bremmer took a deep breath and plunged in.

"After your late husband ejaculated, Ms. Haas, what happened?"

"Well, there was this sudden shudder through his whole body and then he just stopped moving. Completely. He just sort of froze up."

"Like he was dead?"

"Objection. Leading."

"Sustained."

"Froze up like what, Ms. Haas?"

"Like he was dead."

"And what did you think?"

"I didn't know what to think. He'd never done that before. Usually, well, usually he would . . . kind of whimper and whisper things in my ear and . . . well, he was usually very grateful . . ."

"But this time he didn't say anything?" Bremmer cut her off before she shared too many details of their affectionate sexual intimacy.

"No. He was dead quiet. I couldn't even hear him breathing."

"What did you do then?"

"I called his name. I shouted it into his ear. I pinched him, hard . . ."

"What else did you do?"

"Else?"

"Yes. Didn't you do something else?"

"Oh, right. I checked his pulse."

"And was there any?"

"No. I couldn't find any at all."

"What conclusion did you reach after you were unable to locate a pulse?"

"That he was dead."

"Then what did you do, Ms. Haas?"

"I tried to get loose. I pushed with all my might and then I tried to wriggle out from under him, but he was just too heavy and his . . . his thing was wedged inside me. It was like we were bolted together down there."

"So you did your best to escape, and when you were unable to, what did you do?"

"Well, then I cried."

"For how long did you cry?"

"I don't know, fifteen, twenty minutes, maybe."

"And then?"

"I started to think about what to do. I couldn't reach the phone to call for help. I couldn't reach the refrigerator or the sink to get anything to eat or drink. The keys to the handcuffs were on the table in the plate with the soy-sauce packets. All I had was the TV remote."

"Did you think about someone coming to rescue you?"

"Well, that was the problem. It was Friday night. We had no plans for the weekend except maybe to go bowling Saturday night. Doltha wasn't due until Wednesday, and by then I probably would have died of starvation, not to mention Siggy, who had nothing to eat, either."

"So you acted to save your life and your dog's life?"

"Objection. Counsel is completing witness's sentences for her."

"Try to be a little more circumspect, Ms. Bremmer," said Fenetre, peering over her glasses.

"What was your plan then?"

"I thought if I could somehow get free of Ernie, I could reach the drawer with the knives and cut myself free. But I couldn't move with him on me. And then I started to feel his skin get cold. That's what really freaked me out. I thought that he was going to start to . . . to decay right on top of me. I decided that if I was going to die from starvation, I didn't want to die attached to a dead man. I mean, the thought of being riveted to a dead man, even if it is your own husband . . ."

And Audrey started to cry. Right on cue. It wasn't rehearsed. The sense memory was enough to set her off. She cried for a good minute. In the jury box the pregnant woman cried along with her. Rappaport began to envision nooses around the necks of the jury.

After Audrey stopped crying and dried her eyes with a monogrammed Georgina Lindsey handkerchief, there was dead silence in the courtroom. You couldn't even hear the usual low background noise of laptop keyboards clicking. There was nothing, as Jason Rappaport was to say later, but the sound of hormones secreting.

"And so, locked in a death embrace with a decomposing body and acting out of fear for your own life and that of your dog, you removed the weapon that had you pinioned naked against your stove, using the only means available to you—the electric carving knife that you had purchased from the Home Shopping Network three months before?"

"Yes. That's what I did. And I'd do the same thing again."

Bremmer allowed the words to sink in before turning to the judge and saying, "No further questions."

Fenetre gaveled a lunch recess before the beginning of cross-examination, and Audrey rose from the witness stand and returned to the defense table. D'Imbroglio turned to Jason Rappaport and asked, "Anybody on the jury got a dog?"

"I don't know."

"Because we just lost the fucking dog lovers . . ."

Though Audrey's testimony had gone off better than she had anticipated, Susan Bremmer wasn't ready to pop champagne corks just yet. Jason Rappaport would get Audrey after lunch, and that wasn't going to be a pretty sight.

"Just remember, Audrey," she reminded her client, "your three best answers under cross-examination are 'yes,' 'no,' and 'I don't recall.' "

"Can I cry if he gets unpleasant?"

"Just don't overdo it. Once'll probably be enough. Toward the end."

Meanwhile, in D'Imbroglio's office, Jason Rappaport, Martha Demerest, Clint Wells, and the district attorney were huddling over lunch.

"Whatever you do, Rappaport, don't make it look like you're bullying her," Martha Demerest said.

"Bully her? *Moi?*"

"Yes. You can be very sarcastic."

"Just nail her on premeditation," interjected D'Imbroglio. "Rush to judgment. The body wasn't even cold yet. I mean, the guy's cock was still hard. She said so herself. Hammer her on the cock and then go for the carving knife. See if you can get her to describe exactly how she cut it off. Ask her to hold the knife and demonstrate."

"Fenetre won't allow it."

"Why not? They allowed O.J. to try on the gloves, didn't they?"

While both sides were caucusing, the early-afternoon news reporters were trying to determine how much of the cross-examination they could cover before deadline; the evening-news crews were already going over film from the feed to lay in the sound bites; and Carl Furillo was watching Lilian Wong on her cell phone maneuvering to get Jason Rappaport right after the cross-examination.

He had never met a woman who looked so good with a cellular phone to her ear. If they ever got to do it, he would ask her if they could do it while she was on the phone.

The very thought of possessing Lilian Wong while she was on the phone was enough to distract Furillo throughout most of the afternoon, which featured the long-awaited cross-examination of Audrey Haas. He may have been the only person in the courtroom who wasn't hanging on every word.

Jason Rappaport began with some small-arms fire around the perimeter, just to loosen things up a bit.

"You mentioned this morning, or, to be more precise, your attorney mentioned, that you engaged unwillingly in certain sexual activities with your late husband. Is that correct?"

"Yes."

"For approximately five years?"

"Yes."

"During this period of five years, in which you allege that your late husband forced you to engage in certain sexual acts against your will, did you ever seek outside help?"

"I don't recall."

"Let me be more specific. Did you ever call the police to inquire about pressing charges of spousal abuse against him?"

"No."

"Did you ever complain about these practices to friends or relatives?"

"No."

"Did you ever seek out the help of one of the many groups and organizations for abused and battered women, whose 800 numbers are listed in telephone books and on billboards all over the country?"

"No."

"If these activities were so abusive, Mrs. Haas, why is it that you never expressed dissatisfaction about them to anybody?"

"I don't recall."

"You don't recall having spoken of these activities, or you don't recall why it was you never spoke of them?"

"I don't recall."

"Your Honor, the witness is using *I don't recall* for questions she simply doesn't want to answer. By testifying in her own behalf she has already waived Fifth Amendment protection against self-incrimination."

"The witness is directed to address the question more specifically."

"What was the question again?" Audrey asked.

The court reporter read back the question.

"Both."

"You neither recall having spoken of these activities *nor* why you didn't speak of them?"

"Right."

"Mrs. Haas, do you recall the reason you're on trial?"

"Objection. Badgering the witness."

"Excuse me, Your Honor, but I just wanted to ascertain the extent of the defendant's memory loss. I withdraw the question."

"Moving right along . . . now, Mrs. Haas, you said that after Dr. Haas ejaculated, you attempted to determine whether he was still alive before you cut off his penis. Is that correct?"

"Yes."

"And you testified that you shouted into his ear, pinched him, and checked for a pulse. Then you concluded he was dead and decided to cut off his penis because it was impeding your ability to get to the drawer where the knives were, which, you claimed in your testimony, you wanted to cut yourself loose with. Is that correct?"

"Well, actually, I had forgotten about the carving knife until I saw an ad for one on the Home Shopping Network."

"You were *watching television* while this was happening?"

"The TV was on."

"Let me understand this. You testified this morning that you were so frightened and disgusted at the thought that your husband might be dead that you panicked. Nevertheless, you still had the presence of mind to watch a TV ad for an electric carving knife?"

"The sound was very loud."

"Didn't the remote have a volume control?"

"I was too upset to think."

"But not upset enough, apparently, to prevent you from listening to an ad about electric carving knives, were you?"

"Objection. Badgering."

"Mr. Rappaport, please refrain from posing rhetorical questions."

"All right. So now you hear about the electric carving knife on TV, and this suggests a solution to you—get to your electric carving knife in the drawer and cut yourself free with it. Was this your thinking?"

"Yes."

"Then you managed to maneuver yourself to the drawer and get a hold of the electric carving knife you saw advertised on the Home Shopping Network, which you were watching while having sex with your husband? Is that correct?"

"Yes."

"Now, you plug in the electric carving knife in the outlet above the stove, which you manage to reach in spite of your shackles, and you cut your husband's penis off. Is that correct?"

Audrey nodded, then crossed her legs and looked at Bremmer. She wondered whether this was the time to cry.

"Your Honor, would you direct the witness to answer verbally."

"Yes," Audrey said in a barely audible voice.

"Did it occur to you, Mrs. Haas, to use that same carving knife with which you severed your husband's penis to sever the handcuff chains that were binding you to the stove?"

"It's not made for handcuffs. It's made for cutting poultry."

"Well, presumably it wasn't made for cutting penises either, but it did the trick, didn't it?"

"Objection, Your Honor!" Bremmer roared.

"I'll withdraw the question," Rappaport said.

"What question?" retorted Bremmer, and the judge gaveled them quiet.

"So, Mrs. Haas, after using the carving knife that was advertised on the Home Shopping Network to cut off your husband's penis, did you then try to cut the handcuff chain with another implement from your kitchen drawer?"

"No . . . I mean, I couldn't reach the drawer—"

"Pardon me, but didn't you manage to reach the drawer to get the carving knife?"

"I meant the . . . table with the keys or the telephone—"

"So, cutting off your husband's penis to be free wasn't such a hot idea after all, was it?"

"Objection!"

"Mr. Rappaport, I don't want to have to warn you again about rhetorical and inflammatory questions."

"I'm sorry, Your Honor, but the witness doesn't seem to want to answer the questions."

"I'll be the judge of that," Fenetre retorted.

Rappaport turned back toward Audrey and wheeled himself a little closer.

"All right. You were able to do nothing, you claim, until Mr. Long-house arrived. Then what did you do?"

"I tried to get him to let me loose."

"Did you ask him to see if your husband was still alive?"

"No."

"How come?"

"He was obviously dead."

"Did you ask him to call the police?"

"He was a burglar. He wouldn't have called the police."

"He apparently fed your dog and then provided lasagna and Diet Coke for you, which was something most burglars wouldn't bother doing. Didn't that give you a somewhat different picture of him?"

"I don't recall."

"So you asked him to let you loose. Anything else?"

"I asked him to get my Prozac."

"Your medication?"

"Yes."

"And did he?"

"No."

"So you merely watched him feed your dog and put the lasagna in the microwave. Is that it?"

"I was afraid he was going to rape me."

"Rape you?"

"Yes."

"And why was that?"

"Well, you know . . ."

"No, I don't know. Could you tell us?"

Bremmer tried to catch Audrey's eye as she saw her client approach the land mine, but Audrey wasn't looking in her direction.

"Well, he was very big. And he had an earring."

"Is it your judgment, then, that most large men with earrings are rapists?"

"He was an Indian—"

Audrey's words exploded in the courtroom. She had stepped right on the mine, and it had blown up in her face, scattering bomb fragments everywhere.

Eyes turned toward Emmanuel Longhouse, who had been sitting there lip-reading her testimony. The six-foot-five-inch Native American with the small pearl earring in his left ear rose from his seat. Glaring directly at Audrey over the turned faces of the spectators, he spoke for the first time in twenty-seven years.

"Shame," he said. And then he repeated the word several times in a high, lilting incantation that settled over the courtroom like a divine judgment.

Emmanuel Longhouse continued to cry, "Shame!" until he was removed from the courtroom by the bailiff. Outside on the steps of the courthouse and in their parked buses listening to the trial on portable TVs were all the Native Americans who had come to Schenectady for the trial. Emmanuel Longhouse stood at the top of the steps, his raised fist high in the air, shouting, "Shame!"

Before long State Street was filled with a thousand voices crying, "Shame!" Their voices carried back inside the courtroom, where Jason Rappaport, recognizing a good exit line when he heard one, said that he had no further questions to ask the witness.

Chapter 36

EMMANUEL SPEAKS! was the headline plastered across the front page of more than one newspaper following the dramatic interruption of Jason Rappaport's cross-examination of Audrey Haas by the formerly deaf-mute Native American. The *Albuquerque Journal* preferred the simple, one-word headline SHAME! *The New York Times* gave it three columns on page 1: HAAS CROSS-EXAMINATION INTERRUPTED BY ANGRY WITNESS, and in the subhead: TRIAL THROWN INTO TURMOIL BY RACIAL SLUR.

The full effect of Jason Rappaport's searing cross-examination was buried in the fallout from the explosion caused by Audrey Haas's remark and Emmanuel Longhouse's response. There were suddenly two new ingredients to the already murky moral stewpot that the Audrey Haas trial had become: racism and duplicity.

There was not much you could do with Audrey's blatant implication that Indians are rapists. It stood out there, naked and indefensible, to be embraced by no one except the hard-core racists. Even though she maintained, in a prepared statement given to the press a half hour after adjournment, that she had "never discriminated against any person according to race, gender, color, sexual preference, or religion," Audrey had taken a serious self-inflicted shot across her own bow.

But it was Emmanuel Longhouse's sudden regaining of the power of speech that was more widely debated by the spinmeisters. Interpretations ran the gamut from it being a miracle brought on by his conversion from thief to exemplar, to a sudden unblocking of the psychological trauma caused by his mother's suicide twenty-seven years before, to a cynical manipulation of the trial, the media, and the world.

It was this latter theory—that Emmanuel Longhouse had never really lost the power of speech and hearing but had only pretended to be a deaf-mute in order to lessen his own guilt and garner sympathy from the jury—that mitigated the damage caused by Audrey's testimony. Proponents of this theory went even further, implying that the prosecution had been aware of Emmanuel Longhouse's ability to speak all along and had capitalized on it, that it had all been disingenuous—the eleventh-hour appearance in St. Catharines, the return to Schenectady, the public refusal to sign an immunity deal, the bad spelling, the graphologist.

SHAME ON *YOU*, EMMANUEL! was the headline of one Boston tabloid, convinced that his disability was a sham. There were calls to force him to undergo medical tests to discover if he really had been unable to speak and hear all this time. There was pressure on D'Imbroglio to arrest him on the original burglary charge. There was a deluge of demands that he speak out and explain himself.

But Emmanuel Longhouse had nothing more to say. After his outburst in court and his incantation from the top of the courthouse steps, he repaired to the Endicott Tavern and had no comment for anyone except the bartender—he asked for a Narragansett in his usual manner of raising an imaginary bottle to his lips. Even Stanley Bluefinch, his putative attorney, could get nothing more out of him. Fighting his way through the throngs of Native Americans who had crowded into the Endicott Tavern to drink to their spokesman's health, the lawyer elbowed his way to the bar.

"Emmanuel, what happened?"

His client put his arm around his shoulder and signaled for the bartender to set him up with a Narragansett. And that was that. Have a beer. Turn on the ball game.

D'Imbroglio, meanwhile, was completely baffled by the turn of events. His spin guy told him that the talking Indian pretty much balanced out the rapist remark.

"It looks like a push to me," the spin guy said. "You lost whatever Indian vote you were going to get, which, between you and me, you could do without. You're probably going to pick up five to ten percent with women and maybe fifteen percent with minorities, and I don't think the needle moved on the religious right."

D'Imbroglio hung up and called Jason Rappaport at home.

"What do you want to do?" he asked his lead prosecutor.

"There's nothing to do until we find out if Bremmer's going to put her up there again for redirect."

"What if she tries to recall the Indian?"

"On the basis of what—that he can speak?"

"Yeah. New circumstances."

"I don't see how it alters his testimony whether he speaks it or writes it."

There was a pause on the line, then, "Rappaport, do you think we should make a statement about the Indian?"

"What kind of statement?"

"That he never spoke to us, that he was mum as a . . . cigar-store Indian."

"Probably not a good idea."

"You don't think so?"

"I think 'cigar-store Indian' is one of those terms you ought to put in your paper shredder, Ralph."

"Jesus, what *can* you say these days?"

"Not much."

The ball was very much in the defense's court. That evening Susan Bremmer and Lizzie Vaught debated whether to call Audrey for redirect, to call Janice Meckler to impugn Ernest Haas's reputation further, or simply to rest and go out with a blazing closing argument.

"What is Audrey going to say on redirect?" Lizzie Vaught argued. "That she didn't really mean to imply that Indians were rapists?"

"That Rappaport put words in her mouth."

"The question was, if I recall, 'Why did you think he was going to rape you?' "

"He was inflammatory."

"Of course he was. That's his job. Look, I think all we do is put a mustache on it by bringing it up in redirect. We put Audrey up there again, and god knows what she's going to say this time."

Bremmer sat back in her swivel chair and rubbed her eyes. She was exhausted. They had been doing damage control since adjournment—on the phone to the networks trying to tiptoe through the carnage Audrey had left in her wake.

"It was an ill-thought remark brought on by the stress and exhaustion of the trial," she had told Larry King by telephone on his coast-to-coast show.

A full-blooded Shawnee woman from West Virginia called in wanting to know why, if Audrey was so stressed out and exhausted by the trial, she looked like she spent two hours getting dressed every day.

"As a woman," Bremmer had responded, "Audrey Haas has been subjected to sexism and discrimination her entire life and would never indulge in it herself."

"Cowshit," the full-blooded Shawnee woman said, and Larry King went directly to commercial.

Now, as she sat in her office with Lizzie Vaught and Cissy Weiner, staring morosely over take-out Chinese food, she wondered if she had the strength to go on.

"Why don't we just throw her on the mercy of the goddamn court," she muttered. "We're defending a racist bimbo whose ambition in life is to be on the Weather Channel."

Lizzie Vaught and Cissy Weiner exchanged a concerned look. For the first time since the beginning of the case, Susan Bremmer was sounding like a defeatist. Now, at the eleventh hour, just before closing arguments, she wanted to throw in the towel.

"You want me to close?" Lizzie Vaught asked gingerly.

Bremmer got up and stretched painfully. The taste of sesame oil rose in her throat. She looked at Lizzie Vaught, drop-dead gorgeous in her Donna Karan suit at 10:30 at night after fourteen hours of work and a take-out Chinese dinner, and shook her head.

"I opened this goddamn case, and I'm going to close it," she announced, and, stuffing her notes into her hand-woven Schenectady Battered Women's Shelter briefcase, she walked out the door.

The networks sent their top people back to Schenectady for closing arguments. The press section was a veritable who's who of the fourth estate. Lilian Wong, of course, managed to get a seat between Dan and Peter and directly in front of Ted and Barbara.

Furillo was three rows back, sitting between Dominick Dunne and Katarina Witt, who was covering the trial for *Der Spiegel*, so he could admire Lilian Wong's beautifully tailored charcoal-gray Florence Cromer blazer only from the back.

Whatever doubts the defense attorney may have had about her client the night before, she appeared to have buried them this morning. At 10 A.M. in Section 63 of the Schenectady County Courthouse, Susan Bremmer, looking almost stylish in a dark-green corduroy suit, was loaded for bear. She came through the door with both guns blazing and didn't let up for hours.

"Ladies and gentlemen of the jury," she began, "this trial is not about the rights of Native Americans or about the racial attitudes of Audrey Haas. Nor is it about the behavior of the male sex organ upon death, the matching of an electric carving knife, the disposition of a dead man's body parts, or the laboratory analysis of a dog's fecal matter, no matter how much the prosecution would like you to believe it is.

"This trial is about the basic right of a woman to defend herself against a man who regularly came home at night, put on women's clothes, and forced her to have sex with him in dangerous and insalubrious venues.

"Specifically, this trial is about the night of March twenty-seventh, when this man came home and chained his wife to her own stove, in wanton disregard of her safety as well as her inalienable right not to be forced to have sex against her will with any man, including her husband, a right specifically protected by the Thirteenth Amendment's proscription against involuntary servitude, and used her as a vessel for his own aberrant desires.

"This trial is about the basic right that Audrey Haas, or any other citizen of this country, has to defend herself against this behavior and take whatever remedy may be available to her, under the circumstances . . ."

Furillo listened to Susan Bremmer depict Ernest Haas as a modern-day Marquis de Sade—a sex criminal, wife-batterer, and all-around shit—while simultaneously elevating Audrey to the role of the martyred Saint Everywoman, chained to her proverbial stove—used, abused, penetrated, impaled upon the very instrument of her subjugation.

It was pretty strong stuff, and the jury sat there trying to digest it all, their emotions riddled by the incendiary devices fired off by the little defense attorney with the big mouth. By the time Bremmer was through with Ernie, he was not only dickless but heartless, gutless, and ruthless.

"And so I appeal to you," Bremmer said in her eagerly anticipated peroration, "to put aside your prejudices and affirm the basic right of a woman not to be abused. By reaching a verdict of not guilty, you have it in your power not only to vindicate Audrey Haas but also to vindicate the system that so unfairly indicted her in the first place. I am confident that you won't disappoint us."

Bremmer left the microphone to the vacuous silence of the entire courtroom, their breath momentarily taken away by the grandiloquence of her language. She walked slowly back to the table and took her seat between Lizzie Vaught and Audrey.

Judge Fenetre gaveled a lunch recess in order to spare the jury another closing statement on an empty stomach. Bremmer turned to the woman whom she had just finished martyrizing and said, "I think it went very well, don't you?"

Audrey nodded, then said, "You think there's enough time to go over to the Pizza Hut on Van Buren?"

Jason Rappaport wheeled himself to the microphone, lowered it to chair level, then made a three-quarters turn to face the jury box. He verified the location of the pregnant woman, sighting her for eye contact, before beginning.

"Ladies and gentlemen," he said, "you must be pretty confused by now. You must be wondering just who's on trial here. After listening to my distinguished opposing counsel's closing argument, I'm wondering, too. Are we trying Audrey Haas? Or are we trying Joan of Arc?

"The point, ladies and gentlemen, is that it doesn't matter. It's not who you are; it's what you did. You can be a bag lady or the Queen of Sheba—it makes no difference. You are answerable to the law.

"Since the beginning of this trial, the defense has labored to describe Audrey Haas as the victim of a pattern of sexual abuse on the part of her late husband. Between you and me, I don't think that long-standing relations between consensual adults, no matter how exotic, constitute sexual abuse. But let me for the sake of argument concede them this point. Let's say that Audrey Haas was intimidated, forced, cajoled, or what have you, to engage in sex with her cross-dressing husband while handcuffed to the stove.

"Forget the fact that, according to her own testimony, she had done it countless times before. Forget the fact that she never once complained to anybody about this manner of sexual relations. This particular night she didn't want to do it. She wanted to watch television instead of making love to her husband standing up in the kitchen. In any event, at the critical moment her husband suffers what appears to be some sort of seizure. She checks his pulse. She cries for a while. Then what does she do? Struggle to get free, so that she can call 911? Scream, so that a neighbor might hear and come to the rescue? Wait, on the off chance that someone just might arrive, as in fact someone did a few hours later? No. Audrey Haas hears them advertising an electric carving knife on TV, relates it to the Thirteenth Amendment to the Constitution's proscription against involuntary servitude, and cuts her husband's penis off.

"Ladies and gentlemen, though I wasn't there when they drafted the Thirteenth Amendment to the Constitution, I don't think they had this in mind."

He paused briefly for rhetorical effect before going on. "Now, according to the medical examiner's report and subsequent testimony, Dr. Haas's death took place sometime between nine P.M. and midnight. We have the testimony of an eyewitness that when he arrived on the premises at approximately midnight, the penis had already been severed. So, let's put an hour on that, just to be conservative. At one A.M. Ernest Haas's penis is gone. According to the defendant's testimony, she and her husband began having sex at a quarter to nine. On the outside, then, we have just over four hours elapsing between Ernest Haas's ejaculation and seizure and his wife's severing of his penis."

Locking his eyes on the pregnant woman, he moved in for the kill. "Let me ask you something—how long do you wait before dismembering someone you love? Four hours? Four days? Four years? There are people who have waited a lifetime, nursing and tending to their tragically ill mates. There are people who have died along with their loved ones rather than do anything that might jeopardize their chances of survival.

"Ladies and gentlemen," he said slowly and gravely, "I have been disabled since the cab I was riding in hit a guard rail on the West Side Highway in New York and tumbled into the Hudson River. The reason I am disabled and not dead is that the driver of that cab, an African-American, as it happened, and a man whom I had never met before and with whom I had not spoken beyond communicating my destination, took the time to pull me out of the water. He didn't think about his own safety or the lifelong abuse he had suffered at the hands of the white man. He didn't think about how awful it might be if he died in the clutches of a drowning man, how it would feel to touch the skin of a dead man. He didn't think about the Thirteenth Amendment.

"I hadn't been married to this man for eleven years. I hadn't slept in the same bed with him and shared my meals and the joys and sorrows of life. I hadn't been his life partner. All that mattered to him was that I was a fellow human being."

Rappaport could feel the estrogen seeping out of the jury box. He slowly squeezed the trigger.

"Ladies and gentlemen, when you go into that room to begin your deliberations, think about that man. Compare him to the defendant. Ask yourself this: Shouldn't Ernest Haas have expected more from his wife than four hours of discomfort? Didn't he deserve more than a few tears and the carving knife?

"By finding Audrey Haas guilty of having killed her husband with depraved indifference to his well-being, you will restore to him, albeit posthumously, one last shred of human dignity. Which, sadly, is all that Ernest Haas has left now."

Rappaport held the pregnant woman's eyes an extra half second before wheeling himself back to the prosecution table amid the hushed silence of the courtroom.

Fenetre gaveled a twenty-minute recess before jury instruction. As reporters rushed to the press room to plug in their modems, Clint Wells watched Jason Rappaport wheel himself toward the handicapped-accessible men's room, passing the throngs of reporters shouting questions at him. Then Wells turned to Martha Demerest and asked, "You ever hear about the cab driver?"

She shook her head. "I've heard about the truck driver and the pregnant woman, though."

"Huh?"

"Last year in a multiple homicide, a Hispanic truck driver pulled him out of the Mohawk. Couple of years ago in a rape case, a pregnant woman pulled him out of a burning Amtrak car."

"You mean, it never happened?"

"Oh, it happened, all right. Half a dozen times at least."

She loaded her notes into her briefcase, and, as she turned toward the door, she said, "In fact, I wouldn't be surprised if it keeps happening."

Jury instruction was short and sweet. Judge Fenetre was not a woman to waste words. She began with the boilerplate instruction that the burden is on the prosecution to prove its case beyond a reasonable doubt and went on to restate the criteria for a second-degree-murder conviction in New York and to provide several precedential legal definitions of "depraved indifference."

She reviewed the admissibility of evidence, the doctrine of the fruit of the forbidden tree, multiple sources of evidence, the impeaching of witnesses. In what was considered a point for the prosecution, she stated that perjury must be proved in a court of law and, without such proof, must be disregarded.

You could see Bremmer's ears go red at that particular instruction. She opened her non–animal-skin synthetic-leather folder and copied it down as another addition to her appeal file.

The judge concluded by thanking the jury for their months of hard work and personal sacrifice and asking them to go the last mile in determining a verdict. She encouraged the members to keep their minds open during deliberations, to try to see both sides of the argument, and not to become locked into a position one way or the other.

"Coming to a verdict," she said, "is not unlike buying a house. It would be nice if there were a perfect house somewhere, a house with every single thing you wanted. But, unfortunately, most houses have one or two things you don't like—maybe a shake roof instead of a composition, maybe shutters with blue trim instead of green, maybe a powder room off the kitchen instead of the entry hall. Well, that's the way it often is with a case. Don't let a powder room in the wrong place convince you to turn down the whole house."

Carl Furillo watched the jury file out of the courtroom. Actually he watched Lilian Wong watch the jury file out of the courtroom. As soon as Fenetre disappeared into her chambers, Furillo worked his way toward Lilian Wong, passing Dan, who was hurrying up the aisle to the door.

"Double-parked?" Furillo said as they passed.

But Dan didn't even break stride. He just flashed him a noblesse oblige smile and was gone. By the time Furillo reached Lilian Wong, she was already on the phone.

"Uh-huh, uh-huh . . . uh-huh . . ."

Furillo studied the back of her neck, tracing with the tip of an imaginary tongue the faint outlines of veins, all the way to the edge of the phone cradled in the soft flesh between the neck and the shoulder.

"Uh-huh, uh-huh, uh-huh . . ."

God, he loved the way she said *uh-huh*.

When she folded the phone and turned around, they were face-to-face in the almost-empty courtroom. She slipped the phone into her pocket and looked at him. Her eyes were porous. Furillo thought he saw promise in them.

"The jury's out," he said as romantically as possible.

"Yes, it is."

"They'll be out for a while."

"Do you think so?"

"I'm counting on it."

She looked at him, tilting her head in that quizzical manner he had grown to cherish.

"The banks of the Mohawk. The grapes and pâté. The pinot grigio," he reminded her.

She remembered the conversation from the bathtub the night the decision was announced to call Audrey to the stand. She had been lying there, feeling the water get cold around her, thinking about how, with winter approaching, it was time to make some fundamental changes in her life.

She remembered that moment, and others—the trip to St. Catharines, the confession in the hallway of the Ramada Inn, the interrupted kiss in the Henry Hudson Room, the margaritas in Pablo's Cantina . . .

While she was remembering this, Furillo stood with his hands deep in his pockets contemplating exactly the type of wildly self-destructive evening he would spend if she said no. Just how many vodka shooters would it take to kill him?

The moment hung suspended in the air. Furillo thought he could hear the drawbridge creaking. She scratched her calf with the tip of her shoe and said, finally, "You don't mind if I take my cell phone, do you?"

"Actually, I was going to suggest it."

Chapter 37

Saturday morning, October 3, broke clear and warm, a chamber-of-commerce Indian summer day in Schenectady. The foliage was nearing its peak, lush and decadent, an extravagant palette of color strung out along the city's network of old maples. There was a tartness in the air. The city smelled of apples and car polish.

People put up their storm windows and raked the leaves into piles, keeping their radios on the all-news stations, whose reporters were camped out in the press room at the courthouse, along with two hundred other reporters. They were down the hall from the jury room, where the jurors, ordered into weekend session by Judge Fenetre, had convened at ten that morning to begin their deliberations.

Even though most experts were predicting the jury wouldn't be back in until Monday at the earliest, there was nonetheless a national vigil being kept that weekend, as there had been throughout the trial. Having gone this far with Audrey, you didn't want to miss out on the finish line.

The London bookmakers had Audrey at 3–2 for conviction, 2–1 for acquittal, and 7–3 for a hung jury. One bookmaker had a trifecta going that paid 20–1 if you correctly predicted the verdict, and the day and the hour it was announced.

But for the lawyers and the defendant there was nothing to do but stare at the closed door of the jury room and wait. Audrey sat in Bremmer's office answering her fan mail.

She'd had stationery printed up with AUDREY embossed in raised letters on the top of the card, no return address. "Dear Phyllis," she would write. "Thanks for your kind letter. You don't know how much your support means to me. Best wishes, Audrey."

Now and then an ugly one slipped through: "Dear Cunt: You know what you can do with your fucking carving knife?" Nonplussed, Audrey would write back, "Dear Vince: Thanks for your kind letter . . ."

Meanwhile, at the district attorney's office, all other business had pretty much ground to a halt. Files piled up on the prosecutors' desks. Depositions were postponed, court dates continued. Junior members were sent to handle the arraignments.

In spite of Ralph D'Imbroglio's campaign slogan—"You don't want to commit a crime with Ralph on the job"—he wasn't on the job very much, spending most of his time with his spin guys trying to figure out how to get reelected. He avoided commenting on the Audrey Haas case except to say that spousal dismemberers better hope he didn't win in November.

Jason Rappaport suggested to Clint Wells and Martha Demerest that D'Imbroglio change his campaign slogan to "Cut it off, go to jail." He declined a Barbara Walters heart-to-heart on his near-death experience in the Hudson River, as well as first chair on Oprah, Phil, Sally Jessy, Leno, and Letterman. He sat in his office reading *Bleak House* for the ninth time and waited along with everyone else for the white smoke.

Barney Abelove was waiting, too, but not for a verdict. He was on the living-room couch of Renata's apartment waiting for the kickoff of the Notre Dame–Michigan game. He had taken the Irish and four and a half points and wasn't happy with the rain in Ann Arbor. Notre Dame didn't have a mudder in the backfield.

During the pregame ceremonies, one of the sideline analysts was talking with the offensive coordinator of the Irish. Microphone in his face, Kyle Rotunda, former tight end for the Green Bay Packers, was asked his prediction of that afternoon's contest. He thought a moment and then said with a perfectly straight face, "Audrey, twelve–zip."

Abelove grabbed the remote and zapped the game. Fuck this. You weren't even safe in your own home anymore.

The pinot grigio was from Veneto—$19.99 a bottle. He could have gone with the California chardonnay at $6.99, but Furillo was pulling out all the stops. He had to drive to Albany to get pâté soaked in Calvados and a baguette that didn't taste like Wonder bread tortured into the shape of a stick.

It was all set out on a blanket in a clearing at a bend of the Mohawk, not far, as it happened, from the place where Susan Bremmer and Ralph D'Imbroglio had had their secret plea-bargain meeting. Furillo had brought two Steuben-glass wine goblets, borrowed from William in the Henry Hudson Room, and a portable cassette recorder with Tchaikovsky's *Romeo and Juliet* overture.

It didn't get any better than this, Furillo thought. If Manet had wandered by, he would have painted them. *Déjeuner Sur l'Herbe au Bord de la Mohawk.*

Lilian Wong sat cross-legged on the blanket, gingerly nibbling on a Camembert-smeared piece of baguette, a glass of wine in her hand. She was wearing her studded jeans—the same jeans she had been wearing the night he'd had six vodka shooters and passed out in her room—and a loose-fitting crew-neck sweater.

Conversation was desultory. They watched a barge wend its way lazily west toward Lake Erie.

"All we're missing is poetry," Lilian Wong said after a long moment of perfect silence.

"Any requests?"

"Something that rhymes with *pinot grigio.*"

Furillo reached back into the database for a poem that would live up to the moment. It took him a few seconds to access his Brooklyn College senior-English-course memory bank and was surprised to learn that Marvel's "To His Coy Mistress" had survived all these years relatively intact.

Stretched out beside her, he turned up Tchaikovsky a notch and downloaded Andrew Marvel.

" 'Had we but world enough, and time, / This coyness, Lady, were no crime. / We would sit down and think which way / To walk and pass our long love's day. / Thou by the Indian Ganges' side / Shouldst rubies find: I by the tide / Of Mohawk would complain. . . .' "

"You're making this up."

"No. Just adapting it to the circumstances.

" 'I would / Love you ten years before the Flood, / And you should, if you please, refuse / Till the conversion of the Jews. . . .' "

He saw the wine in her eyes and pressed on, " 'An hundred years should go to praise / Thine eyes and on thy forehead gaze; / Two hundred to adore each calf; / But thirty thousand to the rest . . .' "

He had changed *breast* to *calf*, ruining the rhyme with *rest*, and with that change the middle of the poem disappeared, drifting off down the Mohawk along with the barge, gone but not forgotten.

All that was left was the argument, the bottom line for the coy mistress. He recited it just as the andante movement of *Romeo and Juliet* began.

" 'But at my back I always hear / Time's wingèd chariot hurrying near; / And yonder all before us lie / Deserts of vast eternity. . . . / The grave's a fine and private place, / But none, I think, do there embrace. . . .' "

As the words penetrated the pinot grigio, Lilian Wong suddenly darkened. Her eyes went liquid, as if the poem had struck a vein of melancholy deep within her. She held the glass of wine against her cheek, trying unsuccessfully to hold back the tears, which came bursting through the dam with unexpected fury.

Furillo moved to put his arms around her. She folded into his embrace. Soon she was weeping spasmodically, big, wrenching sobs that made her whole body tremble.

He could feel the depth of her sorrow. Time's wingèd chariot had gone crashing through the dry moat right onto the drawbridge.

As he sat there holding her, Furillo realized he had overdone it. The wine, Tchaikovsky, the poetry—it was overkill. You had to be careful with a woman with a creaky drawbridge and a dry moat.

He had finally stormed the castle and carried her off on his horse. And now he had no idea where they were going.

Judge Fenetre was in her chambers trying to digest a bacon burrito she had made the mistake of sending out for at lunch when Wayne Somers, the bailiff, knocked on the door with news that the jury was coming back in.

"All right, Wayne," she said. "Round up the usual suspects."

The news went directly to the press room, and from there out over the wires. Lawyers were quoted trotting out the old saw that a quick deliberation meant a guilty verdict. Other lawyers were pointing out that just because the jury was coming in didn't mean it was bringing a verdict in with it. The whole world stood still for the next fifteen minutes.

Except Furillo and Lilian Wong. They were speeding the three miles from the Mohawk to the courthouse in Furillo's Taurus. Lilian Wong had gotten a call on her cell phone from her editor in New York, who had heard it on an all-news radio station.

Recovering with remarkable speed from her catharsis in Carl Furillo's arms, Lilian Wong threw it in reverse, zipping it up almost as quickly as she had let it fall apart. She was on her feet, brushing grass off her jeans and blowing her nose on a cocktail napkin before heading for the Taurus, leaving Furillo to scoop up the rest of the picnic and the Tchaikovsky.

They made the courthouse in ten minutes flat, getting to their seats only seconds before the judge entered. They were out of breath, woozy from the pinot grigio, redolent of Camembert. There was a grass stain on Lilian Wong's right buttock. Furillo's press badge was askew. To look at them you'd have thought they'd been going at it in the parking lot.

But no one was looking at them. All eyes in the courtroom were on the jury as they filed into the jury box. The TV cameras slowly panned the defense table, where Audrey sat between her lawyers. Then, the quick cut, for contrast, to the prosecution's table, where Jason Rappaport, Martha Demerest, and Clint Wells sat expectantly.

The camera tilted up to the bench to capture Judge Fenetre settling into her executive leather chair and gaveling the session to order.

"Has the jury reached a verdict?" Fenetre asked.

The jury foreperson, an asthmatic florist from Delanson, rose and, wheezing, announced, "No, we haven't, Your Honor."

The air went out of the courtroom as the foreperson handed the bailiff a note, who brought it to the judge. The camera followed the note right into Fenetre's hands. The judge put her reading glasses on, unfolded the note, and read it.

When she was finished, she carefully placed it in her file folder and turned to the spectators.

"The jury has asked for further instruction in the matter of admissibility of evidence," she announced to the courtroom and the world. "Specifically, should the evidence provided by the witness, Emmanuel Longhouse, which was written and read to the jury and not directly transmitted, be considered as hearsay and therefore inadmissible?"

Fenetre tried not to let her annoyance show. The question was frivolous, if not malicious. She had a good idea who was behind it—juror number 5, a mechanical-drawing instructor at R.P.I., who had had a supercilious smirk on his face during most of the testimony.

Looking directly at the mechanical drawer, she said in clipped tones, "Questions of law, such as admissibility, are the domain of the judge and not the jury. Once I have admitted evidence, you may consider it in your deliberations. I urge you to confine yourselves to questions of fact and try to reach a verdict with regard to all evidence that has been admitted."

Rappaport was waiting for the powder room, but it didn't come. The jury was sent back to their deliberations, and the reporters filed out, trying to figure out how to make what was apparently going to be the day's only development into a story. JUDGE RULES INDIAN'S TESTIMONY ADMISSIBLE would be wringing it dry in order to produce a drop of drama.

HAAS JURY IN CHINESE FIRE DRILL was more like it, thought Furillo, as he ruminated on his own Chinese fire drill of less than an hour ago. It already seemed like the distant past. The pinot-grigio buzz was gone, replaced by a dull headache. The pâté and Camembert lay heavily on his stomach. He was running on Calvados fumes.

But Lilian Wong, the cell phone to her ear, was already on the radio to headquarters, calling in the bombing coordinates. His coy mistress had transformed herself back into the tough field lieutenant she had been before falling apart in his arms on the banks of the Mohawk.

She uttered a final *uh-huh*, folded the phone, and turned to Furillo. "I got to do a stand-up outside the jury room."

Her eyes softened, sensing his melancholy.

"It was a lovely picnic," she said.

"Yeah."

"I didn't mean to—"

But he put his hand over her mouth to stop her. He didn't want an apology. On the contrary. She had no idea how grateful he was for that moment of intimacy.

"Maybe . . . tomorrow . . ." she started to say, but he shushed her again.

There was only one perfect picnic by the Mohawk in a lifetime, and they had already had that. The leaves would never be as rich, the breeze as light. How often could you count on a barge floating down the river at exactly the right time, its stern disappearing into the autumn haze just as the cellos signaled the beginning of the andante movement?

His hand moved from her mouth to the side of her face and lingered there. It was a strangely tender moment, given the surroundings. She put her hand on top of his and held it briefly before saying, "Got to change and round up my crew."

He watched her hurry away, tottering just a little in her high-heeled boots. She walked back across the moat and into the castle. The last thing he saw before the drawbridge went up was the grass stain on her ass.

Now that he had regained the power of speech, Emmanuel Longhouse found that he had very little to say. Speech, he was discovering, was as much a liability as an asset. When you were a deaf-mute six-foot-five-inch Indian, people gave you a wide berth. Now he was besieged by people asking him his opinions at all hours of the day or night.

He had blown off the reporters. They had clamored for an elucidation of his one-word condemnation of Audrey Haas. They had called his room, left messages, followed him to the Endicott Tavern at night. But as far as he was concerned, he was already on the record. He had said it loudly and unequivocally. What more did they want from him?

So in the evening Emmanuel Longhouse sat silently drinking Narragansett and feeling a growing nostalgia for the days when he was able to paddle his canoe wordlessly down the river of life. A peculiar melancholy settled upon him as the season shifted and the days grew shorter. What clarity he had attained in the heady days of late summer was starting to cloud over with the weather.

He had begun to realize that a man without baggage was also a man without resources. The fact that he had cleared customs and had nothing to declare didn't, in itself, solve his problems. He may have had no baggage, but he also had no money.

As soon as the trial was over, they would pull his comp at the Holiday Inn. They would no doubt pull his tab at the Endicott Tavern as well.

He suspected that a certain amount of baggage was necessary for the voyage, after all. A man without baggage was a man without weight or substance—a leaf on the water's surface, at the mercy of the river's shifting currents.

His particular river was moving west. That much he knew. And he would head west with it just as soon as he had put some provisions in the canoe.

Back in his room at the Holiday Inn was the one piece of baggage he would take with him wherever he went. It was his bow and arrow, the source of his sustenance. It lay at the bottom of the airline bag in the closet of his room, buried beneath his Atlanta Braves windbreaker and his flannel nightshirt.

He had managed to slip it through the metal detector when he went through customs. It had lain there unused all the time he had been in Schenectady. Now it was time to go hunting again.

It was almost eleven before Lilian Wong returned to the Van Twiller. After doing the stand-up in front of the jury room, she had gone out for a bite with the crew, then been on the phone with New York trying to coordinate live coverage of the verdict, which no one was expecting now for at least a few more days. If it didn't come in today, they had said on the evening news, it meant that the jury was seriously divided and probably wouldn't be back in quickly.

The lack of a precise date was playing havoc with the networks' prime-time lineups. They were trying to decide whether they should go with their regularly scheduled programming or throw some cannon fodder up there in anticipation of preemptions. Lilian Wong's own producer, Skippy Kaufman, was extremely unhappy.

"Well, what the hell am I supposed to do with the Cindy Crawford story?"

"Hold it."

"Two days from now she could decide she doesn't want him back after all. Then I'm sitting on a dead story."

"Then go with it."

"Yeah, but what if I have to go live to the verdict? In the middle of Cindy Crawford?"

"I don't know, Skippy . . ."

"Well, you should know. You're there. You're supposed to be on top of it. Where the hell were you, anyway, when I called you this afternoon?"

I was on the banks of the Mohawk crying my eyes out in the arms of a People *magazine reporter, Skippy. I'd had a little too much pinot grigio and saw my life floating away, growing smaller and smaller like a barge on the river . . .*

Driving back to the hotel, Lilian Wong thought about her little catharsis with Carl Furillo that afternoon. Had it been the wine? The poetry? The sight of the barge disappearing into the river's haze?

It must have been a reaction to stress. She had been working too hard and neglecting the StairMaster. She'd get back to the hotel, do thirty minutes on the StairMaster, get into the bathtub . . .

But as she drove into the underground parking garage, she suspected that it would take more than thirty minutes on the StairMaster to put her emotions back in order.

She pushed the elevator UP button and waited. And as she waited she tried to remember what it felt like to have a man inside her. The dim memory made her flush. Her knees suddenly went watery on her, and her breath shortened.

The elevator arrived, and she got in. She looked at her watch. Eleven. She took a deep breath and controlled the impulse to press 9, his floor. She pressed 7 and waited for the door to close. She stared at the lights hypnotically as they went from P3 to P2 to P1 to L. The elevator stopped.

The doors opened, and Carl Furillo walked in, direct from the Henry Hudson Room, six vodka shooters to the wind, the cowlick sticking straight up.

She stared at him, convinced it was a vision. He looked back at her, stunned into silence. The elevator doors closed behind them. She was in shock. He was less drunk than he ought to have been.

They moved simultaneously into each other's arms.

The kiss was surprisingly tender, given the vodka shooters, the time of night, and the years of deprivation that Lilian Wong had visited on herself. By the fourth floor the tenderness had melted into passion, and they were deeply enmeshed in each other.

By the seventh floor, they were going for buttons and zippers. The door opened, revealing Eddie, the bellhop. Furillo and Lilian Wong didn't even see him.

Barely disengaging, they waltzed past him into the seventh-floor hallway. Eddie wheeled his room-service cart onto the elevator and said, just as the door closed, "I'll see that you're not disturbed."

Furillo picked Lilian Wong up and carried her in his arms down the hallway to 723. She had her key card out and ready. He unlocked the door, carried her over the threshold, kicked the door closed behind them.

The room was illuminated only by a nightlight coming from the lilac-scented bathroom. Trying to remove clothes and walk at the same time, they danced a slow two-step toward the bed. The Claudia Steel blazer and Furillo's $29 corduroy jacket, containing their cell phones, went at approximately the same time. So did the crew-neck sweater and the $16.95 Ivy League Arrow shirt.

Furillo's Dockers were no problem, but Lilian Wong's studded jeans kept getting caught on the heels of her skin-tight leather boots. He pulled as hard as he could but couldn't get the boots off.

"My feet swell at night," she whispered in his ear.

Furillo looked madly around for a sharp instrument.

"Never mind," she said, pulling him down on the bed beside her. They kissed again greedily, and she pushed the jeans as far down as she could, leaving nothing but her Victoria's Secret fanny-flosser underwear. Furillo slowly tugged them down over her thighs and down her legs, where they, too, got caught on the boots.

Down to his Calvin Kleins, Furillo started to remove them, but she stopped him.

Moving on top of him, she slipped her lips around the waistband of his briefs and, engaging the Calvins with her teeth, slowly began to slide them down over his hips.

It was at this point that they heard a muffled ring coming from the mound of clothes strewn haphazardly on the floor. Her mouth disengaged abruptly from the waistband of his briefs.

They looked at each other as the muffled ring continued. Was it hers or his? Did it matter? It was 11:30 at night. The jurors were asleep in their hotel rooms.

They lay there, the two of them, panting like steam engines, waiting for the phone to stop ringing.

On the thirteenth ring, she rolled off the bed and, her jeans and panties around her ankles, crawled through the clothes trying to locate the ticking bomb to silence it.

She finally found it in the pocket of her blazer, still ringing. Angrily, she unfolded it and shouted, "What!"

After a moment of silence she heard the rarely used voice of Emmanuel Longhouse say, "I'm very confused."

"Emmanuel?"

"I can't travel without baggage."

"What?"

"I wanted to get to Saskatchewan before the snow fell. I was stocking the canoe."

The charge was petty larceny. There was only twenty-three dollars in the four parking meters he had rifled before being arrested by a roving squad car on Erie Boulevard. Emmanuel Longhouse did not resist arrest. He put his one-size-fits-all lockpicking tool down on the ground when ordered to do so, raised his hands, and allowed them to frisk him and read him his rights.

He had said nothing to the arresting officers or to the booking sergeant. When informed that he could make a phone call, he dialed Lilian Wong's cell phone from memory.

Lilian Wong put the $100 bail charge on her Visa card and signed papers accepting responsibility for assuring Emmanuel Longhouse's appearance to face misdemeanor petty-larceny charges. They walked out of the police station together, through a small gauntlet of local night-shift reporters, and into Lilian Wong's car.

The bar at the Holiday Inn was closed, so they sat in the corner of the deserted Holidome, beside the Ping-Pong tables, drinking vending-machine coffee.

"I have cleared customs and opened my suitcase," he said after a long silence. "I have spoken the truth. People don't believe me. Soon they are going to stop comping my room. Winter is on the horizon. If a man can't hunt, then he has to fish."

Lilian Wong nodded sympathetically.

"There are blood banks in Saskatchewan. But I haven't the means to get there."

She nodded again.

"People don't mess with you when you're silent. The only noise they hear is the sound of your oars in the water."

"Emmanuel," she said, after more silence, "what is it you want?"

Finishing what was left of his coffee, he put the paper cup down on the table and sat reflectively for a long moment. When he spoke, it was with a quiet but compelling voice.

"I would like very much not to speak again."

Chapter 38

The jury was out all day Sunday and Monday morning. By Tuesday afternoon, the odds on conviction were up to 2–1; acquittal was down to 5–3; and mistrial was holding steady at 7–3. Outside the courthouse, book publishers with satchels full of cash were roaming like packs of feral animals, ready to descend upon the jurors as soon as the verdict was in.

All three networks pulled their prime-time schedules and substituted reruns of TV movies. NBC was showing *A Cry of Rage: The Gilda Johanssen Story*, the Meredith Baxter movie about the woman suing the doctor who performed the unnecessary hysterectomy on her. They took a full-page ad in *TV Guide*, saying it was "the movie Audrey was watching when Ernie came home with the pantyhose."

People was holding eight pages in Monday's edition for Carl Furillo. As far as Furillo was concerned, however, they could keep them. His aborted assault on Lilian Wong's castle had left him dazed and unfocused. He wandered around the press room like a man who didn't know what he was doing there. Sharon Marcuzzi called every few hours with a different idea. The latest was an entire issue devoted to the members of the jury.

"We'll do stories on all of them—husbands, wives, children, families, dogs . . ."

"They're not that interesting," Furillo protested.

"You kidding? At the moment, they're the twelve most important people in the world. Our readers care more about what they eat for breakfast than about Elizabeth Taylor or Yasser Arafat."

Mostly he daydreamed about Lilian Wong and their moment of interrupted foreplay. Though technically accurate, *foreplay* hardly did justice to what had transpired before she was called away to bail the Indian out of jail.

She walked around like a hastily capped volcano, still smoldering but no longer erupting, doing sidebar interviews with the bailiff, the stenographer, and anybody else who would talk to her. She walked the *Hard Copy* audience past the closed door to the jury room, down the courthouse corridor to the press room, and then outside to the satellite trucks.

They had a brief moment on Wednesday, when she nearly ran him down hurrying out of the press room to gather her crew for the arrival of the jury.

"Hi," she said a little breathlessly.

"Hi," he replied.

"About the other night . . ." She skidded to an abrupt halt, dug in for traction, couldn't find any. She stood there, her tires spinning, the uncompleted sentence hanging between them. Lilian Wong was not strong on completing sentences, he had noticed, except on *Hard Copy*, where she nailed them into the ground like fence posts.

"Why don't we just leave it at that," he suggested.

She looked at him with sudden concern.

"I meant the sentence," Furillo hastily added. "It's unresolved. Unresolved sort of sums things up, doesn't it?"

"Furillo, you have no idea . . ."

"Believe me, I do."

And that was the last time he saw her until Thursday afternoon. Furillo was sitting in the press room, playing gin rummy with the guy from *Newsweek*, when the fire alarm went off again.

In the stampede down the hall, Lilian Wong materialized, as if by miracle, in the corridor. She took the lead, passing on the inside, a few lengths ahead of the pack. By the time Furillo reached his seat, two rows behind her, she already had her laptop booted up.

Out of breath, Furillo rose for Fenetre and waited till she took her seat. The bailiff opened the door to the jury room, and the twelve jurors filed in. They looked cranky and tired, as if they'd taken a three-day bus ride over bad roads, sleeping in their seats.

Audrey was wearing black. Furillo wondered if it was an omen. It was a knit suit with a subtle gray pinstripe, but it would have worked for a funeral.

Once again the cameras panned, zoomed, and jump-cut in an effort to capture the mood of nervous expectation that ran through the courtroom. All hands were on deck. No one knew whether this was the verdict or just another fire drill.

The foreperson handed a note to the bailiff, who carried it to the judge. Fenetre unfolded it, read it, then sighed audibly. The sigh went out live over the satellite to the four corners of the earth.

"The jury," Fenetre announced, "has requested that the witness Emmanuel Longhouse's testimony regarding his providing the dog Siggy with dog food be read back."

Consternation ran through the courtroom as the clerk went back through the volumes of trial transcript to locate the requested testimony. At their desks the anchorpeople stared at their TelePrompTers, vamping as best they could, waiting for their legal experts to interpret this development.

Finally, the clerk located the testimony and brought it to the bench. Fenetre examined it, then said, "You may read it to the jury."

The clerk turned, faced the jury, and read: "Question: 'What did you do?' Answer: 'I opened the cupboard.' Question: 'Did you find dog food in there?' Answer: 'No.' Question: 'What did you do then?' Answer: 'I looked at her.' Question: 'What did she do?' Answer: 'She said, "Under the sink." ' Question: 'Were you able to understand her?' Answer: 'Yes.' Question: 'How were you able to understand her?' Answer: 'I read her lips.' Question: 'What did she mean by "under the sink"?' Answer: 'She meant the dog food was under the sink.' Question: 'Was the dog food there?' Answer: 'Yes.' "

The WSCH legal expert was the first to deem this development favorable to the defense. Carrie Castle had him on a split screen with Audrey and the defense table. As Lizzie Vaught and Susan Bremmer exchanged whispers, Albany State law professor Arnold Kantrow said that the testimony went to undermine the criterion of depraved indifference, which was the cornerstone of the prosecution's case. Providing the dog food, he maintained, was an indication of her concern for her late husband's dog—an act of kindness at a difficult moment.

The chairperson of the Association of American Trial Lawyers, Mildred Katzelas, disagreed. The request, according to her, indicated the jury's fixation on Audrey Haas's lucidity and her lack of remorse for what she did. "The woman is concerned with *feeding her dog* with her husband lying dead at her feet? Surely that speaks to the most depraved form of indifference."

"She's on trial for depraved indifference to her husband, not to her dog!" growled Ralph D'Imbroglio in a phone interview with *USA Today*. "The woman ate *frozen lasagna* three feet from her dead husband. Can you get any more *depraved* than that?"

But regardless of what interpretation was put on the jury's request, it boiled down to more waiting. They were back behind closed doors, presumably discussing the relationship between Audrey's providing the location of the dog food and the concept of depraved indifference, while the reporters continued to scramble for experts to explain the significance of the day's events.

Nobody left the courthouse until 9:30, when the jury, still without a verdict, retired for the night. Lilian Wong taped a quick stand-up in front of the courthouse, reviewing the day's events, and then went back to the hotel.

As she entered her room, she made eye contact with the StairMaster and shook her head. "Not tonight, honey," she muttered, grabbing a half-bottle of Chablis from the minibar and going into the bathroom to run the tub.

She used the last of Philippe Paringaux's Coeur des Lilas. She had been in Schenectady long enough to have gone through an entire economy-sized jar of the lilac-scented bath salts. Would this ever be over? Would she be able to go home?

Go home *where*? To her small, immaculately decorated apartment on East Seventy-ninth Street? To her 857 square feet of tongue-and-groove hardwood floors, Flocatti throw rugs, and indirect lighting? To her off-white, lavender-trim walls, covered with Ansel Adams prints and framed posters of openings she hadn't been to? To her overwatered dieffenbachia, her cupboard full of albacore tuna and tasteless English tea biscuits? To her large four-poster bed with the fluffy white bedspread and the pink silk mail-order sheets?

The glass of Chablis in one hand, her Japanese loofah sponge in the other, she lowered her body into the steaming lilac. As she laid her head against her inflatable rubber bath pillow, she thought about that large, clean, cool bed, with the orthopedically certified mattress and the coquettish ruffled skirt.

The bed was perfectly centered in the middle of the bedroom with the pink-and-gray patterned wallpaper and the sliver of a view of the East River. She saw herself lying there, dressed in a white flannel nightgown buttoned to the neck, slowly ripening with the years, her lustrous black hair taking color, her eyes gradually shaded by intricate cataracts, her calf muscles going progressively flaccid.

She tried her best to blot out that image. She flagellated herself with the sponge, ridding herself of dead skin cells until she hurt. She stuck her head beneath the water and dared herself to open up her lungs.

She came up roaring for air and crying. For the second time in less than a week, Lilian Wong sobbed uncontrollably. But this time there was no one there to comfort her.

Two floors up, in room 923, Carl Furillo was sitting crossed-legged on his bed, composing his letter of resignation. He had been at it for hours, scribbling draft after draft longhand on the legal pad, wanting it to be perfect before he typed it on the PowerBook and modemed it to New York.

The current draft read:

> Dear *People,*
>
> Over the past seven and a half years, I have faithfully rendered whatever services were required of me with little caviling or complaint. I have worked long hours, made deadlines, and padded my expense account a good deal less than is customary in this business.
>
> During this time, you have sent me to the ends of the earth to transform people's lives into 500 words of digestible copy. I have produced this copy faithfully and gone back for more, regurgitating it over fax lines and modems from wherever I found myself.
>
> I have trafficked in hyperbole and half-truth. I have elevated the banal to the sublime, the mediocre to the outstanding. I have turned human misery into anecdote, and anecdote into mythology.
>
> I have invaded the sanctity of people's homes and the privacy of their grief. I have reduced their anguish to adjectives, their pain to metaphor.
>
> Like Eichmann, I have been efficient in my work, following orders to the letter.
>
> But as I sit here in my hotel room in Schenectady waiting for the verdict of the trial of the century, I find myself unable to go on. I am out of gas, with the finish line in sight. The bile has risen in my throat and is starting to dribble down my shirt. My rivet gun is empty.
>
> So here's the lead: I quit! Effective immediately. So long. Good-bye. Have a nice life.
>
> Please tell Sharon Marcuzzi that Barney Abelove's ex-wife got remarried to a snap-on-tool distributor from Kiamesha Lake and the

Young Turk who gets my office that the classified Rolodex is in the bottom right-hand drawer of my desk, behind the Rolaids and the condoms.

You may donate any severance pay you might feel obliged to pay me to the Ernest Haas Memorial Fund. (If anybody ever deserved severance pay, it's Ernie.)

Yours faithfully,

Furillo continued to work on his letter well into the night—cutting, trimming, modulating the passion with the sarcasm, looking for just the right balance. It was after two when, bleary-eyed, he decided to quit. He'd take one more pass at it in the morning and then send it off.

He brushed his teeth, swished a little brandy around his mouth, took off his clothes, and crawled naked between the covers. In less than a minute he was out like a ten-watt bulb.

She made for the barge, swimming as fast as she could. But hard as she swam, she wasn't making progress. The barge kept disappearing around yet another bend in the river, its stern dissolving in the mist.

Though it was deep autumn, the leaves resplendent, the Mohawk felt like a bathtub. Her arms and legs were heavy, but she couldn't stop now. Not when she was this close.

She could see them standing on the long flat deck doing a square dance—Audrey in a gingham dress, doing a dos-à-dos with Susan Bremmer, Ralph D'Imbroglio swinging Martha Demerest, Jason Rappaport sitting in his wheelchair playing the harmonica. And at the edge of the barge, his arms open to her, was Carl Furillo. In his Calvin Klein briefs.

Furillo beckoned to her, called her name. She called back, fighting to swim and call his name at the same time. Water began to fill her lungs. She started to cough.

The barge disappeared into the mists again, and she went down into the water. And as she sank down into the soft muddy floor of the Mohawk . . .

She woke up gasping for air, her heart pounding. She sat straight up in bed and started to scream before she realized that she was in her room in the Van Twiller and not at the bottom of the Mohawk.

She squinted at the luminous face of the bedside digital clock radio: 4:23 A.M. The hour of nightmares. Her heart was still beating furiously and she was drenched.

It took her a moment to realize that it wasn't just perspiration.

She got out of bed and stood there shivering in that dark, chilly hotel room. She was wearing baby-blue balbriggan pajamas. Underneath them was the residue of lilac, mixed with the warm waters of the Mohawk.

The clock face changed to 4:24. Soon it would be 4:25. The barge would disappear forever, and with it Carl Furillo. If she didn't go now, she never would.

The pajamas had no pockets. Still, in an act of passionate redundancy, she turned off the cell phone lying on the night table. Then, without bothering to take her room key, she walked out the door into the pathetically subdued lighting of the Van Twiller hallway.

She took the stairs two at a time, afraid that if she stopped and thought about what she was about to do, she'd turn back. And then she remembered that she had no room key and would have to take the elevator down to the lobby and get Eddie to let her in.

She laughed to herself and kept moving. By the time she reached room 923 she was giddy. Not to mention wet. She knocked on the door loudly. Then again almost immediately. She continued knocking as the moat filled up.

By the time Carl Furillo opened the door, it was overflowing.

Chapter 39

At 10:02 the following morning, October 7, a little more than an hour after deliberations had begun for the day, the jury buzzed the bailiff to inform him that they had a communication for the judge.

"This it?" asked Wayne Somers, with a cracked smile. The foreperson gave him a stony look and shut the door in his face.

Judge Fenetre scheduled a session of open court for 11:00. Fifty-eight minutes of lead time and counting. The announcement was greeted in the press room with a certain amount of cynicism. The fire drill was getting routine.

"What do they want to have read to them this time—the dog's testimony?"

"No, they want to try out the carving knife on juror number five—to see if it works."

Nevertheless, the world ground to a halt one more time. Reporters scrambled down the hallway to the courtroom; press passes were carefully scrutinized; regularly scheduled programming was interrupted; Dan was beeped off his Exercycle.

Audrey came down from the attorney's room on the sixth floor and entered the courtroom. She waved absently to her parents, as she did every day, and took her seat at the defense table. Wardrobe-wise, it was not her best day: a maroon blazer over a white blouse and gray skirt, and a pair of low-heeled burgundy loafers that had seen better days.

She had slept badly the night before, having dreamed of being stuck with Zadek during a snowstorm in a funicular hovering over the Alps. He was eating sunflower seeds and spitting the shells out over the Jungfrau.

She was tired and premenstrual. Her horoscope warned of ongoing struggle and counseled patience. Easy for them to say.

She watched Jason Rappaport wheel himself into the courtroom, down the aisle, and right past her table with that superior little grin on his face. If only that taxi driver hadn't pulled him out of the Hudson.

Rappaport took his place beside Martha Demerest and Ralph D'Imbroglio.

"Hung jury—eleven to one," he said to Martha Demerest.

"If it's eleven to one, she'll send them back to redo the powder room," Martha Demerest replied.

The door to chambers opened, and Judge Fenetre made her entrance. She moved to the bench, sat down, and instructed the bailiff to bring in the jury.

As the door to the jury room opened, the twelve members filed in. All eyes were on the foreperson. There was a sudden buzz when those in the courtroom who were familiar with criminal trials saw the brown manila envelope in the foreperson's hand.

Legal experts in newsrooms around the world told their anchors that a sealed brown manila envelope usually contained the signed jury forms that accompanied a verdict.

Judge Fenetre gaveled the session to order and said, "Madame Foreperson, has the jury reached a verdict?"

"We have, Your Honor," said the foreperson in a voice that would be rebroadcast throughout the day, the night, and for many days thereafter. These words would be the epigraph of her book, *Reaching for the Truth: Diary of an Audrey Haas Juror.*

The world waited with bated breath as the foreperson handed the sealed envelope to the bailiff, who delivered it to the judge. Fenetre broke the seal and, donning her reading glasses, examined the forms as the TV cameras tried to get in tight enough to read them.

Audrey closed her eyes and berated herself for having worn the old maroon blazer. Susan Bremmer fingered her gold-plated intrauterine pendant. Lizzie Vaught checked out the open toes of her Manik Bialy shoes. Martha Demerest took a series of deep, calming breaths. Jason Rappaport tapped his fingers on the smooth rubber of the wheels of his chair and wondered who had browbeaten the mechanical drawer. Ralph D'Imbroglio passed gas.

"Would the defendant please rise and face the jury," Fenetre ordered. As Audrey rose along with her attorneys, Fenetre handed the verdict to her clerk.

"The clerk will read the verdict."

Valerie Esplanade stood with the verdict in her hand, but the camera was not on her. The camera was on Audrey, as she stood facing the twelve people who would decide whether she was going to prison or Mazatlán.

Unaccustomed to public speaking, Valerie Esplanade's voice was cracked and low.

Her hands were shaking as she read, "In accordance with statute 125.25 of the New York State Penal Code, we the jury in the case of the State of New York versus Audrey Roberta Haas find the defendant not guilty of murder in the second degree, to wit, causing the death of Ernest Arthur Haas, a human being, by depraved indifference to the value of life."

Audrey's knees went weak as Susan Bremmer, for the first and only time, hugged her. The camera locked onto Audrey as she sagged in Susan Bremmer's arms and let her hand be shaken by Lizzie Vaught, who, unlike Audrey, had sensed a possible verdict and was wearing a gorgeous beige Armani suit with a green plissé blouse.

Audrey never heard Fenetre thank the jury, dismiss them, and gavel the case closed. It was all a blur of meaningless words to her. She disengaged herself from her attorney's embrace and started to say something but found herself too giddy to speak.

Her parents were suddenly beside her, and there was more hugging and more tears. Jack and Frances Myers had to hug Susan Bremmer and Lizzie Vaught as well. It was a hugfest—lapped up by the cameras.

Meanwhile, at the prosecution desk, Ralph D'Imbroglio tried to gather his thoughts for a statement. He would have to say something for the cameras. He looked at Jason Rappaport anxiously. "Got any ideas about what I should say?"

"Yeah. Hormones," Rappaport replied before turning away and wheeling himself up the aisle.

It was later reported that 86 percent of all TV sets in use in the United States had been tuned to the verdict—lower than O.J. but higher than the first day of the Gulf War or Neil Armstrong's moonwalk. By noon there were very few people on the planet who didn't know that Audrey Haas had been acquitted that morning in Schenectady, New

York, of having killed her husband with depraved indifference to the value of human life.

Among them were Lilian Wong and Carl Furillo, who at 11:11 A.M. on that Wednesday, October 7, were asleep in room 923 of the Hotel Van Twiller behind a DO NOT DISTURB sign. They lay, dead to the world, on what was left of the bed, their bodies tangled up in the sheets, recovering from several hours of tumultuous sexual activity that had only just recently ended. They had collapsed into each other at approximately the same time, as it happened, that the Haas jury had reached a verdict.

Before they even began, Lilian Wong had dramatically eviscerated Furillo's cell phone, ripping out the battery and flinging it across the room. She then grabbed the phone on the night table and dialed the do-not-disturb option on the voice-mail menu. Only when this was accomplished did she turn to him and remove her baby-blue balbriggan pajamas.

The first time was just a degree or two below mortal combat, as Carl Furillo's pent-up ardor was equally accommodated by the thirst of Lilian Wong's deprivation. They went at each other with such appetite that had they not fit so well together they would have done each other harm.

The second, third, and fourth times were more lyrical, passion being slowly phased into tenderness, then back into passion—each time a little less turbulent, like waves slowly receding on the shore.

They didn't speak. They dozed, drank imported beer from the minibar, and came back for more as dawn broke and light tried to insinuate itself from behind the heavy brocade curtains.

But they ignored it. At a quarter to eight the alarm on the clock radio went off, and Furillo silenced it with one swift kick that sent it flying off the night table onto the faded Persian carpet, where it lay beside the disarmed telephone, Lilian Wong's pajama bottoms, an empty beer bottle, and a paperback copy of *The Brothers Karamazov*.

The last dance was a sloppy paso doble in the dusty midmorning half-light, and by the time they finally disengaged, they were both already in never-never land.

While all hell broke loose around them, Carl Furillo and Lilian Wong had checked out. Which is what Eddie the bellhop told the concierge, who had sent him up to knock on the door after Sharon Marcuzzi, unable to get through, called the hotel and demanded that someone rouse Carl Furillo.

"What do you mean—he checked out? The *verdict* just came in!" she screamed into the phone.

But Eddie told the concierge, who told the desk, who told Sharon Marcuzzi that Mr. Furillo was not responding and presumably had left in the middle of the night. Did she have any idea who might be taking care of the bill?

Meanwhile, at *Hard Copy*, Skippy Kaufman left a half dozen messages on Lilian Wong's voice mail, after being told by the cellular-phone company that Ms. Wong was away from her instrument.

And so at the biggest moment of the biggest day of the biggest trial in years, two of the biggest guns in the tabloid business were incommunicado. As Audrey Haas walked down the stairs of the Schenectady County Courthouse a vindicated woman, Lilian Wong and Carl Furillo were asleep in their small room above the railroad station, hundreds of versts from St. Petersburg, as the snow gently fell outside their window and the wolves howled mournfully.

Susan Bremmer didn't wait to call a press conference. She gave one right on the courthouse steps, Audrey at her side. With every camera in Schenectady trained on her, she spoke extemporaneously and at length.

"This is not merely a victory for Audrey Haas," she proclaimed, "but a victory for women everywhere—a ringing affirmation of our basic rights under the Thirteenth Amendment to the Constitution. We will no longer allow ourselves to be enslaved—we will no longer sit by and passively tolerate being the victims of sexual abuse, degradation, and violence . . ."

And so forth.

After a while, there was a clamoring for Audrey to say something. Questions were shouted at her. How did she feel? What was she going to do now?

"I feel great," Audrey said, "because, like my attorney said, this was a victory not just for me but for all women who are victims. This is going to send the message out there that we're not going to tolerate abuse anymore and that we're going to move forward, under the Thirteenth Amendment, to dignity and lack of slavery . . ."

As for what she was going to do now, Audrey said, "I'm going to get on with my life. It's time to rebuild bridges and self-esteem. This is a whole new chapter for me, and I'm going to take it one day at a time."

Did she foresee ever getting married again?

"Why not? There're men out there who aren't abusive, aren't there? But I'd have to be careful and make sure he is sufficiently evolved with a raised consciousness . . ."

Bremmer dragged her away to the Saab as a young man with a Leica and a forged press pass shouted after her, "What about Ernie? He certainly got his consciousness raised, didn't he?"

Eugene Zukoff squeezed off round after round until Cissy Weiner ran up to him and, with one clean leg thrust, separated him from his camera, and, then, raking downward, nearly separated him from his equipment.

Lilian Wong didn't wake up so much as rise to the surface. It was a slow, luxurious ascension up through the warm water toward daylight until she broke the surface and lay floating on her back, like Ophelia among the willows, wondering if she had died and gone to heaven.

He was lying with his head buried in the pillow, sheets twisted promiscuously around him, snoring very quietly. The cowlick was up at attention, one of his ears squashed into the pillow, the other sticking out like an orange peel. She inched slowly toward him, inhaling the newly familiar scents of his body. With great tenderness she smoothed the cowlick and then let her tongue run over the edge of the orange peel.

He stirred but didn't wake. She managed to separate the sheet from his body, and then, try as she may, she was unable to stop herself from running her lips down the small of his back, and, as she moved lower, he uttered a moan of pleasure but kept his head buried in the pillow. He may have been a reporter for *People* magazine but he wasn't an idiot. Carl Furillo drifted into semiconsciousness with just enough clarity of mind to realize that if he did nothing but turn over, the next few minutes of his life would be as close to ecstasy as he would get on this earth.

He wasn't wrong. Lilian Wong may have been *hors de combat* for a long period of time, but she read *Cosmo* regularly and had fabulous lips. Furillo thought he would go right through the acoustic ceiling.

When he finally opened his eyes, she was on top of him, bouncing gently up and down, in a smart, rhythmic, ladylike trot. He reached up and put his arms around her neck, pulling her down to him so that he could taste her lips. They kissed for minutes at a time without coming up for air, moving, as they did, into a canter and then a gallop.

Fortunately, the Van Twiller had been built in the days when walls were adequately soundproofed. Otherwise, Eddie would have been up there with the fire brigade. When they finally crashed, parts of the wreckage were scattered over several miles of countryside.

It was some time before either of them could speak. Not that they had a great deal to say to each other at that point. After what they had been through for the last few hours, it was hard to know where to begin.

Eventually, Furillo managed to get up and pad over the wreckage to the bathroom. On his way back he saw the clock radio staring up at him from the floor: 2:15 P.M. Could ten hours have disappeared off the face of the earth?

She pulled herself up on one arm and looked at the strewn shambles of the hotel room. The place looked like a rock group had been partying there.

"Wow," she said.

"Hungry?"

"You kidding?"

He went looking for the room-service menu, crawling on his hands and knees until he found it under her pajama bottoms. He opened it and scanned it.

"How about some Eggs Vincent Van Gogh and a pitcher of Bloody Marys?"

"Sounds good to me."

A few minutes after Furillo called in the order, an envelope was slipped under the door. Lilian Wong got up and went to get it. She opened it up and found two faxes, one addressed to each of them.

She handed him his and read hers. When they were finished, they exchanged and read each other's.

While they waited for their breakfast to arrive, Furillo read her his resignation letter. Then he hooked up the modem and sent it to New York, even though at this point it was academic. He was already fired.

She was fired, too. Her fax had stated a gross dereliction of duty. His had used similar language. Eddie had read both of them and decided that they didn't need to know until the early afternoon, when they'd be either dead or ready for breakfast.

Barney Abelove heard about the verdict on the car radio on his way back from a homicide in a 7-Eleven on South Rotterdam. The shooter had plugged an eighty-one-year-old Pakistani in the face before making off with $112 from the drawer and a carton of Merits.

It was reassuring to Abelove that the world hadn't stopped entirely while the Audrey Haas jury was deliberating. He took what statements there were to take and waited for the meat wagon.

Coincidentally, it was Milton Zieff who got the call. They had barely spoken to each other since last March 28, when they had stood together in Audrey Haas's kitchen and discussed the forensic probability of finding traces of Ernest Haas's penis in Rottweiler shit.

"So what do you think, Abelove?" Zieff asked him, as he bagged the 9mm Beretta slug they had dug out of the wall behind the register.

"Drugs, probably. Shooter needed a hundred for a quick score—"

"No. I mean what do you think the jury's going to come back with?"

"Fuck do I know," Abelove muttered.

"Looks to me like she's going to walk. It's that goddamn reasonable doubt. You could drive a truck through it. You know what I mean?"

Abelove nodded and shoved his pad in his jacket pocket. "Send me the paperwork," he said and headed abruptly for the door.

"Hey, Barney—no one's blaming you," Zieff called after him.

Abelove didn't reply. He continued out the door and into the Cutlass. He started the car and turned on the radio to get the morning line at Saratoga. He got the all-news-radio Carrie Castle instead.

She announced that just minutes before, the jury of nine women and three men had found Audrey Haas not guilty. There was both consternation and joy at the verdict. Susan Bremmer declared it a victory for the Thirteenth Amendment of the Constitution. Ralph D'Imbroglio said the defense inflamed the jury with feminist rhetoric and claimed that not even a dead man could get a fair trial by a jury with nine women on it.

Speaking for the jury, the mechanical-drawing teacher explained that they had reached their verdict because the prosecution simply did not make its case.

"They just didn't get the job done," he said. "Their witnesses were not credible. Personally, I didn't believe anything that cop told me, and as far as the Indian is concerned, the guy robs parking meters for a living."

"You really don't think Audrey did it?" he was asked.

"It doesn't matter whether she did it or not. Bottom line, they didn't prove she did it with depraved indifference. That's the name of the game. Isn't it?"

Abelove played with the radio dial. Every station had the same story. Not guilty. Thirteenth Amendment. Hormones. Reasonable doubt . . .

He turned the radio off and drove slowly up Rotterdam to Van Ecyk, hung a right, and headed toward State Street. As he drove past Erie Boulevard, he saw a man walking by the side of the road with his thumb out. His long black hair was coming out of his baseball cap, and he carried a duffel bag on his shoulder.

Abelove was already past him when he looked in the rearview mirror and recognized Emmanuel Longhouse. He jammed on the brakes and pulled over. The six-foot-five-inch Indian opened the passenger door and got in.

"How're you doing?" Abelove said.

Emmanuel Longhouse nodded.

"Where're you heading?" he asked.

Emmanuel Longhouse took a cardboard sign from his lap and showed it to him.

SASSCATJEWON was written on it.

"That's a long way from here," Abelove said.

The Indian nodded again.

"I'll drop you at the thruway entrance," Abelove volunteered. "Keep going west, you'll run into it."

They rode to the thruway entrance in silence. Abelove pulled over, and Emmanuel Longhouse got out of the car. He didn't say thank you and he didn't say good-bye. He just turned and headed west into the late-morning sun.

As Emmanuel Longhouse walked away toward the thruway, Abelove could hear the quarters jangling in his pockets.

Epilogue

In November, Ralph D'Imbroglio was soundly defeated for reelection to the Schenectady County district attorney's office by a theretofore-unknown cement contractor named Julia Ferragamo. Ms. Ferragamo carried 72 percent of the registered women voters and a majority of the cross-dressers. The Native American vote was split.

Resigning her tenured post at Skidmore College, Susan Bremmer moved to Washington, D.C., to occupy the Audrey Haas Chair in Women's Studies at Georgetown University. Just before Christmas, Professor Bremmer made national headlines again when she punctured the kidney of an alleged mugger in Rock Creek Park with an umbrella equipped with a specially designed retractable bayonet, marketed as a self-defense weapon for women. Criminal charges against her were not filed, but there is a civil suit pending, brought by the family of the kidney-challenged man.

After pictures of her wardrobe appeared in *GQ*, in an article entitled "The Best-Dressed Woman of the Audrey Haas Trial," Lizzie Vaught began dating a multimillionaire apparel wholesaler named Irv Saugus. They plan to marry in May and move to Montecito. She recently turned down $100,000 from *Playboy* for a tastefully nude photo spread.

· · ·

When Clint Wells was passed over for promotion by District Attorney Ferragamo, he left the prosecutor's office and took a job in Rochester representing plaintiffs in product-liability actions. In his first case, a suit against a manufacturer of defective hernia trusses, he came away with $345,000 as his share of the damages awarded by the jury. He is presently involved in litigation against a prominent low-fat-yogurt maker.

Refusing all book and interview offers, Martha Demerest stayed on to work under the new district attorney. In January she began seeing a prominent African-American talk-show host and Scientologist from Albany. She credits this relationship with finally making her clear about the Audrey Haas trial. She attends Scientology sessions regularly with her boyfriend and tithes her $68,500 salary.

Following the trial, Jason Rappaport left for a vacation in Europe, where his specially equipped handicap-operable rental car skidded off a rain-slick road in the Swiss alps and plummeted nine thousand feet onto the rock face below. Because the seatbelts were defective, Jason Rappaport did not go down with the car but instead through the windshield, emerging with only facial lacerations and a broken bicuspid. He has nonetheless initiated legal action against the rental-car company, the canton of Zisseldämmer, and the federal government of Switzerland.

Janice Meckler left her job at the Motor Vehicle Bureau and married the writer with whom she collaborated on her book, *A Perfect Size Eight: The Ernie and Janice Story*. They are now living in Poughkeepsie and selling motivational seminars. The suit against her filed by the estate of Ernest Haas for restitution of the $400,000 she withdrew from their joint bank account is pending on appeal, after a trial court ruled that Audrey Haas's grounds for punitive damages based on alienation of affection were not apposite to the issues of the case. Janice Meckler, for her part, is countersuing Audrey Haas for a share of the value of Ernest Haas's urology practice.

Jack and Frances Myers returned to Phoenix after a dizzying week of appearances on *Oprah*, *Letterman*, and *Sally Jessy Raphaël*. Their book, *The Audrey We Know and Love*, is still being written. An outline of the yet-to-be-completed manuscript is being circulated by Brad Emprin of the Brad Emprin Talent Agency in Los Angeles. According to Emprin, there is a lot of interest in the property.

• • •

Pauline Haggis's book, *The Right Place at the Right Time: How I Blew the Whistle on Audrey*, spent one week on *The New York Times* bestseller list before sinking like a cement block. Her publisher was stuck with 475,000 copies of the original 500,000-copy printing, and the book can still be seen littering remainder tables everywhere. Soon after the trial Pauline Haggis made restitution of the four hundred sheets of Xerox paper illegally appropriated from the Schenectady Police Department's public relations office.

Judge Carmen Fenetre resigned from the bench and moved to Mykonos, where she invested in an espresso bar. She lost eighty-five pounds in six months and met a poetess from Delphi named Lydia Lynkiotis, with whom she shares a small beach house, along with Eudora, Virginia, and a Pekinese named Alice B. Toklas.

Thanks largely to her exposure during the Audrey Haas trial, Carrie Castle was offered the weekend anchor job on the ABC-owned-and-operated station in New York. She has been spotted dining at Manhattan nightspots with Peter Jennings, Ted Koppel, and Boutros Boutros-Ghali.

The script for Charlie Berns's TV movie, entitled *Flight from Violence: The Audrey Haas Story*, was rewritten by four writers before being offered to Holly Hunter. Holly Hunter passed, as did Farrah Fawcett, Joanna Kerns, Marilu Henner, Stephanie Zimbalist, Lindsay Wagner, Valerie Bertinelli, Helen Hunt, Leigh Taylor Young, Veronica Hamel, and Meredith Baxter.
The script went into turnaround and was eventually shot by a Croatian director named Dinak Hrossovic in Vancouver for $1.8 million, with an unknown Canadian actress in the lead. It was released straight to video, where it can be found under the title *Vengeance Is Mine*.

Instead of being drummed off the force, Barney Abelove was quietly transferred back to Burglary after it was decided that prosecuting him for perjury would only rekindle the passions raised by the trial. He married Renata, and they bought the condo in Scotia with the health club downstairs. He refuses to discuss the case with anyone, including his new wife, and spends his evenings watching ESPN. His blood-cholesterol level hovers around 225.

• • •

Though Carl Furillo was fired from his job at *People*, as far as he is concerned, he resigned, and it was only the fact that he hadn't sent the E-mail resignation letter until the next morning that made it seem as if he had been fired first.

Lilian Wong moved into Furillo's large and sloppy West Village apartment. In December, they rented an RV and took off for the Southwest, spending their days photographing wildflowers in the desert and their evenings in trailer parks, watching TV and making love. They are expecting a child in August. If it's a boy, they'll name him Ernest.

Emmanuel Longhouse arrived in Saskatoon in late October. Three weeks later he hit a $3,500 Bingo jackpot and was able to put a down payment on a double-wide trailer on the outskirts of town with a 150-channel satellite dish.

He spends his evenings at the Yukon Bar and Grill with the occasional 4 A.M. hunting foray among the parking meters of Saskatoon. He has not uttered a single word since his last conversation with Lilian Wong in Schenectady.

Audrey Haas spent two weeks at the Club Med in Mazatlán immediately following the trial. After the first few days, the market for pictures of her collapsed abruptly, and the paparazzi pulled up their tents and left town.

When she returned to Schenectady, her new business manager informed her that most of the money she was given for the rights to her story was depleted by her legal bills and that the Audrey Haas Legal Defense Fund had been shut down due to irregularities uncovered during an IRS audit.

The Audrey Haas Battered Women's Shelter was closed when it was unable to pay the utilities bill. Its store front, formerly the triage and reception area, is now an adult bookstore.

In February Audrey found a job on the Weather Channel. She works out of the regional office in Albany, giving the weather for the tri-cities area. She remains in therapy three days a week with Marvin Zadek, who has switched her off Prozac and onto Zoloft. He says she is making good progress and anticipates that someday she may be able to function without antidepressants.

On March 27, the one-year anniversary of Ernest Hass's dismemberment, Siggy, the Haases' Rottweiler, went into the Happy Valley Animal Hospital in Costa Mesa, California, for nonintrusive surgery on a bleeding duodenal ulcer, caused, the veterinarian speculated, by stress and poor eating habits.

In the turmoil of events the previous March, Audrey Haas had forgotten to give Siggy's new owners his organ-donor card along with his license and medical records. As it turned out, there was no need for it. The dog pulled through the operation with flying colors.

With his survival, however, extradition proceedings to bring Siggy within the jurisdiction of the State of New York in order to perform a forensic autopsy have been postponed until such time that "it would not cause undue suffering to the animal—to wit, his death."

The prospect of retrieving traces of Ernest Haas's penis through DNA samples of the dog's intestinal tissue thus continues to become dimmer with each passing day.

ABOUT THE AUTHOR

PETER LEFCOURT lives in the Hollywood Hills with his son, Alex, and a geriatric golden retriever called Doggie.